E-8

Very
Sweet

W9-CKT-053

The Wedding Night

The
Wedding Night

JAYNE ANN KRENTZ

Jefferson-Madison
Regional Library
Charlottesville, Virginia

Thorndike Press • Chivers Press
Waterville, Maine USA Bath, England

1763 0938

This Large Print edition is published by Thorndike Press,
USA and by Chivers Press, England.

Published in 2002 in the U.S. by arrangement with Harlequin
Books, S.A.

Published in 2002 in the U.K. by arrangement with Harlequin
Enterprises, II BV.

U.S. Hardcover 0-7862-4142-X (Romance Series)
U.K. Hardcover 0-7540-4947-7 (Chivers Large Print)
U.K. Softcover 0-7540-4948-5 (Camden Large Print)

Copyright © 1991 by Jayne Ann Krentz.

All rights reserved.

All characters in this book have no existence outside the
imagination of the author and have no relation whatsoever to
anyone bearing the same name or names. They are not even
distantly inspired by any individual known or unknown to the
author, and all incidents are pure invention.

The text of this Large Print edition is unabridged.
Other aspects of the book may vary from the original edition.

Set in 16 pt. Plantin by Christina S. Huff.

Printed in the United States on permanent paper.

British Library Cataloguing-in-Publication Data available

Library of Congress Cataloging-in-Publication Data

Krentz, Jayne Ann.
    The wedding night / Jayne Ann Krentz.
        p. cm.
    ISBN 0-7862-4142-X (lg. print : hc : alk. paper)
    1. Family-owned business enterprises — Fiction.
    2. Married women — Fiction. 3. Large type books.
    I. Title.
PS3561.R44 W43 2002
    813'.54—dc21   2002019900

The
Wedding Night

ONE

The voluminous satin skirts of Angie Townsend's wedding gown sailed out behind her as
her new husband took her hand and whisked
her down the steps to the waiting limousine.

A shout went up and a hoard of Angie's
laughing relatives charged on to the lawn to
form a cheering gauntlet. It was easy to tell
the Townsends from the rest of the multitude. Most of them had copper-tinted hair
and eyes the color of a tropical sea, just as
Angie did. They were all throwing themselves wholeheartedly into the festivities. It
was the way the boisterous Townsend clan
did things.

"I forgot about this part," Owen Sutherland muttered as he plunged into the crowd
with Angie in tow.

Birdseed and flower petals descended like
rain as the throng of well-wishers parted reluctantly to allow the bridal couple to pass.
Several of the male guests offered racy ad-

vice about the wedding night, causing Angie to blush furiously.

"It's all your fault," she said to Owen. "If you'd wanted a quiet wedding you should never have put us Townsends in charge of things. We don't do things by halves."

"I can't say I wasn't warned," Owen admitted.

Angie turned to wave goodbye to her parents and her brother, Harry, who stood in the doorway of the elegant country club, glasses of champagne in their hands.

Angie's mother, one of the few non-redheads in the clan, was sobbing happily into a hankie. She had once confided to Angie that she had been quite restrained and proper in her younger days. Marrying a Townsend had ruined all her good breeding, she claimed.

Palmer Townsend, a robust, broad-shouldered man whose formal clothes did not quite conceal a small paunch, beamed at his daughter with paternal pride. He lifted the hand holding a champagne glass and toasted her as she was led toward the limousine.

Harry, at twenty-nine, three years older than Angie, merely grinned at her. He had his father's broad shoulders and strong build. He also still had plenty of the brilliant

Townsend red hair, which had gone gray and somewhat thin on his father.

"The full production was worth the effort," Owen said. "You look like a fairy-tale princess in that gown." His crystal gray eyes slid over her in swift, satisfied appraisal as the uniformed limo driver stepped forward to open the car door.

Angie felt Owen's glance as though it were a living thing made of fire. Excitement bubbled inside her. There was something so incredibly vital about her husband, she thought. He was so intensely, overwhelmingly *male*. From his midnight black hair and hawklike features to his lean, solidly built body, he radiated a primitive masculine vitality.

The heat rose in Angie's cheeks as she saw the cool possessiveness in his eyes. Tonight Owen would be touching her even more intimately than he was now looking at her. Tonight he would make love to her for the first time. The thought took her breath away.

It was lack of opportunity, not lack of desire that had kept Angie out of her fiancé's bed until this point. Owen's incredibly busy schedule combined with the whirlwind nature of his courtship were the main reasons they had not yet made love. His arrogant insistence on not having his bride become the subject of tacky gossip in the local press or at the country club where he and Angie's father were both members had played a part, too. And of course, the overly protective, old-fashioned attitudes of the Townsend men had also been factors.

On top of everything else there had been a considerable amount of just plain bad timing, Angie decided regretfully. She had, after all, known Owen for only three months, and for the first two of those months she had been secretly terrified of him.

With a hunter's instincts Owen had wisely not pressed Angie into an intimate relationship. He had been content to court her gently, and in this manner, he'd drawn her into his force field with a sure hand.

He'd had a great deal of help from Angie's family, all of whom were delighted with the prospect of a marriage between Angie and Owen. As usual the members of the Townsend clan were convinced they knew what was best for Angie and took pains to tell her so.

Angie knew it was not just the fact that she was the youngest that made all the others adopt a paternalistic and protective attitude toward her. It had more to do with the fact that she was the only one in the family who had shown little interest in and even less aptitude for the family business, Townsend Resorts.

From an early age, Angie's interests had been in the realm of the artistic rather than the corporate world. This lack of flair for something everyone else in the family took for granted had given the rest of the Townsends the notion that Angie was naive by nature. As a result, the clan had gone out of its way to shelter Angie from the realities of big business. While her brother, Harry, was being groomed to take over his father's position as head of the Townsend empire, Angie was encouraged to pursue her artistic endeavors.

Angie tolerated her family's indulgent attitude for the most part, only putting her foot down when someone went too far in trying to organize her life for her. But in the matter of Owen Sutherland, she had come to the conclusion that for once everyone was right. Owen Sutherland was the man for her.

It was during the past month that Angie had finally dared to admit to herself that she was enthralled by Owen. She had also come to the incredible realization that he genuinely needed and wanted her. But it seemed that after coming to that shattering conclusion, she had seen less of him than ever.

Sudden, unexpected business demands had taken Owen out of Tucson for much of the time. When opportunities for privacy had presented themselves, she discovered her father or brother or mother was somehow in the way. Owen had not seemed to mind.

No one had been more surprised by her reaction to Owen Sutherland than Angie herself. Sutherland was not the kind of man she had envisioned marrying or becoming involved with. One look at him today, dressed in austere black and white formal attire, the sun revealing the hint of silver in his black hair, was enough to explain why. He was tall, dark and dangerous.

When Palmer Townsend had first introduced Owen to Angie, her initial impulse had been to run very fast in the opposite direction. Her reaction was not based on the knowledge that the Sutherlands had been business rivals of the Townsends for years. She cared little about the hotel business and considered the rivalry silly.

It was rather that she had taken one glimpse into the depths of Owen's unfathomable crystal eyes and known the man was going to be a serious problem. At that very first meeting Angie had been shaken by some secret, inner knowledge she could not explain. It was as if she had been existing in a world of sunlight, and now the Lord of the Underworld had come to carry her away with him.

That was before she had gotten to know him, of course — before she had come to understand the extent of Owen's need for her. Not that he had discussed that need the way a Townsend would have. Owen was a very private man, unaccustomed to voicing his emotions. Angie sensed that it might be a long while before her husband was able to discuss his feelings with her, but she was in love and fully prepared to wait.

Her new husband was a hard man in many ways and possessed of a formidable willpower and an iron-clad self-control. There was a natural arrogance about him that was not unlike that of her father and brother. It was the arrogance of men who were accustomed to leadership and power. But unlike the arrogance of her father and brother, Owen's arrogance had never been tempered with love.

No, Owen would never find it easy to admit he needed the gentleness of a woman in his life. But Angie knew he did. She was certain of it. Deep down inside Owen longed for the softness and intimacy she could give him. He needed a woman he could trust with his heart and soul. And

13

Angie knew that Owen would never renege on a commitment — especially one as serious as marriage. In that respect he was very much like a Townsend.

Today Owen had stood in front of three hundred people and committed himself to Angie in no uncertain terms. *Until death do us part.* Shyly, but with all the determination of a woman in love, Angie had, in turn, promised herself to Owen Sutherland forever.

She had never been happier than she was at the moment Owen had slipped his ring on her finger. The smile she had given him had held her promise of love and faithfulness for a lifetime. Owen had looked deep into her eyes, and Angie sensed he had understood and valued the gift she was giving him.

A microphone came from out of nowhere as Angie and Owen reached the open door of the limousine. A fast-talking journalist moved in behind it. He was followed by a young man who had a videocamera perched on his shoulder. Angie caught a glimpse of the familiar television-station logo.

"Where's the honeymoon going to be, Sutherland?" the reporter demanded. "One of your own hotels? Or one of the Townsend resorts?"

Irritation flickered briefly in Owen's eyes,

but Angie saw him suppress it almost at once. He gave the reporter a cool, fleeting smile. "The location of the honeymoon is a secret. I'm sure you can understand why. The last thing I want to do is find an inquiring journalist under the bed tonight."

The young man wielding the camera grinned, but another journalist was already moving in to corner Angie.

"Congratulations on your marriage, Mrs. Sutherland. This is going to be big news in the business world, as well as here in Tucson, isn't it? Everyone knows Sutherland Hotels and Townsend Resorts have been fierce rivals for years. And now a Sutherland has married a Townsend. I take it this means the rumors of a merger are valid? What about the possibility of a stock offering? Any chance the new Sutherland and Townsend might go public?"

Startled, Angie shook her head quickly. Microphones made her nervous. She was not accustomed to them the way Owen and the members of her own family were. She had always been shielded from the assaults of the business press. She did not like or understand the rough-and-tumble environment in which Owen and her relatives played expensive, dangerous games.

"You have it all wrong," she said to the reporter. "This is a wedding, not a business arrangement."

"A wedding that could spell a fortune for the two chains if it's true the two families have decided to bury the hatchet after all these years and join forces. Can we assume the merger will officially be announced today?"

"You mustn't assume anything of the kind," Angie said, frustrated by the man's persistence. "There is no merger. This marriage has nothing to do with business. Explain it to him, Owen."

Owen took charge before Angie could protest further. "I'm afraid you'll have to excuse us," he said smoothly as another reporter shoved a microphone forward. "We've got a plane to catch. You can talk to my new father-in-law and brother-in-law if you want more information."

"So Palmer and Harry Townsend are going to make the announcement?"

Angie held her veil out of her eyes and scowled at the man. "For the last time, there is no announcement to be made. This is a *wedding*."

"My wife is right. This is a wedding," Owen said as he guided Angie into the backseat of the limo. "And the groom is getting impatient. We have to be on our way."

He got in beside Angie. The driver closed the door very firmly and hurried around the big car to get behind the wheel.

As the vehicle drove off Angie turned to wave one last time at her mother, father and brother, who were still occupying the doorway of the country club. Her mother waved a hankie. Angie caught a glimpse of her father grinning broadly and saw Harry's bright red hair shining in the warm desert sunlight. Then both men were inundated by a sea of reporters and cameras.

"That was very sneaky of you to sic those journalists on Dad and Harry." Angie sat back in the seat and turned her head to smile at Owen.

"Better them than me. I've got more important things to do today." Owen's hand closed over Angie's. He lifted her fingers to his lips, and his eyes met hers as he brushed a kiss against the plain golden band she was wearing. His ring was a wide circle of carefully beaten gold, as utterly masculine as the man. Angie had designed and created it for him.

Owen looked ruefully at the plain ring he had given her. "I probably should have let you design your own."

Angie shook her head swiftly. She gazed at her ring thinking that even though she loved designing jewelry and had taken great pleasure in creating Owen's ring, nothing she could have designed for herself would have been as perfect as the gold band Owen had given her. The bold simplicity of the ring appealed to her. Moreover, Angie knew her wedding ring was not just a piece of jewelry; it was an ancient symbol, and she would treasure it as such.

"No. It wouldn't have been the same," she said fervently. "I love this ring because you chose it and you gave it to me."

Owen's mouth curved faintly, his satisfaction obvious. "And what about me, Mrs. Sutherland? Do you love me, too?"

"You know I do." Impulsively Angie leaned forward and kissed him full on his hard mouth.

"Umm." Owen's eyes gleamed as she lifted her mouth off of his. "Remember that, will you?"

"How could I forget?"

"You're right. I'm hardly likely to let you forget, am I? Not after everything I just went through."

Angie tipped her head slightly at the odd tone in his voice, but she could not think of a way to ask him what he meant. He would tell her that he'd meant what he said. He was a very private, very controlled man, and she'd promised herself she would respect that. He would change. Love would open him up soon enough, she knew. *How naive as was that of us*

"I suppose that reporter was right about one thing," Angie murmured as she gazed out the tinted windows at the lush green fairways of a golf course. "The business world will be speculating about Sutherland and Townsend for a while because of the wedding, won't it?"

Owen shrugged as he unknotted the elegant black tie that circled his throat. "It doesn't matter what the press says. Palmer and Harry don't mind, and neither do I."

Angie frowned. "It's just that it's annoying to think that some people might assume our marriage was for business reasons."

Owen slid her a quick glance as he reached for the champagne bottle chilling in a bucket on the console in front of them. "Your father warned me that you had a wide romantic streak in your nature. Better resign yourself to the fact that people are going to talk for a while. It's bound to happen. After all, everyone in the industry knows that the Sutherland and Townsend hotel chains have been rivals for years."

Angie gave him a wry smile. "Yes, I know. Ridiculous, isn't it?"

"The old rivalry? I wouldn't say that."

Owen handed her a glass of champagne. "It's had its uses over the years. The public relations people on both sides got a lot of mileage out of the fact that each chain was always trying to outdo the other."

She turned her head quickly. "You're talking as if the famous hotel feud is now in the past."

"Maybe it is, in a way." Owen lifted his glass to her. "Maybe what we've got here is Romeo and Juliet with a happy ending. I've just married my rival's only daughter, haven't I?"

Angie bit her lip, thinking that over. "Yes, you have. But that's not going to change the way either chain does business, is it? I mean, not in the immediate future, at any rate."

"Would it matter?"

"No, of course not," Angie assured him in a soft rush. The hotel business was the last thing she wanted to talk about. She smiled again. "I've never been particularly interested in Townsend Resorts, anyway."

"I know." Owen's voice was dry. "Your parents and Harry made that very clear. They said you started drawing and designing things at the age of three and you've never stopped."

Angie glanced at her hands as they lay

folded on the skirts of her gorgeous gown. "It's lucky my father has Harry to follow in his footsteps because I would never have been any good in the hotel business. I hope your family and friends won't expect me to become an expert."

Owen reached out to catch her chin between thumb and forefinger. He turned her head so she met his eyes. His gaze was very cool and very firm. "No one is expecting you to start taking an interest in the hotel business. Hell, that's the last thing I want. Stick with your jewelry designing and the business of being my wife and leave the corporate stuff to me, okay?"

She nodded, relieved. "Okay."

"This is our wedding day," he added meaningfully. "The last thing I want to do is talk about Sutherland Hotels or Townsend Resorts."

Angie smiled tremulously. "I understand. I don't want to talk about the hotel business, either. Owen, I'm so happy."

"Good." He smiled, clearly satisfied. "So am I."

"So where *are* we going to spend our honeymoon?" Angie gave him an impish grin.

Owen's brow rose with easy arrogance. "A Sutherland hotel, of course. The new one on the California coast near San Luis

Obispo. You didn't think I'd choose a Townsend resort, did you?"

Angie laughed and relaxed against his side. His strong arm went around her, holding her close. "No, of course not. The last thing a Sutherland would do is stay at a Townsend resort."

Owen kissed the curve of her shoulder that was exposed by the heart-shaped neckline of Angie's wedding gown. His mouth was warm and tantalizing against her bare skin. "But tonight a Townsend will sleep in a Sutherland bed, and when she wakes up tomorrow morning she will no longer be a Townsend."

Angie shivered and knew it must have been with desire. It was strange that such a fiery emotion could send such a cold chill through her.

Wedding day nerves, no doubt, she told herself.

There was another limousine waiting at the airport when the Sutherland corporate jet touched down that evening. The sun had set in a blaze of fire off the rugged California coast. A velvet darkness descended as Angie and Owen were driven north to the magnificent new Sutherland hotel and spa.

The hotel crowned a jagged bluff that overlooked the sea. It was a wonderland of crystal blue pools, lush landscaping and exotic architecture. On the premises were a golf course, tennis courts and spa facilities, as well as several different restaurants, a nightclub and a poolside bar. Sutherland hotels were known for being worlds unto themselves.

"Well, well. Not bad. Not bad at all." Angie glanced around with an air of cautious approval as she stepped out of the limo. "Almost as nice as a Townsend resort, in fact."

"Bite your tongue, woman," Owen growled. "You're a Sutherland now, remember?"

"Funny, I don't feel like a Sutherland."

"You will by tomorrow morning. I'll make certain of it."

Angie blushed under the impact of the sensual promise in his gaze.

An hour later she stood on the terrace of the spectacular silver and white bridal suite and gazed over the night-shrouded Pacific. She had changed into the silver gown her mother had chosen for her. Not quite a nightgown and not quite an evening ensemble, the silk peignoir made Angie feel sultry and feminine. The only jewelry she wore — aside from her wedding ring — was a pair of sculptural silver earrings that almost reached her bare shoulders. Angie had designed them herself.

The luxurious honeymoon suite behind her was empty. Owen had vanished a few minutes earlier, saying he wanted to touch base with the hotel manager. He had told her they would be dining in the room when he returned.

Angie took a deep breath of the fragrant night air. This was the first time she had been alone since she'd awakened that morning, and it was something of a relief.

The Townsend clan was an exuberant bunch, always up for a celebration. Anything from a christening to a wake would suffice. But although they enjoyed a good party, it was no secret Townsends were very family oriented. One of the things her mother and father had liked about Owen Sutherland was that he did not have a reputation as a womanizer. Nor was he noted for being highly visible in the social world. He was rarely in the public eye and would expect his wife to stay out of it, also. That suited Angie just fine.

One small fact had bothered her during the past three months, however. She had yet to meet any of Owen's family.

24

It was another unfortunate example of bad timing and lack of opportunity, Angie reflected. The headquarters of Sutherland Hotels had been moved to Arizona a year ago, but Owen was the only Sutherland who had come south with it.

She did not know all that much about his past. He had lost his mother when he was very young, and his father had died in a plane crash two years ago. The rest of Owen's family, which apparently included an ailing stepmother, a sister who was traveling in Hawaii with her husband, a somewhat senile uncle and an aunt who was unable to travel because of a recent knee operation, all lived in California. Owen had told her that the family home was on an island in the middle of Jade Lake in the mountains north of San Francisco. He had also mentioned that his stepmother and his aunt and uncle spent a great deal of time there. Beyond that, Angie knew very little.

It was odd to be marrying a man whose family she had not met, Angie thought as she gazed into the darkness. Even odder that not a single Sutherland relative had been able to make it to the wedding of the head of the family. But Palmer Townsend had seemed unconcerned when she had broached the subject and had vetoed the notion of postponing the wedding until the families had gotten to know each other.

"Now, don't go worrying about the old feud, Angie," Palmer had assured her. "Owen Sutherland runs that clan just like he runs his hotel chain. They'll all do what he tells 'em to do. And he'll tell 'em to welcome you with open arms. Besides, what does it matter if they're a trifle upset about the idea of him marrying a Townsend? You'll be living down here in Arizona, not over in California. You won't have to deal with his family very much."

Owen had said something along the same lines when she had tactfully raised the issue with him.

"Don't worry about my family, Angie. You're marrying me, not them."

"It's not as if his mother and father were still alive and refusing to come to the wedding, dear," Angie's mother had pointed out. "These are just some rather distant relatives."

"One of them is his stepmother," Angie had reminded her.

"I don't think he's very close to her. Owen was raised almost entirely by his father, from what I understand. And you must remember that families are different. Sutherlands apparently aren't outgoing and emotional like us Townsends. Just look at Owen. Calm and cool as a stone."

Angie was still not entirely certain everyone was correct in his reasoning but she had been too much in love to argue. The wedding had been rushed through on the schedule Owen had requested.

And now, for better or worse, the deed was done. Angie glanced again at the ring on her finger. *For better or worse?* That seemed a bit morbid for a wedding night. Another of those strange little chills went down her spine.

The white phone on the clear glass table beside the bed rang, breaking the pall of moody uncertainty that had taken hold of Angie. Grateful for the interruption, she hurried through the open French doors to pick up the receiver.

"Hello?"

"Mrs. Owen Sutherland?" The voice had a dry, raspy sound, as if the speaker was deliberately trying to pitch it abnormally low.

"This is Angie. Angie Sutherland, I mean." Her new last name felt strange in her mouth.

"Congratulations, *Mrs. Sutherland.* I hope you're satisfied with the bargain you've made. I know your family certainly is."

"I beg your pardon?"

"Tell me, how does it feel to find out you've been used as a pawn in a business deal this big? I hope you had the sense to at least get a prenuptial agreement guaranteeing you your fair share. If not, you're going to be very sorry, *Mrs. Sutherland*."

"Who is this? What on earth are you talking about?"

"So I was right. You really don't know about the plans your husband and your father have made, do you? How naive you are. I was told you were. They said you were an artistic type who never paid much attention to the realities of the business world. Easy game for Owen Sutherland."

"If you don't explain yourself immediately I am going to report this call to the police."

"He's going to divorce you as soon as the stock offering takes place, you know. The Romeo and Juliet marriage was strictly for publicity purposes, although the Townsends think it's for real. Townsends are so emotional, aren't they? Even when they're doing business. They fell for Sutherland's scheme hook, line and sinker."

"Please, you've got to tell me what this is all about."

"Why it's all about business, *Mrs. Sutherland*. Don't you understand? The whole

28

thing is about business. It always is with Owen Sutherland."

"Stop it."

"Think about it. The wedding and news of the ending of the big feud will draw enormous attention to the stock when it goes public next month. Investors will love it." The raspy voice was almost conversational in tone now. "Your family all think they've pulled off a coup but they'll soon find out they've been duped. They thought they could deal with a Sutherland but they're way out of their league."

Angie told herself she should hang up. This was nothing less than an obscene call. But a trickle of a premonition was back. Something was horribly wrong. She could feel it.

"In two years or less the Townsends will find themselves powerless on the new board. Owen Sutherland will be running everything. After that it will be just a matter of time before the Townsends are eased out of the picture entirely."

"I don't understand what you're talking about."

"Of course you don't, you naive little fool. Why don't you try dealing with reality for a change? Ask yourself this question: Why should Sutherland keep you around after you've served your purpose? Oh, one more thing. Take a look outside the front door of your hotel room. I think you'll be very interested in what you find there."

Angie did not hesitate another instant. She dropped the phone into the cradle as if it were a snake. She should have hung up immediately, she told herself. Owen would be furious when she told him what had happened.

Why should Sutherland keep you around after you've served your purpose?

Angie found herself at the door of the hotel room before she was aware she had crossed the thick, white carpet. She turned the knob with cold fingers and opened the door.

An envelope lay on the floor outside the room. Angie picked it up and stared at it numbly. Inside the envelope was a fax of a press release from the corporate offices of Sutherland Hotels. A note in the right-hand corner advised that the release was to be held until the day following the wedding, then sent to all major stock analysts, business news dailies and a variety of other media.

Sutherland Hotels and Townsend Resorts today announced a merger. The two premier hotel chains, long rivals for the high-end market, have joined forces in order to expand into the global arena. To raise capital, the new corporation, which will be known as Sutherland and Townsend, will go public with a stock offering next month.

Anticipation of such a merger has been keen among industry insiders and stock analysts since the engagement of Owen Sutherland, president and chief executive officer of Sutherland Hotels, to Angela Townsend, the daughter of Palmer Townsend, was announced a few weeks ago. The merger agreement was signed on the day of the wedding.

Owen Sutherland and Palmer Townsend were both quoted as saying the marriage heralded a new era in the growth of the hotel chains.

Angie stared at the press release until a noise at the end of the hall made her look up. A maid pushed a cart around the corner and smiled quizzically when she saw Angie standing in the open doorway.

"Good evening, ma'am. Was there something you needed?"

Angie shook her head distractedly and started to step into the room. Then she thought of something. "Wait, please. Did you by any chance notice who left this in front of my door?"

The maid shook her head. "Sorry, ma'am. I didn't see anyone."

"Thank you." Angie closed the door and sagged against it, clutching the press release. She took a deep breath and tried to think.

It can't be true, she thought wildly. Then she remembered the reporters at the wedding and remembered how Owen had calmly suggested they talk to her father and brother.

Her father and brother. They must have plotted this with Owen weeks, perhaps even months ago. Mergers the size of this one did not get planned overnight or on a whim.

It was so like the other members of the Townsend family not to bother naive little Angie with pesky business details, she reminded herself bitterly. They had all approved of Owen and that was enough. As usual, they thought they knew what was best for Angie.

Angie leaped for the white phone and frantically punched out her parents' home number. There was no answer.

The hotel room door opened as she was slowly replacing the receiver. She whirled to face Owen.

"Angie? Is something wrong, honey?" Owen was wearing the beautifully tailored gray slacks and white shirt he had changed into earlier. He came quietly into the room and closed the door. He frowned at her in concern. "You look like you've seen a ghost."

"What I've seen is this," she whispered. She held out the press release with trembling fingers. "There appear to be a few minor details about this wedding someone forgot to mention to the bride."

TWO

Owen recognized the Sutherland corporate logo as he took the fax from Angie's hand. He knew instantly what he was looking at and decided quickly that somebody's head was going to be on the chopping block within the next twenty-four hours. It would most likely be the neck of his vice president in charge of public relations that would feel the ax, although it was hard to believe Calhoun had screwed up this badly. Calhoun, like everyone on Owen's staff, knew that when the president of the Sutherland Hotel Corporation said he wanted something kept under wraps, he meant it. People got fired for this kind of mistake.

It was possible, of course, that someone on the Townsend staff had been responsible for leaking the news a day early. The Townsends were a notoriously excitable bunch, not cool and controlled like the Sutherlands. Still, everyone had agreed the news of the merger should be kept secret until the day after the wedding.

Palmer had been as insistent on that point as Sutherland. He had said that Angie, with her romantic, artistic ways and her lack of a proper business perspective, might not understand why her wedding had been timed to coincide with the merger announcement.

No, the Townsends had no reason to leak the news, and there was no getting around the fact that the fax had been sent from Sutherland corporate headquarters in Tucson. This was a Sutherland error.

"Damn." Owen scanned the release. "This wasn't supposed to hit the streets until tomorrow."

"I'm not sure it has hit the streets," Angie said with an unnatural calm. "Perhaps it was meant for me."

Owen narrowed his eyes as he looked up from the release. It occurred to him that he had never heard that curious brittleness in Angie's voice before. Her words were almost always laced with some easily identified emotion: warmth or laughter, feminine curiosity or sweet, reckless passion — never this shaky coolness.

Owen studied his wife as she stood in front of him with her arms defensively crossed under her breasts. Slim and delicate, her fiery red hair pulled into a sleek knot at her nape, she looked at him with an injured, womanly pride.

Owen was fascinated, as he always was, with the startling turquoise of her faintly slanting eyes. Angie looked like one of her own jewelry designs, he had often told himself: elegant and feminine, with a quiet kind of strength and power.

The silk gown she was wearing clung to her gently curving breasts like liquid silver. Owen could see the outline of her nipples. He was suddenly, vividly aware of the rising heat in his own body. He had, after all, been anticipating his wedding night for three long months. Not nearly as long as he had been anticipating the merger of Sutherland and Townsend, of course, but long enough to play havoc with his fierce Sutherland self-control.

"Why do you say it was meant for you?" he asked, buying time while he tried to assess Angie's reaction. He was not certain what was going on in her mind. It was the first time he had found himself unable to tell what she was thinking.

"There was a phone call." She tilted her chin to indicate the phone on the bedside table. "Someone told me about the merger and then suggested I take a look outside the door."

Owen stilled as he assimilated that bit of information. Then a cold anger flared to life. "Someone called you to tell you about this?"

"Yes."

"What did he say?"

"I'm not sure it was a he. It could have been a woman. Whoever it was did not say much, only that I had been used as a pawn in one of your business maneuvers."

Owen waited. When Angie did not volunteer anything more he prodded carefully. "Was that all the caller had to say?"

"No."

"Don't you think you'd better tell me the rest?"

She shrugged. The silver silk flowed over her breasts with the movement. "There wasn't much more. Just that within a couple of years the Townsends would discover they were out in the cold and you would be running everything. Oh, yes, there was also the strong suggestion that when my usefulness was past, which would be immediately after the stock offering, you would divorce me."

"I'll destroy whoever made that call," Owen said. He crumpled the fax in one fist.

"Will you?"

"Count on it. I won't allow anyone to

upset you like this and get away with it. Angie, you didn't take any of that nonsense about being a pawn seriously, did you?"

Hope instantly brightened her eyes. "Are you telling me it's all a lie? That there's no truth in the press release? Owen, I'm so relieved. You don't know how . . ."

Owen exhaled deeply as he walked across the room to the liquor cabinet and poured himself a glass of the French brandy he had ordered earlier. "The merger is a fact. Your father and I signed the papers this morning shortly before the ceremony."

The hope in her eyes died a quick death. "I see."

"No, I don't think you do." He turned to face her, drink in hand. "You're reading far too much into this."

"Am I?"

"Angie, you weren't told about the merger because the entire deal was meant to be kept strictly confidential until tomorrow. It was business. You're not involved in your family's business, and there was no reason to tell you what was going on."

"I don't think I believe that, Owen. I think I wasn't told about the merger because it would have made me wonder exactly why you were marrying me. Tell me, did my father make me part of the deal? Was that his way of trying to insure that my family didn't come out the loser in this arrangement? Or did he just see it as a fitting ending to an old feud? Townsends are all romantics at heart. He would have liked the Romeo-and-Juliet-with-a-happy-ending bit."

"The business side of this thing had nothing to do with the personal side."

"Do you swear that's true?"

"Come on, Angie, you know things don't work like that in this day and age." Owen smiled reassuringly. "This isn't a marriage of convenience or whatever they used to call them. I'm not a masochist. I'll admit I wanted the merger badly, but not badly enough to tie myself for life to a woman I didn't want."

"But you're not permanently tied to me, are you? You can get rid of me as soon as the stock offering is made. Whoever called me on the phone was right about one thing. The Romeo and Juliet gimmick is dynamite PR. Even I can figure that much out."

"Angie, calm down."

She ignored that, waving a hand wildly for dramatic emphasis. "I can see the headlines in the business press already. *Sutherland and Townsend end the feud with a wedding. New firm goes global.* People will love it, won't they?"

"Angie, listen to me," he said gently. "You've got it all wrong."

"Have I? Are you telling me that the timing of our marriage had nothing whatsoever to do with the timing of the merger? That it was all one incredible, amazing coincidence?"

Owen's jaw tightened. He wished he could cut this argument off with some smooth, simple explanation that would pacify Angie, but he knew that was impossible. The damage was done. "No, it wasn't a coincidence. But it wasn't nearly as Machiavellian as you're assuming it was, either."

"How can I believe that?" Angie challenged him with stormy eyes.

Owen felt his usually well-controlled temper start to rear. He made a deliberate grab for the reins of his calm, rational side, which had always served him so well in business. There was no reason it should not serve him equally well in his marriage, he told himself.

"I had been interested in doing the merger for over a year," Owen said. "I approached your father about it six months ago. He was receptive and we started talks. Then I met you and decided I wanted to marry you. The two events were entirely unrelated."

"Oh, is that so?"

"Yes. But when we realized there would be both a wedding and a merger, your family and I decided it made good business sense to combine them. The public relations opportunity was simply too good to ignore, what with the stock offering coming up soon."

Angie's chin came up angrily, her turquoise eyes sparkling with brilliant rage. "Why wasn't I told?"

Owen took a sip of brandy. "Because we knew you'd probably react exactly as you are now. You're a designer, an artist, not a businesswoman. Palmer and Harry agreed with me that you'd no doubt leap to a lot of wrong conclusions. Your mother thought we could tell you and that you'd understand if it was all properly explained, but she got outvoted."

"I don't believe this. It's as if you called a meeting of a board of directors and voted on my whole future."

Owen set his teeth. "Angie, we did it for your own —"

"*For my own good.* I know. Owen, I really detest it when people make decisions for me for my own good. Just when was I supposed to find out about the business side of this marriage?"

Owen sighed. "Tomorrow morning."

She stared at him. "Why wait until then? What difference was that supposed to make?"

"You'd have been my wife in every sense of the word by then," he reminded her quietly. "You would have known for certain that what I feel for you is totally separate and distinct from the business angle."

Her eyes widened. "You thought I'd be so overwhelmed with your magnificent love-making I wouldn't stop to put two and two together when I found out about the merger? That I'd be in some sort of sexual thrall to you by tomorrow morning? Good grief. I know you think I'm emotional and romantic, but I'm not stupid."

He shook his head, smiling slightly. "I never said you were stupid. I have nothing but respect for your intelligence." He glanced significantly at his ring. "And for your talent. But you are not business oriented, Angie. Even you admit that."

"Tell me something," she shot back. "Would you have courted me and asked me to marry you if you hadn't been interested in merging the two companies? Would you have gone ahead with the wedding if it hadn't been coupled with a good business opportunity?"

"Angie, you're not being logical," he said

patiently. "I would never have met you if I hadn't decided I wanted the merger. Townsends and Sutherlands never socialized in my father's day. The feud was useful as a publicity gimmick, but it wasn't ever a mere PR creation. It was for real. It goes back thirty years and it would probably still be going on if my father hadn't died two years ago and left Sutherland Hotels to me. I decided it was time to end the feud and your father agreed with me."

"It was crazy," she whispered. "Years of craziness. I've always wondered what started it all."

"Something to do with the two companies attempting a merger thirty years ago. The deal fell through, and Sutherland lost some important financial backing, which Townsend later picked up. My father blamed yours. Your father thought it was all my father's fault that the deal went sour. After all these years no one knows for certain what went wrong, and as far as I'm concerned, it doesn't matter."

"Are you sure about that?" she demanded.

"Damn sure. Angie, I don't care what happened thirty years ago. I'm concerned about the future of my company, not the past. And I give your father credit for being willing to settle the feud. My father would never consider it. Lord knows we quarreled over it often enough."

Angie turned her back to him, giving Owen a view of her vulnerable nape and her glorious hair. His gaze skimmed hungrily down the graceful line of her spine. He watched the play of the silver silk gown over her sweetly curved buttocks and his fingers flexed tightly around the glass in his hand. *This is my wedding night,* he thought.

"Owen, I want to ask you something. Something important. Is the real reason no one from your side of the family came to our wedding that they all feel as strongly as your father did about the feud?"

"Old quarrels die hard," he admitted. "My family isn't like yours. Sutherlands aren't noted for being easygoing and open-minded."

"Did you think your people might like me once they got to know me? Were you counting on my charm and personality to win them over?"

"I'm not concerned with winning them over. I am only concerned that they treat you with the respect that is due my wife," Owen said softly. And if any of them did not, he vowed silently, he would cut off their income from Sutherland Hotels. He had the power to do it.

"On the other hand, why should they bother to get to know me when it's entirely possible I won't be a Sutherland after the stock offering is made?" Angie asked in a suspiciously bland tone.

Owen felt his temper start to slip again. He was not accustomed to the sensation and he did not like the feeling. He was always in control of himself, his business and everyone around him. Nobody manipulated Owen Sutherland.

His father had taught him to dominate any situation in which he found himself. This marriage would be no different. He would be in charge. The first step was to maintain his self-control.

"This has gone far enough," Owen said coolly. "For the last time, Angie, I didn't marry you because of the merger."

"Why did you marry me?" she asked. She did not turn to look at him. She was still hugging herself very tightly.

"Because I want you as my wife."

"Owen, do you love me? Really love me?" Angie asked in a small voice, still not turning. "You've never said the words, you know. I've been assuming so much. I've been telling myself that you have a hard time talking about your emotions, but maybe I've been making excuses for you because I was so desperately in love myself."

The brandy glass made a sound like the crack of a pistol shot when Owen slammed it on the liquor cabinet. He stalked across the room and caught Angie by the shoulders, whirling her to face him. He saw her beautiful eyes widen in surprise and trepidation.

"You don't need to make excuses for me," he bit out. "I married you. You are the only woman I have ever asked to marry me. You are everything I want and need in a wife, and I knew it the minute I saw you. We are in this together, you and I. We will make it work. You have my word of honor on it."

"If only I could be sure —"

He looked into her tumultuous gaze, gave a low, frustrated groan and pulled her into his arms. He covered her trembling mouth with his before she could finish the sentence.

Deliberately Owen set about using his own desire to ignite Angie's. He was positive he could do it. She had been responding to him beautifully during the past few weeks — sweet and hot, hovering on the brink of total surrender. Owen had gloried in the knowledge that he could make her react completely to him. He had used his sensual power gently, cautiously, not wanting to alarm her or take advantage of her. But he was getting desperate.

And she was his wife. He had a right to coax the response he knew she was longing to give him. If he could get her into bed, everything would be all right again, he was certain of it.

"*Owen.* Owen, please . . ."

He heard the feminine desire in her soft, pleading cry and felt her begin to lean into him. Her soft breasts were crushed against his chest. Her arms stole around his neck and her lips parted as he deepened the kiss.

Owen let his tongue probe the warmth of Angie's mouth as he slid his hands slowly up her spine. She sighed softly and her eyes closed. Owen felt her hips against his thighs, and his already aroused body tightened even more with a fierce, compelling need.

Owen was suddenly swamped with desire. He wanted to pull Angie onto the bed, strip off the silver silk and plunge himself into her. He inhaled the scent of her, part perfume and part feminine arousal, and he knew she was already becoming moist, welcoming, responsive. . . .

He could not wait any longer. She was clinging to him. Owen scooped Angie up in his arms and started toward the huge, white, canopied bed. He could only think of one thing, and that was his overpowering need to make Angie his wife in every way. This was his wedding night, and he was on fire for his bride.

In the morning she would understand that his need for her had nothing to do with the merger of Sutherland and Townsend. He would convince her here in their wedding bed. *With my body, I thee worship.*

"Owen . . ."

"Hush, sweetheart. We'll talk in the morning. It's all right. Trust me, Angie. Everything's going to be just fine. This is the way it's supposed to be between us."

He put her on the bed and leaned over to slide the tiny straps of the gown over her shoulders. Angie did not move as he slowly eased the fluid fabric to her waist to reveal her breasts. Owen sucked in his breath at the sight of her rosy nipples.

He gently caught one hard little berry between his fingers and squeezed carefully. Angie gasped, and Owen felt the shiver that went through her as if it had gone through himself.

Owen smiled and straightened. He watched her as he started to yank at the buttons of his shirt. Angie lay there looking at him with a growing wonder and a deep, questioning awareness that made him want to soothe and reassure her even as he ached to take her completely.

In another few minutes she would be his.

The knock on the door jolted Owen as violently as if he had touched a live electrical wire.

"*Damn.*"

"Room service, sir," said the disembodied voice from the other side of the door.

Owen closed his eyes in brief, savage annoyance. Then he got a fresh grip on his self-control and managed a slight smile for Angie. "That'll be dinner. When I ordered it, I actually believed we might want to eat tonight. Obviously, I made a mistake. You stay right there, honey. I'll take care of it."

He went to the door and jerked it open, startling the waiter. The young man smiled nervously.

"Excuse me, sir — Mr. Sutherland. Uh, you ordered dinner, sir?" the waiter stammered.

"Right. I'll handle it. We won't need any help. We can serve ourselves." Owen summoned up his patience and reminded himself that he always had this effect on employees when he stayed in one of his own hotels. Tonight he probably looked even more forbidding than usual. He knew he was scowling.

"Yes, sir, Mr. Sutherland. And, uh, the chef sends his congratulations, sir." The waiter backed away, his face turning a bright red as he took in the state of Owen's clothes. "Sorry to interrupt. Let us know if you need anything else."

"I'll do that," Owen said dryly. He wheeled the cart into the room and closed the door.

He turned to look at Angie, who was sitting up on the edge of the bed, fumbling with her silver gown. She did not meet his eyes. "We don't have to eat this right now," he said suggestively. "It'll keep."

"No!" She leaped to her feet. "No, I'm . . . I'm very hungry. I hardly ate at the reception. And I couldn't eat breakfast. I haven't had much to eat all day, now that I think about it."

"Angie . . ."

"Here, I'll help you set that up." She darted forward and began yanking the silver lids off the serving trays. Fragrant aromas wafted up from artichokes and golden hollandaise sauce and perfectly broiled swordfish steaks. "Doesn't this look wonderful?"

Owen stifled an oath, aware that the moment had been lost. Angie had clearly gone from being on the point of sensual surrender to being a nervous wreck. His mouth quirked as he obligingly began dealing with the contents of the dinner cart.

"Shall we eat out on the terrace?" Owen asked politely.

"Yes. That sounds delightful." She carried the fish to the glass and white wrought-iron table on the terrace.

Owen followed more slowly, taking a long, deep breath of the night air to cool his clamoring senses. "Fog's coming in," he remarked casually.

"It is, isn't it? A bit chilly."

"We can eat inside, if you like."

"No, no, this is just fine," she said hastily. "It won't turn really cold for a while yet. And there's something very pleasant about the fog coming in off the ocean, isn't there?"

"If you like fog."

"Yes. Well, I do." She perched on the edge of one of the chairs and made a production of serving the food from the trays.

Owen sat down, watching her with indulgent amusement. "Why so nervous all of a sudden, Angie? I've kissed you before. I was always under the impression you enjoyed the experience. And this is our wedding night, after all."

"Please, Owen. Could we talk about something else?"

"Something other than our wedding night, you mean?"

"*Yes*, damn it."

He blinked lazily at the flash of temper and calmly reached for a crusty roll. "Whatever you like, honey."

The more agitated Angie got, the more Owen relaxed and told himself everything was going to be fine. She was such a fiery, hot-blooded creature, and that put her at a distinct disadvantage when dealing with someone coolheaded and self-controlled.

As long as she was nervous, Owen knew he would stay in command of the situation. It was only when she caught him off guard with that oddly brittle persona, as she had earlier, that he was at a loss.

They ate in silence for several minutes. Owen made no attempt to ease the situation. *Let her stew a bit,* he decided. When he eventually took her into his arms, she would no doubt collapse against him in total surrender, and that would be the end of the problem. The thing to remember when dealing with nervous, excitable creatures such as Angie was that they were their own worst enemies.

Owen was eating a slice of Brie from the cheese tray when Angie suddenly put down her knife, folded her hands in her lap and sat back in her chair.

"All right, Owen. I have done a great deal of thinking during dinner and I have made some decisions."

"Interesting."

"I would appreciate it if you could refrain from being sarcastic. This is a very serious matter."

"Making love for the first time? I agree with you. It is a serious matter, but I think we can handle it."

"Owen, please. This is not a farce."

"I know, darling. But you're on the verge of turning it into one, aren't you?"

She stood abruptly, liquid silver swirling around her slender frame. She went to stand at the terrace railing and gazed at the fog-shrouded ocean. "I have concluded that I cannot make a rational, intelligent decision about the future of our relationship tonight."

"You don't need to make any decisions about it," Owen said quietly, setting down his cheese knife. "The decision was made today when I put that ring on your finger in front of three hundred witnesses."

She shook her head quickly but did not turn around. Her hands were clenched around the railing. "I can't seem to think clearly tonight. Don't you understand? I'm confused and I'm frightened. I need time to consider everything."

"I see." Owen finally began to perceive where this jumbled conversation was heading. He tossed aside the monogrammed napkin and got to his feet. He crossed the terrace to stand directly behind Angie but he did not touch her. "Just how much time do you think you'll need to figure out that you really are married to me?"

"Until after the stock offering," she said in a soft, determined little voice.

Owen saw red. For one blistering instant he nearly lost his temper completely. It took him several seconds to regain his self-control, and even when he was sure he had himself in hand again, he still did not dare to touch her.

He forced himself to speak slowly and deliberately on the off chance that he had misunderstood. "What, exactly, are you trying to tell me, Angie?"

"That I don't want us to . . . to consummate our marriage until after Sutherland and Townsend goes public."

Owen could not believe what he was hearing. "The stock offering doesn't take place until the first of next month. That's three weeks from now."

"I know."

He put out a hand and closed it firmly around her shoulder. Very carefully, fully aware of his tightly leashed anger and his fierce desire, he turned her to face him. "You're saying you don't want to go to bed with me until after you find out if whoever called you tonight was telling the truth?"

She nodded mutely.

"How do you think that makes me feel, Angie?"

Tears welled in her beautiful eyes. "I'm sorry. But I'm scared, Owen. I've allowed you and my family to rush me into this marriage and now I'm wondering if I've made a terrible mistake. You know what they say about marrying in haste."

"You haven't made a mistake."

"Don't you see? You and my family should never have kept me in the dark about the merger. The telephone call and press release hit me like a ton of bricks tonight. They made me realize how willfully naive I've been about our whole relationship."

"Honey, that's not true."

"It is true. When you stop and think about it, you must realize I don't know you very well, Owen. I don't even know your family, let alone the true depth of your feelings for me. I need some time."

"Three weeks, to be precise, right? You

want to see if I'm going to file for divorce after we take the company public. You want to see if this courtship and marriage have merely been a clever business ploy."

"That's part of it," she admitted in a choked voice. "But mostly I just want time to be sure of what I'm doing."

"Angie, don't forget the fact that your parents approved of this marriage. Your father and brother had no problem with the idea of doing the merger and the wedding at the same time. You know your family would never have gone for the idea of you marrying me if they hadn't believed you'd be happy."

"I know. What I don't know is how good you might have been at convincing them that you really care for me. Don't you understand?" Her voice rose in frustration. "That's the problem. There's just too much I don't know about you."

"Like what?" Owen demanded.

"I want to meet your family and find out the reasons none of them could be bothered to come to the wedding. I want to think about the fact that you kept the merger a secret from me. I feel I've been caught up in a whirlwind and now I want a chance to get my feet on the ground and make up my mind about our relationship."

"And you don't feel you'll be able to think

clearly if you're sleeping with me?" he demanded, his fingers still clamped on her shoulder. "Is that it?"

"Yes, that's it."

"Damn it, Angie," he muttered, "you don't know what you're doing."

"I know. That's why I want time to think."

Owen shook his head ruefully. "That's not quite what I mean." He tugged her gently against him. Her body was stiff and unyielding, but he felt her tremble. He wondered what would happen if he kissed her. She was so responsive to his touch. . . . "My family is not going to be a good advertisement for me, honey. I see as little of them as possible myself."

"Owen, that sounds awful," she said into his shirt.

"I know. You say that because you Townsends are really into family. But that doesn't mean everyone else is."

"But don't you see? Sooner or later I'll have to deal with your family. I need to know what I'm getting into."

"Angie, I want you to trust me on this. Let me handle my family and the business. You just concentrate on being my wife and everything will work out fine."

"You're forgetting something, Owen," she said quietly. "That phone call tonight proves that you can't separate our relationship from the business of Sutherland and Townsend."

She had a point, and Owen knew it. He had kept the choice of which hotel he would be using for the honeymoon completely confidential, just as he and Palmer had kept the merger confidential. Yet someone had learned both secrets and had used them to drive a wedge between himself and Angie.

"And I seriously doubt that we can ignore your family, either," Angie continued. "No matter how much you want."

"We can give it a damn good try," he muttered.

She stirred restlessly against him and lifted her head. Her eyes were stark in the pale light that filtered from the hotel room. "And there's something else we have to resolve, Owen. Something I hadn't allowed myself to examine too closely until tonight."

"Damn. This list is getting a little tedious, isn't it? What else do you need time to think about besides my family and my business and my honorable intentions?"

She took a deep breath and looked at him, her face more sweetly serious than Owen had seen it. "I need to know if you really love me, Owen. That's actually the only thing on the list, when you get right down to it. Everything else I'm wondering about stems from that basic question. I don't know the answer."

His insides clenched. "Angie, I've told you, you're everything I want and need in a wife."

"Yes, but do you *love* me? That's what we need to find out. And then we need to see if you can admit it to me and to yourself. I need to discover if your feelings toward me are merely a result of your being physically attracted to me and feeling that I'm also an extremely useful business asset."

"Damn it, Angie . . ."

She straightened her shoulders. "I have decided we should delay our wedding night until we know for certain exactly what our relationship is based on and how long it's going to last."

Owen set his teeth. "I see. And just where the hell do you plan to spend tonight, Mrs. Sutherland?"

She blinked and gazed anxiously into the room behind him. "Well, this is a hotel. There should be plenty of rooms available."

Through an extraordinary act of will, Owen managed to quash his rage. But he brought his face very close to Angie's so that she would have no trouble seeing just how blazingly furious he was. "I'll be damned if I'll have my wife going down to the front desk of a Sutherland hotel on her wedding night to ask for a different room so that she won't be obliged to sleep with me."

Angie bit her lip. "I wouldn't want to humiliate you, of course."

"A very wise decision."

"I can see where it would be a bit embarrassing to have it get out that we didn't spend tonight together," she murmured apologetically.

"Embarrassing? I'd be the laughingstock of the entire hotel staff, not to mention the whole damn industry."

"Yes, we must maintain appearances, mustn't we?" she snapped. "After all, this is business. Everyone knows there are hundreds of thousands, maybe millions of dollars worth of Sutherland and Townsend stock about to go on the block. If you don't mind, I'll sleep out here on the lounger."

"You will sleep on the damned bed," Owen said through his teeth. "And so will I. We'll put a sword or something equally appropriate between us. Does that suit you, *Mrs. Sutherland?*"

Angie eyed him cautiously, obviously aware that she was on extremely thin ice. "Yes, thank you," she said very politely.

THREE

In the end, they used two king-size pillows Angie discovered in the closet rather than a sword. But as she lay wide awake on her side of the huge bed, counting down the minutes until dawn, Angie decided the pillows might as well have been made of steel. The barrier they created between her and her husband was certainly as sharp and formidable as any sword would have been.

She felt miserable. Guilty and hurt and angry and uncertain and just plain miserable. And the worst part was that Owen had apparently gone straight to sleep the moment his head had hit the pillow.

I'm doing the right thing, Angie repeated to herself over and over again as the hours crawled past with painful slowness. It became a mantra. *I'm doing the right thing.*

She realized she must have dozed off at some point because she came awake with a start shortly before dawn. She opened her eyes and found herself staring straight at a dull gray sea. For a few disoriented seconds she could not figure out where she was or why there was a huge white canopy overhead.

"You awake?" Owen asked from the other side of the bed.

Angie cringed at the coldness in his voice. *Well,* she asked herself, *what did you expect from your new husband after a wedding night like the one we've just had?* "Yes."

"Good. I've made some plans."

"Oh."

"Don't tell me you had any?" he drawled.

"No. Not exactly. I mean, I hadn't really thought about what we would do next. I know we're supposed to spend a couple of weeks here."

"That would be a bit awkward under the circumstances, don't you think?"

"I don't know about that," she said, thinking it through. "It's a lovely hotel and we're here now. We could spend the next two weeks getting to know each other."

"Angie, I am not about to waste the next two weeks playing the devoted bridegroom in front of a couple hundred people who happen to work for me and who will be watching us every time we leave this room," he stated flatly.

"I can see where that might be difficult," she retorted. "Playing the devoted bridegroom, that is. Especially if you're not. Devoted, I mean."

"Let's try this from a different angle," he muttered.

Angie turned to look at him, propping herself up on her elbow. Her first sight of him lying there, big and dark and dangerous against the snowy pillows, made her catch her breath.

Owen had undressed in the shadows last night, and she had carefully not looked at him as he'd climbed into bed beside her. Now she realized he was not wearing anything above the waist. She could not tell if he was wearing anything below the waist because the lower half of his lean, hard body was cloaked in a white satin sheet.

"Angie, are you listening to me?"

She realized she was staring at the broad expanse of his chest, thinking about what it would be like to twine her fingers in the crisp, curling dark hair there. She jerked her gaze up quickly, aware that she was turning pink. "Yes, of course."

He studied her, his crystal eyes narrowed behind his dark lashes. He had his hands laced behind his head and he looked very much at ease lying there in a strange bed with a woman who was not quite his wife. "All right, here's what we're going to do. I'm taking you to Jade Lake until after the stock offering."

"Jade Lake? I thought your stepmother lived there. And your aunt and uncle."

"They do. One big happy family. If we're real lucky my stepsister and her husband might drop in."

"If you don't like your family all that much why are we going to spend three weeks with them?"

"You said you wanted to get to know them, as I recall. I've got an office at the house. I don't use it very much because I don't go to Jade Lake often. But I should be able to get some work done from there during the next few weeks so the time won't be entirely wasted."

Angie sat up suddenly, pushing the strap of her silver nightgown hastily back up on her shoulder. She saw Owen's gaze rest on her breasts and realized her nipples must be thrusting at the silk. She hunched her shoulders to reduce the stress on the fabric.

"Now hold on just a minute," Angie said. "You're not going to dump me into a houseful of strangers for the next three weeks while you bury yourself in an office."

"This is the most logical way of dealing

with the problem. It'll give you the chance to meet my family, and it will give you the time you said you needed to come to a decision. It will also keep our relationship off-stage while we wait for the stock offering."

"I'm not so sure I like this. I think you've decided to stash me out of sight until after the new company goes public. You're afraid I'll jeopardize the interest in the stock, aren't you? People will start to question the strength of the merger if everyone starts talking about our shaky marriage, won't they?"

He shrugged against the pillows. "It's a strong possibility."

"Right. And if they question the merger, then they'll question the value of the stock. If they question the stock, you and Dad won't be able to get a good price for it when it goes public. And if the stock doesn't do well in the market, Sutherland and Townsend won't raise the capital it needs to expand."

"You've got it in one," Owen said roughly.

"I am not nearly as naive about corporate business matters as everyone likes to think," Angie declared with a touch of pride.

Owen inclined his head mockingly, but his eyes were grim. "The bottom line is that I sure as hell don't want you running around giving interviews for the next three weeks."

Angie was outraged. "I wouldn't give interviews."

"Reporters and competitors have a way of getting innocents like you to talk. If you were a starry-eyed bride who thought I was Prince Charming, that would be one thing. You'd just be shoring up the image of love conquering all every time you opened your mouth. But in your present mood I'm not taking any chances. I want you under lock and key until this whole deal is concluded."

"Lock and key."

"A figure of speech. Let's just say I want us to have a lot of privacy in the next few weeks. The family home is on an island in the middle of the lake. No one can get to it without a boat and no one comes ashore without an invitation. Believe me, we won't be inviting anyone."

"You've got a hell of a lot of nerve to talk like that. If you think for one minute that I'm going to let you lock me up until you've launched the new company stock, you're out of your mind!"

"Angie . . ."

"You're right about one thing, however — you're no Prince Charming."

He moved so quickly Angie never even saw it coming. Owen clamped a hand around her

66

wrist, hurled the pillows out of the way and dragged Angie across his chest. His eyes glinted.

"You owe me this much, Angie. I'm putting up with a hell of a lot from you. I think I'm beginning to figure out how the original feud might have gotten started. Apparently you Townsends have a nasty habit of trying to wriggle out of a bargain once you've made it. So far I've been deprived of a wife, a wedding night and a honeymoon."

"Now, Owen . . ."

"I'll be damned if you're going to screw up this stock offering on top of everything else. And if you've got doubts about behaving yourself for my sake, think about your own family. The Townsends have just as much at stake in this as I do. You're going to Jade Lake Island and you're going to stay there for the next three weeks. Understood?"

"My, God, you're cold-blooded, aren't you?"

"I'm trying to deal with a potentially disastrous situation here. This is called damage control. You're a walking time bomb for both the Sutherlands and the Townsends. And since you're legally a Sutherland, now, that makes you my problem."

"Thanks a lot." Hot, furious tears burned

her eyes. "If I have to be kept out of sight, why don't you take me home to my own family, instead? I'm sure I'll be a lot happier there, and they'll be just as anxious to make certain I don't talk to the wrong people."

He slanted her a derisive glance. "Where's your sense of pride, Angie? Doesn't the idea of having your groom hand you over to your family the morning after the wedding night seem just a trifle embarrassing to you?"

He had a point. Angie had a sudden vision of trying to explain everything to the hot-headed, emotional members of her family. There was no telling how they would react, but one thing was for certain: the reaction would be loud and explosive.

Owen was right — she was not prepared to deal with Townsend dramatics yet. It would be humiliating to be returned to her family by a disgusted, cold-eyed husband the morning after the disastrous wedding night. She doubted that her father and brother would find her excuses satisfactory, and her mother would be in tears. They simply would not understand that this time, their so-called protection of her had backfired. Angie realized she needed time to figure out how to deal with her own clan as well as her problems with Owen.

She summoned up all her courage and

tossed her hair over her shoulder in a defiant gesture. "I'll think about your suggestion to spend the next three weeks at your Jade Lake place."

"Yeah, you do that. Think about it real hard. On the way to Jade Lake." Owen sat up. "Start packing. We're leaving in an hour."

Much later that evening Angie decided she ought to have considered a third option to the problem of how to spend the next three weeks. She should have run away. Perhaps she could have hidden herself in one of the laundry carts at the hotel. Or taken a long walk on the beach and not returned.

The difficulty would have been managing to stay hidden. She knew Owen well enough to realize he would have tracked her down and dragged her back. *Anything to avoid embarrassing him and jeopardizing the merger,* she thought irritably.

The Sutherland family house crouched like a dark, predatory beast above a small cove on the eastern tip of a small, thickly forested island. Jade Lake was a large, deep body of water set in the mountains. The water was an unusual shade of jade green that darkened with the setting sun into a black, bottomless moat around the Sutherland fortress.

Fortress was the only word Angie could think of that suited the heavy, brooding old house. It had windows on all three levels, but no light seemed to enter through them. Everything inside the heavily paneled interior was dark, from the old Oriental carpets on the aging wooden floors to the heavy furniture in the rooms. The depressing avocado walls in the hallways made Angie long for a bucket of white paint and a large brush.

The moment Angie had stepped reluctantly through the front door shortly before sunset, she had known the next three weeks of her life were going to be extremely unpleasant.

On the other hand, as she sat down to the evening meal, she realized she could take cold comfort in the knowledge that Owen was not going to have a terrific time of it, either. He certainly did not seem to be enjoying the prospect of dinner in the bosom of his family any more than she was.

Angie toyed with her salad as she risked a speculative glance down the length of the polished dark oak table. The members of the Sutherland clan were a grim, depressing bunch — completely opposite in nature to her loud, cheerful, redheaded relatives.

"I must say, it was certainly a surprise

having you show up on our doorstep this evening, Owen. Not that we aren't pleased to have an opportunity to meet your new bride, of course." Celia Sutherland gave Angie a wintry smile.

Owen's stepmother was a handsome, rather intimidating woman in her early fifties. She reigned at the far end of the dining table, a natural aristocrat with her patrician features and her beautifully tailored, tastefully restrained black dinner dress. Her hair, cut into a fashionable bob, was far too perfectly laced with silver to be natural in color; the artful shade was obviously maintained by an excellent stylist.

"Thanks, Celia." Owen gave his stepmother a laconic glance. "Knew you'd be delighted to meet Angie."

"I must admit we are all wondering why you're here, however," Celia continued coolly.

"We certainly are," Helen Fulton murmured from midway down the table. "Do we assume this has something to do with the merger?"

Owen's Aunt Helen was about the same age as Celia but she had allowed her hair to go elegantly white. Her pale gray eyes and high cheekbones testified to her Sutherland genes. The gray dress and pearls she wore gave her the look of a demure dove, but the icy glitter in her eyes indicated a more predatory sort of bird. That expression marked her as pure Sutherland, in Angie's estimation.

"You can assume whatever you want," Owen said. "Just so long as you bear in mind that this house is mine and I've got a right to bring my bride here."

"Hell, that's true enough, isn't it, Owen?" Derwin Fulton, Helen's husband, gave his nephew a grim look from beneath bushy white brows. "Your father left it to you along with everything else, including the business, didn't he? Wonder what he'd say if he knew you'd gone and married a Townsend."

Whitehaired and broad-shouldered in spite of his years, Derwin appeared quite imposing in his dinner jacket. And he did not look the least bit senile, she thought in annoyance.

"I don't see that it matters much what Dad would have said," Owen replied with a bored, icy calm. "The only instructions he gave me were to take care of the business and make sure nobody in the family wound up on welfare. So far I've managed to do that."

Celia frowned. "Speaking of business, don't you think you owe us all an explanation, Owen? This news of the merger has been a great shock to everyone. You must have been plotting it for months."

"Mergers take planning. And that planning is best carried out in secret." Owen picked up his wineglass and took a sip. His eyes met Angie's in a warning glance.

"Well, I must say, your decision to rush ahead with the wedding to a Town . . . to *Miss Townsend,* here, was certainly unsettling enough," Helen murmured. "But to spring this other surprise on us is a bit much. We all know you run the company the same way my brother did, without regard for anyone else's opinion. But the least you could have done is consult us before carrying out something as drastic as a merger. With Townsend, no less. Derwin's right. Your father would have been appalled. And as for marrying a Townsend —"

"Don't worry, Sutherland Hotels is going to triple its net worth within the next few months," Owen interrupted coldly. "That should make the shock of the merger a little easier to take."

"Are you certain of that?" Celia demanded sharply. "Triple our net worth?"

"If the stock offering is as successful as Palmer Townsend and I think it will be, yes. The Townsends and the Sutherlands all stand to do very well out of this. Try to keep

73

that in mind when you are being less than welcoming to my new bride."

Celia cast a quick, speculative glance at Angie. "Am I to understand, then, that this marriage is more in the nature of a business alliance?"

Helen looked up with acute interest. "That would certainly explain the matter, as well as your peculiar behavior lately, Owen. But if the marriage is just a business arrangement, why didn't you tell us at the start?"

"Yes, we might have gone to the wedding if we'd realized it was only a short-term arrangement for business reasons," Celia added briskly. "After all, it would have added a convincing touch to have had us there, don't you think?"

Angie sat frozen as the full impact of the women's words hit her. "I was told you were ill, Mrs. Sutherland, and that was the reason you were unable to attend." She looked at Owen's aunt. "I heard you were unable to travel because of recent knee surgery, Mrs. Fulton. Tell me, is Owen's sister Kimberly actually in Hawaii with her husband, or can I expect her to pop out of the woodwork any minute now?"

"She's in Hawaii, all right," Derwin said. "Bought the tickets right after Owen announced his intention to marry you. Tell me, what excuse did he make for me?"

Owen stepped in before Angie could respond. "I told her you had gone senile, Derwin. Actually, I had considered telling her the whole damn family was senile, but then it occurred to me that Angie and her folks might start to worry about the strength and durability of the Sutherland genes. I was afraid she'd back out of the marriage."

There was a collective gasp from the Sutherland clan.

Angie started to giggle. She could not help herself. The outrageousness of the remark appealed to her sense of humor as nothing else could have done in that moment.

Everyone at the table turned to stare at her.

The giggle escalated into a laugh. Angie blotted her eyes with her napkin. "Excuse me. But the picture of Owen sitting there at his desk trying to think up excuses for everyone . . . it's just too much. . . ."

Helen gave her a severe look. "Really, Miss Townsend."

Angie tried unsuccessfully to control her mirth behind her napkin, but it was useless. "Just wait until I tell Mom and Dad and Harry." She was aware of Owen watching her with wryly elevated brows, and her laughter increased until she thought she would fall off her chair.

Owen's dour relatives sat in stony silence. Derwin flushed a deep red and his eyes darkened in frosty annoyance. Aunt Helen looked pained, and Celia's disapproving frown tightened into a scowl.

"I'm afraid I fail to see the humor in this," Celia began coldly.

"That's one of the things you have to get used to when you're dealing with Townsends," Owen explained softly to his stepmother. "They frequently fail to react quite the way you expect them to react. And they find the strangest things extremely amusing. A very emotional bunch."

"Not like you Sutherlands," Angie recovered her composure enough to respond. "Your family appears to have a range of emotions that runs all the way from grim to depressing, Owen. I'll bet you guys have a really fun time when you get together at birthday parties and Christmas."

"Of all the nerve," Helen whispered ominously. "You have the manners of a street urchin, Miss Townsend."

Owen turned to his aunt with a cold, furious expression. Angie held her breath, afraid of the confrontation that was clearly about to erupt.

It was the housekeeper, Betty, a gray-haired, stoutly built woman in her early sixties, who saved the day. She came through the door at that moment and began clearing the table for the next course. She made quite a production of it, rattling dishes and causing a general commotion. When she reached for Angie's plate, she winked broadly. Angie hid a smile.

The moment of imminent confrontation passed. Owen subsided in his chair. He still looked ready for a fight, but it was clear he was not going to start the battle. Helen picked up her wineglass and took a deep swallow.

When a serving of poached fish was set in front of Angie, she discovered her appetite had suddenly increased dramatically. She picked up her fork with relish. The fish was excellent.

"About the merger and stock offering, Owen." Derwin spoke bluntly, having obviously made the decision to change the subject. "Don't you feel you should have consulted the rest of us before taking such a radical step?"

"No," said Owen. He took a bite of his fish.

"Well, I find that bloody damn arrogant," Derwin sputtered. "Your father would have discussed it with us, at least. Given us some indication of his intentions."

"No, he would have discussed it with me, but not with the rest of you. You know that as well as I do, Derwin. Now that Dad's gone, I make my own decisions. It's time Sutherland Hotels went after a piece of the international market, and the quickest, fastest, most efficient way to do that is to merge with Townsend. Now, if you don't mind, I'd like to discuss something besides business. I am on my honeymoon, after all."

"But if this marriage is just a temporary business alliance, why pretend to be on a honeymoon?" Helen asked with a pointed glance at Angie.

Owen looked at his aunt. "You seem to be laboring under a misconception here, Helen. This marriage is not a temporary affair. It's for real. Until death us do part and all the rest. You and everyone else had better get used to the idea."

Angie knew the warning was meant for her as well as the others. She wrinkled her nose in silent defiance and concentrated on her fish.

"If this was a genuine marriage and a genuine honeymoon, why on earth did you show up here today?" Celia demanded.

"For privacy. I figure it's the last place the

reporters, insiders and analysts will be looking for me. They'll be busy staking out all the Sutherland and Townsend hotels."

"I wouldn't put it past 'em to find you here," Derwin warned him.

Owen smiled grimly at his assembled relatives. "I've given Jeffers orders not to allow anyone who is not family to dock a boat and come ashore without my personal authorization. Betty has been told to refer all phone calls to me."

"What on earth?" Helen looked stricken. "You're going to intercept our personal phone messages? You can't do that, Owen."

"Now see here, Owen, you can't just drop in here like this and start giving orders right and left to the staff," Celia informed him in frozen accents.

"Why not? I pay their salaries," Owen said. "And as I am also directly responsible for everyone else's income around here, I will give all the orders I want while I am in residence. This house is large. I'm sure we can all manage to move around in it for the next three weeks without tripping over each other too frequently."

Celia looked incensed. "Of all the high-handed, intolerable things to say. Your father always intended me to have this house. You know he did."

"Then he should have left it to you instead of me," Owen said easily.

Celia stared at her stepson in fulminating silence then apparently decided there was no point arguing. She swung her steely-eyed gaze toward Angie. "What about you, Miss Townsend? I take it you are going along with all this because of the money involved in the forthcoming stock offering?"

Angie looked down the long length of the table and smiled politely. "Were you speaking to me, Celia? In that case you made a mistake. My name is Mrs. Sutherland now. Mrs. Owen Sutherland. Not Miss Townsend."

There was another appalled silence. This time it was broken by Owen's shout of laughter. "Be warned, everyone," he said with a wide grin. "If you back a Townsend into a corner, she'll come out fighting."

It was one of the few times Angie had ever heard her husband laugh out loud. She turned to look at him in surprise, along with everyone else at the table. He got to his feet, still chuckling, and held out his hand to her.

"And on that note, I think we will say good-night, wife. Come with me, *Mrs. Sutherland*. We are, after all, still on our honeymoon. I believe it's time we went upstairs to bed."

Angie blushed under the gleaming possessiveness of his gaze. Then she folded her napkin the way her mother had taught her years ago, rose and put her hand in Owen's.

His fingers closed around hers in a crushing grip that spoke volumes about the fierce emotion coursing through him, but as usual his hard, arrogant face showed no trace of whatever he was truly feeling.

He led her out of the oppressive, dark-paneled dining room and started up the wide staircase toward the second level of the huge old house.

"That pretty much settles it," Owen said softly halfway up the stairs. "Looks like it's you and me against the rest of the family."

"Is it?"

"Afraid so. Sorry about that. I'm not well liked around here, as you may have gathered, even if I am one of the family." He reached the landing and led her down the hall to the suite of rooms they were sharing.

Angie considered his words. "You know, Owen, I don't see them as your family, precisely."

"No? What would you call them?"

"Your responsibilities, I think."

He glanced at her in surprise as he opened the door of their suite. Then he nodded slowly. "They're definitely that, all right.

Dad told me from the time I was a small kid that someday I'd have to be responsible for everyone else in the Sutherland clan. He said it went with the territory. He left the whole damned bunch of them to me along with the business. Sometimes I wish I'd become an astronaut."

Two hours later Owen lay in the massive four-poster bed that had belonged to his father and listened for small noises from the adjoining room. It had been quiet for some time in the small sitting room that formed part of the bedroom suite. Angie had been scratching around in there earlier but she had apparently settled down at last and gone to sleep on the cot.

Owen figured he would be awake for a long time, judging from the uncomfortable tightness in his loins. The thought irritated him. It was not right that a newly married man should be spending the second night of his honeymoon alone.

He had hoped the frustration factor would be minimal tonight since Angie was not sharing a bed with him, but he had been wrong. He had found himself aware of every movement she had made nearby, and his imagination had supplied plenty of vivid mental pictures to go along with the soft sounds of her undressing and getting ready for bed.

In fact, he realized ruefully, it was too damned easy to summon up an image of her high, gently curved breasts and elegantly shaped hips. He ached to see the sweet passion kindle in her beautiful eyes and watch her gorgeous red hair fan out on the white pillow. When he thought of all the times he could have taken her and had not, he wanted to kick himself.

The cautious policy had seemed wise at the time. He knew Angie had been as nervous around him as a doe in hunting season for at least two months. He had wooed her slowly, not wanting to rush her any more than necessary. He'd had to move fast enough as it was because of the merger announcement — which he and the Townsends had agreed should come at the same time as the wedding. But he had also taken things carefully with Angie because he had found himself feeling curiously protective of her. It was a new experience for him.

But his overriding concern had been to make Angie his own. Owen had been certain that once he had put a ring on her finger, everything else would fall into place.

He was learning just how mistaken he had been.

He'd taken one hell of a risk bringing her to Jade Lake after things had gone so wrong last night. He did not bother to run through the reasoning he had used on the others and on Angie. None of it was valid. He'd invented that nonsense about needing privacy. This house was far from private what with Celia, Derwin and Helen hanging around. When he'd married Angie, he'd had absolutely no intention of letting her spend a single night under the same roof as Celia and the others.

It was perfectly true the house would be useful for keeping the financial world at bay for the next three weeks. But Owen knew very well he could have found a way to insure privacy for himself and his unwilling bride without having to stay at the old family place.

That morning when he had awakened from his botched wedding night, however, Owen had made an uncharacteristically impulsive and reckless decision. He wanted to find a way to force Angie to confront the reality of their marriage. The fastest way to do that, he'd concluded, was to make her see herself as Mrs. Owen Sutherland.

Celia, Helen and Derwin had obliged him very nicely by attacking him as soon as he and Angie had walked in the front door.

Owen had known they would, of course. It was inevitable, given his relationships with the members of his family.

It had definitely been a risk, but it had paid off.

Owen groaned and turned over on the wide bed. He stared out the window at the moonlight on the lake.

He had wanted to force Angie to start seeing herself as his wife and he had known that there was no faster way to accomplish that than to make her choose sides. Tonight she had passed the first test with flying colors. There had always been the possibility that she might choose her own side. Therein had lain the real risk. She could have declared herself a Townsend and thereby taken a stand against all of them, her husband included.

But she had not. Owen had tossed the dice and he had gotten lucky.

Were you speaking to me, Celia? In that case, you made a mistake. My name is Mrs. Sutherland now. Mrs. Owen Sutherland.

"Sooner or later," Owen muttered to the shadows, "you really will be Mrs. Owen Sutherland. We'll have our wedding night, Angie. And when we do I'll prove to you that you were never part of a business arrangement."

FOUR

Angie crept past Owen's bed with all the silence of a ghost. Her bare feet made no sound on the carpet. The hem of her nightgown, another daring concoction of lace and satin from her trousseau, floated around her ankles. She was carrying a quilted robe and her slippers in one hand.

Moonlight streamed in through the windows. It revealed Owen's bare shoulders and smoothly muscled back as he lay sprawled facedown on the white sheets. Angie felt a sharp pang of longing and a deep, feminine curiosity as she studied her sleeping husband. He occupied the huge bed with a magnificent male arrogance that was not the least bit diminished by the fact that he was sound asleep.

She could have been in that bed with him, Angie told herself sadly as she tiptoed to the door. She had every right to be there. But she was afraid. That was the problem. She was *afraid*.

All the anguished questions that had sprung up on her wedding night haunted her more than ever now in the small, dark hours before dawn. She had to get some answers and she knew only one place to start. Harry might not appreciate being awakened at three in the morning, but that was his problem. In fact, he deserved it after what he had done to her. She was not going to forgive him readily for participating in the family conspiracy to marry her off to Owen Sutherland. Even if he had thought it was in her best interests.

Her brother could be as overbearing and paternalistic toward her as everyone else in the clan but Angie knew from past experience that he would level with her if she asked a point-blank question. And she intended to do exactly that tonight.

She let herself into the hall and closed the door gently behind her. Hurriedly she slipped into her coral-colored robe and slippers. Then she stood still for a moment, allowing her eyes to adjust to the darkness. There was a faint light glowing at the top of the stairs. Someone had obviously seen the wisdom of illuminating such a treacherous area at night. The soft glow would guide her.

Angie trailed silently along the hall then started cautiously down the stairs. She moved slowly, testing each carpeted tread for squeaks before putting her full weight on it.

At the foot of the stairs she paused again, orienting herself. She recalled seeing a phone in the kitchen and another in the study Owen said he occasionally used as an office. There were probably others but she did not want to traipse through the big house searching for them. Owen's study was closer than the kitchen. Angie turned toward it.

The door was closed but it opened easily when she tried the knob. Angie let herself into the dark room and went to the desk. The moonlight provided enough illumination for her to see a microcomputer on the desk. A telephone sat next to it.

Angie withdrew a tiny flashlight from the pocket of her robe. She held it in one hand while she picked up the receiver and began to punch out her brother's number.

She was still on the Tucson area code when a man's hand came out of the darkness behind Angie, cut the connection and calmly removed the phone from her fingers.

"Owen!"

"What's the matter, Angie?" He calmly replaced the receiver in its cradle. "Couldn't sleep?"

Angie struggled for composure. Adrenaline pumped through her, causing her to tremble violently. "Good grief, Owen. You scared the daylights out of me."

"Did I?" He leaned negligently against the desk, his arms folded. He studied her intently in the moonlight. He had put on a pair of jeans before following her downstairs, but he was wearing nothing else. He looked menacing and thoroughly male.

"Yes, you did and you have absolutely no right to intimidate me like this."

"Who were you calling, Angie?"

"None of your business."

"Your brother?"

She glowered at him. "I said, it's none of your business. But, as it happens, you're right. I was going to call Harry. He owes me some answers."

"Why don't you try asking me the questions?" Owen suggested softly.

She lifted her chin. "Because I can't be certain I'll get truthful answers. Who knows what you'll tell me? *For my own good, of course.*"

Owen's face hardened. "Damn it, Angie, you make it sound like you're the victim of a conspiracy."

"That's precisely how I feel."

"Do you have to be so melodramatic about the whole thing?"

Angie took a deep breath. "I feel I can't

trust anyone in this house. You've made it clear I'm virtually a prisoner here for the next three weeks. It's plain none of your family wants me here. And it's very obvious they all wish you had never married me. I do believe they actually have the nerve to think you married beneath yourself."

"Angie, honey —"

"I'm nervous and I'm angry and I just wanted to talk to someone from my own family. What's wrong with that? How would you feel if you were in my position?"

Owen groaned. He reached out to hold her. He eased her stiff, resisting body gently against his hard frame. "Angie, I'm sorry things turned out this way. I never wanted it to be like this."

"Then let me go," she mumbled into his bare chest. The warmth of his skin was oddly comforting.

"I can't. Where would you go?"

"Home."

"We already went over that." Owen stroked her spine with strong, soothing hands. "It would be embarrassing for you to go back to your family."

"I've decided I can live with the embarrassment. I'm more angry than embarrassed now, anyway," she muttered. "I'm going to strangle all of them."

Owen dropped a soft kiss into her hair, threading his fingers through her thick mane. "If you're going to try to strangle anyone, it should be me."

"Don't think the thought hasn't crossed my mind. Unfortunately, you're too big. Stop kissing my ear. I do not want any romantic gestures from you."

"Damn it, things wouldn't be like this between us if we had just had a normal wedding night."

"Sex wouldn't have solved the kind of problems we've got." She trembled and quickly moved her head as Owen deliberately lifted a swath of her hair and kissed her nape. "I said stop it, Owen. I meant it."

He reluctantly lifted his head and gazed broodingly at her. "You still want me, Angie, even though you're angry. I can feel it. You shiver when I touch you."

"That's a sign of nerves, not passion."

"Is that right? Well, I've got news for you, it seems like the same kind of trembling I felt when you were aching for me to make love to you."

Angie glared at him. "If you can't tell the difference between nerves and passion, that only proves how insensitive you are." She stepped out of his arms.

Owen sighed and ran his fingers through

his hair in a gesture of pure frustration. "Three weeks, Angie. That's all I'm asking. Just stay here with me for the next three weeks until the stock goes public. Afterward you'll see I didn't marry you for business reasons."

"And then what, Owen?" Angie walked to the window and gazed forlornly into the night. "What kind of marriage can we possibly have after getting off to such a disastrous start? How can I ever trust you again?"

He caught hold of her shoulder. "Don't call me a liar."

She eyed him wonderingly, startled by the fierce pride in his words and the hawklike expression in his eyes. It occurred to her that there was real fury in him.

"All right," she said stiffly. "I won't call you a liar."

Owen released her shoulder with a muttered oath and turned his back to her. He shoved his hands into the rear pockets of his jeans. "I can't believe this. No one has ever questioned my word. *No one.* I do business with a handshake — my word is considered as binding as a contract. That's the way my father always operated and it's the way I operate. And now my own wife dares to imply I'm a liar and a cheat."

"I didn't say that exactly," Angie murmured. It was obvious she had seriously offended him.

"You sure as hell came close. If you were a man, I'd —" Owen shook his head in disgust. "Forget it. I've had enough of this stupid conversation." He swung around to confront her, his eyes still glittering. "If this marriage is going to start off on a battlefield, we're going to make some ground rules."

"You mean *you're* going to make some ground rules, don't you?"

He shrugged. "If that's the way it has to be, yes. Rule number one is that you can believe anything I tell you. I have never lied to you and I never will lie to you. Ever. Got that?"

Angie crossed her arms beneath her breasts and hugged herself as a strange chill went through her. She had never seen Owen in this mood. He was always so cool and calm and controlled.

"Well, all right," Angie said thoughtfully.

Owen's jaw tightened. "I suppose I'll have to be satisfied with that, won't I? My own wife will kindly deign to show a modicum of trust. Lucky me. Hell, I can't believe this."

"Obviously you had the wrong impression of me, Owen. I am not quite as naive or as gullible as you seem to believe. I am fully capable of thinking for myself and of evaluating the evidence I see."

"You think so?"

She smiled grimly. "I can reach my own conclusions. Provided I am given all the evidence to evaluate, of course."

"What's that supposed to mean?"

She drew herself up proudly. "It means, Owen, that as long as we are setting ground rules for this battle, I have a rule of my own."

"And that is?" He eyed her warily.

"And that is, that in the future, you will not deliberately withhold important information from me. I am not a child, and I will not allow you to treat me like one."

He scowled. "You are also not involved in the hotel business. I fail to see why I should inform you of every little decision I make that involves my business."

"I am not asking you to inform me of every little decision. Just those decisions that directly affect me."

"The plans for the merger and stock offering didn't affect you, but you're holding me responsible for not telling you about them," he shot back.

Angie nodded. "Definitely. Because as far as I am concerned they did affect me."

"Only to your way of thinking. How am I

supposed to know which decisions you'll think affect you?"

Angie smiled. "Beats me. You'll have to be very careful and conscientious, won't you? Probably best to err on the liberal side, Owen. Just get in the habit of telling me everything and that way you won't go far wrong."

He stared at her in outrage. "Why, you little . . ." He broke off, shaking his head again. "I can't believe this. Who do you think you are?"

"Mrs. Owen Sutherland. For better or worse, apparently." Angie strode past him, feeling vastly more cheerful than she had a few minutes ago. She went through the study door.

"Angie, come back here. I'm talking to you." Owen stalked out of the study behind her. "Damn it, where are you going?"

"To get something to eat. I'm starving." She went down the hall toward the kitchen. "Dining en famille had a bad effect on my appetite earlier this evening. But arguing with you has sharpened it again. I hope your housekeeper is big on storing leftovers."

Owen did not say another word as he followed her down the long hall. When they reached the huge, immaculate kitchen he stood in the center of the tiled floor, hands on his hips, and watched in bemusement as Angie opened one of the two large white refrigerators.

Angie stood bathed in the glow of the refrigerator light and surveyed the shelves of neatly wrapped and packaged items. "We're in luck. Looks just like the deli section of a first-class supermarket." She bent to lift the lid of one plastic container. "Aha. Tuna." She tried another container. "Pasta salad. This gets better and better. Now all we need are a few crackers."

Angie chose two or three items from the refrigerator shelves and carried them to the table in the corner. She set down her haul and went across the room to flick the switch on the wall. The fluorescent lamps overhead winked and came on, illuminating the sparkling white kitchen. Angie started opening cupboards.

"You're going to eat all that?" Owen asked, his gaze on the cartons of food waiting on the table. He did not move from the center of the room.

"I told you, I'm hungry. Arguing always gives me a voracious appetite." Angie smiled with satisfaction as she spotted a box of crackers. "Here we go. All set."

She found a couple of knives and two forks in a drawer, then sat at the table. Owen still did not move as she arranged the goodies and started piling tuna onto crackers. When she had a plateful, she sat back and looked at Owen.

"Would you like some?" she asked politely.

Still wearing his bemused expression, Owen came slowly across the room and sat across from her at the small table. Without a word he picked up a cracker and took a large bite out of it. He chewed reflectively for a moment. When he was finished he popped the rest of the cracker into his mouth.

Angie helped herself to two crackers then eyed the pasta salad with interest.

"Angie?"

"What?" She scooped out a spoonful of the salad and put it on a plate.

"Would you mind telling me what is going on here? A few minutes ago you were mad as hell. Now you're eating like a horse and acting as if nothing happened."

Her eyes widened as she munched a forkful of salad. "Something happened, all right. We had a major fight. But now it's over and I'm hungry."

"Is this the way you always are after a fight?" Owen picked up another cracker.

"Usually."

"Even when you don't win?" Owen's eyes mocked her.

"Who says I lost?" she smiled sweetly. She was feeling sweeter, she realized. It was amazing what food could do for a bad mood.

"I've still got you locked away here in my gloomy castle, surrounded by a moat and several irritating relatives," Owen pointed out dryly.

"They are irritating, aren't they?"

"Very." Owen brushed that aside, his gaze intent. "Angie, why don't you feel you lost that argument we had in the study? Why aren't you still ranting and raving?"

"I never rant and rave."

"Don't fence with me. Tell me why you're suddenly in a much better mood than you were fifteen minutes ago."

Angie sighed and put down her fork. "I suppose because I realized something during our argument. Something important."

"What was that?" he pressed.

She met his eyes. "You have a great deal of pride, Owen. As much pride as any member of my own family. I understand that kind of pride. It makes me feel that maybe I wasn't entirely wrong about you, after all. You do have feelings about a few things besides business. It's kind of reassuring, if you want to know the truth."

He stared at her. "You find it reassuring

that I lost my temper? If that's all it takes to make you feel more at home around here, believe me, I can accommodate you."

"I just said I appreciate your sense of pride, that's all. I understand it, and it makes me feel as though we might perhaps have something in common, after all. And now I do not wish to discuss this any further."

"Is that right?" Owen drawled, looking dangerous.

Angie picked up a cracker, heaped tuna on it and stuffed it into Owen's mouth. "Mother always said the easiest way to make a man shut up was to feed him."

Angie woke the next morning feeling surprisingly well rested. She lay quietly for a few minutes, listening for sounds from the adjoining bedroom. When she heard nothing she got up cautiously and peeked around the corner.

Owen's bed was empty. The covers on the bed had been carelessly thrown to one side. Owen evidently expected the housekeeper to perform the chore of making up his bed.

Either that or he expected his new wife to do it, Angie thought in annoyance. She stalked into the bathroom and turned on the shower. She certainly was not going to fall into the trap of waiting on Owen Sutherland hand and foot.

When she had finished showering, she pulled on a pair of jeans and a sunny yellow sweater. She saw the note stuck on the mirror over the dressing table when she went to brush her hair.

Angie:
I'd appreciate it if you would make up your cot before leaving the bedroom. Betty will be in later this morning to clean. I'd just as soon she didn't notice we're using two beds. Felt certain you'd understand.

Owen

Angie grimaced in exasperation, put down her brush and went into the sitting area she was using as a bedroom. She was not particularly surprised by the note. It was little wonder Owen did not want the housekeeper speculating on their sleeping arrangements. He had his male pride. It would no doubt be extremely humiliating for him if Betty noticed he was not sharing a bed with his new bride.

She had fully intended to make up the cot, anyway, Angie reminded herself as she tucked in the sheets and arranged the comforter. She was quite accustomed to making her own bed in her Tucson apartment.

The memory of the chic, Spanish-style apartment she had given up shortly before marrying Owen made Angie wistful for a moment. She went to the window and looked out. The sunlight had finally risen above the surrounding mountains and was sparkling on Jade Lake.

Angie considered the prospect of breakfast with Owen and his relatives and decided she would rather take a walk around the small island.

She hurried into the hall and nearly collided with Betty.

"Oh. Good morning, Betty." Angie smiled distractedly.

" 'Morning." Betty eyed her sharply. "In a hurry?"

"Just going to take a walk," Angie explained.

Betty nodded grimly. "Don't blame you. This house can start to close in on a person. Been working here for over thirty years, so I'm used to it, but I expect it's a little hard on someone like yourself. Hear you come from Tucson. You're used to a lot of sun, I'll bet."

Angie examined the woman curiously.

"This place is a little dark, isn't it?"

"In more ways than one. But there ain't anything wrong around here that couldn't be fixed up just fine if the right man and the right woman was to set their minds to it," Betty declared firmly. "All this house needs is some love."

"Love?"

"Yep. Houses need love just like their owners do. Owen Sutherland's gone a little short of a woman's love for too much of his life. Mother died when he was just a baby, you know. Father was all right in his way, but tough as nails, if you know what I mean. Raised his son to be just like him. Never give an inch. That's the motto of the Sutherland men."

"I see."

"Yep. Like I said, ain't nothing a good woman can't fix. You going to attend to that problem, Mrs. Sutherland?"

Angie was so startled by the personal question she did not know what to say. She blinked. "Uh . . . Betty, if you'll excuse me, I've got to be on my way."

Angie fled down the long staircase and out the front door. She spotted none of the Sutherlands as she made her way across the lawn, through the gardens and to the boat house. Jeffers, the combination gardener and handyman, waved and went back to work on an outboard motor.

Angie waved back then turned and started walking along the shoreline. The fresh morning air felt clean and exhilarating. As she strolled along the pebbly beach she got her first good look at her surroundings. Yesterday she had been too upset about the mess she was in to note much.

Today she could see a sprinkling of cottages and the small town of Jade on the shore of the lake. There were several boats scattered on the shimmering, smooth surface of the water. Early morning fishermen, no doubt. It all looked very picturesque, Angie decided as she heard footsteps approaching from behind. She knew without turning around that whoever it was, it was not Owen.

"I saw you walk down here," Helen said coldly as she came up behind Angie. "Thought I'd join you. I always take a morning walk, myself."

"Good morning, Mrs. Fulton," Angie said quietly.

"You may as well call me Helen. Owen will insist upon it. Owen's just like his father was. He usually gets his own way."

Angie shrugged. "Whatever you prefer."

"What I would prefer," Helen said, gaze

sharpening, "is that this whole merger business had never occurred. But it appears we're all going to be obliged to go along with it. It's going to be a long three weeks, isn't it?"

"It certainly will be if we all work at it." Angie smiled grimly as she turned to face the older woman. "I'm sure that with a little effort we can all make each other perfectly miserable. You Sutherlands seem to have a talent for it."

Helen's eyes narrowed angrily. "You don't know what you're talking about. Take my word for it, whatever ability we Sutherlands have for causing unhappiness pales in comparison to the skill you Townsends have. I, for one, have not forgotten what happened thirty years ago."

"Really? What did happen?"

"That's none of your affair. It is family business, and I am not about to dredge it up at this late date merely to satisfy your curiosity. My brother wanted it buried forever, and I intend to respect his wishes. I just wish Owen had consulted the rest of us before he opened up this hornet's nest. I know this merger will cause nothing but trouble in the long run."

Angie studied her. "You seem very certain of that."

"I am. Townsends are nothing but trouble." Helen sighed. "We shall just have to hope that Owen knows what he is doing and trust that he's got the whole thing under control."

"He usually does, doesn't he?" Angie murmured.

Helen shook her head, her expression dark with foreboding. "He thinks he does, but the truth is, he's not enough like his father when it comes to running the business. Too many modern notions, that boy. My brother was always single-minded about Sutherland Hotels. Did things the old-fashioned way. Put the company first. And he would never have trusted a Townsend. Not after what happened thirty years ago."

"I don't know what happened thirty years ago, and you obviously are not going to tell me, Helen. But I can guarantee that when it comes to business, my family honors its contracts."

Helen jerked her gaze away from Angie's face and concentrated on the distant shore. "How long do you expect to remain Mrs. Owen Sutherland, Angie?"

The bald question shook Angie. Whatever doubts she was experiencing about her future, she certainly was not going to confide them to this bitter woman. She managed a polite smile. "The members of my family take wedding vows quite seriously, Helen. Just as seriously as they do their business contracts."

"Never mind the romantic nonsense. Just tell me how much," Helen said flatly.

Angie pushed a lock of hair out of her eyes and frowned. "How much what?"

"How much will it take to get you to leave after the stock offering? If you're reasonable, I'm sure we can come to terms. I should warn you, however, that if you're planning to clean up in a messy divorce, you had better reconsider. Owen is no fool. He'll make certain you get the bare minimum."

Angie sucked in her breath. "Are you offering to buy me off, Helen?"

"That's putting it crudely, but yes, that's exactly what I'm offering. You'll have your share of the new stock, I suppose. That should be enough, but it probably won't satisfy you. So I'm asking you how much cash you want to go quietly out of our lives."

"I've got news for you, Helen. Townsends never go quietly." Angie turned on her heel and walked into the woods.

Owen stood at the breakfast room window, a cup of coffee in his hand, and watched broodingly as Angie turned her back on Helen.

"I suppose Helen tried to buy her off," Celia said calmly as she carried her coffee to the window and looked down. "Looks like the first offer was too low."

Owen's fingers locked violently around the handle of the cup but he kept his voice cool as he responded to his stepmother. "If Aunt Helen had any sense, she'd know that was the wrong approach to use with Angie."

Celia arched one brow. "Why would it be the wrong approach?"

"Angie's got her full share of the Townsend pride." Owen took a swallow of his coffee. "Believe me, it's the equal of the Sutherland pride any day. You think a Sutherland would allow himself or herself to be bought off?"

"Don't be ridiculous." Celia frowned as she watched Angie stride into the trees. "Your father always said there was no comparison between Sutherlands and Townsends when it came to matters of personal pride and integrity. He always said a Townsend would sell his soul if the price was right."

"Dad was never very rational on the subject of the Townsends."

"You think your judgment is better than his?"

Owen shrugged. "Dad never met Angie."

"Maybe not. But he certainly knew her father."

"He thinks he did. But I'm not so sure." Owen turned away from the window. "Palmer Townsend is as straightforward and honest as the day is long. I don't know exactly what happened thirty years ago, but I seriously doubt it was all Townsend's fault."

Celia gave him an odd look. "Be that as it may, we all know that Sutherlands have very little in common with Townsends. I still cannot believe you've actually married one, Owen."

"Why do you say that?" Owen poured himself another cup of coffee from the silver pot. He realized he was genuinely curious about Celia's answer.

"Well, for one thing, it's quite obvious this young woman is not your type."

"You don't think so?" Owen smiled. "What is my type, Celia?"

"Someone a little more refined. More sophisticated. Definitely someone with better manners than those that young woman displayed last night at the dinner table," Celia said tartly. "She was downright rude, and you know it."

Owen shrugged. "She had cause, as far as I'm concerned. No one was going out of his or her way to make her welcome last night."

"What did you expect? You ought to have known better than to bring her here. Why did you, anyway? I don't believe you just wanted privacy from the business world. You could have found that somewhere else."

"I had my reasons and I don't feel like discussing them. Let's just say that I expect my wife to be treated with the respect and courtesy due her from now on. Clear?"

Celia sipped her coffee. "I cannot guarantee how she will be treated. You know Uncle Derwin. He hates the very name Townsend. And your aunt isn't much better."

"What about you, Celia?" Owen asked softly. "How do you intend to treat her?"

"I feel very strongly that I have an obligation to honor your father's wishes in this sort of thing. You know as well as I do what he would have said if he'd known you intended to merge the companies and marry a Townsend. He would have preferred Sutherland Hotels to go bankrupt."

"I doubt it. Behave yourself, Celia. I'm giving you and the others fair warning. Anyone who hurts Angie will answer to me."

Celia slanted him a questioning glance. "You're very protective of her."

"She's my wife. I take care of what belongs to me."

"What a pity you aren't as concerned about the members of your own family. It seems to me charity should begin at home."

"Are we by any chance discussing my sister's new husband again?"

Celia's mouth tightened. "Yes, we are. You have no right to keep Glen out of the business, Owen. You know how much it hurts Kimberly. You have the power to give him a high-level position. Why won't you do it?"

"Langley's an engineer. He has zero background in the hotel business. I'll be damned if I'm going to put him into Sutherland at a high-level position, and we both know Kimberly won't be satisfied unless I do. Besides, what kind of man marries a woman and then expects her brother to hire him into the family firm?"

"Glen did not marry Kimberly in order to get a piece of Sutherland Hotels. He genuinely loves her."

"Is that so? Then let him go find a job and start supporting his wife in the style to which she has become accustomed. I'm not interested in financing that marriage." Owen slammed down his coffee cup. "Damn it, I should have known we couldn't avoid that particular subject. Thank God they're both in Hawaii."

"Kimberly and Glen are due back in California today," Celia said quietly. "They're planning to drive up here tomorrow."

"Great. That should certainly liven things up around here." Owen headed for the door. "Just wait until Angie meets my adoring little sister and her freeloading husband. She's really going to start wondering what kind of family she married into, isn't she?"

FIVE

The following morning Owen hung up the phone and sprawled in his chair, thoroughly frustrated. He gazed thoughtfully out the study window as he analyzed what he had just learned from the head of his public relations department.

Owen had been coldly furious with Calhoun when he made the call. He had fully expected to fire someone before the conversation was finished. But after talking to Calhoun, he had opted to wait for more information before making any decisions. The truth was, no one in the head office seemed to have been aware that the merger announcement had been leaked.

For the moment, at any rate, Owen was inclined to believe Calhoun.

The situation left a lot of unanswered questions, and Owen intended to get the answers. But, he told himself, the damage had been done and he had a more pressing problem on his hands. Namely a marriage that was a marriage in name only.

The knock on the study door was brisk and peremptory. Owen wondered which of his relatives had come to corner him.

"Come in." He did not bother to turn as the door snapped open.

"Either you take me across the lake to Jade or I shall steal a boat and make a run for it on my own," Angie announced dramatically.

Startled, Owen swung the chair around so he faced her. She was wearing snug-fitting jeans and a bright green pullover. Her fiery hair was drawn back at the nape of her neck and fastened with a gold clip. She looked regally defiant as she confronted him.

"Why do you want to go to Jade?" Owen asked cautiously.

"Because I shall go crazy if I do not get out of this prison for a while." She gave him a challenging smile. "Just think of how it would look in the financial press, Owen. 'Hotel tycoon locks bride away on remote island and drives her mad.' "

"I'm the one being driven mad." Owen stood up slowly. "For your information there's nothing to do over in Jade. There's nothing there but a couple of small shops, a grocery store, a café and a gas station."

"No offense, but that sounds a heck of a lot more interesting than what we have here. Are you coming with me or do I commandeer the boat from poor Jeffers?"

"I'll take you over to Jade if that's really what you want to do."

"It's not what I really want to do. What I really want to do is leave permanently and never come back. However as that does not appear to be much of an option for the next three weeks, I'll go to Jade for the day instead."

Owen looked at her and wondered how everything that had once felt so right could have gone so wrong. "Damn it, Angie, I keep telling you it doesn't have to be like this."

"I'll be ready to leave in ten minutes," Angie told him, spinning away as he took a step toward her. "I have to pick up something in the kitchen."

"What's that?"

"A picnic lunch Betty is making for us."

Angie vanished down the hall, leaving Owen staring after her in amazement. He pondered matters for a few minutes then strolled out of the house and down to the dock.

He found Jeffers puttering with an outboard. The laconic handyman did not bother to look up from what he was doing with a small oilcan.

"Goin' over to town?" Jeffers asked.

"Yeah. Need anything?"

"Nope. Use the launch. It's runnin' real good. Your uncle's been fiddlin' with all the boat motors. Figured out some way of fixin' 'em up so they run cleaner. Use less gas. Seems to be workin'."

"Derwin's still tinkering?"

"You know him. Loves to fiddle with things. Always has."

"Yeah." Owen watched Jeffers work for a few minutes.

"Might be a good idea to take the little lady away from here for a few hours. Betty says things are kind of tense in the house."

"It's going to work out."

"Maybe. Then again, maybe not."

"Jeffers, you're a real ray of sunshine, you know that?"

"Bull. You got a lot of your father in you, boy. Going to be interestin' to see if the little lady can soften you up a bit."

Owen scowled. "I don't need softening up. I just need a little time to get everything back on track around here."

"If you say so." Jeffers hunkered down with the oilcan.

When Angie appeared a few minutes later

with a wicker basket slung over one arm and a wide-brimmed straw hat on her head, Owen had the small launch ready.

He eyed the picnic basket as he helped Angie into the boat but he carefully refrained from commenting on it. He had a hunch that if he showed any sign of hope due to the fact that she had gone out of her way to arrange a picnic, Angie might just dump the contents of the basket overboard. He did not know quite what to expect from her.

Still, this business of arranging a picnic lunch was definitely a good sign, he told himself as he untied the launch. He was feeling much more cheerful now than he had been a short time earlier. Owen decided to reopen the topic of their marriage, but this time, he promised himself, he would be more subtle.

"You know, Angie," he said as the craft began to move. "I've been thinking."

"Careful. I'm not so sure thinking is one of your niftier talents. It's your clever thinking that got us into this present mess." She clung to her straw hat as the launch skimmed across the mirror-smooth lake. Her attention was focused on the little town perched on the opposite shore.

"Very funny." Owen sent her a glowering

look. "The truth is, Angie, our present situation is not exactly normal."

"You can say that again." Angie pulled a pair of oversize sunglasses out of her purse. She put them on and peered at the shore. "What a lovely picture this would make. I wish I'd brought my camera."

"Angie, I'm serious." Owen wished he was not obliged to pitch his voice quite so loud, but doing so was necessary if he wanted to be heard over the roar of the engine. "Try to look at this objectively. We are married but we aren't. Not yet, at any rate. It's an unnatural state of affairs. It's causing a lot of unnecessary stress in our relationship."

"No kidding."

He glanced at her in annoyance and saw she was still concentrating on the upcoming shore. "Sarcasm isn't going to get us anywhere, honey."

"Nothing is going to get us anywhere until after the stock offering." She looked at him. "So I suggest we don't try to discuss it."

"You're being irrational and deliberately stubborn."

"I've got a right to be irrational and deliberately stubborn. I'm the offended party, remember?"

"What about me?" Owen retorted. "I'm a bridegroom with an unconsummated mar-

117

riage. Talk about offended parties.”

“You’re just feeling grouchy because things didn’t go quite the way you expected, that’s all.”

“I’m feeling damned annoyed because I haven’t had a wedding night.”

“Sex isn’t everything, Owen,” Angie said primly.

“It’s sure as hell a start in the right direction when it comes to marriage.”

“Time you got used to the fact that you can’t always have your own way. Things are going to be a little different around here.”

Owen took a firm grip on his resolve. He had to stay calm and rational if he was going to win this war. Logic told him that sooner or later Angie would be defeated by her own volatility. Self-control was the key here. He had it. She did not.

“Maybe you’re right,” Owen conceded as he eased the throttle back and let the launch glide into the small marina. “Maybe I am accustomed to getting my own way most of the time. I suppose it’s a habit. I’ve been making decisions for Sutherland Hotels for so long that I guess I just naturally make them in the other areas of my life, too.”

Angie slanted him a suspicious glance. “Well, if you can admit it, I suppose that’s a step in the right direction.”

"Thank you." Owen tried to sound humble and ingratiating. It was not easy and it definitely did not feel normal.

She smiled hesitantly. "It's not so surprising. Your arrogance, I mean. My father and brother have a major streak of it, too. Sometimes it drives Mom and me nuts."

"Maybe we all three feel protective toward the women we care about," Owen suggested gently as he coaxed the launch close to the dock.

"That's what Mom says. But I don't think that's it. I think men like you are just naturally arrogant."

So much for the subtle approach, Owen thought as he vaulted out of the launch and set about securing it to the dock. "Angie —"

"What happened between the Sutherlands and the Townsends all those years ago, Owen?" Angie scrambled out of the boat, clinging to her hat and the picnic basket.

"I told you, I don't know." Owen reached down to grasp her arm. "Dad would never talk about it very much."

"Do you think your aunt and uncle know the full story?"

Owen frowned. "Maybe. They've dropped a few dark hints over the years. But it's difficult to tell if they really know what occurred or if they're just being loyal to my father."

119

Angie removed her dark glasses and peered at him from under the brim of her huge hat. "Aren't you curious?"

Owen shrugged. "I asked your father straight out about it when we started the merger talks. He swore he doesn't know the whole story. All he knows is that the first merger fell through when the financial backers pulled out of the deal. He says the Townsends got the blame but no real explanations. As far as he's concerned, it's history, and that's exactly the way I feel about it."

Angie considered that. "I'm not so certain, Owen. It seems to me that your family is as upset today about whatever happened thirty years ago as everyone must have been at the time."

"I told you, my family is different than yours. Sutherlands know how to hold a grudge." Owen took the picnic basket from Angie and clamped a firm hand around her arm. He steered her along the bobbing dock toward the shore. "What have you got in here? It weighs a ton."

"A picnic's no fun unless there are a lot of goodies." Angie hesitated. "About your family, Owen."

"Forget my family."

"I can hardly do that," she snapped. "I'm

surrounded by them, thanks to you."

Owen swore softly. "I meant, forget about whatever happened thirty years ago. It's not important any longer."

"Hmm. I'm not so sure about that."

He glanced at her and decided to change the topic. "Welcome to beautiful downtown Jade," he said, indicating the short street with its handful of small, worn-looking shops. "What would you like to do first? Watch them check dipsticks at the gas station? Or perhaps you'd like to tour the grocery store. I hear they recently installed a new freezer unit. Should be exciting."

"Let's just walk, okay?"

Owen shrugged. "Whatever you say."

"So long as I don't say I want to leave, right?" She gave him a challenging glance.

"Right," Owen growled. He paced beside her in silence for a while, mulling over tactics. Finally his curiosity prompted him to ask a question. "How much did Helen offer you to go quietly after the stock offering?"

Angie shot him a quick, searching look. "How did you know about that?"

"It was an obvious move. One of the three of them was sure to try it. I saw you and Helen together yesterday morning and figured she'd been elected to make the approach."

"I see. You're very cynical, aren't you?"

"I'm realistic."

Angie sighed. "No amount was mentioned. We never got that far."

Owen nodded. "She probably figures you're going to hold out for a big divorce settlement instead."

"She did warn me that I'd get a lot less out of you than I would if I took her offer. Said I wouldn't stand a chance against you if I tried to fight you in court."

"The issue will not arise. There's not going to be a divorce, Angie. We're going to work this thing out sooner or later."

She did not respond. Instead she strolled beside him in silence as they left the tiny village behind and moved among the trees that fringed the lake.

"I think this would be a good spot," Angie finally announced, coming to a halt.

Owen glanced around. They were standing on a bed of pine needles not far from the lake's edge. "A good spot for what?"

"The picnic, of course." Angie took the basket from him and set it on the ground.

Owen watched as she shook out a checkered cloth and spread it on the ground. Then she crouched beside the basket and began laying out an assortment of interesting sandwiches and snacks.

Owen settled down on the cloth. "I think I recognize that tuna."

"Nope. Fresh batch. Betty made it up special for us this morning." Angie handed him a sandwich and took one for herself. She lounged back on one elbow and studied the big house on the island in the middle of the lake. "Who built that fortress you call a home, Owen?"

Owen followed her glance. "My great-grandfather. Came out west to make his fortune. Did it with cattle. Then he went back east for a bride. Built that monstrosity of a house for her. It's been in the family ever since. One of these days I'll sell it to somebody who has some fantasy about turning it into a bed-and-breakfast place."

"You're not going to make it into a Sutherland Hotel?"

Owen grimaced. "Hell, no. It would cost a fortune to upgrade it to the level of the rest of our hotels. Not worth it."

Angie tilted her head. "You don't like that house very much, do you?"

"No. And it wasn't convenient for business, either. Dad and I never spent much time there. But after Dad married Celia, we came up here more often."

"Celia likes the house?"

Owen smiled wryly. "I think she sees it as

the grand old family mansion or something. Celia's very big on old family stuff. Likes to play lady of the manor. Dad humored her, for the most part. That's why he never sold the place. But now that he's gone, I'm going to get rid of it."

"Have you told Celia and your aunt and uncle that you plan to sell the place?"

"Haven't really discussed it with them."

"They're not going to appreciate it."

"No," Owen admitted. "But they're not the ones paying the bills on that monstrosity, either."

"You can afford them."

He scowled. "That's not the point. The house can't be run in a cost-effective manner, so eventually I'll get rid of it. If I can. Lord knows, it's going to be tough to unload in this market."

"Do you view everything in terms of cost-effectiveness, Owen?"

He sensed a trap. "No, not everything."

"What about a wife? Would you expect your wife to be cost-effective? Hypothetically speaking?"

"That is not a hypothetical question." He put down his sandwich, reached out and caught her chin on the edge of his hand. She did not attempt to pull away. "I've got a wife. And she is definitely not cost-effective at all at the moment. But I'm not going to get rid of her."

Angie said nothing. Her eyes were very wide as she searched his face. Owen waited a moment before slowly lowering his head. He gave her every opportunity to avoid the kiss, but she did not even try.

"Angie . . ." Her name was a soft growl of swiftly mounting desire on his lips as he eased her onto her back.

He felt the initial resistance in her and then her arms stole softly around his neck. *She still wants me,* he told himself with hot satisfaction. No matter how much she challenged him, she still reacted with passion when he took her into his arms. Relief roared through him.

"Angie, honey, it's going to be all right," Owen muttered against her throat. He was aroused already, straining against the tight denim of his jeans.

"Owen, I shouldn't let you do this. I know I shouldn't."

"Relax, darling." He slid his hand down to her hip. "We're married, remember? This is the way it's supposed to be."

"Not yet. There's too much that has to be settled between us first. I have to know for certain —"

He slipped his hand beneath the green

125

pullover and found one soft breast. Angie gasped, and whatever else she was going to say was lost forever. Owen slid one jeaned leg between her thighs. He was wildly impatient with her clothing now. Everything — buttons, snaps and zippers — seemed to be conspiring to get in his way. He finally realized that Angie was batting ineffectually at his hands.

"Owen, stop."

"Angie, relax. We both want this. It's natural for us to want it. We're married. Take it easy, honey." He soothed her with kisses that trailed down her throat to the V of her pullover. Underneath it, his thumb slid over a nipple, and Owen thought he would go out of his mind with the craving he felt.

"Owen, I said *stop.* There's someone watching," Angie hissed.

Her urgency finally got through to him. Owen lifted his head. "What the hell?"

The sound of an idling boat motor finally caught his attention. He glanced over his shoulder and saw the grinning teenagers in the speedboat cruising just offshore. He swore again — an earthy four-letter word that most adequately expressed his emotions at that particular moment.

The kids hooted with laughter and gunned the speedboat, racing off across the lake.

Owen scrambled to his feet hastily. "A married man should not have to go through this," he grumbled. "He should be able to make love to his wife in privacy."

"Just as well we were interrupted." Angie sat up quickly and began shoving items into the picnic basket. "I'm really not ready for that sort of thing yet, Owen. I've told you I want to wait. I would very much appreciate if you would stop trying to seduce me at every opportunity. It's not fair."

He glowered at her. "Not fair? I'm your husband, damn it. I'll seduce you whenever I please."

Angie shook her head firmly, closing the basket. "No, I'd rather you did not do that." She sighed. "I didn't think it was going to be a problem."

"Now what are you talking about?"

"I've been so annoyed with you since I found out about the merger and the stock offering that I thought I'd be able to handle the physical side of our relationship."

"You mean you thought you'd be able to resist me simply because you're mad at me, is that it?" Owen felt his spirits soar as he realized what she was admitting. He started to grin slowly.

"Something like that."

"But you can't resist me, can you, sweetheart? You want me just as badly as I want you, and when I take you in my arms the way I did a few minutes ago, you melt. Warm honey on a summer day. That's only right, Angie. I'm your husband. Why fight it?"

"I *can* resist you and I shall continue to do so," she announced imperiously as she got to her feet, "until I am satisfied with the other elements of this relationship."

"Stop calling it a relationship. We're married." But there was no real bite in his voice now.

Owen was aware that he was suddenly feeling much better than he had since his wedding night. He should have tried the physical approach last night, he told himself. Tonight he definitely would take a new tack with his recalcitrant bride. Sex, not subtlety, was the solution to his dilemma.

Angie glared at him. "You can wipe that stupid grin off your face, Owen Sutherland. I am not a complete pushover, you know. I would have stopped you even if those boys hadn't come along."

"Yes, dear."

"I am not going to let you use the —" she licked her lower lip "— the physical attraction between us to manipulate me."

"I wouldn't think of it." Owen reached

down, picked up the cloth they'd been sitting on and started to fold it. He hoped the action hid the laughing triumph he knew was probably showing in his eyes.

"I mean it, Owen."

"I hear you, honey." He packed the cloth and hoisted the basket. "Ready to start back?" He gave her an innocent smile. "Or would you prefer to continue our hike?"

"I'm ready to go back to the dungeon," Angie muttered.

"Hey, look on the bright side. I'm not trying to get you to wear a chastity belt. Just the opposite."

Angie was quiet on the return trip across the lake. She had started out this morning feeling very much in control of herself and the situation. Looking back on it, she realized that the midnight confrontation with Owen the night before last had given her a dangerous confidence.

She had sensed the passionate pride in her husband and had told herself it meant he had other strong passions, as well. She understood pride and passion. She could deal with those powerful emotions. Or so she had thought.

But now she had to face the fact that she was still as vulnerable to Owen's mesmerizing sensuality as she had ever been. She must be careful, she warned herself. She had to maintain her equilibrium in this volatile situation. She was very much afraid she would lose what little advantage she did have if she succumbed to her husband's lovemaking.

There was another boat tied up at the Sutherland dock when Owen eased the launch into the small cove. He frowned when he saw it.

"Visitors?" Angie asked eagerly. She would not mind having a friendly face around, she thought.

"More family." Owen got out of the boat and reached down to help Angie. "My stepsister and her husband. This should be amusing."

"I take it you're not on speaking terms with them?"

"Oh, we speak to each other. Kim and I used to get along fairly well. But things have been different since she married Glen Langley six months ago."

"Why? Don't you like Glen?"

Owen lifted one shoulder as he started up the path toward the big house. "The problem with Langley is that Kim and Celia seem to think he should be put straight into management at Sutherland Hotels just because he's married into the family. Apparently Langley feels the same way."

"And you don't?" Angie asked.

"Hell, no. The man's an engineer. He's never been involved in the hotel business."

"And you think he may have married Kim in order to get a chunk of Sutherland Hotels, is that it?"

Owen glanced at her. "I think there's a very good possibility that's exactly why he married her."

Angie smiled. "You don't think there's just the slightest possibility he might have fallen in love with her? Or is he too much like you in that respect?"

Owen came to a sudden halt and rounded on her, his eyes coldly furious. "What the hell is that supposed to mean?"

Startled at the sudden change in his mood, Angie took a step back. "I was just wondering if you're assuming your brother-in-law is not in love with Kim because you don't happen to believe in love."

"So help me, Angie —"

"Owen, you've practically admitted you're not in love with me. Yet you married me. What are we supposed to conclude? That you may have married me for business reasons, after all? In which case, how can you fault Glen Langley for marrying your sister?"

"You are really walking close to the edge, lady." Owen's expression was ominous. "I'd advise you to stop baiting me about what I supposedly feel or do not feel for you before you go too far. You said you didn't want to be manipulated with sex? Well, I damn sure don't want to be manipulated with words. Understood?"

"Oh, yes, Owen. I think we have an excellent understanding of each other. I guess it's true what they say about never really getting to know a man until after you're married to him." Angie swept past him to the front door.

She drew a deep breath when she realized she was out of Owen's reach. Mentally she wiped her brow in relief. She had pushed him a little too far that time.

"Well, well, well," an amused masculine voice drawled from the doorway. "You must be the latest addition to the clan. Nice to know I'm not the only one who had the nerve to marry a Sutherland. I'm Glen Langley."

Angie looked up quickly and smiled when she saw the good-looking, sandy-haired man on the top step. Glen Langley looked relaxed and athletic in casual slacks and a sweater. He had an open face with blue eyes that seemed to watch the world with a hint of sardonic humor. She liked him on sight. He reminded her of her brother, Harry.

"I'm Angie." She smiled. "I expect you've already been told who I am and why I'm here."

"Right. You're Owen's latest business acquisition, according to the relatives. But I don't pay much attention to them — a dull and depressing bunch."

"You noticed that, too?"

"The problem is they're all much too concerned about their precious hotel business. I'm trying to break Kimberly of the habit."

"Fascinating observation," Angie murmured as Owen came up beside her. "I've been having a few thoughts along those very lines, myself."

"Hello, Langley." Owen arched a brow. "How was Hawaii?"

"Sutherland." Glen acknowledged Owen with an affable inclination of his head. "Hawaii was fine until I found out why Kimberly was so hot to go on the spur of the moment. I didn't realize until we got there that you'd recently told everyone you were getting married. As you can see, we're home early. Sorry we missed the big event."

"Don't worry about it. No one else from my side of the family bothered to show up, either. Believe me, it wasn't a problem. No one was missed. Where's Kim?"

"Inside talking to her mother." Glen glanced over his shoulder into the dark hallway. "Here she comes. Kim, darling, meet your new sister-in-law. I've already made our apologies for having missed the wedding."

The attractive young woman who came to stand beside him had the grace to blush. Kimberly Langley was tall and sleek. She was wearing gray trousers and a cream-colored shirt that added to her look of patrician elegance. Her dark brown hair was cut in a heavy bob. She nodded brusquely at Angie.

"Hello. Mother and Aunt Helen have been telling me about you."

"Nothing good, I imagine," Angie said cheerfully.

Owen shot Angie a warning glance then looked at his stepsister. "For the record, Kim, I expect Angie to be treated with respect. She's my wife and anyone who doesn't treat her as my wife will answer to me."

"Nobody's arguing with you, big brother," Kimberly said smoothly. "We all understand that this is a difficult situation for everyone concerned. For the sake of the company, I think we can all manage to stay civil until the stock offering."

"Yeah, I had a hunch you'd see it that way. I'll be in my study if anyone wants me." Owen climbed the stairs, stepped around Kimberly and went into the house.

Kimberly followed him with her eyes, then turned to study Angie. "I hope you knew what you were getting into when you married my brother."

"As a matter of fact, I didn't," Angie admitted, smiling brightly. "But I'm certainly learning fast. Always nice to find oneself surrounded by a warm, welcoming family, isn't it?"

"Mother was right. You are rather rude, aren't you?" Kimberly swung around on one well-shoed heel and disappeared into the house.

Glen waited until his wife was out of sight, then his blue eyes met Angie's. The sardonic humor was gone and in its place was a more serious expression. "I apologize on behalf of my wife. I assure you, she only gets like this when she's in the bosom of her family. I've concluded that Sutherlands tend to bring out the worst in everybody. I always feel like an outsider when I come here."

"I understand." Angie went up the steps. "I've had the same feeling since I got here."

Glen chuckled as he followed her indoors. "I can't tell you how glad I am to make your acquaintance, Angie. Something tells me you and I are going to discover we have a great deal in common. I suggest we combine forces and stick together against these dark, brooding Sutherlands. What do you say?"

Angie smiled, grateful for a friendly face in the gloomy house. "It's a deal."

At that moment she felt the hair on her nape prickle. She glanced down the hall and saw Owen lounging in the doorway of his study, his thumb hooked in his belt. She knew he had overheard Glen's remark about joining forces against the Sutherlands.

Owen held her gaze for a moment, his eyes unreadable. Then without a word he went into the study and closed the door very softly.

SIX

He should have seen it coming, Owen told himself later. It was a natural alliance. The two outsiders in the family, Angie and Glen Langley, were bound to discover just how much they had in common.

Owen had watched the pair covertly during dinner. Now, as everyone made a polite show of having a cup of coffee together in the living room, he could see the battle lines shaping up rapidly. He wondered if he had made a major miscalculation. The possibility made him go cold inside.

When it came to business, he always knew just what he was doing. But when it came to dealing with family, he was not nearly so sure of himself.

Langley and Angie were sitting by themselves on a sofa near the window. They were having an animated conversation about Angie's jewelry design business. Langley appeared fascinated. In a very short while it would be Angie and Glen in a united stand against the whole Sutherland clan. If he was not careful, Owen realized, he was going to lose what little ground he had gained when he had brought Angie here. She was no longer going to see him as the lone wolf defending himself against the rest of the pack. He swore silently, remembering the feel of Angie's sweet breast filling his hand earlier that afternoon.

Owen wondered if this particular sort of frustration, the kind experienced by a bridegroom deprived of a wedding night, was fatal, or if the torture could go on indefinitely without actually killing the victim.

"Those two seem to have found something to talk about," Kimberly murmured as she sat beside Owen.

"Looks like it." Owen concentrated on the view of the night-darkened lake through the window. He thought once again of how little he liked this place. In the distance he could see the glimmer of lights in the cottages along the shore. The deep, endless darkness of the forests loomed behind them, and beyond the trees crouched the inky black mountains. The sight gave Owen a vague sense of claustrophobia. He realized just how much he had come to prefer the endless expanse of the desert to these deep-shadowed valleys and the vast lake.

"Owen, please tell me what is going on," Kimberly begged softly. "This whole thing is getting extremely confusing. At first Mother and Aunt Helen and Uncle Derwin said you'd gone crazy when you announced you planned to marry a Townsend. They said Dad would roll over in his grave if he knew. They said you'd betrayed his memory by getting involved with a Townsend."

"Nice to know everyone was so concerned about my selection of a wife."

"Owen, this is not some kind of joke. You're playing a very dangerous game with our futures, and as usual you're not consulting the rest of us. Now Celia and the others tell me the marriage is part of a business arrangement. They say you're merging the two companies and that the wedding was strictly for show. Is that true?"

"No. But I don't expect anyone to believe that." *Hell, even Angie doesn't believe it,* Owen thought glumly. *Not even Angie. The one person who really matters.*

Kimberly knitted her well-shaped brows in a delicate frown. "Owen, I know we haven't exactly been close in the few months since I married Glen, but you are my brother. Don't you think you owe me an explanation, even if you don't feel you owe the others one?"

"I've given everyone the only explanation they're going to get. It's not my fault no one's buying it."

Kimberly's eyes widened. "Don't tell me you've actually fallen for her? I don't believe it . . . I won't believe it. You've never let any woman have that kind of power over you. You're the original iceberg when it comes to love. You expect me to believe you got yourself seduced by a Townsend?"

"You could say that." Owen thought of how alive he had felt the first time he had met Angie, the sense of certainty he could not put into words — the need to have her that had pulsed through him like electricity.

He recalled how cautiously he had wooed her in the beginning, how carefully he had worked to coax her into marriage. How passionately she'd responded when he'd taken her into his arms, even when she was furious with him. There was no doubt about it. He had gotten himself seduced.

Strange. He had never thought of it in quite those terms. He had assumed from the beginning he had been in control. Now he wondered.

"Owen, be serious. We both know you're not the type to be swept away by a grand passion." Kimberly studied him intently. "You've never been in love in your life. I doubt if you even know the meaning of the word."

"I think we'd better change the subject, Kim."

"But I have a right to know what is going on."

"You know everything you need to know. I'm married. The Sutherland and Townsend chains have merged. There's going to be a stock offering in a little less than three weeks. What more do you want to know?"

Kimberly stirred her coffee, her eyes mutinous. "All right, be that way. If you won't tell me what you're up to, I certainly can't force you, can I? Lord knows you're in charge of the business. Dad made a point of leaving everything to you, just as I knew he would."

Owen turned his head to look at her. "What's that supposed to mean?"

"You know what it means," she replied bitterly.

"I make damn sure everyone gets his or her share, you know that."

"But ultimately you're the one in charge, just as Dad was when he was alive. You hold the reins and crack the whip. The rest of us are just along for the ride. You were always the son and heir. The firstborn. The one he cared about the most. The one he groomed to take over Sutherland Hotels."

"Be reasonable, Kim. You never had any interest in the business."

"I was never encouraged to have any interest in it," she retorted. "But that doesn't mean I don't care about it. Everyone in this family cares about it. Unfortunately we're all dependent on you. You run things single-handedly and you never ask any of us for our opinions."

"Who should I ask?" Owen demanded softly. "Uncle Derwin, who never showed an ounce of business sense and who has spent his whole life tinkering with gadgets? Or maybe Aunt Helen, who spends most of her life researching Sutherland genealogy and sitting on the boards of her favorite charities?"

"You're not being fair, Owen."

"Maybe I should ask Celia for her input, is that what you're suggesting? Come on, Kim. We both know your mother only cares about doing things Dad's way. If she doesn't think he would have done something a certain way, then she doesn't think I should, either."

"She's very loyal to Dad's memory, that's all," Kimberly said defensively.

"To the point of not being able to tolerate the idea that I'm now in charge. Look, Kim, the bottom line here is that no one in this family is qualified to run Sutherland Hotels except me. They all just want to be certain they're going to get what they think is their fair share. Dad was right not to leave everyone a chunk of the chain. I can see the board of directors' meetings now. We'd fight tooth and claw over every single decision, and nothing would get done."

"With this merger you'll be letting Townsends help make the decisions. How do you think Dad would have felt about that?"

Owen shrugged. "He'd have chewed nails. But he's not here, is he?"

Kimberly's mouth tightened. "Glen is here," she reminded him quietly.

"I've noticed." Owen slanted another brooding glance toward the pair on the sofa. Angie was discussing some element of jewelry design. As Owen watched she took off her ring and blithely handed it to Langley for inspection.

Owen wanted to get up, cross the room, snatch the ring from Langley's hand and shove it on Angie's finger. She had no business taking it off like that.

"Please, Owen."

Owen frowned as he realized he'd missed something his sister had said. "Please, what?"

"Please give Glen a chance. It's only fair.

Give him a position in the company. Something important. Let him prove himself."

"We've already had this conversation. The answer is still the same. Langley can prove himself someplace else besides Sutherland Hotels."

"Damn you, Owen Sutherland." Kimberly got up abruptly, the coffee cup clattering on the saucer in her fingers. "Who appointed you king and emperor? You don't care about anyone else's feelings, do you? You just do what you want. You make all the decisions regardless of who gets hurt and the hell with everyone else."

"If Langley wanted to prove himself, he should have done it before he rushed you into marriage," Owen said roughly.

"You still think he married me because of Sutherland Hotels, don't you?"

Owen saw the suspicious brightness in his sister's eyes and felt a stab of remorse. He realized Celia was glaring furiously at him from across the room. He wished he'd never come to Jade Lake. *A mistake. The whole thing was a monumental mistake.* "I don't want to get into that argument again. Forget it, Kim."

"I'll try." She slid a meaningful glance toward the sofa where Angie sat talking to Glen. "After all, who are you to talk, big brother? It seems to me that if anyone around here got himself married because of Sutherland Hotels, it was you."

A raw fury roared through Owen. He clamped down on it with every ounce of self-control he possessed as he got to his feet. With an enormous effort of will he succeeded in keeping his voice very even. "I don't want to hear you say that again, do you understand? The one thing I know for certain is that Angie did not marry me because of Sutherland Hotels."

"Then why did she marry you?" Kimberly took a nervous step backward but she did not turn and flee. "Don't stand there and tell me she married you for love or for sex. You two aren't even sleeping together."

"Who the hell told you that?"

"Betty, of course." Kimberly took another step back and put down her coffee cup. "She says one of you is sleeping in the cot in the sitting room off your bedroom. She can tell because whoever it is makes it up very carefully each morning using a different method of folding the sheet corners than the one Betty uses."

"Maybe it's time good old Betty found herself another housekeeping job," Owen said through his teeth.

"Oh, come on, Owen. If you're going to

blame anyone for the secret getting out, blame me. I asked Betty what was happening and she answered honestly, that's all. You may pay her salary, but you're hardly ever here. She's been loyal to the rest of us for years."

Kimberly turned on her heel and joined her mother on the other side of the room.

Owen watched her for a moment then headed for the terrace. He had never needed fresh air more in his life. He forced himself not to look at Angie and Glen Langley as he left the room.

"It's eating her up, you know," Glen said quietly to Angie.

"What is?"

"The fact that she can't coax her brother into offering me a job with the chain. Kim felt badly rejected two years ago when she found out her father had left everything to her brother. Now her brother won't accept me and she sees that as another kind of rejection. Her mother and Helen and Derwin are encouraging the idea."

"Do you want a job with the hotel chain?" Angie asked curiously.

"Hell, no. I wouldn't work for Sutherland if he was the last guy on earth offering a pension plan and paid benefits." Glen grinned faintly. "But I'd give my right arm if he'd at least make the offer."

"For Kim's sake?"

"You've got it. It would mean a great deal to her if her brother would bend far enough to offer me a position with the company. In her eyes it would mean he was at least accepting her choice of husband." Glen shrugged. "Of course, that would leave me with a really big problem on my hands."

"Which is?"

"Not knowing what Kim would do if I turned Sutherland down. I've got a great offer up in Seattle. But I haven't told her about it yet because I'm not certain how she'll react."

"You're afraid she won't want to go with you to Seattle?" Angie asked gently.

"Yeah. That's about the size of it. Celia has really been pushing the idea that I should be working for the family firm. And she doesn't just want me to get any old job in the Sutherland chain. She wants Owen to make me a vice president or something equally impressive."

"She probably thinks that if her son-in-law had some status, she and the others would have some say in the business," Angie said thoughtfully. "Right now they're all totally dependent on Owen's goodwill and sense of responsibility, aren't they?"

Glen chuckled. "I see you've got this crazy family figured out already."

Angie frowned. "Not completely, but I'm working on it. I've got one really big question I'd like answered."

"What's that?"

"I'd like to know what happened thirty years ago to set off the original Sutherland–Townsend feud. No one seems to know all the facts."

Glen narrowed his eyes over the rim of his coffee cup. "More likely no one's talking. This crowd can be real secretive. Especially Helen and Derwin."

"I've noticed." Angie started to say more but she was interrupted by the arrival of Derwin, who had wandered over to the sofa.

"You two look as though you're enjoying yourselves," Derwin muttered darkly. His bushy brows were drawn together in a straight line. "Glad someone is."

"It is a bit grim around here, isn't it?" Angie observed dryly. "Do you folks always have this much fun after dinner?"

"You think you're very clever, don't you, young lady?" Derwin scowled at her. "But you're not half as smart as you think you are."

"I've suspected that, myself," Angie admitted. If she was all that bright, she would not be in this situation, she thought.

Derwin flushed a dull red. "Go ahead and laugh, but we know the truth. Won't pretend to know how you got Owen dancing on the end of your string. Always thought that, whatever else he was, he was too smart to be taken in by some fast-talking female, let alone a Townsend female. Guess I was wrong on that score."

Glen started to frown. "I think that's enough, Derwin."

"Not near enough," Derwin declared. "Miss Townsend here thinks she's fooling all of us, but she isn't. Want her to know it."

Angie set down her coffee cup with great care. "Just how am I supposedly fooling everyone, Derwin?"

Derwin's face grew redder. His eyes slid away from hers. "You aren't Owen's wife," he sputtered. "Not for real, at any rate. The housekeeper told Kimberly that you and my nephew don't even sleep together. Ha. Pretty odd behavior for newlyweds, if you ask me."

"No one asked you, Derwin," Glen said harshly. "I think you've said about enough, don't you?"

"Not by half," Derwin declared, gaining momentum. "She's a Townsend, and we all know Townsends can't be trusted as far as you can throw 'em. Like I said, I don't know how she pulled the wool over Owen's eyes, but she can be damn sure she hasn't pulled it over ours. She's up to some sneaky Townsend trick, by God. And she won't get away with it. Owen will come to his senses sooner or later."

Derwin turned and stalked off to join his wife. Helen's face was rigid with anxiety.

There was a short, uncomfortable pause before Glen spoke.

"Don't pay any attention to Derwin. He's been bitter for years because neither Owen's father nor Owen trusted him with an important role in the family business."

"Where is Derwin from?"

"Poor old Derwin came from a proper sort of background. He was the son of an established wine-making family in the Napa Valley. But he was never interested in the wine business. He likes to tinker."

"Tinker?"

"Sure, you know. Gadgets. He invents them. Even holds a couple of patents, although he's never made a lot of money on any of his inventions. Owen's father always considered him something of an eccentric mad scientist or something, from what Kim tells me. He and I have something in common, when you think about it."

"You mean the fact that neither of you can get a high-ranking position in the Sutherland family business?"

"Right. The difference is that Derwin would sell his soul for the privilege of being treated as an important member of the family. I'd sell mine just to be asked to take the job."

"It sounds like the real problem is that neither Owen nor his father ever bothered to find a tactful way of handling Uncle Derwin. The policy appears to have been to ignore him as much as possible. Which Derwin and no doubt Aunt Helen and the others all resented." Angie shook her head. "What a mess."

"Yeah, you can say that again." Glen lifted his cup in a mocking salute. "Welcome to the war zone, Angie. As you can see, we're all just one big, happy family around here."

For some reason it was the fact that everyone knew she and Owen were not sleeping together that bothered Angie most of all. It should not have mattered to her, she told herself. Surely it was Owen's pride that had taken the blow, not hers. She had not wanted to carry out this stupid charade of a real marriage in the first place.

Owen's pride. Angie had been raised with a dynamic brother and a powerful father. She knew that a man's pride was a formidable and extremely vulnerable thing. It was all tied up with his ego and his need to feel in control of his life and his world.

Her mother had ruefully explained to Angie that a man's pride was both a source of strength and his greatest weakness. A wise woman handled it with great care.

Angie glanced across the room and saw that Owen had gone onto the terrace. Someone — Kim, no doubt — had probably told him the rest of the family was speculating on his sleeping arrangements.

Angie recalled the little note requesting her to make up the cot, which had been stuck on the dressing table mirror that first morning. She had obliged, but now the truth was out, thanks to Betty.

Owen's pride would be so much bloody meat at the moment.

Angie smiled wryly at Glen and got to her feet. "Will you excuse me?"

"Sure." Glen gave her an odd look. "I don't pretend to know what's going on between you and Sutherland, but my advice is not to let the rest of the family get to you."

"The only one who gets to me is Owen," Angie told him softly.

"I know how you feel. The only one who gets to me is Kim."

Angie nodded in understanding and moved toward the French doors that opened onto the terrace. She could feel the eyes of the Sutherland family on her as she stepped into the cool darkness.

She did not see Owen at first. Angie went slowly toward the low stone wall that surrounded the terrace, wondering if Owen had taken a walk. She decided to leave the terrace and see if he had taken the path to the boat house.

"Hello, Angie. Thinking of making a run for the boat?"

"Owen! Good grief, I didn't even see you."

"Obviously." He was standing so still in the shadows of a tree she would have walked right past him if he had not spoken.

"Did you come out for some fresh air?" she asked hesitantly.

"You could say that. Why did you come out? It looked to me like you were having a great time talking to Langley."

"I like Glen," Angie said softly. She took a couple of steps closer to him, trying to gauge his mood. Her eyes were adjusting to the shadows, and she could see that Owen had one shoulder propped against the tree trunk. His arms were folded across his chest in that subtly arrogant manner he had.

"I know you like Langley. How could you

not like him? After all, you two have so much in common," Owen said. "Just you and him against the rest of us, isn't it?"

Angie shivered at the dangerous softness in his voice. She realized how coldly angry Owen was. A startling notion occurred to her. "Are you jealous, Owen?"

"Hell, no. I've never let a woman make me jealous in my life. But I can recognize an explosive situation when I see one and that's just what I see shaping up here. You get any more friendly with my sister's husband and we're all going to have a big problem on our hands."

"There is nothing between Glen and me. He loves your sister very much. As far as I can figure out, that's the only reason he's willing to put up with you and the rest of the family," Angie said.

"So he's started crying on your shoulder already, is that it? Didn't take long. But, then, maybe you cried on his shoulder first, hmm? Did you tell him you haven't slept with your new husband yet?"

Angie felt her temper start to flare. "I never said a word about our sleeping arrangements."

"Is that a fact? Everyone sure as hell seems to know about them."

"That's not my fault. As a favor to you, I've

made up that stupid cot in the sitting room every single morning since we got here."

"Yeah? Well, you didn't do a very good job of it, did you? Apparently Betty noticed right off that someone was sleeping in the sitting room."

"If you don't like the way I make the bed, you can do it," Angie retorted.

"If you were sleeping with me like you should be, nobody would have noticed a damn thing. There wouldn't have been anything to notice. Now the whole blasted family knows I've got a wife who won't even share my bed."

Angie took a deep, steadying breath. She sensed that the argument was threatening to roar out of control, and she was not certain what to expect if it did. "I'm sorry, Owen. I tried to make it look as though we were both using the main bed."

"I should never have brought you here."

"No. On that we agree." Angie looked at him. "We can always leave."

He gave her a disbelieving look. "Are you out of your mind? I'm not walking out of here now. I'll be damned if I'll let them force me out of my own home."

"Owen, you don't even like this place."

"That's not the point. The point is I won't let that bunch drive me off. And I won't let them think I've fallen victim to some Townsend con job."

Angie lost her fragile grip on her temper. "As it happens, we have something in common there, Owen Sutherland. I do not appreciate the fact that your entire family seems to feel I've pulled a fast one. Your Uncle Derwin believes you've been duped by Townsends. He says I've got you dancing on the end of my string. He implied I seduced you or something."

"Why don't you try it?"

"Try what?" Angie was completely exasperated.

"Seducing me. You're my wife, aren't you? You were supposed to be on my side in this war, Angie. I thought you'd figured that out. You said you understood about pride. It seems to me that if you really cared about my pride, you'd do your duty as a wife."

"I do understand your pride. But I've got some pride of my own," she shot back. "And a wife isn't supposed to sleep with her husband out of a sense of duty. She's supposed to sleep with him because she loves him."

"So where's the problem? You love me, Angie. You said so yourself on our wedding day."

"That was three whole days ago," she raged.

156

Owen smiled dangerously, showing his teeth. "No kidding. Three whole days and already you've fallen out of love with me. And here I thought your love would last a lifetime. I guess everyone in there was right, after all."

"What are you talking about?"

"I was duped by a Townsend. Had the wool pulled over my eyes in a major way. Yes, ma'am, you've made a real fool out of me, haven't you? I'm the laughingstock of my own family."

Angie was so furious she resorted to stamping one foot. "Damn you, Owen Sutherland. You're twisting this all up and you're doing it deliberately."

"You're the one who's twisted everything up, Angie. If you'd behaved like a wife is supposed to behave, we wouldn't be in this idiotic situation."

"Don't you tell me how a wife is supposed to behave. You know nothing about how a marriage is supposed to work. I have never met anyone less qualified to lecture on the subject of a proper marriage."

"Don't worry, I'm learning how this marriage works real fast. My wife sleeps in her own bed and gets real chummy with my sister's husband at the first opportunity. Should be interesting to see what happens next."

"Don't you dare drag Glen into this. He's got nothing to do with any of it." Angie was seething.

"I didn't drag Langley into this. You did."

"It's your own fault you don't get along with him, you know."

"Is that a fact?"

"Yes, it is," Angie informed him stoutly. "And I'll tell you something else. It's your own fault you've got troubles dealing with your sister. You want some advice, Mr. Sutherland?"

"From a wife who's a wife in name only? Not particularly."

"Well, you're going to get it, whether you want it or not," Angie told him through clenched teeth. "I can tell you how to solve a lot of your family problems in one blow."

"Oh, yeah? How?"

"Offer Glen a decent position in your company."

"*What?*" Owen stared at her, his eyes glittering with astonished fury. For a moment he did not move. "That does it," he finally bit out in a savage voice. "That really tears it, lady. I've been damned patient with you, but this time you've gone too far. You are not going to start telling me how to run my company."

"Owen, *no*." Angie hastily stepped back

again, but it was too late.

Owen came away from the tree trunk in a swift, fluid motion that gave Angie no chance to escape. Before she realized what he intended, he had bent low, caught her around the waist and slung her over his shoulder like a bag of laundry.

"Owen, put me down this instant." Angie pounded on his broad back as he started up the terrace steps.

"The next time I put you down, lady, it will be in my bed."

He strode across the terrace, the heels of his boots ringing on the stones. He carried Angie through the open French doors and into the living room where the rest of the family fell into shocked silence.

"Good night, everyone," Owen said calmly as he walked through the room. "I realize it's early yet, but Angie says she wants to go to bed. I've decided to join her. You know how it is with newlyweds."

Angie groaned, torn between an insane desire to laugh and an equally strong wish to yell like a shrew. This was certainly a side of Owen she had never before witnessed, she thought ruefully.

A man's pride was, indeed, a dangerous thing to attack. She should have known the risk she was taking when she confronted

Owen on the terrace. She had done nothing less than wave a red flag at an already seriously annoyed bull.

SEVEN

Owen carried Angie down the second-floor hall and into the master bedroom where he dumped her unceremoniously onto the big, four-poster bed. He braced one hand on a heavily carved post and stood glowering at her with a gleaming challenge in his eyes.

"Well?" he demanded.

"Well, what?" Angie sat up, brushing hair out of her eyes. She curled her legs beneath her and primly straightened her calf-length skirt so that it covered her knees.

"Aren't you going to start screaming or something? Don't you want Langley to rush to the rescue?"

"Not particularly." Angie fussed with the clip in her hair, which had come undone. Her fingers were trembling so badly she could not manage to close it. She tossed the clip onto the bedside table, hoping the seemingly casual action would conceal her nervousness.

Owen deliberately put one knee on the

bed. The thick mattress gave beneath his weight. "Why don't you want Langley to come running?"

"I don't need rescuing from my own husband." Angie smiled tentatively, knowing where this scene was going.

The die had been cast in the heat of the moment downstairs. She accepted that the time had come to stop rejecting Owen on the physical level. She was beginning to understand that this was the only way in which he knew how to communicate with her. She had been depriving him of this source of intimacy because it required such an emotional risk on her part. But maybe it was time to take that risk. He was her husband and he wanted her.

She had to be brave tonight, Angie decided. Her intuition told her things had reached a flashpoint in her relationship with Owen.

"So you don't need rescuing from your husband?" Owen's hand closed around her leg, warm and strong and relentless. "If you're talking about me, I should warn you I don't feel much like a husband yet, Angie."

"Do you feel single?"

"No." He shook his head slowly and deliberately, his gaze brilliant and intent. "Definitely not single. I feel trapped in some kind of no-man's-land. I want my wife but she doesn't want me."

Angie swallowed tremulously. "That's not true, Owen. You know it isn't true. I've never said I didn't want you."

He lowered himself slowly on top of her, pushing her into the pillows. His eyes never left hers.

Something primitive and utterly feminine deep inside Angie stirred under the impact of Owen's glittering gaze. She felt her whole body respond to the heavy, sensual weight of him.

"You want me?" Owen asked.

"Yes."

"Show me." Owen threaded his fingers through her hair, anchoring her gently. "Show me you want me, wife. Lord knows I ache for you. I'm going out of my mind with wanting you."

She could read the truth in his eyes. He might not understand love, but tonight Owen could have written the book on frustrated desire. And all that volatile masculine passion was focused on her.

With my body, I thee worship.

Owen was her husband. She loved him. She had never wanted anything or anyone as much as she wanted this man, whom she loved with all her heart.

"Owen," Angie whispered. "Owen, I want you. I have always wanted you. You know that." She saw the flare of response in his eyes. Angie framed his hard face between her palms and brought his lips gently down to hers.

"Angie."

Owen's mouth closed over hers with a desperate hunger that Angie had never before felt in him. In the past there had been passion in Owen's kisses, but it had always been controlled. She had sensed its presence, even had strong hints of its power, but she had never experienced the full force of it. Tonight Owen's passion was a fire storm that would swamp them both.

Owen caught Angie's face between his hands as his mouth ravished hers. He invaded the sweet, vulnerable warmth behind her lips with an intimate aggression that seared her senses. When she started to respond, her fingers clenching around his shoulders, he groaned.

Angie felt Owen lift himself away from her. She started to protest then went still as she felt his fingers on the buttons of her silk blouse.

When she felt him fumble she realized she was not the only one shivering with need. *It's so unlike Owen to be clumsy,* she thought in growing wonder. Somehow, Owen's loss of sensual finesse at this crucial moment charmed her and endeared him to her as nothing else could have done.

"Stupid buttons," Owen muttered. He gave up the task of trying to undo them and yanked at the delicate fabric of the blouse.

Angie bit back a gasp of astonishment as buttons popped and went flying across the room. "Good heavens, Owen."

"It's all right," he assured her roughly as he dropped hot, urgent kisses along her throat. "I'll buy you all the blouses you want, I swear." He stroked her breast, his thumb grazing her nipple. "A hundred blouses. A million blouses. Just let me touch you, sweetheart. I need to touch you like this. Need to feel you." And then his mouth was on her breast.

Angie sucked in her breath, her fingers biting into Owen's shoulders. She arched herself against him as his hand moved across her stomach to the curve of her hip.

"Yes, love. Yes. It's going to be so good, Angie. So good." Owen found the fastening of her skirt, made one or two attempts to undo it and abandoned the attempt in frustration. His hand swept lower. He found the hem of the skirt and shoved the entire mass of fabric up to her waist.

Angie shuddered when she felt his fingers on the inside of her thigh. She started panting when he parted her legs with one of his own. His trousers were excitingly rough against her skin. She realized vaguely that she was clutching at him now, lifting herself, straining for a more intimate touch.

"Angie, tell me again that you want me. *Tell me.*"

"I want you. I want you. I want you." She covered his hard jaw and strong throat with small, hungry little kisses.

Owen groped for and found the waistband of Angie's silken panty hose. He tugged them over her hips and pushed them impatiently along her legs to her ankles. She kicked them off, and when she was free of them, he brought his hand up her leg until he was inches from the hot, damp core of her.

Then, with a low, husky groan, he found her and closed his hand possessively over her.

"Owen. Oh, please, Owen. Please." Angie writhed against his hand. She felt him teasing her with his fingers and thought she would go mad. She clung to him, pleading for more.

Everything was happening so fast, she could no longer think clearly. It was like being caught in a lightning storm.

"Oh, yes, sweetheart. So good. I knew it would be like this. You all hot and soft and clinging." As he spoke, Owen eased one finger into her, his thumb simultaneously gliding over the secret swell of flesh hidden in the dark thatch of hair between her thighs. "You're ready for me. You want this as much as I do."

Angie cried out softly. Every nerve in her body was alive with tension now. She knew Owen felt it. She heard his thick exclamation of satisfaction, then she heard the hiss of his zipper being lowered.

"Owen?" She opened her eyes and looked at him through her lashes. He was watching her face with a fierce intensity.

"Now, sweetheart. Tonight. You're so beautiful, so ready for me. I can't wait any longer to make you my wife."

"Yes."

She closed her eyes and once more her fingers gripped his shoulders as he slowly, deliberately thrust himself into her.

He filled Angie with a steady, relentless pressure that nonetheless made some allowance for her sensitive flesh.

"Am I hurting you?" Owen's brow was damp with sweat.

"No. Never."

Angie trembled as she took him into her. She felt as though she was taking all of him, his strength, his male power, the very essence of Owen Sutherland. Now, in this moment, he belonged to her completely, and she knew beyond a shadow of a doubt that she belonged to him.

When he had buried himself deep within her, Owen trapped her face between his hands. For a timeless moment he looked at her with so much glittering emotion in his eyes that Angie wanted to weep and laugh and cry out with joy.

"Hello, Mrs. Owen Sutherland," Owen whispered. His voice was unbelievably tender but unmistakably laced with male triumph.

She should have been appalled by the satisfaction in his gaze, Angie told herself ruefully. But she was not. Probably because in addition to the triumph she saw there, she also saw the unshakable promise of commitment.

Owen was giving himself tonight, just as surely as he was claiming her.

And then Owen started to move within her and Angie could no longer think at all. With a soft, choked exclamation, she surrendered to the glittering storm of sensation that swept over her.

★ ★ ★

Angie stirred in Owen's arms a while later. She started to turn and realized her skirt was bunched around her waist. She was still wearing her blouse, too. It was open, revealing one breast and only partially concealing the other. Her panty hose lay on the floor beside the bed.

Owen was sprawled beside her, one arm curved possessively around her, the other behind his head. One of his legs was covering hers. She could feel the crisp texture of his trousers against her skin.

Angie looked down the length of their entwined bodies. Owen's zipper was still unzipped. His shirt was half undone. Tantalizing glimpses of crisp, curling dark hair were visible through the openings of both shirt and trousers.

"Sure looks like the shocking aftermath of a scene of unbridled lust, doesn't it?" Owen did not open his eyes.

"Well, yes, as a matter of fact, it does." Angie smiled. "I do feel a bit ravished, now that you mention it."

Owen opened one eye. "This wasn't quite the way I had planned it, you know."

"I know how you had it planned. Champagne, room service and the honeymoon suite. I was there, remember?" Angie slipped her fingers inside his shirt.

"So you were." Owen's mouth curved faintly. He opened both eyes, revealing the lazy satisfaction in his gaze. "Things didn't go according to schedule, but it doesn't matter." He brought his hand along her bare leg. "Everything is just fine now."

"Is it?"

"Uh-huh." He closed his hand around the back of her head and brought her mouth down to his. He kissed her slowly, lingeringly and with a deep, tender possessiveness. "Everything is just perfect. About time, too. You kept me waiting long enough, lady."

"Owen —"

"Hush." He rolled on top of her, trapping her between his hands. "We haven't finished our wedding night yet."

"We haven't?"

"No. But don't worry. This time we'll do things with a little more class. Hell, this time, I'll even take off my pants first."

The next time Angie stirred and stretched in Owen's arms, she realized he was wide awake, studying the darkened ceiling. She sensed the change in his mood.

"Owen? Is something wrong?"

His arm tightened around her reassuringly. "No, honey. I was just thinking, that's all."

"About what? Us?"

"No."

Angie made a face in the shadows. "Thanks a lot."

He turned his head, looking at her in surprise. "What do you mean by that? Why should I be thinking about us? Things are okay now. We've finally got this marriage on track. Everything's settled between us."

"Oh, I see. Everything's settled. Just like that?"

He wound his fingers in her hair and tugged gently. "Kiss me."

She obliged, leaning down to brush her mouth across his. He nipped playfully at her lower lip, then caught and held her close for a deeper kiss.

"Like I said," Owen murmured. "Everything's settled between us. What I was thinking about was something you said earlier out on the terrace."

"The something that turned you from a civilized gentleman into a caveman?"

He ignored that. "About offering Langley a job."

"Oh, that."

"Yeah. That. What was it all about, Angie?"

"You'll probably lose your temper all over

again if I try to explain," she said.

"Try anyway."

"All right, here goes. I think you should offer Glen a good position with the company. You could do it. You have the power to hire anyone you want at a high level."

"Give me one good reason I should offer Langley a high level position."

"I'll give you three good reasons. The first two are Celia and your sister, Kim. They would both appreciate it more than you know. They already feel rejected enough by the terms of your father's will. Your rejection of Kim's husband has added to that feeling. Making an offer to Glen would reassure both Kim and Celia that you at least respect their wishes — that you care about them. It would be a nice gesture, Owen."

"You don't run a company like Sutherland Hotels with nice gestures."

"One nice gesture isn't going to hurt. You can afford this one."

"You said there were three good reasons I should make Langley an offer. What was the third reason?"

Angie smiled as she readied her *coup de grace*. "You can make your grand gesture with perfect safety. Glen's going to turn you down."

"He's going to *what?*"

172

"You heard me. Glen has no intention of working for you. I can't blame him, either. I think you'd probably be a terrible boss. But that's beside the point. He's had an excellent offer from an engineering firm in Seattle and he intends to take it."

"If that's so," Owen said, sounding suspicious, "why should I go through the charade of making him an offer?"

"I've told you, for Celia and Kim's sake. Glen says Kim is tearing herself apart because you won't show some sign of being willing to accept her husband."

"Why should that bother her?" Owen muttered.

"Because you're her big brother, of course. It's perfectly natural that she would want your approval. I'm a little sister, Owen. I know what I'm talking about. Glen wants you to make the gesture for Kim's sake. Then he will very nicely decline and take the Seattle job."

"Langley told you this?"

"Yes. Tonight, when we were talking on the sofa."

"And you believed him?"

Angie got the first inkling that her suggestion was being met with some skepticism. She frowned. "Of course I believed him. Why would Glen lie to me?"

173

"To get you to do exactly what you are doing, maybe?"

Angie was immediately incensed. "Owen, how can you say such a thing?"

"Easy. I've had a little more experience with men like Langley than you've had, honey. You've led a sheltered life. It's only natural that you'd be a bit gullible. Unfortunately, it looks like Kim has the same problem. She fell for Langley's line, too."

Angie sat up, angry all over again. "Tell me the truth, Owen. Do you have any real evidence that Glen married your sister because of her connection to Sutherland Hotels, or are you just suspicious of him on general principles?"

"I don't need hard evidence. Just look at the facts. The guy swept her off her feet with a whirlwind courtship. They were married less than three months after they first met. Two months later Kim is hounding me to give Langley a position with Sutherland. You tell me if that doesn't sound suspicious."

"A whirlwind courtship, hmm?" Angie smiled slowly. "Three months, you say? That's just about as much of a courtship as I got, isn't it?"

Owen scowled. "Don't try to draw any comparisons here, Angie. It's not the same situation at all."

Angie pursed her lips thoughtfully. "Let's see, a mere three-month courtship and right after the wedding we discover the groom has some serious interest in the bride's family business. Very suspicious situation, if you ask me. I can certainly see why you were alarmed. In fact, I know exactly how you feel."

"Damn it, Angie, don't start. As of tonight I don't want to hear any more about that."

"Whatever you say, Owen."

He eyed her warily. "That's better." When she did not argue, he smiled slowly and reached for her. "Much better."

Owen awoke shortly before dawn. He lay quietly, relishing the feel of Angie's warm, soft body curled against him. It felt good. Right. The way it was supposed to be. She was his. *His wife.*

He turned his head to study her in the predawn light. Her hair was a tangled wave of fire against the pillow, and her dark copper lashes were closed, concealing her turquoise eyes. Her soft mouth was slightly parted, inviting his kiss, even in sleep. The elusive, womanly scent of her tugged at his insides, arousing him.

Owen considered awakening her so that he could make love to her again. Then he thought about how much she had given him last night. Reluctantly, he decided to play the gentleman and let her sleep.

He certainly had not been much of a gentleman last night, he thought as he eased himself from under the covers. His first night with Angie had not gone according to plan at all. But this morning that no longer mattered. The marriage had been consummated. He and Angie were man and wife.

A surge of euphoric satisfaction hit Owen as he went into the bathroom and turned on the shower. He could not remember the last time he had felt this good. He was laughing silently by the time he finally stepped under the water.

Owen was still grinning twenty minutes later when he loped down the stairs and sauntered into the breakfast room. Betty was setting a pot of coffee and a basket of freshly baked muffins on the table.

" 'Morning, sir."

"Good morning, Betty." Owen sat down and picked up the coffeepot. The aroma of freshly ground and brewed beans was terrific. "By the way. A word to the wise. If you want to make it to retirement around here, I suggest that in future you refrain from commenting on my personal habits to others in this household."

Betty smiled complacently. "You can't fire me, Owen Sutherland. I've worked for this family for over thirty years. I remember you from the days when you used to sneak around stacking chairs to make a ladder to get to the cookie jar."

"A touching memory, I'm sure, Betty, but I no longer have to steal my cookies. I just reach out and take them. As many as I want."

"Ruthless, huh? That what you're trying to tell me?" Betty chuckled, obviously unintimidated. "Save your threats, boy. You don't scare me. And if you want to know why I told your sister you and your new bride weren't sharing the same bed, I'll tell you."

"Okay, why did you tell Kim about that?"

Betty grinned widely. " 'Cause I knew it'd get back to you in no time, of course. Figured you'd do something about the problem. And it was clear from the look on your face when you came in here a minute ago that you did do something about it last night."

Owen managed a severe scowl. "Your idea of playing Cupid, I take it?"

"Sure. Knew right off something was wrong between you and your missus. I could tell she was head-over-heels in love with you but feelin' kind of uncertain, too. When I realized you weren't even sleepin' together, I decided that was a big part of the problem."

"Is that right?"

"Yep. Thought I'd give you a little shove. Easiest way to shove you is right in the middle of your Sutherland pride."

"Lucky for you I'm in such a good mood this morning, Betty. That's all I can say." Owen picked up a hot muffin, sliced it open and dribbled honey into it.

"A good mood, huh? A good woman does that for a man. And there ain't no doubt you got yourself a mighty good woman." Betty picked up a tray and headed for the door.

Owen decided he had no quarrel with that conclusion. He bit into the muffin. It was perfect. He finished it and reached for another.

Glen Langley strolled through the door, yawning. He eyed the muffin basket as he sat down. " 'Morning, Sutherland. You planning on eating all of those muffins yourself?"

"You can have one."

"Gosh, thanks. I guess the lord of the manor is feeling generous this morning." Glen reached for a muffin and poured himself a cup of coffee.

Owen ignored that and munched thoughtfully for a moment. "You really want to work for me?"

Glen blinked in surprise. "Hell, no. No offense, Sutherland, but I think you'd make a miserable boss. What I want from you is a job offer. And I want you to make it in front of Kim."

"Angie says if I make the offer you'll turn it down. What guarantee do I have you'll do that?"

Glen shrugged. "None at all. You'll be making it in front of a witness — namely, your sister. If I change my mind and decide to accept the offer, you'll be stuck with me."

"That's what I'm afraid of."

"I can understand that," Glen said. "You've got good reason to be nervous. Believe me, Sutherland, you may be the world's nastiest CEO, but I can promise you that if I ever came on board as an employee, I would make your life a living hell."

Owen smiled slowly, appreciating the threat. "Yeah, I'll bet you would. Why'd you marry Kim?"

"The usual reasons. Fell in love with her first time I saw her. Realized I'd better grab her fast or I'd lose her. Didn't want to give her too much time to think. Give women enough time to think and they start inventing all sorts of problems that a man has a tough time solving. Know what I mean?"

Owen thought about what he had gone through since his wedding day. He winced. "Yeah, I know what you mean."

"Figured you did. I sized up the situation with Kim and your family and then I went in fast. I knew you were going to be the biggest stumbling block. I swept Kim off her feet and married her before she had a chance to fret too long about getting your approval."

"What made you think I wouldn't approve?"

"You're a big brother, right? Big brothers hardly ever approve of the men who marry their little sisters. Hell, I'm a big brother myself. I know what I'm talking about. On top of that perfectly normal state of affairs, Kim had lost her father two years ago. That meant big brother was going to be playing father figure, too. It would make the test even tougher to pass."

"So you decided to short-circuit the situation with a whirlwind courtship and a quickie marriage."

Glen's eyes met Owen's. "That's about it. Now, of course, I've got to clean up the mess. But at least I've got my wife and I can take my time getting you to see the light."

"Damn," said Owen.

"Yeah, I know. But I think you and I have

a lot more in common than you realize, Sutherland. I'd say we tend to operate the same way."

"Go in fast, get the job done and clean up the mess later, is that it?" Owen finished the last of his muffin. He folded his arms and rested them on the table.

"Isn't that what you're doing right now?" Glen asked quietly. "Cleaning up a mess? From what I've heard, you don't spend much time here at Jade Lake if you can help it. The fact that you brought your bride where you knew she wouldn't be welcome means you've got a drastic situation on your hands. Probably something to do with the merger. Am I getting warm?"

Owen said nothing.

"I'll make a deal with you, Sutherland. Make me an offer, a good one. I'll turn it down and then I'll take Kim away from here. It'll give you one less thing to worry about."

"What if she won't go with you, Langley?" Owen asked softly. "Kim wants you to go to work in the hotel business. So does her mother."

"That's a risk I've got to take. I'm banking on the fact that she loves me and she knows I love her. I think she'll trust her future to me."

Owen swore softly and sat back. He shoved his hands into his pockets and stretched his legs out under the table. Langley was tough. Tougher than Owen realized. Angie's judgment of the situation had been accurate, after all.

She didn't know much about the hotel business, but he was beginning to acknowledge she might know a lot more about what made families tick than he did.

He was still pondering that and Glen was still drinking coffee when Kim wandered in a few minutes later. She went straight to her husband and kissed him lightly before she sat down and helped herself to coffee.

"Good morning, Owen," Kim said coolly.

"Hello, Kim."

"You certainly made a spectacle of yourself last night."

Owen decided his mood was still too good to be ruined this early in the morning. "I married a Townsend. Townsends tend to get exuberant when they get excited. We Sutherlands, on the other hand, are a touchy bunch. We tend to get mad as hell when someone offends our pride, don't we?"

Kim eyed him uncertainly. "What are you talking about, Owen?"

"Never mind." Owen made up his mind. "I was just about to offer your husband, here, a position as vice president of engineering with Sutherland and Townsend. He can go straight to work in the head office planning our first hotel in the South Pacific. There will be some travel involved as the planning stage moves into the construction phase, but you can go with him."

Kim's fork clattered to her plate. "Owen, are you serious?" She stared at him in astonishment. "You mean it?"

Owen met and held Langley's eyes. "You know me, Kim. I never say anything I don't mean. The job is Glen's, if he wants it. Something tells me he'll work out just fine at Sutherland and Townsend."

"Owen, this is wonderful. I know you won't regret it." Kim jumped to her feet, darted around the table and threw her arms around Owen. "Thank you, Owen. Thank you so much."

Owen realized there were tears shining in his sister's eyes. He smiled faintly. "Hey, it's okay, kid. Least I can do for a member of the family, right?"

"Right." Kim laughed. She released Owen and went happily to her seat. "This is perfect, isn't it, Glen?"

"Yeah," Glen said. "Just perfect. Except for one small fact."

Kim frowned. "What fact?"

"I've got a better offer in Seattle. And the truth is, I'd rather work on aircraft control systems than on hotel air-conditioning and plumbing systems. I'm grateful to your brother, but I'm going to turn down his offer."

"But, Glen —"

Owen overrode Kim's protest. "The offer's good, Langley," he said quietly. "I wouldn't have made it otherwise. Like I said a minute ago, I always mean what I say."

Glen smiled. "I know. I appreciate it. But I think it'll be better if Kim and I go to Seattle."

Owen got to his feet. "I hear you. You and Kim talk it out. Whatever you decide is fine with me. See you later."

It was a beautiful day, Owen thought as he left the house and walked into the morning sunshine. He did not recall Jade Lake ever looking quite this shade of emerald green. Even the mountains seemed more picturesque this morning. Not quite so dark and forbidding. For once the atmosphere around Jade Lake wasn't making him claustrophobic.

Owen glanced at the window of the master bedroom. It was open. He saw Angie leaning out, taking in the sight of the lake. She was wearing her quilted robe, sleep-tousled hair swirled around her shoulders. When she saw him watching her, she smiled and blew him a kiss.

Owen grinned and waved at her. He could see her blush even from where he stood.

He started to whistle as he sauntered down the path to the boat house to see what Jeffers was doing.

EIGHT

Celia was alone in the breakfast room when Angie arrived. She was standing at the window, gazing at the boat house while she absently stirred her coffee.

"Good morning, Celia." Angie poured herself a cup of coffee.

"Good morning, Angie." Celia turned slowly. She smiled uneasily. "I suspect we have you to thank for Owen's sudden change of heart."

Angie hovered over the muffin basket, dithering between blueberry and bran. "What change of heart?"

"Kim tells me he offered Glen a position with Sutherland Hotels. A good position."

"Did he?" Angie decided on the blueberry muffin. "Don't thank me. I didn't have anything to do with it."

"I have a hard time believing that, Angie. Owen is one of the most stubborn men I have ever met. Takes after his father."

Celia's smile turned wry. "Once he makes a decision, he almost never changes his mind. His Sutherland pride won't allow it. But this morning he seems to have done exactly that."

Angie bit into her muffin. "Owen is stubborn, but he's not completely unreasonable."

"Perhaps unreasonable is the wrong word. Implacable might be better."

Angie grinned around a mouthful of muffin. "Or intractable? How about impossible? Imperious? Immovable? Occasionally even a touch idiotic?"

"You find this all very amusing, don't you?" Celia asked quietly.

"Not really. I'm sorry if I seem facetious, Celia. Another annoying Townsend trait, no doubt."

Celia looked at her for a long moment. "No doubt. Be that as it may, I owe you my thanks for patching up things between Owen and Kim. It was very painful watching their relationship being torn apart. Of course Kim did rush into marriage with Glen, and his motives did appear suspect for a time. But I knew Kim loved him and after I got to know Glen, I felt he was an honest young man who cared deeply for my daughter."

"I happen to agree with you. I like Glen."

"I thought once Owen got a chance to

know Glen, he would come to accept him. But then Kim came up with the notion of Glen going to work for Sutherland Hotels and Owen exploded."

"It was probably Kim's way of trying to force Owen to accept her husband," Angie mused. "Nobody forces Owen to do anything."

"Very true." Celia sighed. "I assure you, he was just as stubborn and unreachable when he was a boy. Owen was thirteen years old when I married his father. And he already considered himself an adult. The boy never did accept me as his mother. Oh, he was always polite, mind you. Always well-behaved. But there was a distance between us. He was cool and self-contained, even as a boy."

"I can't see Owen as a little boy."

"Neither can I," Celia admitted. "He was certainly not a little boy when I first came into his life. More like a younger version of his father in many ways. From the day I met him, he made it quietly clear that he knew he was being groomed to take charge of Sutherland Hotels and the Sutherland family. You could see that he had accepted the responsibilities before he even knew what they would entail."

"And the last thing he wanted was a new mother, right?" Angie asked gently.

Celia put down her coffee cup. "Precisely. As I said, he was always polite to me, but he never saw me as his mother. I think that to Owen, I have never been anything but one more responsibility he was expected to eventually shoulder. And he has done his duty by me, I'll grant him that. He has done his duty by all of us. One thing you can say about Owen, he fulfills his responsibilities. In his own arrogant way."

Angie heard an old, sad regret in Celia's voice. She was searching for the right words with which to respond when Kim breezed through the door, followed by Glen. Kim looked happier and more lovely than Angie had yet seen her.

"Hi, Angie. There you are, Mom. I came to tell you that Glen and I will be leaving soon. There's no point staying. We've talked it over and I realize that he would much rather work in the aircraft industry than the hotel business. He's had the most wonderful offer from a firm in Seattle, haven't you, darling?"

Glen smiled at his glowing wife. "I think it will be a good job. And I think Kim will like Seattle."

"I'm going to love Seattle," Kim assured everyone.

Derwin appeared in the doorway, his

bushy white brows locked in a deep scowl. "What the devil is going on here? I heard Owen offered you a vice presidency, Glen. Is that true?"

"It's true," Glen said easily. "But I've turned him down."

Derwin stared at him. "Turned him down? You can't be serious."

"Afraid so." Glen looked at his watch then at Kim. "We'd better get packed, honey. Your brother's going to take us across the lake so we can pick up the car. Got a long drive home ahead of us."

"Don't worry. I can be ready in half an hour." Kim turned to Angie and smiled. "Thank you, Angie. I know you had a hand in this. That brother of mine can be so darned stubborn."

"I think he was just feeling a little over-protective," Angie murmured. "I've seen the same syndrome in my own brother, Harry. Big brothers get that way about their little sisters, I guess."

Kim tilted her head thoughtfully. "Maybe you're right. I never thought of it that way. I just assumed Owen was being his usual arrogant self." She went across the room and gave Angie a quick hug. "You know, I think it's going to be interesting having you in the family."

"Thank you," Angie said, surprised and touched by the unexpected show of warmth.

Glen laughed softly. "Something tells me things are going to be a little different around here from now on. See you at the next family reunion, Angie." He came forward and gave her a quick, affectionate hug. "And thanks," he murmured. "I owe you."

"No," Angie said quickly, but Glen was not listening. With a nod to Celia and Derwin, he took Kim's hand and tugged her toward the door.

Derwin's scowl deepened as the pair left the breakfast room. "I can't believe that boy turned down a decent offer with Sutherland Hotels."

"I think it was for the best," Celia said. "A young couple should stand on their own feet right after marriage. Gives them a sense of independence. All Kim really wanted was to know that Owen accepted Glen. She's satisfied. And that's what counts, don't you think, Derwin?"

"I was never offered a vice presidency," Derwin growled. "I was never even offered a job in the damn mail room." He turned to confront Angie. "This is your doing, isn't it?"

"Now, Derwin," Celia began quietly.

"It is her doing. And I, for one, would like

to know what is going on around here. We all witnessed that caveman spectacle Owen put on for us last night. I've never seen anything so undignified in my life. Typical of a Townsend, perhaps, but totally out of character for Owen. She's doing things to him. Changing him."

"Please, Derwin," Celia said.

He ignored her, still glowering ferociously at Angie. "You've seduced Owen, that's what you've done. You caused that boy to make a fool of himself in front of his own family. And now you're starting to interfere in family matters. You're up to something. I know it."

"*Derwin,*" Celia snapped, "I think that's quite enough."

"My guess is it hasn't even begun." Derwin threw down his napkin and stalked to the door. "Never could trust Townsends. They're always scheming. Always using people. You'll see, Celia. Mark my words. Owen will live to regret the day he married a Townsend. He'll learn his lesson the hard way."

An uncomfortable silence descended on the breakfast room. Celia smiled apologetically. "I'm sorry, Angie. Derwin and Helen are rather set in their ways. Old habits die hard, and they have been in the habit of hating Townsends for a very long time."

"I wish I knew why," Angie said. She met Celia's eyes. "Do you?"

Celia shook her head. "No, not really. I just know it all goes back to the first merger attempt between the two companies. I wasn't married to Owen's father then so I don't know the details. Whatever happened left a bad taste in everyone's mouth, apparently. I'll admit that out of loyalty to the family, I've been as suspicious of Townsends as everyone else, although you're the first one I've actually met."

"We're quite lovable when you get to know us."

Before Celia could respond to that Owen came through the door.

His eyes found his stepmother first. " 'Morning, Celia. Seen Angie?" Then he spotted Angie at the table. His eyes gleamed. "Ah, there you are, honey. I've been looking for you. I've got to run Kim and Glen across the lake in a few minutes. While I'm gone why don't you have Betty make us up another picnic lunch? We'll take the boat out this afternoon and we'll hit a couple of the islands at the south end of the lake."

"All right," Angie said. "How long will you be gone?"

"After I see Kim and Glen on their way,

I'm going to pick up some supplies Jeffers ordered at the hardware store." Owen shrugged. "I shouldn't be gone more than a couple of hours."

"Fine." Angie felt herself blushing under the expression in Owen's eyes. She knew very well he intended to make love to her on one of those islands at the south end of the lake. Hot memories of the previous night flooded her, making her senses dance with expectation.

"See you." Owen started for the door.

"Owen?" Celia called him quietly.

He turned. "Yeah?"

"Thank you," Celia said quietly.

"For what? Offering Langley a job? Forget it. No big deal. He turned me down, anyway."

"It meant a lot to Kim. And to me."

Owen hesitated, then his mouth curved faintly. "Langley's okay. Dad would've liked him. Guy's got guts."

Much later that afternoon Owen anchored the launch in a tiny cove on one of the miniature islands that dotted the south end of Jade Lake. He glanced at Angie, who was eyeing the short walk to shore.

"It's not very deep. Just roll up your jeans and take off your shoes," Owen advised.

"Unless you want me to carry you ashore?"

"I think I can manage. You take the lunch." Angie handed him the basket. Then she kicked off her loafers.

Owen rolled up his jeans. Then he went over the side with the basket in one hand, his shoes in the other. He stood knee deep in the clear water and watched as Angie gingerly swung one bare leg over the edge of the boat.

A rush of pleasure went through him as he vividly recalled the feel of that soft, curving leg against his own last night. He could hardly wait to make love to his wife again.

Angie glanced up at that instant, and she must have seen the warm anticipation in his eyes because she blushed furiously. She looked down quickly, concentrating on her footing. Owen saw the flash of gold on her hand as the sun glinted on her wedding ring, and a hot, possessive feeling surged through him.

"I thought we came here for lunch." Angie splashed into the water and waded ashore.

"Lunch and other forms of nourishment." Owen swung the picnic basket, feeling light-hearted and curiously content with life. "Besides, it's not lunch, it's a midafternoon snack. Too late for lunch."

"Thanks to the fact that you were over an

hour late getting back from Jade," Angie reminded him.

"There's something about hardware stores," Owen said. "Once I get into one, I suddenly think of all kinds of stuff I need. And I don't even like to tinker the way my uncle does. Hell, I don't even have to do my own household repairs."

"Must be a male thing. I've seen my father and brother in a hardware store. It's not a pretty sight." She reached the small, pebbly beach and stood gazing at a fern-choked grotto. "This, on the other hand, is a lovely sight."

"Lovely," Owen agreed, watching the way the sunlight gleamed on Angie's red hair, turning it to fire. He wondered if he could get away with making love to her before he fed her or if she'd insist on eating first. He decided to try his luck. "How about that spot right over there?"

"Okay." Angie plucked the checkered cloth out of the basket and arranged it in a small clearing among the ferns. She sat in the shade of a tree and began unpacking the lunch. "Betty certainly outdid herself this time. Pâté, French bread and a bottle of wine."

Owen grinned as he sprawled on the cloth beside Angie. "She probably wanted to promote the romantic element. Can't blame her." He put his hand on Angie's thigh, squeezing gently. "I'm feeling kind of romantic, myself."

Angie laughed. "You mean you're feeling sexy."

"What's the difference?" Owen slid his hand a little higher up her jeaned thigh. She felt warm and soft, even through the denim. He bent his head and kissed her knee. When he looked into her eyes he saw the wealth of emotion there. He smiled encouragingly, sensing she was about to tell him she loved him.

"Did you get those supplies?" Angie asked as she unwrapped the pâté.

"Huh?" Owen frowned, surprised by the unexpected change of topic.

"Those supplies you said Jeffers asked you to pick up at the hardware store in Jade. Were they in?"

"Oh, yeah. Those. I got them." He watched as she industriously spread pâté on a slice of French bread. "Angie, I'm really not that hungry right now."

"Aren't you?"

"No." He gently removed the slice of bread and the knife from her hands, put them into the basket then reached for her. "Come here, wife."

"I'm here," she whispered.

"Closer." He eased her down onto the checkered cloth and slid his leg between her thighs. She put her arms around him and watched him from beneath lowered lashes. Her smile was soft and inviting, telling him in that timeless, feminine way that she was his. Owen felt his whole body tighten with desire.

"Owen?"

"It's all right. This time we've got privacy. No one can see us from the water."

Owen lowered his mouth to cover Angie's. The picnic lunch was forgotten, and a very short time later she was lying naked and soft beneath him and he was buried deep in her feminine heat. He could feel her clinging to him, feel her tightening deliciously around him. Her nails were digging into his shoulders.

Owen lifted his head to watch hungrily as Angie shivered in his arms the way the sunlight shimmered on the surface of Jade Lake. Her soft cries of sensual fulfillment were the most incredibly exciting sounds Owen had ever heard. He was poised on the brink of his own pounding satisfaction when he vaguely realized he was waiting for something.

But the tiny, delicious contractions deep within Angie's body pulled Owen inevitably into the storm. He forgot why he had been waiting, forgot why he had been holding back a moment earlier. He surrendered to the hot whirlwind with a hoarse exclamation of triumph and pleasure.

It was not until after he shuddered and eventually lay still, his body still damp with perspiration, that Owen remembered what he had been waiting to hear in those final seconds of lovemaking.

He had been waiting to hear Angie tell him she loved him. He frowned slightly as he realized she had not done so since he had started making love to her. But he was too relaxed to worry about it now. He closed his eyes and let himself drift into a state of deep lethargy. . . .

Owen did not realize he had fallen asleep until he awakened some time later to the sound of Angie rustling around in the picnic basket. He opened his eyes and saw that she had already dressed and gone back to the task of spreading pâté on French bread. This time the pâté and bread combination looked great. Owen decided he was ravenously hungry.

"I could eat about half a dozen of those," he said. He got to his feet, pulled on his jeans and went to wash his hands in the lake water.

"I've got a head start on you. Better hurry if you want your fair share." Angie handed him a slice of bread covered with a thick chunk of the pâté.

Owen downed it in two bites. "I'll open the wine." He busied himself with the corkscrew Betty had remembered to provide. "Angie?"

"Um?"

"I've been thinking."

"I've warned you before about that."

He grinned, feeling too lazy and too satisfied to take offense. "How about we go finish this honeymoon someplace else?" He poured the wine into two glasses and handed her one.

"I thought you wanted me here where I couldn't do any damage to the stock offering."

"Hell, that never really entered into it," he admitted. "I knew I could keep the press and anyone else away from you at one of the hotels. I'm the boss, remember?"

Angie slowly lowered her slice of French bread, her eyes never leaving his face. "Then why did you insist we come here?"

"I had this wild idea that if you saw me surrounded by the rest of the Sutherlands, you'd feel obliged to come to my defense." He grinned. "You're the sort who naturally champions the underdog. I thought if you saw the way things are between me and my family, you'd get over being mad and start remembering how you really felt about me."

"I see."

"Matters didn't go quite the way I had planned," Owen admitted. "But everything worked out." He slanted her a deliberate look. "And you do remember now how you really feel about me, don't you, Angie?"

Angie drew up her knees and wrapped her arms around them. Her expression was thoughtful. "You want this marriage to work, don't you, Owen?"

"Damn right, I do."

She nodded. "So do I."

He smiled with deep satisfaction. "I know. I've known it all along. You just needed time to get over your anger. And your fear that you'd been used. Some of the problem was my own fault. Maybe I didn't give you a chance to get to know me well enough before the marriage. I rushed you. If there'd been more time, you'd have been more secure with me."

"I think you're right. I feel I know you much better now, Owen," Angie's expression was intent and serious.

"You can say that again." He leaned over, kissed her soundly and smiled. "I was hoping that after we'd turned this marriage into a normal one, you'd come to exactly that conclusion."

"You're very sure of yourself, aren't you, Owen?"

He laughed softly. "I'm not going to answer that. It's one of those no-win questions. But if it's any consolation, you did manage to throw a monkey wrench into most of my big plans for the perfect honeymoon. But now I think we can get this wedding trip back on line, don't you?"

"All right."

"Is that all you can say?" He gave her a mocking glance. "Don't tell me you actually like it here at Jade Lake?"

"I won't tell you that. But I will tell you I've learned more about you in the past few days than I learned in the three months before we arrived here, Owen."

That annoyed him. "That's not true, damn it. You just came to your senses here, that's all."

"If you say so."

Owen realized his good mood was starting to evaporate. "Angie, what is it with you? Are you mad or something?"

"No, I'm not mad. I've just been doing a lot of thinking." She rested her chin on her folded knees. "We both agree we want to give this marriage a chance."

"I didn't say that," he muttered. "I said it was going to work. Period."

She nodded in acquiescence. "I think there's a good possibility it will."

"A *possibility?*"

"Yes, the way I see it, we've got a lot going for us. There's a strong physical attraction, for one thing."

"That's for damn sure." Owen took a swallow of his wine.

"And there's that strong business connection between us, too, especially now that Sutherland and Townsend have merged. I was angry at first, but now I've come to the conclusion that having business interests in common could be a binding element in our relationship."

Owen lost his temper at that comment. "Damn it, Angie, our mutual business interests have got nothing to do with this relationship!"

"Yes, they do, Owen." Angie's voice was very calm, very soothing, as if she was dealing with a recalcitrant child. "You can't deny it. You said yourself that we would never have met if it hadn't been for the fact that our families are both in the hotel business. Don't worry, I'm beginning to see it as a strong point in our marriage."

"Angie, will you just give it a rest?"

She gave him an innocent look. "Why are you getting so upset, Owen? I'm telling you what you want to hear, aren't I?"

"I do not want to hear about the business aspect of this marriage," he said through his teeth. *What game does she think she's playing now?* he wondered. "The hotel business is not what is going to hold us together."

"What will hold us together, Owen?"

"All kinds of things."

"Physical attraction? I already mentioned that."

"Not just physical attraction," he growled. "Affection. Mutual respect, mutual interests." *Your love for me,* he shouted silently.

"I mentioned mutual interests, too. The hotel business."

"Not just the hotel business."

She smiled, humoring him. "All right. Picnics. We do seem to have a mutual interest in picnics."

"There's more. A lot more."

"Like what?" she prompted gently.

Owen felt as if he was being driven into a corner. "Trust. Commitment. A sense of responsibility."

"Yes, I think you're right. Those are all wonderful things. Valuable things. Precious things."

"Damn right." *And none of them are as wonderful or as valuable or as precious as your love for me,* he thought savagely. *Why aren't you saying the words, Angie? Why aren't you telling me how much you love me? We're married now. Really married. But you haven't said the words since we became lovers.*

"Owen? Is something wrong?"

"What could be wrong?" He smiled grimly. "I'm alone on an island with the woman I . . ."

"Yes, Owen?"

Owen looked at her and finally saw the soft, anxious, distinctly hopeful expression in her clear turquoise eyes. It hit him. He knew now what she was doing. Unfortunately for Angie, he could read her like a book. If she thought she could manipulate him this easily into vowing his undying love, she could think again.

Nobody manipulated Owen Sutherland. Not ever. A man who allowed himself to be manipulated was weak. His father had taught him that.

"I'm alone on an island with the woman to whom I happen to be married," Owen said smoothly. "An extremely convenient state of affairs, wouldn't you say?" He reached for her and pulled her on top of his chest.

The sunlight glowed in Angie's hair and the sweet, sexy weight of her thighs against his was already arousing Owen. He forgot his anger over her futile attempt to control him the moment he captured her mouth.

He was alone on an island with his wife and his wife loved him as no other woman had ever loved him. Owen was certain of it, even if she was too proud to admit it at the moment.

He understood pride. He could wait. Angie was much too soft and gentle and too in love with him to hold out for long. She would surrender first in this small undeclared battle she had instigated.

She understood pride, Angie told herself the next morning as she started out on yet another walk around Jade Lake Island. She could wait.

She stopped amid a stand of fir and watched the Sutherland launch skim across the lake toward town. The boat's wake cut a clean swath across the green water. Owen had left a few minutes earlier to exchange one of the parts he had picked up yesterday for Jeffers at the hardware store.

Angie suspected that Jeffers could have handled the task but Owen had obviously been looking for an excuse to get off the island. He had volunteered to take the launch to town.

Angie knew Owen was getting restless. It was time to leave. He had started to talk about finishing the honeymoon elsewhere yesterday but she had sidetracked him with her puny attempt to get him to admit he loved her.

Her mouth curved downward at the memory of how her efforts to force him to recognize his love for her had backfired. So much for the subtle approach. The man was as stubborn as a mule. Maybe she should get herself a stick and thump him between the ears until she got his full attention, she mused.

It was clear Owen was content to wallow in her love for him — equally clear he had no intention of dealing with such dangerously soft emotions in himself. Owen, indeed the whole Sutherland family, seemed uncomfortable with intense emotions.

It was easy enough to see why Owen was so reluctant to admit to his own feelings. Angie had learned enough about him since she had come to Jade Lake to understand where the problem lay. As a boy he had lost his mother before he had ever really known her. He had been raised by a father who had no doubt encouraged such solid, masculine traits as willpower, the ability to command others and arrogant authority — all characteristics that had served Owen well in his role as heir to the throne of the Sutherland empire.

Celia had come into Owen's life much too late to effect any real change. Owen's path had been clearly marked by the time he was thirteen. In any event, Celia had soon found herself busy with a child of her own and had been content to let Owen continue to grow up under his father's guidance.

Helen and Derwin were clearly too bitter about their own roles in the Sutherland hierarchy to waste much affection on the boy who would be taking his father's place . . . the boy on whom they would someday be dependent for their income and position in the Sutherland corporation. The boy whom they must have resented even then, on some level.

Angie turned at the sound of footsteps approaching. Derwin was striding briskly through the fallen pine needles. He appeared to be in a hurry.

"Good morning, Angie." Derwin nodded coolly. "Pleasant day."

"Yes, it is."

"I see Owen is underway. Heard him say he planned to go over to Jade this morning." Derwin peered across the water at the wake of the small launch. "Don't imagine he'll be back for a couple of hours."

"Probably not. He was mumbling something about crescent wrenches and valve fittings when I saw him off a few minutes ago." Angie smiled. "I have no doubt but that once he gets into that hardware store, he'll think of all kinds of interesting things to check out."

"No doubt." Derwin's thick brows drew together in a frown as he continued to stare out over the lake. "Well, now, I wonder who this is coming toward us."

"Who?" Angie turned to face the lake again and saw that the small boat Derwin had noticed was slowing as it neared Jade Lake Island.

A young man who could not have been out of his teens waved to get their attention. Then he cupped his hands around his mouth.

"I've got a message for Mrs. Sutherland."

"I'm Mrs. Sutherland," Angie called back.

"From a guy who says he works for your brother. He says it's important. Wants to see you right away. Asked me to give you a lift across the lake."

A sudden, overwhelming fear enveloped Angie. "I'll meet you at the dock," she shouted.

She started to run toward the boat house.

NINE

~

"Said his name was Rawlings and that he worked for Harry and Palmer Townsend. That's all I know, ma'am." The teenager, a thin young man dressed in jeans and a T-shirt, squinted at Angie from the boat. "He asked me to come over here and get you. Said he needs to talk to you right away. Said nobody would take his phone calls here at the Sutherland place."

Angie glanced at Derwin, who stood beside her on the dock. "Do you know anything about any phone calls from a Mr. Rawlings?"

Derwin grimaced dourly. "No. But Betty was instructed to refer all calls to Owen, if you will remember. The rest of us aren't even allowed to answer the phone in our own home anymore."

Angie recalled Owen's instructions to his family. All phone calls were to be directed to him and no one outside the clan was allowed ashore without an invitation. She had assumed all that had changed since the night she and Owen had made love.

But now that Angie thought about it she realized she had never heard Owen revoke his orders. Why should he have altered the rules, she thought grimly. Nothing had really changed between them, had it?

Of course it had. If the big, stubborn, arrogant idiot didn't realize that, he could darn well figure it out for himself!

"I'll come with you to see this Rawlings," Angie said to the teenager. "Can you bring me back across the lake?"

"Sure."

"Okay." Angie climbed into the boat. "Derwin, please tell the others I'll be back shortly."

"Very well."

As the boat sped away from the dock, Angie glanced back and saw Derwin staring after it. The craft was halfway across the lake before she saw him turn around and start up the path to the main house. She looked at the young man who was piloting the boat.

"What did you say your name was?" Angie called out above the roar of the engine.

"Dave. Dave Markel. My family owns that

house over there to the left of town. I work at the marina."

Angie brushed wind-whipped hair out of her eyes. "Lived here long?"

"All my life. Be leaving this fall, though. Going off to college."

"Congratulations."

"Thanks." Dave grinned. "I'm looking forward to getting out of this burg, I can tell you."

Angie grinned. "I suppose you've known the Sutherlands ever since you were born?"

Dave shrugged. "Just to say hello to if I see one of 'em on the street. They don't socialize around here much. Kind of stand-offish, if you know what I mean. At least the older ones are. Don't see much of the head honcho who runs the hotel company or his sister. Didn't even know Owen Sutherland had gotten married until this Rawlings guy showed up and asked if I knew you."

"When did he show up? Rawlings, I mean."

"Don't know when he got into town. But he came down to the marina about an hour ago and said he was looking for someone who could take a message across the lake. Maybe pick you up and bring you back, if you were willing."

Angie realized she was not going to get much more information out of Dave. She sat back in her seat and watched as the marina grew larger on the horizon.

Soon, the outboard bumped against the marina dock and Dave bounded up to assist Angie out of the craft. She glanced around expectantly. The Sutherland launch was tied up a few yards away. There was no sign of Owen.

"Where is this Mr. Rawlings?"

"In the marina café." Dave angled his chin in the direction of a ramshackle little restaurant at the end of the pier. "Said he was going to have a cup of coffee while he waited for you."

"Thanks." Angie walked down the dock, climbed the small flight of steps that led to the shore path and headed for the café.

It was not at all difficult to pick Rawlings out of the crowd at the small burger and coffee joint. He was the only one wearing a tie. It was silk and it went very nicely with his expensive suit.

Angie eyed him curiously as she walked toward him. Rawlings appeared to be in his mid-thirties. Dark-haired and dark-eyed, he had the alert, aggressive look of a man on the way up. He got to his feet as Angie approached.

"Mrs. Sutherland?"

"Yes."

"I'm Jack Rawlings. Please sit down."

Angie slid into the booth across from him. "Is something wrong, Mr. Rawlings? The boy who brought your message said you worked for my brother."

Rawlings flashed her a charming smile. "Not exactly. I admit I told the young man that, but only because I wanted to talk to you in a hurry and I couldn't think of any other way to reach you. I tried calling, but no one returned my calls."

"I see." Angie frowned. "Who are you exactly, Mr. Rawlings, and why did you want to see me?"

Rawlings pushed aside his coffee cup and folded his arms on the plastic tabletop. He fixed her with an intent gaze. "Mrs. Sutherland, I'll be frank. I represent a group of investors who are interested in acquiring a large block of shares in Sutherland and Townsend when it goes public."

"What's that got to do with me?"

"To be perfectly blunt, there have been some unsettling rumors to the effect that your marriage to Sutherland was pure hype. The gossip on the street is that the merger isn't going to work for long. People are saying the old feud is as strong as ever and that Owen Sutherland won't be able to patch things up for more than a year or so."

Angie froze. "That's ridiculous. Where on earth did you hear that?"

Rawlings shrugged. "Street gossip, like I said. Please understand, Mrs. Sutherland. My people are preparing to put a lot of money on the line. If the Sutherland and Townsend merger is shaky from the start and management is going to be bickering constantly because of the old feud, my investors stand to lose a great deal of cash."

"You brought me here to find out if my marriage is solid so you could figure out if the merger is solid?" Angie asked incredulously.

"Let's just say I'm looking for a little clarification. If your marriage to Sutherland was nothing more than a publicity gimmick, then, yes, my people are going to be concerned about just how secure the merger itself is. I'm told the feud between the two companies left a lot of bad blood on both sides."

Angie was furious. "That's ridiculous."

"Look," Rawlings said with an ingratiating smile, "you see my problem, don't you? If those feelings are still strong, they're bound to affect management. And bad management of Sutherland and Townsend will adversely affect my group's investment."

Angie slipped out of the booth and got to

her feet. "I certainly do see your problem, Mr. Rawlings. Your problem is that you listen to gossip. I can assure you that in this case, your inside information is wrong. I am very much married to Owen Sutherland. Furthermore, I resent your lying in order to get me to meet you here. If that is the way your group of investors works, then as far as I'm concerned, I don't particularly want them putting money into my family's company."

"Take it easy, Mrs. Sutherland." Rawlings hurried out of the booth when he realized she was turning on her heel to leave. He started after her. "I was just trying to find out what was going on."

Angie refused to turn. She was striding toward the door of the café when it opened.

Owen strode into the restaurant. His gaze found her immediately then went to the man who was following her. Angie saw the cold flames leap in Owen's eyes.

Owen took two long strides forward, reached out and caught Angie's arm. He pulled her close. "What's going on here?"

"This is Mr. Rawlings," Angie said quickly. "He represents some investors who are interested in the Sutherland and Townsend stock."

"I know who he is." Owen pinned Angie

to his side as he confronted Jack Rawlings. "If you've got any questions, you can talk to me, Rawlings. My wife does not get involved with the family business."

"Hey, give me a break, Sutherland. I'm just trying to do my job. You know that. This is just business."

"The hell it is. I'm on my honeymoon. I'm not interested in talking business at the moment." Owen flashed Angie an intimate smile that did not quite wipe out the seething anger in his eyes. He flicked his gaze to Rawlings. "And for the record, I don't like the way you do your job, Rawlings. Maybe you and your little group of sharks had better go find more interesting meat."

"Don't give me that, Sutherland," Rawlings said. "My people have a lot of cash to invest. You need them."

"Sutherland and Townsend doesn't need your group and we both know it. The stock is going to be red-hot when it goes public and you're well aware of it. Your efforts to drive down the offering price are useless. Now get out of here before I toss you into the lake."

"Look, I'm acting on solid information. I've got a right to know whether this merger is for real or if you've got potential problems. I've heard a lot of talk that says the old feud isn't dead."

"It's dead, all right." Owen shot Angie another dangerous smile. "Angie and I buried it personally, didn't we, honey?"

Angie felt Owen's fingers biting into her arm. She managed a sweet, wifely expression — the sort of look a woman on her honeymoon was expected to give her husband. "We certainly did, darling."

"The feud is old news," Owen said easily to Rawlings. "There never was all that much to it, anyway. Just a publicity ploy for both companies. It served its purpose in the past, but times have changed. Sutherland Hotels and Townsend Resorts can grow faster together."

"That's not the way I heard it," Rawlings muttered.

Owen shrugged. "Then you heard wrong. Now, you'll have to excuse us, Rawlings. My wife and I are going to head across the lake. Like I said, we're still on our honeymoon. We've got better things to do than talk business with you."

Without a backward glance, Owen steered Angie out of the café. He said nothing as he guided her to the dock where the launch was tied. He handed her into the boat and leaped lightly in behind her. Then he fired the engine and shoved the throttle forward.

A moment later the launch was tearing across the lake toward the island. Aware of Owen's dangerous mood, Angie sat in thoughtful silence. Her hair flew in the wind. She pushed a lock absently behind her ear as she reran the scene with Jack Rawlings in her mind.

Halfway across the lake Owen eased back the throttle. The roar of the engine faded to a murmur and the launch continued toward the island at a much slower speed.

Owen turned his head to look at Angie. "All right, what the hell was going on back there?"

"Just what you thought was going on. Rawlings wanted inside information on the merger." Angie watched him warily.

"I know that. What I want to know is how you came to be with him in that café. How did you get across the lake?"

"Actually," said Angie, "that's a rather interesting story, now that I think about it."

"Yeah, I'll just bet it is."

"Rawlings sent a kid in a boat over to the island to tell me that someone who worked for my brother wanted to talk to me."

Owen's hand tightened on the wheel. "I should have knocked his teeth down his throat."

"The kid said that Rawlings had tried to call me but couldn't get through to me on the phone." Angie studied Owen's hard profile. "Is that true?"

"No. No one's called." Owen was concentrating on the approach to the island.

"Are you sure, Owen?"

His head came around abruptly; his eyes were as hard and challenging as those of a hawk. "Are you accusing me of lying again?"

Angie shook her head slowly, watching him. She remembered his pride and his promise to her. "No. You told me you would never lie to me. I believe you."

Some of the anger faded from his gaze. "Good. I guess we've made some progress, at any rate. I ought to be grateful for small favors. Damn, Angie, you should never have fallen for that trick. Your father and brother were right when they said you're too naive when it comes to business."

That infuriated Angie. "I am not naive. If people would just take the trouble to keep me informed, I wouldn't fall for any tricks. But nobody bothers to keep me posted, do they? You all keep me in the dark and then get angry when I blunder around on my own or come to a false conclusion."

"Blundering around is exactly what you're doing. You should have used your common sense with Rawlings. You should have known there was something wrong when some jerk sent a message saying he worked for your brother."

"Stop chewing me out, Owen. I reacted in a perfectly normal and reasonable manner, given the circumstances."

"Just what were the circumstances?"

"The guy said he'd been trying to get hold of me on the phone, and I knew you had ordered Betty to direct all phone calls to you. For my own good, of course. Because I'm so naive and all."

Owen glared at her. "Calm down, Angie. You're getting emotional."

"I can't help it. That's the way I am, remember? Furthermore, I do not appreciate being called on the carpet like an employee who screwed up."

"You did screw up," Owen insisted.

"It wasn't my fault."

"It was your fault." He turned and scowled, his feet braced against the gentle motion of the launch. He leveled a finger at her. "You should have known better than to get into some stranger's boat. You should have been suspicious of the message in the first place. You should have waited until I returned before you went rushing off to see what was going on. You should have used a

221

little common sense, damn it."

"You're just mad because you're afraid I might have said something that will hurt the stock offering," Angie muttered.

"Wrong. I don't give a damn about the stock offering right now. I'm mad because that jerk, Rawlings, was trying to use you and you let him trick you into doing exactly what he wanted."

Angie lifted her chin. "I think we had better postpone this discussion until you're in a more reasonable frame of mind."

"Reasonable? You expect me to be reasonable about this?"

"Yes."

"Well, think again, lady." Owen shoved the throttle forward. The engine roared. "We'll finish this conversation later," he yelled above the noise. "You're right about one thing — this is not a good time to talk. At the rate things are going, I might decide to let you swim back to the island."

When they arrived Owen was still feeling irritated. But at least he was in full control of his temper once more. As he tied the launch up at the small island dock he thought about how incredibly easy it was for Angie to transform his moods. Around her he could go from rational, deliberate and calm to a state of complete masculine outrage in the blink of an eye.

Discovering Angie in that café with Rawlings had been the final straw. All morning, he had been restlessly mulling over Angie's refusal to admit she loved him. It was a childishly transparent attempt to manipulate him. He'd told himself the best way to handle the situation was to pretend to ignore it. He was sure his reasoning was correct. Angie was too soft and emotional to hold out for long. Sooner or later, she was going to forget herself when she lay in his arms. She would say the words he wanted to hear. And when she did, Owen could tell himself he had won the small, silent battle.

"Owen?"

"Yeah?" He glanced up from where he was coiling a yellow nylon line. Angie was climbing out of the boat, a thoughtful look on her face.

"How did you know I was in that café with Rawlings?"

Owen's hands stilled on the line. Then he stood up and reached out to grasp her arm to steady her. "A kid at the marina said you had gone into the place to meet someone."

"That would be Dave, I suppose."

"Right. Dave." Owen eyed her as she stood in front of him on the dock. "And?"

"I just wondered."

He put his hands on his hips and studied her. "What exactly did you wonder about, Angie?"

"Well, to be perfectly honest, it occurred to me that the timing of this little incident was rather interesting," Angie said slowly.

"Go on."

She frowned. "Okay, look at it this way. You leave the island in your launch and within a short while I get a message that someone representing my brother is trying to get in touch with me."

"Rawlings could have been watching the island with a pair of field glasses. As soon as he saw the launch leave, he probably sent the kid with the message. He knew it was the only way to get you alone."

"True." Angie nibbled on her lower lip, considering that angle. "He referred to what he called the gossip on the street."

"Gossip about what? The old feud?"

"Yes. He seemed to think it was far from settled, and he said that was what worried his investors. They thought it could make for trouble in the new management lineup."

Owen shrugged. "If they're that nervous, they can pass on the offering. I'm not worried about losing Rawlings's group. I checked with my headquarters this morning. The business world is eating up the story of our marriage and the merger. Believe me, there's plenty of interest in Sutherland and Townsend stock."

"That's not my point, Owen."

"What is your point?"

She looked up at him with serious eyes. "On our wedding night someone deliberately tried to drive a wedge between us by making certain I saw an advance copy of the press release about the merger."

"Did a damn good job of it, too," Owen grumbled. "Every time I think about spending my wedding night with a pillow between me and my bride, I get mad as hell all over again."

"That's very touching," Angie said dryly, "but you're still missing my point."

He folded his arms. "So tell me your point."

"The point is that it's obvious someone is still trying to hurt the merger, Owen. Don't you think you'd better find out who it is?"

"You think I haven't been looking?" he asked softly.

"Well?" She tilted her head to one side. "Have you got any ideas?"

He unfolded his arms and shoved his hands into his back pockets. "None I want to talk about yet."

"Why don't you want to talk about them?"

"Because I'm not sure of anything yet, all

right?" He heard the irritation in his voice and forced himself to relax.

"You're afraid that one of your relatives is behind this, aren't you? You're afraid this is a family thing."

For a second, he was tempted to deny it. But Angie was watching him with those clear turquoise eyes, and he knew she had intuitively arrived at the conclusion he had reached by dint of painful logic. "Yes. Damn it to hell, yes."

Angie touched his arm gently. "It's all right, you know. You don't have to defend any of them to me. I'm family now, too, remember?"

He looked at her. "I hadn't thought of it that way."

She smiled slightly, her eyes warm. "Don't try to shelter me or keep me out of this. We can deal with it together, Owen. I'm your wife."

"It doesn't feel solid yet," he told her.

"What doesn't feel solid?"

"You and me," he admitted. "I've got a legal document that says you're my wife. I've got my ring on your finger. I've taken you to bed. But something's still missing."

"What more do you want?" she asked.

"I don't know."

Angie's brows rose. Then she smiled.

"Let me know when you do figure it out. In the meantime, try treating me like a wife. Let me help you handle this mess."

He wanted to argue. Wanted to demand that she admit she loved him — that she was his as completely as she had been before their botched wedding night at the hotel. But he could not think of how to force the issue while standing on the stupid dock.

He would wait, Owen promised himself. He would wait until he got Angie into bed that night. Maybe then he'd figure out how to get things right between them. He seemed to be able to communicate very well with Angie in bed.

"Owen?"

"There's nothing to handle," Owen said coolly. "Not yet, at any rate." He took her arm and started walking along the dock.

"Owen, please don't shut me out. This is my problem, too."

"It's business, Angie."

"No, it's not. It's family. You know it is."

Owen groaned, sensing that he was not going to be able to deflect her and no longer certain he wanted to. He understood business things. He did not understand family things.

But Angie did.

"I'm used to handling stuff like this

alone," Owen warned her warily.

"I know. But you're not alone anymore. You've got me, remember?"

He smiled slowly. "How could I forget?"

"Right. As you once said, we're stuck with each other. I think we should put together all the facts that we've got and see where we're at," Angie said.

Owen thought about it. "The problem is, we don't have a lot of facts. But I've had a feeling all along that whoever's causing the trouble is probably a member of my own warm and loving family. No one else would stand to gain from disrupting the merger."

"No one in the family stands to gain from disrupting it, either," Angie pointed out. "At least, not financially. Everyone will be better off if the stock offering is successful."

"True." Owen glanced at her. "But I think it's obvious that whoever's trying to hurt the offering has something besides a financial goal in mind."

Angie nodded. "Someone is trying to keep the feud alive. Someone would rather lose the potential profits of the merger than see Townsends and Sutherlands bury the hatchet."

Owen sighed. "Celia, Derwin or Helen. Got to be one of those three."

"Celia wasn't here thirty years ago."

"No, but you know that old phrase about someone who is more royalist than the king? Celia's made a career out of being a Sutherland. And she's violently loyal to Dad's memory. She may have taken it upon herself to hurt the merger because she knows Dad would have disapproved of it."

"What about your aunt and uncle?"

"I don't know. Like Dad, they always refused to discuss whatever happened thirty years ago."

"Why don't we talk to Betty?"

Owen frowned. "Betty?"

"She was working for your family then, wasn't she?"

"I think she'd just started. But I doubt she would have been aware of what was happening in the family's inner circle."

"You'd be surprised at what the hired help knows about what goes on in the inner circle. Let's talk to her."

Owen hesitated briefly then decided there was no harm in trying. "All right."

Betty reached for the whistling kettle. She lifted it off the stove and poured boiling water into a teapot. "Of course I knew something terrible had happened. Nobody talked about it, but everyone went around real tight-lipped for weeks." She looked at

Owen as she carried the pot to the table. "Your aunt cried a lot. Your father was furious. Derwin had been seeing a lot of Helen and was about to get engaged to her. I think he knew what was going on, too. He acted very strangely."

"But you don't know what actually happened?" Owen watched her pour tea for the three of them.

"Just knew it had something to do with business. And that everyone was real mad at anyone with the last name of Townsend." She cocked a brow at Angie. "No offense."

"Her last name is Sutherland now, not Townsend," Owen said. "So you don't have to worry about offending her."

Angie picked up her cup. "Don't pay any attention to him, Betty."

"Right." Betty looked thoughtfully. "You know, it's hard to believe the bad feelings lasted all these years. Never did understand that part. Business deals go sour all the time. I've been around long enough to know that. No one holds grudges for thirty years."

"They do if there was more than business involved," Angie murmured. She looked at Owen. "And we've already decided this isn't a business matter."

"No," Owen agreed, his eyes meeting

Angie's. "For someone in this family, it's very personal."

"I wish I could help you," Betty said. "All I know is that the Townsends caused a lot of pain around here thirty years ago. Far as I'm concerned, it's about time the old feud was buried and forgotten."

"It's been buried," Owen said. "But someone hasn't forgotten."

"It will all be over soon," Betty predicted. She gave Owen a meaningful glance. "I always knew you had more common sense than your father. He was a good man in many ways, but you couldn't reason with him when it came to some things. Dealing with Townsends was one of his blind spots."

"I know," said Owen. He gave Angie a crooked smile. "But it's not always easy dealing with Townsends. You've got to have a knack for it."

Angie stuck her tongue out at him. Owen chuckled.

Fifteen minutes later, having learned nothing more than he already knew, Owen took Angie's hand and led her out of the kitchen.

"What now?" she asked as they went down the dark hall.

"I'm not sure. I could summon everyone together and stage a big confrontation scene.

Try to force the truth out of someone."

"You could cause a lot of pain if you do things that way."

"I don't give a damn about causing whoever's responsible pain. Not after what happened this afternoon."

Angie glanced at him. "What made this afternoon's incident worse than any of the others?"

Owen came to a halt in the middle of the hall. He clamped his fingers around her shoulders. "Don't you realize what happened today?"

Angie wrinkled her brow. "Of course. Someone obviously told Rawlings that our marriage was a fraud. One more attempt to hurt the stock offering."

He groaned at her naïveté. "That was only part of it. What someone was really trying to do was drive another wedge between us, Angie. You and me."

"What are you talking about?"

"Don't you understand? Someone wanted me to see you talking to Rawlings. You were deliberately set up, Angie. So was Rawlings, which is why I didn't flatten him."

"I don't understand."

"You *are* naive, damn it. Listen, I'll try again. It was no coincidence that I was told you were in that café with Rawlings. Someone wanted me to think you were selling inside information to him — maybe arranging a deal on the stock. Someone wanted to prove to me that even after all these years, nothing had changed. A Townsend cannot be trusted."

Angie eyes widened in shock. Then outrage flashed in the turquoise depths. "Of all the nerve," she sputtered. "Of all the sneaky, low-down, rotten *nerve*. A set up. I was supposed to look like a traitor."

"Right. Now you've got the whole picture," Owen said. He could not restrain a small, rueful grin. "And you wonder why us big, bad male chauvinists consider you a trifle naive?"

"But I was innocent," she raged.

"Hell, I knew that," he said impatiently.

Angie blinked. And then she started to grin. A wonderfully smug, utterly feminine grin.

"So you did," Angie said.

TEN

~

Owen eyed Angie coolly. "What's so damn funny?"

"Nothing." She smiled with perfect innocence, more certain of his love than she had been since their wedding day. Euphoria welled inside her.

"Angie, I am not in the mood for any cute games," Owen warned.

"Yes, dear."

He gave her a small shake. "Why are you grinning like a Cheshire cat?"

"Because I have reached a perfectly logical conclusion," she said smugly. "You'll be pleased to know that I have arrived at this conclusion without any excess of emotion and without so much as a trace of unreliable female intuition or wishful thinking. Just cold, clear logic. Your kind of thinking, Owen. Just the facts and nothing but the facts."

"Angie, what the hell are you talking about?"

"Mind you," she said, "I was fairly certain of this conclusion before I arrived at it through sheer, brilliant logic. But I knew you'd be pleased that I got at it your way as well as mine."

"Damn it, Angie, if you don't tell me what this is all about, I'm going to —"

"Of course I will tell you what this is all about. You love me."

He gave her an utterly blank stare. "Huh?"

"I said you love me. You just proved it."

"I did?"

"Certainly." She smiled at him and put her arms around his neck. "You admit you walked into that restaurant this afternoon, saw me with Jack Rawlings in what could only be called a compromising situation, and you never believed for a moment that I was going to ruin the stock offering by telling him our marriage was a fraud."

Owen's eyes started to harden. "You may not have been screwing up the offering, but you were sure as hell guilty of a number of other offenses."

"Ha! Name one."

"Impulsiveness, lack of common sense and a failure to think about consequences. Most of all, you displayed an annoying tendency to act on your own without consulting your husband."

"You weren't around."

"You should have waited until I was around!" Owen bellowed.

At that moment, Derwin stepped into the hall, frowning in deep concern. "Is something wrong out here?"

"No," said Angie. She smiled beatifically at him.

"No." Owen scowled at his uncle. "This is a private matter."

Derwin nodded, looking grave. "I understand. Sorry to interrupt. I take it you were able to keep your appointment at the marina this afternoon, Angie?"

Angie looked at Derwin and suddenly saw the eagerness in his eyes. The happiness she had been experiencing a moment earlier faded. "Yes, thank you, Derwin."

Owen shook Angie off him and turned toward his uncle. "How did you know about Angie's meeting at the marina?"

Derwin gave Owen a surprised look. "Oh, didn't she tell you? I happened to be taking a walk at the same time as that young man, Dave, arrived with the message that someone wanted to see Angie."

"Is that right?" Owen did not move.

"Yes, of course. I saw her off at the dock myself, didn't I, Angie?"

"Yes, you did." Angie reached out and

caught Owen's hand. He resisted, starting to free his fingers. She felt the new tension in him and deliberately squeezed hard. He apparently got the message because his hand relaxed in hers.

"I thought I saw you bringing Angie across the lake awhile ago," Derwin said, pinning Owen with a sharp gaze.

Owen's smile was cool. "So you did," he said easily. "I found her having coffee with Jack Rawlings in the marina café. You may have heard of him. Rawlings heads up a group of investors who want a block of Sutherland and Townsend stock when it goes public."

"I see." Derwin's narrowed eyes skipped between Angie and Owen. "Rather odd, isn't it?"

"Not really." Owen swung Angie's hand gently. "But definitely unethical. Rawlings sent her a message saying he worked for her brother. Naturally Angie went flying off to see what it was all about. But she realized soon enough she'd been tricked. Rawlings wanted to pump her for some inside information. She told him to get lost. Didn't you, Angie?"

"Of course."

Derwin scowled at Owen. "And you believed her?"

"Sure," Owen said. "She's my wife. Why wouldn't I believe her?"

Derwin's gaze turned stormy. "She's a Townsend, that's why. But it's obvious you're too besotted to notice what's in front of your very eyes." He stalked off without another word.

Angie felt the stillness in Owen. She looked at him. He was gazing after his uncle, his expression grim.

"Owen?"

"Let's get out of this damn hall."

He tugged her into the study and closed the door. Angie sat down and watched anxiously as Owen sprawled in the big chair behind the desk.

"I don't think you should jump to conclusions, Owen."

"It's Derwin who's behind all this. Got to be." Owen contemplated the view outside the window. "He's bitter because he's been kept out of the management of Sutherland Hotels since the beginning. He's been angry for years — and now he's furious with me because I haven't given him a position, either."

"You don't know it's him, Owen."

"I know it."

"How?"

Owen slanted her a derisive glance. "You saw him a few minutes ago. He thought we were quarreling because I'd found you talking to Rawlings."

"We *were* quarreling because of that."

"Yeah, but I hadn't jumped to the conclusion Derwin expected. I was just mad because you'd let yourself get fooled into seeing Rawlings. I never thought you'd set up a deal with the bastard. But Derwin looked like he just couldn't wait to hear me say you'd sold out the Sutherlands. He set up that meeting, Angie."

"And the other incidents? The fax I received on our wedding night? The telephone call telling me you were planning to divorce me as soon as the stock offering was made?"

Owen nodded grimly. "All of it."

Angie spread her hands. "But how? He's been here at Jade Lake for weeks. You know he has. And you said yourself the whole merger thing was a state secret. No one knew about it except you and my parents and Harry."

Owen's eyes rested thoughtfully on the computer that sat on his desk. "These days you don't always need spies inside someone's company to find out what's going on. Not if you know how to handle a computer. Derwin never had to step outside this house to learn what was going on or to arrange any of those incidents."

Angie followed his gaze. "You think he did it through this computer?"

"Watch." Owen leaned forward and punched a few keys. Then he sat back and waited as the screen flickered to life. "In this day and age all you need is a computer and a telephone. I should have thought of this a long time ago. It's the obvious answer."

Angie got up and came around the desk. She studied the series of memos that were appearing on the screen. "What are those?"

"I kept the merger information out of the computer until the last week of negotiations for security reasons," Owen explained. "Then, right before the wedding, I had to let the vice president of my public relations department know what was going on so he could make the announcement and handle the press. But once Calhoun had his instructions, the secret was vulnerable."

"Because he started writing memos and press releases on the computer?"

"Right. I knew there was a possibility the information would be leaked to the financial community. Hell, the rumors were already circulating because of our engagement. Remember those reporters waiting for us by the limo on our wedding day?"

"Very clearly," Angie said dryly.

"Your father and brother and I had been seen together enough to generate talk. I wasn't worried about the gossip. Rumors can be useful in a situation like this."

"Why?"

"They heighten the sense of excitement in the investment community. Palmer, Harry and I figured they wouldn't hurt so long as . . ." Owen broke off, frowning darkly.

"So long as I didn't hear them?" Angie concluded sweetly.

"You weren't likely to hear them during the week before the wedding," Owen said. "You had your hands full with wedding preparations. And according to Palmer and Harry, you never paid much attention to the business, anyway."

"My interests have certainly broadened lately, haven't they?"

"Very funny," he growled. "The point is, this computer — plus Derwin's fondness for tinkering with gadgets — explains how he knew what was going on. He's obviously taught himself how to use the computer to access Sutherland files."

"What about the fax?"

"Easy to send a fax with this setup." Owen drummed his fingers on the desk. "Once he knew the fax had been delivered, he simply picked up the phone and dialed our room at the hotel." Owen's hand clenched into a fist. "My own uncle."

"All right," Angie said quietly. "We know how it *could* have happened. But we still don't know why."

"I told you why. Derwin's been resentful and angry for years because Dad never trusted him with a major role in Sutherland."

"But he has a vested interest in Sutherland Hotels, just as everyone else in this family does. Why would he jeopardize the stock offering? There's a lot of money at stake."

Owen shrugged. "He's had years to nurse his grudge."

"I think there's more to it than that, Owen." Angie was silent for a moment, thinking. "It's got something to do with the old feud, not just Derwin's grudge against your father. Betty said that it wasn't just another business deal that went sour."

Owen scowled. "It doesn't matter why Derwin's so bitter. It's enough that we know he had a motive and —" he nodded toward the computer "— opportunity."

"So did everyone else around here. In fact, up until you offered your brother-in-law a job, your sister and Celia had motives, too. Even your aunt is resentful toward the

Townsends. And they all had access to the computer at one time or another. Kim and Glen could have used a computer while they were in Hawaii."

"Aunt Helen knows nothing about computers. She's not into gadgets the way Derwin is. Neither is Celia or Kim. Glen could have managed the job, but I don't think he did. He had no reason to sabotage the merger."

Angie watched Owen's face. "What are you going to do?"

Owen was quiet for a moment, obviously considering his options. "Confront Derwin. Tell him I know what's going on. Tell him that it stops right now or I cut off his income and Helen's, too."

"There might be a better way of handling it, Owen." She perched on the edge of his desk.

Owen swung around to face her. "Yeah? What do you suggest?"

"I think you should find out exactly why your uncle did what he did. Then maybe you should consider doing things a little differently than your father did them. Would it hurt to give Derwin a seat on the new board of Sutherland and Townsend?"

Owen's mouth dropped open. He recovered himself immediately. "Are you crazy?"

"Owen, think about it, please. You could handle him if he tried to stir up trouble. But my guess is he wouldn't be a problem. I think he'd back you in any move you made."

"I don't believe this. First I have to offer Glen Langley a job and now Derwin. Angie, quit trying to tell me how to run my company and my family!"

"I've got a stake in both. Why should I keep my mouth shut?"

"Because you don't know what the hell you're talking about."

Owen got to his feet. "I don't want to hear another word of advice, is that clear? I'll make my own decisions around here."

"You know, while we're on the subject, you really should think about deeding this house over to Celia. Apparently she feels your father had promised to leave it to her. And it's not as if you want the place. You hate it."

"Deed the house over to Celia? Good God, you don't know when to stop, do you?"

"Just a thought, Owen." She smiled her most winning smile.

"*Stop thinking*, damn it."

"Yes, Owen."

"I mean it, Angie. Don't think I haven't realized how you've been trying to manipulate me lately."

"That's not true." She stared at him, appalled. "I haven't been trying to manipulate you."

"Come off it, Angie."

"It's true. I've simply made a couple of suggestions, which you have wisely considered, that's all. I know very well I couldn't possibly manipulate you into doing anything you didn't want to do, Owen. Nobody could."

His eyes narrowed. He leaned back and beckoned with one finger.

"Come here, Angie," he ordered softly.

Wary of the new gleam in his eyes, she eased off the desk and took a step toward him. "Why? What do you want?"

"Come here and I'll tell you."

"I don't like the look in your eye, Owen Sutherland."

"Come here, Angie."

"Not unless you tell me what you have in mind."

"Come here, Mrs. Sutherland." Owen's voice deepened, becoming as smooth and rich as honey. His eyes held hers as surely as if he had reached out and caught hold of her wrist.

A rush of sensual excitement seized Angie. She sensed the desire in him and it drew her like a magnet. She risked another step forward and smiled.

Owen's hand clamped gently around her wrist. He stood, drew her against his chest and pinned her there, one palm curved around her buttocks. Deliberately he spread his legs so that she stood between his thighs.

"Well?" Angie demanded in a voice that trembled with anticipation. "What do you want, Owen?"

"Tell me you love me." His hand slid to her nape.

The request surprised her. It was not quite what she had been expecting. Angie hesitated. "Why should I tell you that? You don't care about love."

"I want to hear you say the words." He brushed his mouth lightly across hers, silently urging her to comply. "You haven't said them since our wedding day."

"I haven't had a good reason to say them." She twined her arms around his neck, vitally aware of the heat and strength in him.

"You do now." He kissed her brow, then the tip of her nose.

Angie shivered as the liquid warmth coiled inside her. "I don't see why I should. You haven't said those words to me."

"We're talking about you, Angie. Not me." He tightened his thighs around her hips, anchoring her. Then he started to slowly undo the buttons of her shirt. "We'll see who can manipulate whom around here."

"Owen, this is not fair."

"I've decided I want to hear you tell me you love me."

"Why?"

"I like it." He parted her shirt and slipped his hand inside to cup her breast.

"Owen, wait . . ."

"Tell me, Angie." He skimmed his mouth down her throat, pushed aside her collar and kissed her bare shoulder.

"Owen, stop. What are you trying to do?" Angie struggled briefly as she realized he was going to put her through sweet torture until she capitulated.

"Say the words, Angie." His hand dropped to the waistband of her jeans.

Angie heard the snap and the sound of her zipper being lowered. She was trembling, her body sensitized and aware. She breathed quickly, trying to steady herself. "Wait. Let's talk about this. I know you're annoyed because you think I've been trying to manipulate you. But I swear, it wasn't like that, Owen."

"Tell me you love me, Angie." He slid his hand inside her panties.

She gasped. "All right, maybe I was trying to pressure you a little bit. But I wasn't trying to manipulate you. I was just trying to give you some guidance. I wanted you to think about your feelings. I just wanted you to realize how you really felt about me, Owen."

"Say it, Angie." His fingers curled against her, seeking her softness. He nuzzled her neck.

"Look at it from my point of view, Owen. You've obviously got a problem admitting your deepest feelings to yourself, let alone to others. But I know your emotions run . . . *Oh.*"

"Do you love me, Angie?"

"Owen, stop! Anyone could walk in on us."

"If anyone does, he or she will turn right around and walk out again." He withdrew his hand, then slid his leg between hers and pushed at her gently with his thigh. "Love me, Angie?"

So much for trying to pressure him into admitting he loved her, Angie thought. When it came to this kind of resistance, he had a lot more stamina than she did. Owen was a pro at standing up to pressure.

"I love you, damn it." Angie gripped Owen's head between her hands and kissed him with a surge of exasperation and enthusiasm. "I love you, I love you, I love you. And you love me, Owen Sutherland. Admit it."

He ignored her passionate demand. Instead, his mouth closed roughly over hers, searing her lips. The masculine hunger in him enveloped Angie, drawing her into the heart of the storm. Owen's need for her was all-consuming.

And so was his love, she told herself as he lifted her and carried her across the room to the couch. *If he could only bring himself to admit it.*

The door of the study opened without any warning. Helen walked into the room. "Owen? Owen, what is going on? I just talked to Derwin. He tells me you found Angie with someone named Rawlings and that you . . . oh, my God."

Angie was flat on her back on the couch. She groaned and closed her eyes, making a quick grab at her parted shirt. Owen, one knee on the couch, turned to glare at his aunt.

"Excuse me," Helen said coldly. She made no move to leave the room. She stood there, glaring with anger and disapproval.

Owen straightened slowly, a resigned look in his eyes. Keeping himself strategically placed between Angie and his aunt, he confronted Helen. "What seems to be the problem here?"

Helen braced herself defiantly. "I demand to know what is going on."

Owen ran his fingers through his hair, a

gesture Angie had come to learn indicated disgust. "Well, since you ask, I was about to make love to my wife. Any objections?"

Helen's face went red and her lips thinned. "I do not particularly care about your ill-mannered personal behavior at the moment. Has Angie been giving inside information about Sutherland to this Rawlings person?"

"No." Owen shoved his shirttails inside his jeans and slanted an amused glance at Helen. "Do you think I'd be making love to her if I'd just caught her in the act of selling me out?"

"Who knows what you would do? It's obvious she's seduced you," Helen said tightly. "Derwin's right. You're just a puppet on her string. I've warned you before about the way Townsends go about deceiving people. But you won't listen, will you? You never listen to anyone. You think you know everything." Helen's eyes glistened with tears.

"Helen . . ." Owen started toward her.

"Go back to your cheap little seductress of a wife. Go on. You'll find out what Townsends are really like." Helen turned and fled. The door slammed behind her.

Silence descended on the study. Angie sat up cautiously, all trace of passion gone. She was silent for a long moment. "Owen, there's more to this than we know. More than just Derwin's bitterness over not being allowed to work at Sutherland. Your aunt's anger is too passionate, and it's all directed at my family."

Owen was staring at the closed door. "You think she was involved in whatever happened thirty years ago?"

"I'm not sure what to think." Angie stood. "All I know is that we've got to find out what happened before we take any further steps."

"Celia?" Owen cocked his brow inquiringly.

"I don't think she'll be able to help us any more than Betty could. But we can try."

"The hell with it," Owen said. He finished adjusting his clothing and strode to the door. "I'm going to get everyone together in one room and we're going to have this out once and for all."

"Owen, wait." Angie fumbled with her clothing and ran after him. "I'm not sure that would be a good idea."

"I'm not particularly interested in your analysis of the situation," Owen called over his shoulder as he went down the hall. "I want some answers and I want them now. Go find Celia. Tell her I want her in the living room in five minutes."

"But, Owen —"

"Just do it, Angie."

Angie trailed to a halt. Maybe he was right. Maybe it was time to force the issue. Assuming Owen could get everyone to talk. "All right."

Ten minutes later Angie sat tensely on the sofa near the window. She watched the expressions on the faces of her new relatives as Owen let the silence hang heavily in the room.

The emotions ran the gamut. There was anxiety and concern on Celia's patrician features. Derwin and Helen sat rigidly upright in their chairs, their expressions reflecting bitterness and something that might have been fear.

Owen stood at the window looking implacable and completely controlled. Angie wondered if this was the way he was when he called a meeting of his board of directors. She was suddenly rather glad she did not work for him.

Owen let the seconds tick past while he gazed over the lake. Night was falling rapidly. Lights were winking into existence on the far shore. Jade Lake was quickly turning from dark green to black.

He finally turned slowly to face the others. "I've had enough of this nonsense about the old Sutherland–Townsend feud. I know full well that certain recent incidents aimed at causing trouble between Angie and me have all been caused by someone in this house."

Derwin looked offended. "How dare you accuse us?"

"Believe me, once the facts are set out, it's damned easy to accuse you." Owen met his uncle's gaze. "Only a fool could miss the pattern. The Townsends are innocent."

"I wouldn't be too sure of that, if I were you," Derwin muttered.

"Derwin," Owen said with cold patience, "I know *how* things were accomplished and I know *when* they were accomplished. I am fully aware that the computer in my study was used. The only thing I don't know for certain is why someone here is so determined to ruin this deal with Townsend. Would you care to tell me?"

"I don't know what you're talking about," Derwin snapped, his gaze focused on the lake outside the window.

"I'm talking about what happened thirty years ago."

Helen straightened her shoulders. "Why don't you try asking the Townsends?"

"I did," Owen said quietly. "Palmer Townsend says he does not know what went wrong thirty years ago, and I believe him. All he knows is that the deal to merge the two companies went sour at the last minute and that my father would never speak to him again."

Derwin narrowed his eyes. "Palmer Townsend knows what went wrong. Hell, he was the cause of the trouble."

Angie was incensed. "That's not true."

Owen threw her a repressive look. "Quiet, Angie. We're going to get to the bottom of this. This is no time for an impassioned defense of your family. Save the emotion for later."

"If you think I'm going to sit here and let your uncle slander my father, you're out of your mind," Angie shot back furiously.

"What I think," Owen said very softly, "is that you should sit there quietly while I sort this out. The last thing I need right now is a display of Townsend theatrics."

He was right and Angie knew it. She subsided, contenting herself with a glare.

Owen turned to his uncle. "Derwin, I think we'll start with you. Tell me what happened thirty years ago."

"I don't see why I should be forced to dredge up the past," Derwin argued.

"Put it this way," Owen said in a softly menacing tone, "either you tell me what happened or you and Helen can dredge up a new source of income."

Derwin stared at him, clearly shaken. "Are you threatening to cut us off from Helen's share of the Sutherland income?"

Angie groaned and closed her eyes briefly. The others looked at Owen in disbelief and outraged shock. Owen took no notice.

"Now you're starting to understand, Derwin. Talk."

Derwin drew himself up stiffly. "Very well, if you insist. But you aren't going to like what you hear."

"Just talk, Derwin."

Derwin glanced at Helen then faced Owen. "It's quite simple. Townsend never intended a genuine merger. What was intended was a hostile takeover of Sutherland Hotels. When it was over Sutherland would have been effectively swallowed up by Townsend Resorts and all of us would have been out in the cold."

"Try another story, Derwin," Owen suggested.

"It's true, I tell you," Derwin sputtered. "Your father found out that Townsend had been quietly buying up shares of Sutherland stock through a third party. Once he had acquired enough stock, Palmer Townsend could have forced the merger on his own

255

terms. He almost succeeded. But your father realized what was going on in time to stop it. It cost Sutherland Hotels a fortune because we had to buy back a lot of the company stock. It was tough going for a while, but we did it."

"My brother managed to forestall the hostile takeover," Helen put in. "Just barely. He made two decisions after that. One was to make certain that Sutherland Hotels never lost controlling interest in its own stock again. The second decision was never to trust a Townsend."

Owen shook his head in disgust. "That is a bunch of crap. Don't expect me to buy any of it."

Celia frowned. "How do you know that, Owen?"

"Because out of curiosity I took a look at the stockholder records from thirty years ago. My father was no fool. He always made certain he held at least fifty-one percent of the stock. He was never vulnerable to a hostile takeover. But something did change his mind about the merger with Townsend, and I want to know what it was."

"Are you saying I'm lying about what happened thirty years ago?" Derwin demanded.

"Yes," Owen said. "I am. The question is why?"

There was an appalled silence. Unable to meet anyone's eyes because of the pain she was afraid she would see, Angie focused on the view outside the window. She noticed a small speedboat roaring toward the island. She frowned, studying the three figures in it closely.

"Owen?" she said tentatively.

"Not now, Angie."

"I think we've got company," Angie said.

"What are you talking about?" Owen turned to follow her glance.

The small boat cut its engine as it neared the island. It closed in rapidly on the small dock. The lights of the boat house revealed the familiar face of the man who leaped out of the boat. The two other people in the craft piled out and started moving swiftly up the path.

The lights from the terrace gleamed on Harry Townsend's red hair and the set, determined faces of Angie's mother and father.

"Well, hell," Owen muttered. "Just what I needed. A landing party of Townsends coming to rescue Angie from a fate worse than death. You know something? This really is the last straw."

ELEVEN

"I'll get the door," Owen told Betty as he stalked into the hall. "Looks like we'll need a couple of extra places set at dinner and two more bedrooms made up for tonight. My in-laws have arrived unexpectedly."

Betty grinned, wiping her hands on her apron. "Well, well, well. This should be interesting."

"If I were you, I'd stay in the kitchen until the fur stops flying."

"Think I'll do just that. You can handle this, Owen. You've got a wife who will help you."

Owen opened the door and found himself confronting an irate father-in-law, a furious brother-in-law and a worried mother-in-law.

"What a pleasant surprise," Owen murmured. "We were just talking about you Townsends."

"I demand an explanation, Sutherland,"

Palmer Townsend said before he was even through the door.

Harry pushed past Owen, searching the hall. "Where's Angie? What the hell is going on here, Sutherland? We got a message this morning that you've got her stashed here until after the stock offering. Some jerk claims you're going to divorce her as soon as the stock goes public."

"Some jerk lied," Owen said calmly. "Come on in, Marian," he said to Angie's mother. "You look as if you've had a long trip."

"You would not believe what I've been through today." Marian smiled uncertainly. "Palmer and Harry went crazy when the message came this morning. We flew to San Francisco and rented a car to drive up here. We've been hours on that winding road trying to find Jade Lake. Neither Palmer nor Harry would stop for directions. It's been incredible."

"You're just in time for dinner," Owen said.

Angie came into the hall. She smiled brightly. "Hi, everyone. What's all the excitement about?"

"Typical Townsend reaction to a family crisis, dear," Marian said. "Everyone is going bonkers."

"I am not going bonkers," Palmer snapped, looking ferocious. "And neither is Harry. But we do want some explanations, by God."

"You'll get them." Owen put his arm possessively around Angie's shoulders. She stepped close, signaling her loyalty in no uncertain terms.

Palmer and Harry did not miss the small but highly significant action. Harry glared at his sister. "Are you sure you're okay, Angie?"

"I'm fine, thank you."

Palmer looked at Owen. "Just what the devil is going on around here? I thought you two were heading to a Sutherland hotel for your honeymoon."

"So did I. Our plans changed." Owen led the way to the living room, his arm still firmly around Angie. "Have a seat, everyone. I'll make the introductions for those of you who don't know each other personally. Then we're going to finish hashing this out."

"I don't see what needs to be hashed out," Palmer muttered. "All I want is an explanation." He nodded brusquely to Helen, his face softening slightly. "Hello, Helen. Been awhile. Almost didn't recognize you."

"Hello, Palmer," Helen said softly.

Owen caught the brief, odd look on his aunt's face as she greeted Palmer Townsend. He studied her more closely out of the corner of his eye while he ran through the introductions. Owen realized Angie was covertly watching his aunt, too.

"When this is all over," Owen concluded, "we're going to have dinner and go to bed. In the morning Angie and I will be leaving to finish our honeymoon at an unspecified Sutherland hotel."

Angie gave him an amused, interested look. "We will?"

"Yes, we definitely will. Now, let's get on with this miserable business." Owen decided to take a chance. "Helen, I think it's your turn."

Helen looked stunned. "But I don't have anything to say about what happened all those years ago. There's been enough damage done. Owen, can't you let things be?"

"No," Owen said deliberately gentling his voice. "I can't."

Derwin spoke up angrily. "What happened thirty years ago has nothing to do with you, Owen. You were just a child."

"You're wrong, Derwin. Whatever happened then is affecting my marriage and my business. This mess has got to be cleared up

261

now. Let's get one thing straight, here. No one is leaving this island until I have the truth." Owen looked at his aunt again. "Helen?"

Derwin leaped to his feet. "Stop badgering her. The least you could do is show some respect for your own aunt, Owen Sutherland. She's your father's sister, after all."

Owen felt Angie's fingers slip gently into his. She squeezed his hand reassuringly, and he knew she was telling him to continue on his present course. "I'm sorry, Helen. But I have to have some answers."

"I know," Helen whispered. "I always knew that sooner or later it would all come out." She burst into tears.

Derwin hurried over to her, thrusting a handkerchief into her hands. "You don't have to tell him a thing, Helen."

She blew her nose and shook her head firmly. "No, Owen's right. This has gone far enough. We've lived with this all these years and I, for one, am tired of it."

Palmer eyed her closely. "This has something to do with me, doesn't it, Helen?"

"Yes. Yes, it does. I'm sorry, Palmer."

Owen saw Marian glance at Angie and raise her brows, but she said nothing.

"All right, Helen," Owen said gently. "Tell us what happened."

"What happened," Helen said, her voice firming as she spoke, "was that I made a foolish mistake thirty years ago. My only excuse is that I was rather young. And somewhat sheltered. And accustomed to being spoiled, I suppose. To put it in straightforward terms, I fell in love with Palmer Townsend the minute I saw him. And, with typical Sutherland arrogance, I convinced myself that he was in love with me."

Owen shot a quick glance at his in-laws. Palmer looked unhappy and uncomfortable. Marian appeared sympathetic. Harry looked surprised.

"There was a great deal of excitement in the air because of the plans for a merger between Sutherland and Townsend," Helen continued. "Everyone was bubbling over with enthusiasm, full of anticipation for the future. I decided nothing could be more romantic than Palmer and I marrying and uniting the companies and the families through a fairy-tale wedding."

"Helen, you don't have to say any more." Derwin gripped her shoulder.

"He's right, Helen. Don't pay any attention to Owen, here," Palmer said. "This is personal. You don't have to spill your secrets to all of us."

She smiled sadly. "But I do. Owen is right.

They aren't just my secrets. They affected all of us in one way or another. The rest of what happened is quite simple. I went to Palmer and told him that I was in love with him and that I wanted to get married. He was startled, to say the least. Stunned would be a more apt description."

Palmer looked at the toes of his shoes. He was turning red.

Helen continued with an apologetic smile. "He tried to be a gentleman and let me down easy. But when I realized he was not in love with me and, indeed, had never considered me more than a casual friend, that he was about to become engaged to someone I had never met, I became enraged. I did something very wrong. Something I have regretted for thirty years."

"Helen, that's enough," Derwin said. He patted her shoulder — an awkward but tender gesture.

"No, not quite." She touched his hand briefly, her eyes going from Palmer to Owen. "In a jealous rage, I became determined to ruin the merger. I'm the one who gave inside information to certain financial backers. It caused them to change their minds about loaning money to the company that would have been formed by the merger. Those same backers later decided to finance some Townsend expansion plans. My brother naturally assumed that had been Palmer Townsend's scheme from the beginning."

There was a collective gasp around the room. Owen leaned forward and propped his elbows on his knees. He frowned thoughtfully. "What was the information, Helen, and how did you get it?"

Helen shrugged. "Just some accounting data about one of the resorts in the Sutherland chain that was having difficulties. I got the information from a secretary. It wasn't difficult. I had heard my brother talking about the situation and knew he wanted to keep it quiet until after the merger. When I sent the information anonymously to the financial backers, I implied that the troubled resort was only one of many. They believed it. You know how gossip affects business deals."

Palmer looked at Owen. "I remember that problem resort. Bad location. Your father planned to sell it off and that's what he eventually did. It never really hurt the rest of the chain."

Helen looked at her folded hands. "My brother was furious when the backers mysteriously pulled out of the deal and turned around and financed Townsend. He was sure a secret deal had been made."

"He thought I'd convinced them that Townsend was a better bet on its own than a Sutherland–Townsend merger," Palmer said slowly. "He decided I'd changed my mind about the merger and used inside information to get the backers to drop their interest in Sutherland and get behind Townsend, instead."

Helen nodded. "My brother turned the company upside down looking for your spy. He eventually came to me. When he pinned me down, I told him another lie."

Palmer looked at her, his eyes narrowed slightly. "You told him I had seduced you in order to get inside information, didn't you?"

"Yes," Helen admitted. "I think my brother could have forgiven a few shady business maneuvers on the part of a competitor. But I knew he'd never forgive you for what I told him you did."

"And that's why he hated my guts all those years." Palmer shook his head in wonder. "Well, at least now I understand why he took such a dislike to me after the deal fell through. But why didn't he confront me?"

"I begged him not to. I told him my pride was at stake. He understood."

"Sutherland pride," Owen muttered ruefully.

Angie smiled at him. "I always knew there was a lot of passion in this family. All kinds of passion."

Owen tightened his grip on her hand. "So much for the cool Sutherlands." He glanced at Helen. "Was I wrong about Derwin being behind all the recent incidents, then? Was it you?"

"No," Derwin answered quietly. "You were right. I was the one who tried to cause enough mischief to ruin the stock offering. I found out about the merger and the marriage too late to head either off, but I thought if the stock didn't do well, you and Townsend might undo the merger and go back to running the corporations separately. It was a long shot, but it was all I could manage on such short notice. I had to try."

Palmer stared at him in exasperation. "For God's sake, man, why? We're all going to make a lot of money out of this merger."

"Some things are more important than money," Derwin said proudly. "I had to try to protect Helen from the pain I knew she would experience if Sutherland and Townsend eventually got together on a permanent basis. I knew what had happened thirty years ago, you see. I knew how passionately she had once loved you, Palmer. I detested you for having caused her so much unhappiness, even though it eventually paved the way for me to become engaged to her."

Palmer frowned at him a moment longer then nodded. "Sure, I can understand that."

Harry shrugged in sympathy. "Yeah. I can see where you'd feel you had to try something now, Derwin."

"Perfectly reasonable of you, Derwin," Marian murmured. "And I certainly understand why you did what you did, Helen. Unrequited love can be dreadfully painful. One can do foolish things because of it."

"It was all a bit drastic," Celia observed. "But I suppose one can understand."

"Absolutely," Angie said. "Poor Helen. How perfectly awful it must have been for you. And it was wonderfully loyal of you to try to protect her from having to confront my father and be humiliated this time around, Derwin."

Helen smiled sadly at Derwin. "The thing is, it was only a matter of pride, not love. I realized that soon enough when I discovered it was Derwin I truly cared for. But I was afraid to confess the truth afterward. It would have been so humiliating and it was too late to repair the damage, anyway. I was hoping everything would be forgotten. But it never was."

Owen scanned the faces of everyone in the room. He groaned and dropped his head into his hands. "Somebody save me from all this *emotion*. Even my father fell victim to it. I cannot believe I am surrounded by people who seem to have no problem at all understanding thirty years of business decisions based on smoldering vengeance and unrequited love. *Thirty years.*"

"Now, Owen," Angie said, patting his shoulder sympathetically. "You're overdramatizing the situation, dear. It's not that bad."

He raised his head and glared at her. "Not that bad? Are you crazy? It's absolutely incredible that either corporation has survived this long with such emotional people in charge. How the hell are we going to run the new Sutherland and Townsend with a board made up of seething, passionate overreactive people like this?"

Everyone in the room turned to stare at him. Owen glowered. Angie smiled gloriously.

"You're going to put some of your family on the board?" Palmer asked, looking interested.

"Why not?" Owen said. "You, as president, and I, as chief executive officer, each get to appoint an equal number of board members, right?"

"Right?"

"You're no doubt going to put Harry on as soon as possible."

"Sure. And my wife. I like to know I've got people I can count on behind me when I get into a fight," Palmer said.

"Yeah? Well, I want people *I* can count on to back me up when you and I get into it, Palmer." Owen looked at his uncle. "I could use the kind of loyalty you've shown to Aunt Helen for thirty years, Derwin. What about it? Will you take a seat on the new board?"

Derwin looked startled then flustered, his surprise obvious. "Well, I . . . Yes. Yes, of course. Be glad to help out on the new board." He stood a little straighter and beamed proudly at his wife.

"And what about you, Celia?" Owen switched his gaze to his stepmother. "If you're on the board you can look after Kim's interests in the company. There will probably be grandchildren one of these days, too. You'll want to protect their futures."

"I'm deeply honored, Owen." Celia studied him closely. "But I don't really know much about running a business like Sutherland and Townsend."

"Something tells me you'll learn fast. And I already know you're loyal to Sutherland interests. That counts for a lot. By the way, while we're on the subject of grandchildren, I want you to know you can have this house for them. It's all yours. I know Dad would have wanted it that way. He just didn't bother to spell it out in the will. You know how Dad did things."

"He expected you to take care of everything. Yes." Celia smiled slowly and nodded. "Thank you, Owen. Thank you very much. And I accept the seat on the board."

Owen turned to Helen with a questioning glance.

"No, thank you," Helen said gently. "I don't need a place on your new board of directors. I trust you and the others to look after the family interests. And I'd really rather spend my time with my charity projects, if you don't mind."

Owen nodded, appreciating the quiet vote of confidence. "Thanks."

"Hey, what about me?" Angie bounced up and down and waved her hand eagerly to get Owen's attention. "I'd like to be on the new board of directors. I'll take the seat Helen doesn't want. It'll be great fun. I've got all sorts of really terrific ideas for the company, including a new logo."

Owen heard Palmer and Harry groan. He ignored them as he turned to his bright-eyed wife. He decided to try logic first.

"You've already got a career designing jewelry, remember?"

"Yes, but I'm sure I could manage two careers," she said quickly.

"Angie, honey, you and everyone else will own shares in the new company. That will give you some say in how things are run. You don't need a seat on the board."

"But, Owen —"

"For crying out loud," Owen exploded, abandoning logic, "you're sleeping with the CEO. How much more clout do you want?"

"It isn't the same," she insisted, blushing furiously as everyone grinned. "Give me a shot at it, okay, Owen? I just know I'd make a great member of the board. I'll attend every meeting and I'll volunteer for special committees and everything."

"I'll just bet you would." Owen grinned slowly. "I'll be real blunt, Angie. I'm going to love you for the rest of my life and then some, but it will be a cold day in Hades before I allow you onto the board of directors of Sutherland and Townsend. Something tells me you're going to cause more than enough trouble just holding a few shares of stock."

"*Owen.*" Angie's lips parted in astonishment. Her eyes widened with delight. "What did you just say?"

"You heard me."

"Owen, you *do* love me. I knew it."

Owen barely had time to brace himself as Angie hurtled straight into his arms.

"Oomph," Owen muttered, his arms going around her immediately.

She clung to him, smothering him with kisses as the assembled majority stockholders of Sutherland and Townsend cheered.

Betty walked into the living room and took in the scene of Sutherlands and Townsends laughing uproariously together. She caught Owen's eye over the top of Angie's head and smiled broadly.

"Always knew there wasn't anything wrong around here that couldn't be fixed up with the love of a good woman. Now, then, dinner is served. I just can't wait to see all you Sutherlands and Townsends sitting down to a meal together."

The following evening Angie stood on the terrace of the honeymoon suite of a familiar Sutherland hotel. The evening breeze rippled the silk of her silver peignoir. She leaned her elbows on the railing and watched the sunset far out over the Pacific. Her long, silver earrings swung gently.

Mentally she began designing a graceful, curving bracelet of beaten silver that would capture and reflect the colors of twilight.

She would start sketching again soon, she decided. She had only been away from her jewelry design work for a couple of weeks, but she was already starting to miss it. Her art was a part of her, and when she was away from it for very long she got a little restless.

She turned as she heard the door of the suite open behind her. Owen walked in carrying a bottle of champagne and two glasses in one hand. He was wearing the black dinner jacket, pleated white shirt and black trousers he had worn to dinner.

He paused long enough to close the door and lock it securely. Then his gaze skimmed over the elegant white and silver room until he saw Angie out on the terrace. He started toward her and began to loosen his black bow tie. His smile was slow and warm and full of sensual promise.

Angie shivered under that warm gaze as if Owen had touched her. She watched him stalk across the white carpet like a jungle cat, moving with sleek power and masculine grace. She saw the love and the hunger in his eyes and she thought again how much she loved him.

Owen came to a halt near her. He put the bottle and glasses on the white wrought-iron table. He opened the champagne with a few smooth, efficient movements. Then he poured two glasses and handed one to Angie. He lifted his own in salute.

"To you, Mrs. Sutherland."

"To you, Mr. Sutherland."

Owen waited until Angie had taken a sip of the bubbling champagne. Then he removed the glass from her hand and put it on the table beside his.

Very deliberately he reached around her waist to grip the wrought-iron railing behind her. He looked at her as she stood gently caged in front of him.

"Now, then, Mrs. Sutherland." He kissed her slowly, taking his time, letting her feel the endless need and love inside him.

Angie smiled and twined her arms around his neck. "Yes, Mr. Sutherland?"

"I believe," Owen said, his lips on her throat, "that you and I still have some unfinished business."

"Is that right?" She trembled under his lingering, compelling kisses. She tipped her head back and let her hair tumble over her shoulders. "And what would that be?"

"A wedding night."

"Ah. That." She laughed up at him with her eyes and started to unfasten his white shirt. "Do we need to call a meeting of the board in order to get approval of this merger, or do you think we can manage it on our own?"

"The board of directors of Sutherland and Townsend has already given this its full approval. I think we can handle the details just fine all by ourselves." Owen's mouth came down on hers. He scooped her up in his arms. He strode into the white and silver room with her and put her on the bed.

When Angie looked at him she saw that he was watching her silver gown slide around her thighs. She smiled at the look in his eyes, reached up and took hold of the ends of his tie. She tugged gently.

Owen laughed huskily as he allowed himself to be pulled down onto the bed. He lay sprawled on top of her and threaded his fingers through her hair in a now wonderfully familiar gesture.

"Tell me you love me, Angie."

"I love you, Owen. I shall love you all of my life." She touched the strong line of his jaw with gentle fingertips.

"Just as well, because I am going to keep you close for the rest of our lives, come what may." He caught her hand and kissed the golden band on her finger. "I love you, wife. Forever."

"Forever."

★ ★ ★

Ten months later Owen paused outside a hospital room door. He was carrying a dozen red roses in one arm and a large manila envelope in the other. He did not bother to conceal his proud grin as he walked into the room. The place was littered with gifts from various members of the Sutherland and Townsend clans. Pink ribbons and brightly colored wrapping paper lay everywhere.

Angie looked up from the infant in her arms. She smiled, her eyes glowing with love and happiness. She looked tired, Owen thought with some concern. But he had to admit he had never seen anything so beautiful as the sight of his wife holding their baby.

Angie looked at the flowers. "Owen, they're lovely. What's in the envelope?"

"The kid's first share of Sutherland and Townsend stock." Owen opened the envelope and removed the stock certificate made out to Samantha Helen Sutherland. "Think she'll like it?"

Angie laughed. "She's going to love it when she graduates from high school, that's for sure. At the rate the stock is climbing these days, she'll be able to finance law or medical school with her share."

"Maybe she'll decide to be the next CEO of Sutherland and Townsend." Owen leaned down to admire his baby. The infant did not open her eyes, but her tiny hand closed tightly around his thumb. Owen laughed at the strength and determination in that small grip. "She knows how to hang on to what she wants."

"Just like her father," Angie agreed.

"Right," said Owen. He looked at Angie. "And I am never going to let go of you, Mrs. Sutherland. Remember that."

"I will," Angie said. And she smiled at him the way she had on her wedding day when he had put his ring on her finger.

The way she would for the rest of their lives.

We hope you have enjoyed this Large Print book. Other Thorndike Press or Chivers Press Large Print books are available at your library or directly from the publishers.

For more information about current and upcoming titles, please call or write, without obligation, to:

Thorndike Press
295 Kennedy Memorial Drive
Waterville, Maine 04901 USA
Tel. (800) 223-1244
Tel. (800) 223-6121

OR

Chivers Press Limited
Windsor Bridge Road
Bath BA2 3AX
England
Tel. (0225) 335336

All our Large Print titles are designed for easy reading, and all our books are made to last.

THE ROMANCE OF LABRADOR

THE MACMILLAN COMPANY
NEW YORK · BOSTON · CHICAGO · DALLAS
ATLANTA · SAN FRANCISCO

MACMILLAN & CO., Limited
LONDON · BOMBAY · CALCUTTA
MELBOURNE

**THE MACMILLAN COMPANY
OF CANADA, Limited**
TORONTO

Photograph by F. C. Sears

SUNSET AT NORTHWEST RIVER

A LABRADOR VILLAGE

The
Romance of Labrador

BY

SIR WILFRED GRENFELL
K.C.M.G., M.D., F.R.C.S., ETC.

ILLUSTRATED

New York

THE MACMILLAN COMPANY

1934

THE LIBRARY
COLBY JUNIOR COLLEGE
NEW LONDON, N. H.

F
1136
G84

Copyright, 1934, by
THE MACMILLAN COMPANY.

All rights reserved—no part of this book
may be reproduced in any form without
permission in writing from the publisher,
except by a reviewer who wishes to quote brief
passages in connection with a review written
for inclusion in magazine or newspaper.

Set up and printed.

15542

PRINTED IN THE UNITED STATES OF AMERICA

Northward Ho!

"THERE is a lure to far-away places on the earth's frontier which only those who have been there can fully understand. It may be the desert, the mountains, Africa, the Orient, the South Sea islands, fever-infested tropical jungles, or barren Arctic wastes. Wherever it may be, and no matter the hardships endured, the lure to go back is always the same, and those who have felt it have truly lived."

Acknowledgment

IN A previous book called "Labrador: The Country and the People" most of the scientific facts concerning Labrador, up to 1922, have been collated. It was intended for a book of reference rather than for popular consumption; and readers desiring information on special subjects must be referred to it.

I wish here to acknowledge my indebtedness to the following authorities: Dr. E. B. Delabarre, Dr. Charles Townsend, Dr. O. Austin, Dr. Charles Johnson, Mr. John Sherman, Mr. Outram Bangs, Miss Mary Rathbun, Mr. William Cabot, Mr. W. G. Gosling, Professor Fernald, Mr. W. S. Wallace—who have all been among my best helpers. Valuable information has been received also from the books and records of: Dr. Loeber in the Encyclopædia Britannica, Dr. Cranz's records, Mr. Rolt-Wheeler, Mr. Meade Minnigerode, M. de la Roncième of Paris, the curators of libraries and museums which I visited in Rouen, Dieppe, Paris, London, New York and elsewhere, the Hudson's Bay Company's magazine, "The Beaver," Dr. Bryant's monograph, Mr. Durgin's letters, Dr. Storer's observations, Dr. Prowse's History, Mr. Dillon Wallace, Mr. Hesketh Prichard, and Mrs. Hubbard.

In "The Romance of Labrador" I owe special debts also to Professor Coleman of Ottawa, Professor Wheeler

Acknowledgment

of Cornell, Mr. Noel Odell of Cambridge, England, and particularly to Dr. Reginald Daly of Harvard, whose monograph written for "Labrador: The Country and the People" I have here largely used again.

The data on which the following chapters are based have been garnered from every source available to an inveterate wanderer, and from more than forty years' personal experience in the country. It is impossible for the author to acknowledge his debts to others as he would like. If any feel aggrieved, he trusts that they will accept this expression of sincere gratitude to everyone who has added to the stock of knowledge of "The Romance of Labrador." All men of science desire to have their contributions to knowledge used to the utmost for the benefit of mankind. Like good coin, the more it is turned over, the greater their reward.

Contents

Contents

Illustrations

Illustrations

Prologue

THIS book is an attempt to record the scientific and historic facts about Labrador, as far as they are known. It is the *"audi alteram partem"* of a medical man, who has spent much of the past forty years on those coasts, and who admires greatly Mussolini's dictum, "We must not be proud of our country for its history, but for what we are making of it to-day."

When the word "Labrador" is mentioned, men shrug their shoulders and shiver as automatically as, when the definition of a spiral staircase is asked, they twist their right forefinger up into ascending whirls.

Quite recently, a university graduate coming to Labrador in June to help me for his summer holidays, unblushingly walked up the wharf carrying a pair of boots with skates screwed on them. Practically no part of Labrador is north of Scotland, and three out of our five hospitals are south of the latitude of London.

The records by which Labrador has been judged are those of disappointed adventurers, of genuine explorers who condemned that which they did not understand how to adapt, of those who in a new era of man's power over Nature have never personally seen the country, and of men who have become so dependent upon the luxuries of so-called modern civilization that they have neither the grit nor the vision to-day for the venture of

Prologue

converting its raw materials to man's use. So far it has been the men who judged it, and never the land itself, which have been "of no use." No stories of the peoples who have passed across the world's stage bring home as vividly the reasons why, under man's hand, the progress of civilization is often deplorably delayed.

We have no fear of being listed in the days to come as among the "false prophets." There is no "dump-heap" —unless it is we, who are free to become such. In God's economy there is no waste.

> *"Lo, the book exactly worded*
> *Wherein all hath been recorded:*
> *Thence shall judgment be awarded."*

THE ROMANCE OF LABRADOR

I: THE PAGEANT OF THE ROCKS

The Stage is Set

"THE Labrador Coast is still one of the most bold and rugged in the whole world," said a famous geologist. "The bareness of the rocks, their freedom from obscuring forest and turf, helps the long coast to tell its own geological story. Mother Nature has there taken off more than the usual amount of clothing which she is wont to bestow on the land elsewhere; and the autographed story of the ages is so imprinted on her naked bones that those who run may read its thrilling pages, and the wayfaring man can enjoy the conceit of being for a while a veritable Sherlock Holmes. To know Labrador is to know her geology. Seldom elsewhere is

I

the explorer's mind so forced to think of the very beginning of things. One day the scientific study of Labrador will bring a rich store to our knowledge of the whole earth."

To follow the story, however, the reader must keep thinking of a thousand years as but a day. The mountains we look at now do not seem to alter one iota in our lifetime, yet whole series of mountain ranges have grown up and then been worn away in the earth's lifetime by the same forces that are acting to-day.

The bedrocks of Labrador are for the most part of remote antiquity and belong to the very foundation of the whole continent of North America, the "oldest series" of rocks. These "Archean" formations constitute a complex mixture of rocks of different ages, a veritable jumble-box of underground history, and yet may be regarded as a vast geological unit, stretching all across from the coast to Hudson's Bay and then on to the Pacific and to Mexico. The whole is often called the "Basement Complex." It bears no fossil remains of animals or plants.

Here and there in the Labrador Peninsula the worn-down surface of the Complex is veneered with nearly horizontal beds of much younger limestones, shales, sandstones, and hardened gravels, some of which enclose fossils of some of the earliest known organisms. Elsewhere in the continent this veneer covers still larger patches and so obscures the true majesty of the Basement Complex, which in reality is continuous underground from the Arctic Ocean to the Isthmus of Panama and from Labrador to California. In Labrador the veneer over three-quarters of the Peninsula has been gnawed away through endless ages by weather, rain, and ice sheets. This ancient surface has thus been resurrected and to-day presents an astonishingly flat surface. Amazing it is when one compares the simplicity of the plain-like relief over most of Labrador with the infinite turmoil through which its constituent rocks passed when the contortions of the crust of the young earth prepared the structure we call the Basement Complex.

Most of the Basement rocks were once molten. They froze into crystalline masses, composed of minerals like those in the familiar granite. These include quartz, glass-clear and without planes of cleavage; feldspar, cleaving in two sets of planes; mica, cleaving in scales; hornblende with its own peculiar cleavages and other properties. In varied combination these minerals formed to make different kinds of granite and, more rarely, such rocks as syenite, diorite, and other species familiar to the geologist. Intermixed with those dominant rocks are lavas and other volcanic products of the old time of storm and stress, and also limestones formed at intervals during the early invasions of the ocean into what we now know as Labrador.

Granites, syenites, lavas, and limestones were all gripped in the vise that made mountain structures, and in this process new molten masses were squeezed up into the writhing mass of older rocks and themselves were cooled to form younger granites and the like. Again and again this kind of thing happened. With each paroxysm of the crust of the earth the rocks were heated by friction and by the temperature of the newer, invading

3

"melts." At the same time, the solid rocks were pressed with unimaginable force, so that their original minerals were flattened and re-crystallized into new flat forms. The result was a general layering of the rocks, of whatever nature originally. The process of this mighty change is technically called metamorphism; the Basement Complex is very largely composed of metamorphic rocks.

The Peninsula is only now being mapped in detail, but studies already made by geologists suggest that one of the main chains of mountains, generated when the Basement Complex was formed, trended along the northeast coast. It seems, then, that well before the earliest known fossil was entombed in the earth's rocks—more than five hundred million years ago—northeastern Labrador underwent tremendous pressure from the northeast, with a great mountain structure as the result. There is some reason to think that the roots of this structure, though greatly worn down, can be detected all the way from Belle Isle Strait to Cape Chidley, Labrador's Land's End.

Dr. Robert Bell discovered in Baffin's Land what looks like another ripple of this same range, in which case it would extend more than thirteen hundred miles. The old Labrador range and the others of the great Appalachian Mountain system, meet at the Straits of Belle Isle. The Labrador range locates one of the most ancient (pre-Cambrian) formations in America; the other is much younger (post-Carboniferous).

Another of the most marvellous underground events occurred very late in the building of the Complex. For fifty miles north from Ford's Harbour and for many miles inland, a vast body of molten rock displaced the

4

old formation. This then crystallized under the pressure of the cover of overlying strata, which have since absolutely worn away. This has left the "intruder" visible over hundreds of miles. This rock is called gabbro. In composition it is like basalt, which is the commonest kind of lava or rock erupted from volcanoes. It has an especially dark colour like basalt and it dominates the island cliffs and mainland mountains all around Nain. These high lands are bare of soil and vegetation, and their black slopes afford a sense of sombre majesty.

Most of this gabbro is a wonderfully beautiful variety of feldspar, called "Labradorite," one of the abundant constituents of the world's crust. In Square Islands and on Mt. Pikey there are other large masses of the mineral. Owing to the peculiar internal structure of this variety of Labradorite, white light penetrating its glassy surface is broken up into its coloured components. Some the mineral absorbs, but some, reflected from myriads of microscopic particles, flash like flame out of the iridescent crystals. Purples, blues, and violets are the predominant colours, but orange, red, green, and yellow are not uncommon.

The finest Labradorite crops out in those ledges. As a gem it is difficult to polish, being cleavable, but from it letter weights, table tops, and pendants of flashing, living beauty have been made, and command a steady market.

After the old mountain structure around Nain was essentially completed, it was broken by countless cracks that reached down to the earth's depths where basalt was kept molten by heat. Into these fissures the basalt was squeezed upward and there it crystallized, set like cement, and so knit the whole range together again.

These frozen "ribs" greatly strengthened the ridge against the onslaughts of weather. All up and down the Coast the gray cliffs and slopes are seamed with these thousands of fissure-fillings, the so-called "dykes of trap rock"—excellent examples of which are seen at Indian Harbour and Ice Tickle. In Cape Uivuk and Cape White Pocket Handkerchief, which rise perpendicularly from the sea, are huge dykes running the whole way up the cliffs—fifteen hundred feet in height. They afford invaluable landmarks whenever one happens to be trying to make a harbour on a coast still without any artificial aids to navigation.

The dykes of basalt or trap rock, being more resistant to weather than the older rock, stand up as palisades across islands, as if these marked abandoned fortifications of cyclopean battlefields. Curiously, however, it resists the assaults of the sea less well than do the granites, so that near the shore thick dykes crop out on the floors of long chasms slicing the land. On Mt. Blow-Me-Down are dykes one hundred to four hundred feet in width, exposed on its face for thousands of feet. Conspicuous for many miles offshore. These dykes compel the voyager to wonder at the stupendous force which so clove the mountains to their mysterious depths, suggesting gigantic preparations for earth's final Armageddon. All this clearly shows that the present-day contour of the land is due much more to the agelong sculpturing by weather and waves, than to the original upheaval of the earth's crust.

6

CAPE UIVUK

CAPE BLOW-ME-DOWN

SHOWING RECENT GLACIAL ACTION

The Pageant of the Rocks

In comparatively recent geological times the Basement was lifted bodily, so that the streams have had to cut through thousands of feet of rock. It was this action which created the present coast relief for one hundred and fifty miles south of Cape Chidley, rivalling in grandeur though not in height the Alps or the Selkirks. These "reconstructed" mountains are called the Torngats, which means "devils." Their bare, jagged peaks, springing abruptly thousands of feet from the fjords or the ocean, are like the forbidding horns of the well-known chief himself. The dark shadows, made the more startling by the brilliance of the high lights of the northern sun or the eerie loneliness of their naked crags under a ghostly, whispering aurora, people these fastnesses with spirits sinister for the savage mind.

Nakvak Bay is one of the great portals to this region of the "Devils." Its narrow entrance, flanked by sheer cliffs two thousand feet in height and usually supporting a ceiling of clouds, suggests to the visitor that he is Jack, timorously entering the Giant's Gateway. One passes along mile after mile between its lofty walls rising abruptly from stygian water sometimes to lone peaks towering nearly four thousand feet in the air. On the northern side the serrated skyline, caused by what is aptly dubbed the Razor Backs, bristles with cyclopean teeth. Mr. Noel Odell points out that these consist of rare granite of unusual formation and resistance called Charnockite, which occurs also in southern India and has close kinsmen on the north side of two other near-by fjords in Labrador, called Komaktovik and Kangalaksiorvik. Between the enamelled teeth immense gullies

7

gouged out in the last ice age end in flat-floored hanging valleys with perpendicular sides. The whole suggests the ferocious jaws of Cerberus, guarding the entrance to Hades.

Here and there are high cornices, huge ice-filled cirques and "glacierettes," reaching about half a mile in maximum length, with occasional glacial lakes of exquisite blue and green tints. On the northern slopes of Mt. Tetragona, so named by Professor Coleman after the beautiful wild heath flower, great precipices, twenty-five hundred to three thousand feet in height, fall perpendicularly to the glacier below.

Twenty odd miles from the mouth a nearly vertical precipice three thousand feet high marks a salient angle where two branches of Nakvak Fjord meet. Its head is twice the height of Cape Eternity in the famous Saguenay River, while from its sides numerous waterfalls tumble from high hanging valleys into the abyss below. Here rise the highest mountains, directly from the sea, between Baffin's Land and Cape Horn. Nothing else in eastern American scenery approaches the ruggedness of the Torngats of Labrador.

Fifty miles south of Hebron is another wholly new element appearing in the landscape. Not only is it new among the wonderful mountain forms of the Labrador Coast, but it possesses unique and imposing features in its architecture. It consists of a range of mountains covering some three hundred square miles, called by the Eskimo the Kaumajet or Shining Tops, which is the exact equivalent of the Hindu Himalaya. Even in summer the Kaumajets always wear caps of snow.

8

The Pageant of the Rocks

One titanic cleft through this range is used by numbers of craft, both as a centre for fishing and as a short cut to the north. It is about two miles wide and both sides rise almost perpendicularly in great terraced bastions of pink rock, three thousand feet high, the whole tipped and lined by green ledges. Especially when the snow outlines the ridges it is a perfect picture of beauty. Here and there over the sides leap sparkling cascades. A large one takes one leap of seventy feet.

It was my privilege to witness that rare phenomenon, a thunderstorm, in this Tickle, which bears the name of a famous man called Mugford. "Tickle" on the Labrador means a ticklish place to sail through—as this unquestionably is. The flashes of lightning gave an even more thrilling effect than the scintillating colours of the Aurora Borealis in the fall, while the rolling cadences of the thunder suggested that old Boreas had seized the hammer of Thor to demolish us puny mortals.

Here is the geological story of this weird region. This section of the well worn-down mountain roots, which here formed the earth's crust, for some reason sank down into the sea, due to some wrench, some pressure, some strain. Then on its back were deposited through long ages under water, mud, sand, gravel, lavas, or volcanic ash, until finally they reached thousands of feet in thickness. Then once more the writhing earth bent its back, carrying the whole up out of the water for thousands of feet, in the form of slates, sandstones, conglomerates, and quartzites, all welded together as before by ribs of trap rock. Here was an entirely new variety of raw material. In shape it was like a series of dromedary humps,

9

yet so vast as to be over half a mile in thickness, fifteen hundred feet of which are volcanic formations. For before the subsidence under the sea, during countless millions of years volcanoes had been belching out enormous volumes of ash and débris, coarse and fine, in violent explosions—witness to which is the fact that still, bedded in the lava, one can see some of the perfectly rounded bombs, which froze as they spun through the air from the mouth of Nature's cannon.

Once again the whole was given over to the "secular arm" of frost and other weathering agents, and the still more destructive action of water streams, patient and resistless. To-day only comparatively small patches of these ancient sea bottoms remain in the superb walls of the great gorges and canyons which now form these appalling waterways and harbours, and in the large islands of Ogualik (cod) and Naunautot (white bear) which rise directly from the ocean, thousands of feet in the air.

This region has well been described as a huge geographic fossil, which was once entirely hidden by the generous covering spread over it; but now that that has been so largely torn off, it lies an open book for all to read.

The range is capped by two massive rock towers, each soaring about eight hundred feet above the ridge. They stand a quarter of a mile apart. Sudden slopes fall full eighteen hundred feet, and then there is a sheer drop into the sea. The aëroplanes of the Grenfell-Forbes Survey Expedition found peculiar pleasure in flying between these ancient sentinels when taking the picture

THE CONTORTED CRUST OF THE EARTH NEAR CAPE MUGFORD

THE KIGLAPEITS, OR DOG-TOOTHED MOUNTAINS

here shown. The light grey colour of the Basement in contrast with the black of the stupendous masonry above gives to the perfect symmetry the impression that the whole is the work of giants with the brains of men.

Yet another of the "high places" of the Labrador is the Kiglapeit or Dog Tooth range. It is a great sierra, again an island, some fifty miles south of the Kaumajets, which in solemn loneliness rears its rocky and giant vertebrae, ten in number, over two thousand feet above the sea. It is like a monster reptile, thirty miles in length, left stranded on the shore. Oddly enough, this time it lies east and west, with its head jutting out towards the Atlantic. Mt. Thoresby, the actual head of this petrified dinosaur, is of sombre gabbro, looming twenty-seven hundred feet into the air.

From this point the mainland, stretching for three hundred and fifty miles to the Straits of Belle Isle, is girt with islands, forming a plateau about five hundred feet in height. The general skyline is so strikingly level that it could scarcely be more so if some titanic shovel had filled in all the hollows. This flatness sweeps right away inland as far as Lake Winnipeg. This is the "almost plain" to which the Archean Mountains have been reduced by wasting.

None of the younger sedimentary deposits, representatives of the lifetime of the earth, have yet been found on the northeast coast. Only far away to the south and west are there sea bottoms of geological epochs, consisting of accumulated mud, sand, and gravels—many miles in thickness—which now constitute the emerged continent known to all of us as North America. But if there was ever more veneer on the Basement Complex than that now remaining in the limited Kaumajet region, it has yet to be discovered. Thus for millions of years Labrador has been above the sea, during which time the onslaught of Nature's forces has laid bare throughout its length and breadth the very foundations of the world. The only remains of Labrador's constructive evolution are the Kaumajet deposits of geological yesterday, called the Glacial Period, and of this morning, the post-Glacial Epoch.

Long years ago an ice cap accumulated in North America, like that of Greenland to-day. It was thickest between the St. Lawrence River and James Bay. Slowly, like other major glaciers, this ice flowed in all directions —out to the seaboard of this long coast, literally ploughing the floor as it moved along.

The Labradorian, or Laurentian, ice cap extended over two million square miles, to the plains of the upper Mississippi and the Northwest Territories of Canada, and as far south as New York City. Even Mt. Washington, six thousand, two hundred and ninety-three feet in height, was covered by the flooding ice. To the northwest Hudson's Bay had an ice cap all to itself, called Keewatin, while Newfoundland boasted also a private white nightcap.

For reasons unknown, the ice caps disappeared. Not one acre was left on the mainland, unless the Grinnell Glacier in Baffin's Land could be counted a last remnant of it. The bared back of Labrador shows marks which glaciers etched there not long ago. For exactly as rivers do, the ice stream tears up its bed at the upper end and carries it along with it until it drops the débris or drift material of its load as it slows down near the end, where the glacier's moraine corresponds to the river's delta. And here we may remember that rivers, like glaciers, have often disappeared, such as the one which the Italians have recently rediscovered in the Libyan Desert.

In the glacial period the outer edges of the ice cap lay far out under the ocean, where the material which the great mill was grinding was then deposited. This vanished ice cap was no idler in its moulding of the present Labrador architecture. One sees endless examples of its work; for Dame Nature often surprised it at its task and forced it to throw down and leave some huge rock after it had just been moved from its still self-evident bed—exactly as at Assuan, where a great granite monolith was being hammered out of the solid rock for the Pharaoh of three thousand years ago, by a hundred thousand workmen tapping incessantly around it with granite stones, held in the hand as hammers. They had almost removed the obelisk by hammering dry, wooden wedges into the holes they had made, and then wetting them, when they, too, were surprised by enemies and fled, throwing down their implements, which are there to this day to show how with almost equally incredible tools, sufficient numbers of puny men, working long enough, achieved impossible results. Just so a glacier uses rocks for crowbar and crane as well as for gouge and chisel.

It was normal cutting by streams long before glacial

days which produced most of the grand features of the Labrador sculpture.

Glaciers, like rivers, write indelible records with veritable graving tools too deeply to be denied. Labrador's glaciers have left grooves a foot deep in soft rocks. They did it by dragging frozen-in boulders over the rock faces of their beds. Occasionally to-day one sees off the Labrador Coast some capsized but triumphant iceberg, aggressively holding aloft just such a graving tool frozen into its now upper surface. The striae record for all time the direction of the ancient ice streams.

Some five thousand feet up on the top of the highest peaks of the central range Odell discovered just such marks, showing that presumably, from the extensive weathering of the near-by summits, in the far older pre-Pleistocene Ice Age the whole of Labrador was buried under the cap. However, all agree that the jagged devil peaks of the Torngats probably maintained their impish heads high above the latest of the four devastating ice floods, the streams from which, with resistless force, tore their way through the central and coast ranges of the North, right into the Atlantic Ocean. The whole for a long period, says Odell, formed a rocky archipelago in the glacial mer-de-glace, which, when it once more disappeared, left the contour of northern Labrador as it exists to-day.

The half million square miles between the Atlantic and Pacific are one vast complex of pre-Cambrian rocks, which have furnished, farther west in its better-known parts, immense deposits of valuable minerals. Iron and copper have been found in the Lake Superior district,

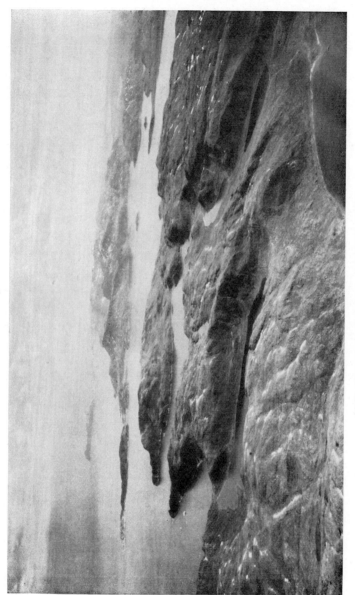

THE GREAT KAUMAJETS (SHINING TOPS)

SAEGLEK FJORD

AN OLD ICE CHANNEL

magnetic iron ores in the Adirondack regions, gold in those of Porcupine, silver and cobalt in those of Cobalt, copper and nickel in Sudbury, and some of the richest gold mines in the world in the famous Hollinger, Timmins, and Flin Flon mines.

Some fine work done by Dr. Low, of the Canadian Geological Survey, showed vast deposits of magnetite in the neighbourhood of the Grand Falls. Also near them, one grant of forty square miles has recently been made for gold mining, since prospecting has been made easier by aëroplane. Gold was discovered "in situ" in the Mealy Mountains some years ago, and a fine iron pyrites mine was begun in Rowsell's Harbour and only discontinued because of the difficulty of transportation.

The latitude of Labrador is that of Britain. The scrubbing of the ice cap and the cold bath in which she lies only partly explain her scanty vegetation. The uplift of her coastline helped further to deprive her of the extra garment of fertile clay or till that was deposited, and still remains in the valleys and prairies farther west.

The distance between Labrador and Greenland does not seem to be getting gradually wider, yet it probably is, for Mother Earth is not rigid, but still a whirling, mobile mass, ever whirling round at a terrific speed as she hurtles through space, and wrinkles on her face keep altering with her age. Thus the Gully, known now as the Gulf of St. Lawrence, is just a smile dimple filled with rich blessings for her children.

The split in the earth's surface between Europe and America left, during the process, Greenland and Iceland as fragments of the ancient bridge between the conti-

15

nents, just as the Aleutian Islands are parts of the old band that once united America and Asia—for the slip tendency is ever to the westward.

All along the Atlantic seaboard of the Americas, from Labrador to Patagonia, runs an undersea shelf, attributed once to the vast débris of the lost continent of Atlantis. However, with the lapse of time, the steep edges of the great cracks naturally sagged and wore down, while the bottoms of the great cracks filled with lava from below and sediments from above.

The soil and rocks torn from the surface of the land by weather, by rivers, or by brutal ice were not lost, but deposited on the growing shelf. The ocean all the while added its quota of remains of animal life. The whole, as well as the great extension known as the Grand Banks, off Newfoundland, has been a veritable nursery of fish through the centuries—a priceless food supply for mankind.

The Labrador Peninsula, like some diffident virgin, is still wrapped in garments of isolation, having turned away her wooers. But there can be no reasonable doubt that, untouched in the thousands of square miles of the Labrador terrain, as well as in her waters, lie vast treasures yet to be wrested from her for the benefit of the world.

II: THE PAGEANT OF THE INDIANS

The Curtain Rises

THERE are still three or four thousand Indians remaining in Labrador's hinterland, feathers in Canada's cap, while the still existing Eskimo are the best tribute to the Moravian missionaries. Labrador has been kinder to the Indians than anywhere else in America, not excluding Puritan New England, judging by the much larger proportion of them to the whites which still exists in the Northland.

The original Indians of North America, like her Eskimo, are Mongoloid in type. Still to-day the eastern Asiatic tribes and the Northeastern Indians have so many traits in common with Eastern Siberians that there is little doubt of their common origin.

No remains of palæolithic instruments, or human remains, associated with those of animals of pre-glacial days or in rocks of those ages, have ever been discovered in North or South America as they have in Europe, Asia, Africa, and Oceania.[1] Moreover, the cultural traits of the rest of the world, except perhaps the ability to make fire and use bows and arrows and harpoons, never reached the American Indian previous to the Russian invasion. The same is true of all the important domesticated animals and plants except the dog.

The toilsome march of Homo Bimana from the Cradle of the Race in the Euphrates Valley to America was therefore probably on foot, and made before "our mobile earth" burned her last land bridges which had connected America with Europe by way of what is now Behring Sea, and so after she (America) had received the Indian contribution.

The Indians of the Labrador unquestionably came from farther south and west, for they are all branches of the great Algonquins who have left their names in endless places from the Atlantic to the Mississippi and the Rocky Mountains, and from the Carolinas and the Gulf of Mexico to Hudson's Bay. Beyond were their enemies, the Indians of the plains to the south, and the Athabascans to the northeast.

History tells us that the Labrador Indians were attacked by the "bloodthirsty" Iroquois and driven north. Though comparatively few pursued, it was with such

[1] A. L. Kroeber, *Encycl. Brit.*

18

"relentless ferocity" that they fled as far as Hudson's Bay and the very northern end of the land. In 1660 the Iroquois raided the country around Lake Tamagami as far as Ottawa. There are pictographs on the surrounding cliffs, supposed to commemorate these raids. Even today the Indian mother uses the name "Iroquois" to frighten her children, as the Spanish did that of Francis Drake. Probably it is on this account that the Labrador Indians received the name Nascopies, which is indifferently translated as "ignorant," "heathen," or "unworthy." Whatever its exact meaning, it was certainly not intended to be complimentary. This Indian invasion in turn drove back the Eskimo to the seaboard, except in the peninsula between Ungava and Hudson's Bay, which is still Eskimo country.

The northern section of these remaining Indians no longer go south in spring to the Gulf. They remain in North Labrador where they trade around Davis Inlet, with Nain or even with Port Chimo. They are now called "Montagnais" or mountaineers, and speak only a dialect of the great Cree language. The southern branch of the Indians can still understand them, a fact which holds true right across to the Rockies—the original language being the same all the way. The Gulf of St. Lawrence, however, has been a barrier between them and their New England relatives, and when an Abnaki sees a Nascopie on the Labrador on a winter trail, they have to speak in French or in sign language.

Dr. Cabot says that the language is without any "r" sound, which has been attributed to the difficulty of facial muscles rendered stiff with cold articulating it. He claims that the Scotch clerks of the Hudson's Bay Company are better able to speak Algonquin than the English, being accustomed from birth to being "stiff with cold."

Less than half the Labrador Indians can speak any language but their own. Another branch of the Indians in Labrador is known as the Barren Ground Indians. They hunt around St. George's River and they, too, trade at Fort Chimo, or Whale River, or Mistassini. The Nascopies called themselves "Nenenot," which means the "ideal" or true people; just as the Eskimo, whose name signifies "raw meat eaters," call themselves with even less modesty "Innuit," or simply "The People." This optimism is the evil of nationalism. The Israelites, who exterminated so many peoples in Palestine of old, always regarded themselves root and branch as "The Chosen People." Every nation at heart succumbs to this temptation. "We are the people and wisdom shall die with us." [1] It is this kind of patriotism which lies at the root of most wars.

It is not inspiring to remember that until the white folk came to the St. Lawrence, Labrador provided liberally for its original owners. When Europeans began to settle the St. Lawrence basin, vast forests spread from the Gulf to the Arctic prairies, except on the highest plateaux. Not till then did the devastating forest fires occur which swept the Coast from the Saguenay to Romaine, and from the Gulf to the Height of Land. They destroyed the game, the timber, and even the soil, and drove the unfortunate Indians from their healthy high-

[1] The Bible.

LABRADOR GOTHIC

Photograph by F. C. Sears

LABRADOR INDIANS—THE NASCOPIES

Photograph by F. C. Sears

BREAKFAST

lands to the few swampy parts which had escaped the
flames, or back to the low ground near the coast, where
tuberculosis and other troubles found them an easy
prey. Possibly wandering hunters were less careful to
observe the rigid fire code of the Indians in other territory than their own.

The Nascopies were first heard of in Europe when
Cortereal's sailors captured a lot of them in Hamilton
Inlet for the benefit of His Most Christian Majesty, the
King of Portugal. They were "tall, strong, and tattooed."

The Nascopies, though without any written code,
have a system of their own which includes a central
meeting ground in the region of the Great Lakes, and a
grapevine telegraph which circulates the news of the
families, who still go every year all the way south by
canoe to meet their priests and sell their catches of fur.
The high plateau has always been a home for the caribou, which has afforded the northern Indians an easier
existence. However, endless fish, speared and netted in
every river and lake, will always be their standard staff
of life. This fish diet is supplemented by eggs, berries,
and birds, and even mammals—small and large, from a
squirrel to a deer. It was this sufficiency which accounted
for the fact that many ceased to roam so far and wide to
earn a livelihood by trapping. As a result, however, now
that modern firearms and traps have reached them, they
are destroying, like children, their own sources of supplies, and they are themselves disappearing more rapidly
than their southern cousins. This is perhaps the more
remarkable since the latter suffer more from contact
with the whites of the St. Lawrence shore, where social

diseases, easy access to "firewater," and the less dramatic nemesis of proximity to specific contagious diseases and epidemics take a larger toll. These results are noticeable even in the size of the Indians and their bodily framework. The northerners are practically useless for the heavy work of guides and porters. The more active life, aided possibly by a mixture with the Scotch fur traders' and the French "Habitants' " blood, render the latter far better risks for any adventurers succumbing to "the lure of the Labrador wild."

On the contrary it is equally true that given a mixed group of Eskimo from north of Cape Chidley and those from the south, nurtured around the Moravian Mission stations and relying on flour and "civilized" diets, it would be possible for any intelligent stranger to separate them correctly, simply by the differences in their physique. The northerners are sturdier, livelier, and have a real red colour in their cheeks.

The introduction of reindeer into Alaska made the natives there happily self-supporting. For Labrador, nothing constructive has been attempted for the Indians. There has been no conservation of forests, or of animals, like the buffalo in Canada or the reinstatement of the fur seal in the Pacific. How could it be otherwise than a simple corollary that the Indians of the Labrador are steadily vanishing, if only by a slower process, than if the sea had not prevented their farther flight when the Iroquois were pursuing them so many generations ago?

Everywhere in Labrador the physically weakest still go to the wall. No white man is yet able to make a home in the interior, where the only law is still the immemorial code of the hunting ground. The high interior, scrubbed bare of soil by the ice ages and burned over by the great fires, can only become a white man's country when the wealth of its minerals justifies the expense of supplying his needs from the outside. The Indians and Eskimo, who die in our environment, can live there happily and can be an asset to human life, which it will take a long time to evolve again once they disappear.

The end of the winter for the Indians is signalized by the sinking of the snow, and by Bruin coming out of his cave after his long sleep. Fur becomes worthless in May. The sun bleaches the bright colours of the hair; the foxes sleeping on the snow, which gets moist during the day, freeze their long hairs to it, and literally pluck themselves. Such pelts are called "trace-galled." Also all furs begin to lose density in the spring, so the season closes and the Indian migration southward begins.

Indians and even the half-breeds are very strict about not killing fur out of season. The trappers once brought out to us a man caught for the second time taking a silver fox in late September. The offender was bound hand and foot. In our capacity as magistrate we had to warn him and his family to leave the country, as the rest of the men were determined to enforce the law of the forest, and send them by a shorter road to the "happy hunting grounds" if they dared to remain.

Though unfenced, hunting lands or fur paths are held by individual trappers. They descend from father to son, or daughter's husband. All relations have a right in the hunting lodge and must be taken care of—even widows, orphans, and the incapacitated. It is a kind of modified Soviet arrangement. Whilst crossing another's land you may kill game for food only. A three-year rotation, hunting only one-third of one's fur path annually, is the custom. To-day a fur path is roughly one mile wide and of indefinite length.

By June, the Leaf Moon, these Indians are back on their southern reserves. July, St. Anne's Moon (their patron saint), is spent in receiving spiritual instruction from their priests. When August comes, the Moon of Flight, the families once more leave for the interior.

The flight really applies to the young ducks, who, like the manna of old, make possible the migration of the Indian families. The Indians are then burdened with supplies and the ducks afford easy meat by the wayside, without delaying progress. Dr. Cabot's description of one such family which he overtook suggests the courage of Abraham. As he got out of his canoe one day, an old, withered Indian woman greeted him on the river bank. Beside her was her still older, totally blind husband, leaning on a staff. The heads of two children peered out through the bushes at the strange canoe. A near-by shot was heard, and a smiling young man carrying a partridge joined the group. This family could not possibly reach their camping ground until the autumn. Yet they were embittered by no worries or regrets. They were perfectly cheerful, though they had none of the frills of life, and though there was only one effective pair of hands to fend for them all. The fact that obstacles are so unending and sources for obtaining supplies so scanty that two American explorers on just such a journey, with a native guide and a perfect equipment, could starve to death, proves that some other than a material factor is necessary to prevent fatalities from being frequent.

Before the white man came the Indians did not have to make these long journeys. There can be no doubt that, although they evolve character, they do tell on the very old, the young, and the feeble. Occasional disasters where whole Indian families have perished of starvation are only too well authenticated. No country is without its tragedies. At the end of a fjord called Nullataktok we ourselves came upon the remains of a camping ground where a dozen or more skulls and other bones told plainly the fate which is never unreasonably far from these Indians. A trader in Fort Chimo said that every year during his long residence there an average of five or six persons had failed to return. Alas, the less the food supply, the farther these Indians must go to seek it. During our own first ten years on the Coast, fifty per cent of the Indian families were reported to have starved or died through deficiency diseases around Fort Chimo away in the north. There are no doles in the interior.

In the summer of 1931 we saw Indians leaving on their winter trail from near Nain with what seemed to us nothing whatever with which to secure a livelihood. Their tents were in rags, clothing almost absent, ammunition and twine practically nil. Not a few were bare-footed; and they did not have enough provisions to last the week out.

Almost always they have a small dog which runs along the bank as they paddle. It barks, treeing birds and small animals which can then frequently be captured merely by a noose on the end of a pole. I have known an Eskimo kill as many as five hundred white partridges in one winter with nothing but his dog whip. The Indians prefer a bow of spruce wood, with a thong or sinew for a string. The arrows are made of spruce with great flat-faced knobs, which strike hard and are easier to hit with than the pointed arrows used by the Eskimo. Moreover, they need no metal tips.

On partridge diet only, however, they cannot keep strong; and "rabbit" starvation is a well-recognized term on the Coast. Both should be accompanied by some flour, or other carbohydrate addition. The great lake trout, or "the fish that swallows anything" as they call it, is their best and most dependable food. It is supplemented by whitefish, pike, salmon, and trout; though the whitefish go into deep water during the winter and are not then available.

In winter neither the Indians nor the trappers use dogs for driving. They haul their supplies and walk themselves. Dog food is heavy. Moreover, their method is quieter for hunting, and requires no trails through the woods or up cliffs. The sledge is very narrow and very light, made of birch or larch which do not "ice up" easily (a serious handicap). Only when the spring sun thaws the snow by day and it freezes at night, are runners attached. No skis are used—only a roundish "bear-paw" snowshoe, which is far better in the woods. Special pairs made very large and with fine meshes are used to run down caribou in deep snow.

The Indians, like the Eskimo, are polygamous. The

ability to maintain the family is the only law. It is their custom to put the old and feeble out of the way, the person concerned preferring that to abandonment and freezing to death.

Those who know have described the Nascopies as mean and inhospitable to strangers, and selfish; in fact, very unlike the rest of the Crees.[1] What can we say, however, who give them little without exacting payment? Towards one another, no people show more generosity. A hunter keeps only the head of an animal; the whole of the rest he gives to the others if in need. They in fact exercise a community of food, such even as they buy at the stores seldom remaining in the same hands more than three or four days.

In spite of their Christian affiliations, their old beliefs are by no means extinct. In this respect, too, these poor Indians are very like the rest of us. Their mental machine, uncrowded as ours is by outside impulses, retains old impressions, especially emotional ones, longer than ours does.

In the Indian lodge the spirit of original evil is called a Windigo. Spirits, however, are not malevolent if uninfluenced by human beings; but the nearer they are to being men the less they are to be trusted! A priest can use any spirit for evil purposes! It is popular to laugh at these poor Indians' conception of the Deity as being anthropomorphic. But whose brain can conceive of God in any other way? At least their great Manitou is wholly good, and these humble folk have even tried to regard him as a trinity—in which the first person gives them

[1] Mackay, "Twenty Years on the Labrador."

27

what is necessary for life, the second person gives them abundantly more than they need, and the third person that of which they cannot have too much. To an Indian, that of course is fur. Every notable feature in Labrador has its spirit, to the minds of both Indian and Eskimo alike.

So long as the language of the old wilderness life persists, so long will these people continue (as we do) to mix inbred with acquired ideas. The Indians, furnished with calendars and pins, mark up the Saints' Days and Sundays, which they certainly observe better than does the average European. Along their travelled routes there are many lonely graves marked by our common token of a cross. Passers-by respect them, and camps, tents, wigwams are not pitched too near them so that their peace may not be disturbed.

Among Indians and Eskimo alike many legends exist. It is less easy to collect those of the Indians. Comeau describes their curious habits of "shoulder-bone reading." As soon as ever a caribou is killed its shoulder blade must be removed. The meat is cut off as close to the bone as possible, which is then boiled for a few minutes, wiped absolutely clean of all meat, and hung up to dry. That night when all the family in the wigwam are asleep, the neck of the bone is held in a split stick over hot coals for a few seconds, until small cracks spread across the bone. The small burnt spots on the branches indicate not only the distance of game from the camp—which is always the largest burnt black spot—but also the direction in which the hunter must go to find it. The hunter fares forth accordingly, and "no Gospel truth was ever more firmly believed in."

The Indian, again like the Eskimo, does not fear the bear but his spirit, and will not use the name "bear" if he can help it. Instead he calls it "black animal." He will talk to the body of a bear in a trap in order that the spirit may not seek vengeance. Women and children never eat the paws of a bear for fear of suffering later from cold feet; just so an Eskimo wears a piece of bearskin sewed on his coat, so that the next bear may see it and keep away from so brave a hunter. He will not even mention the name of an iceberg while passing it, or the name of a dead man until a new man bears his name.

At the Indian Dog Feast, which is especially for their medicine men, the objective is much the same as that of a modern medical college. It is a kind of graduation, intended to turn out efficient practitioners. The course opens with private séances in the tent of the principal doctor. A drum is beaten directly the student enters, and is continued all night for several nights in succession. The door is closely barred and secrets pass continuously between the master and the pupil. The noise which goes on all the time insures that these mysteries do not leak out through uninvited "listeners-in." When exhaustion is reached and the pupil has held communion with all the spirits, both good and bad—for both are regarded as supreme sources of power—the novice is considered to have graduated. His profession insures him a good living as a rule, and much of the same authority as is accorded to a priest in civilization.

Cartier relates that the Huron Indians, when killing a

criminal prisoner, would slash the body and sink it in the river for ten hours, when certain fish which he called "cornibots" would be found in the cuts. These they considered of more value than gold or silver, because they would stop bleeding from the nose! He experimented with some of them and found that the claim was justified. The faith element in healing is a universal human trait.

It is noticeable that Indians rarely intermarry with whites, but though French and English girls have been known to marry Indian men, they never marry Eskimo. The Indian never marries an Eskimo, but cross-breeding between settler men and Eskimo girls is not uncommon.

Jacques Cartier, writing in 1556 from his winter station, says that though he would not have believed it unless he had seen it, the Indians, both male and female, would go naked into the water in winter between the ice-pans in the St. Lawrence, hunting for fish, and apparently did not mind it. They have, alas, lost this physical fortitude long ago, partly because of the doles which they have received.

In South America the Indian race survives. For in spite of our prejudice, "The Spanish Conquest destroyed in order to construct, whereas the Pilgrim Fathers destroyed in order to remove." So writes W. E. Macleod in "The American Indian Frontier." The red man has had his passionate apologists in prose and poetry—such varied writers as Fenimore Cooper, Montaigne, Macaulay, Southey, and Byron—as well as his detractors, who accounted him nothing but a common, ferocious beast, and offered a reward for murdering him at sight. General Braddock offered a bounty of five pounds sterling for every enemy's scalp, "Indian or French," a special reward of two hundred pounds for the chief Wildcat, and a reward of one hundred pounds for Father Le Loutre, a Jesuit missionary amongst the Indians. The Governor of Pennsylvania in 1756 went further and made special rates, with quotations for female scalps also. Wholesale slaughter of Indians for gold was made legal in 1849. To believe this now is difficult, but the definite policy of extermination was undoubtedly established. One has only to read "A Century of Dishonor" to be convinced of it.[2]

It is an unforgettable fact that Mather, on hearing of a massacre of Indians, thanked God publicly from the pulpit "for sending six hundred more heathen souls to hell."

The indictment of the reservation system, as administered in the United States, is official and convincing. This story of failure is simply that of this world. No race has yet been long willing to forego the opportunities of profiting at the expense of a weaker neighbour.[3] The story of Naboth's Vineyard is no monopoly of the Hebrews. Civilized Greeks and Romans, just as much as Huns and Goths, Kings of France, Spain, and England, every bit as much as the Vikings of Norway and Denmark, were all predatory animals. Neither Kubla Khan nor Emperor William held any monopoly in "coveting their neighbour's goods." Students of the Indian side of

[2] "A Century of Dishonor," by Helen Hunt Jackson.
[3] "The Problem of Indian Administration," Institute of Government Research, Baltimore.

the problem will find, however, a recent recrudescence of apologists for it, and among them some of their own highly developed people.[4]

The banishment of the Indians to the Bad Lands, which afterwards proved to be rich oil-fields, ended by the American Government having to enforce a law preventing every male adult Indian from having more than a thousand dollars a month. Yet access to everything which money can buy was far from supplying the "elixir vitae" to this race. On the other hand, in the recent endeavour to use them as herders for the reindeer, unlike the Eskimo in the west, they proved a signal failure. The Indian seems to be entirely unwilling to earn his living by any regular work.

Alas, our Indians of the Labrador are equally slow to envisage their real dangers, exactly as when they fought first on one side and then on the other, for no other reward, as it proved, than their own extinction. The good weapons given them only enabled them to destroy the buffalo and other game—their one source of supply of almost everything they needed.

The problem to-day is exactly reversed. The Government no longer considers the Indian a physical menace, but a moral responsibility as the former owner of the country. The survival of any race depends primarily on itself. The Indian has shown himself capable of exhibiting all our virtues as well as our vices. A hundred thousand once warlike Sioux Indians are living happily in

[4] "Old Indian Trails," McIntosh; "The Soul of the Indian," Eastman; "Indians of the Enchanted Desert," Crane; "The American Indians and Their Music," Densmore; "The Downfall of Temlaham," Barbeau.

Canada, appreciating law and order so well that only a handful of Mounted Police are required amongst them. The Indian beneath his red skin is much the same as we under our white one, but he lacks our background of centuries of education.

The Quebec Government have taken no little trouble to repatriate their Indians on the Côte du Nord. Their endeavours to place him on the land beside the French "Habitants" have, however, so far only confirmed the suspicion that the Labrador Indian is bound for extinction. In spite of the grit of the Montagnais and the Nascopie of the high plateau, firewater, indolence, and other temptations have found them displaying little resistance. The greatest single source of destruction of the Indians has been alcohol. The chiefs of the Aztec Indians, even of the Iroquois, realized this and became the first American prohibitionists; and our traders were the first bootleggers. By the irony of fate, the Latins are to-day returning this compliment to our civilization.

In Labrador the interior seems to offer the only chance left to the Indian. He has never shown any aptitude for competing in sea fisheries. Conservation and adaptation of animal life, coupled with altruistic paternalism, might enable him to hold on there and so justify the Government's attempts. Naturally the Government feels bound to prevent starvation; but the dole and alcohol destroy the very moral fibre on which the survival of the Indian depends.

33

13542

THE LIBRARY
COLBY JUNIOR COLLEGE
NEW LONDON

III: THE PAGEANT OF THE ESKIMO

The "Innuit" Arrive

IN 1796 Major Cartwright wrote in his famous Journal concerning the Arctic:

> *"Here the squat-legged Eskimo*
> *Waddle in the ice and snow,*
> *And the playful polar bear*
> *Nips the hunter unaware."*

Of the Labrador he wrote:

> *"In peace they rove along this pleasant shore,*
> *In plenty live; nor do they wish for more."*

The Pageant of the Eskimo

The second race which crosses the Labrador stage is one of thrilling interest. There is little doubt that, like the Indians, the Eskimo came from Asia after the Ice Ages—but probably later, coming in skin boats instead of on foot. No race, Asiatic or European, is to-day quite like them. They can live happily where no other men on earth can exist. They are the world's best utilitarians. No Eskimo has ever had nervous prostration, and in their simple life they are to-day probably the most contented people on earth. "Me Very Laughing" could well be the legend on their national flag. Their language, called Karalit, is apart from all others; none seems to be related to it. Fifty dialects exist. The words are what one might call "agglutinative," so that in their poetry or hymns one or two words are all that a line can contain. Thus "merngotorvikangilak" is one line which runs in my memory, as being sung by a dying Eskimo patient who had come south to one of our hospitals. It meant "There will be no sorrow there."

It is true that they belong to the "great unwashed," but everyone familiar with them as a medical man will agree with me that it cannot be shown that their physical health suffers in any particular way on that account. In their original snow houses they strip stark naked on account of the heat; and the practice of smearing their bodies with oil and then rubbing it off with birds' skins, and finally scraping it clean with their "ooloos," or broad skinning knives, is much easier and more practical than soap and melted ice in their frigid environment. Their habitat is nearer the North Pole than that of any other human beings.

35

Obliged to be fatalists to a greater or less degree, they are yet individuals as we are. Their love for the family is as "human" as our own. An Eskimo hunter fell ill on the edge of the polar sea just when winter was coming on. To the last he hunted in an heroic endeavour to provide for his wife and little boy. Finally he could do no more. It was obvious that death was near. Day after day, week after week, the wife stayed by and cared for the dying man without thought of herself and child, though she knew that when the end came the nearest spot where help could be obtained lay a hundred miles away. Yet not until she had collected great stones and built a grave and laid her husband in it, together with his clothing and all his belongings, including his rifle, and piled up more stones to protect it from wild animals, did she start with her little son for the almost impossible journey. Though she had four dogs, there was practically no food for them, for the boy had only been able to catch a few foxes in his father's traps.

Day after day they journeyed, trusting to the dogs to lead them in the right direction. Weaker and weaker they grew. But life is just as sweet near the Pole as near the Equator, and still they struggled on. At last they could go no farther, and apparently had resigned themselves to death when a party from the Hudson's Bay Company's Post chanced to find them, "just in time to bring them back to life." Even to Hudson's Bay men it was a new vision of the power of love, when they found a tiny, eight months' baby cooing at the bottom of the sealskin sleeping-bag.[1]

[1] Norman Irwin in *The Beaver*.

ESKIMO GRAVE

Photograph by F. C. Sears

ESKIMO AT MORAVIAN STATION

Photograph by F. C. Sears

NORTH LABRADOR ESKIMO

Per contra, two white settlers coming south to the Moravian Mission station for the Easter Feast a few years ago, missed their way in a blizzard and perished. Later it was found that the dogs, which returned after a few days wild with hunger, had eaten the bodies of both the man and the woman.

The Eskimo, though racially akin to the Indian, are a much whiter race, the young people being often fair and ruddy. It is quite true that exposure to the weather and the fact that the Eskimo never wash have deceived those who only judge of their natural colour by the older people. Stefansson describes the "blond Eskimo." Peary's pictures suggest the same fact. However, there has been much admixture of white blood in some parts of the Arctic.

No study of eugenics can afford to neglect the Eskimo, if only on account of their extraordinary experiment in the extent to which the human body is capable of adaptation. Wherever they came from, their ventures into the Arctic ice fields are really far more dramatic than was Abraham's into the Promised Land. Contact with Europeans, our food, clothing, and habits, are found to lower materially the Eskimo's power of resistance.

Their straight black hair, dark almond-shaped eyes, high cheek-bones and long heads all certify Mongolian origin. It has been said "scratch an Eskimo and find a Tartar," which in the light of the stories of their retaliation on Europeans was quite credible. In justice, however, it must be remembered that everyone's hand was against them. Crees and Iroquois drove them to the coast, where the Vikings caught and slew them, as the Sagas tell us. The French pioneers agreed: *"L'Esquimau est méchant; quand on l'attaque, il se défend."*

Incidentally, the Eskimo are not all of them small or by any means weak. Only Norse Vikings could refer to them as weaklings, or "Skroelings." The men are thick-set, very heavy boned, and may be even six feet in height. Early adventurers to Labrador, who carried off all that they caught for slaves, attest that they made excellent manual labourers, when compelled to work.

Once they were spread across forty degrees of latitude and their number estimated to be seventy thousand. In 1891 forty thousand was the total estimate. In 1930 the estimate for all the Eskimo remaining in the world is twenty-eight thousand. In Labrador only about nine hundred remain to-day.

Two thousand years ago there were Eskimo on the west coast of Newfoundland. They had disappeared, however, with few exceptions, before John Cabot arrived in 1497. The last of them, a few half-breeds, left the northernmost point of Newfoundland the year we arrived on the Coast, 1892. That was the fatal year when an American schooner carried off from North Labrador a large party of Eskimo for a side show in the World's Fair in Chicago. Few returned. One, the little son of the chief, we ourselves picked up two years later, dying of tuberculosis on a stony beach in Nakvak Fjord.

Concurrent with the Eskimo of Newfoundland, who lived by seal hunting, were a race of whale-hunting Eskimo of Hudson's Bay. Recent discoveries and relics preserved in museums of the Hudson's Bay Company suggest that three thousand years ago these men used stones in building houses, though without mortar.

Killing whales indicates no small advance in evolution, for it must have been easier to approach a mastodon or a dinosaur on the land, and after launching your attack to escape by hiding, than to pursue "Moby Dick" to his lair in a sealskin boat—a very poor craft in which to be taken for a "Nantucket Sleigh Ride."

Wood in the extreme North is so scarce that even in Labrador we have seen one of these frail craft with its framework made of fragments of driftwood pegged together with ivory from a walrus tusk. We have also seen bows made of split bone lashed together with deer sinew, coming from Baffin's Land. The pieces were arched away from instead of towards the hunter, to supply the resiliency of which the bone has none. The arc was kept from breaking by heavy thongs lashed lengthwise both in front and behind the bone.

When they could get it they used the long, drooping horns of the musk-ox, which they split lengthwise and then lashed with thongs in the same way. The bowstring was of sinew. Nothing can be cleverer than the Eskimo hunting weapons. Thus walrus tusks are used to weight their harpoon tops and to carry the iron barbs, when they can get any. Only the barb is attached to the line. It comes loose off the handle directly the animal is struck. The line, which is of seal or walrus hide, runs through a ring, or heavy toggle, attached to the shaft and tusk and prevents their being lost. We brought them out some iron heads from Europe, as they cost so little, but the natives preferred their own brand. The line attached to an inflated sealskin is thrown overboard and easily followed.

Before lines of hemp were brought them they made their own of fine shreds or splits of baleen or whalebone, tied end to end. Their hooks were ivory, weighted with soapstone or with granite tied up in bags woven from the tendons of seals. They also wove nets of the same material and used them to dip up fish, especially capelin, for drying. They would catch ducks and even wild geese with bolas like the Indians of the Pampas, using ivory blocks on the walrus or seal lines. They supplemented the darting stick or spear by clever stone traps put out in the water for trout and salmon.

One of their most ingenious devices is the runner or "shoe" of their sledge. Fine mud is mixed with warm water and plastered on the wooden runner, onto which it instantly freezes. This is smoothed down with a rasp. A piece of bearskin is then moistened and run along it several times until a quarter to a half inch of ice covers the whole length. This enables it to run over snow with almost no friction. If a piece does get knocked off they keep it carefully and freeze it on again.

In my possession I have an arrow made from a bit of driftwood, tipped with a small triangular scrap of rusty iron from the keel of an old wreck, with goose feathers to steady it. With this arrow the owner had walked right up to a polar bear and driven it through his heart. Incidentally this same hunter had drifted for three months on the ice floe with his family and also that of a friend who had been drowned. There was only himself to provide for the whole number of women and children. They finally landed at Cape Wolstenholme at five o'clock one Sunday night. The Hudson's Bay Company factor saw them landing and offered to open the store. Extraordinary as it may seem, that Eskimo knew that it was Sunday, and preferred to wait until the next morning to get some supplies. Moreover he and his fellow-voyagers invited the agent to sing a hymn of praise with them on the rocks by the skin tubik as soon as it was pitched. This is another tribute to the Moravians.

"Eskimo" is a name of contempt. In Indian it is "Uskepoo." In the Cree language "Ashki" means raw and "mow" means meat. Hence the derivation "raw-meat eaters." But although the Eskimo appear to have robust stomachs, it is neither personal preference nor recognition of the superior vitamin values of raw foods which induces them to forego cooking. More often, as in the case of the Cherub's explanation to the Archbishop who offered him a seat in the heavenly choir-stall, "*Il n'y a pas de quoi.*" The Eskimo call us "Kablunak"—the people with the big brow. They consider us inferior animals and think we are descended from the red fox!

On long journeys in his skin oomiak, or women boat, though it allows mighty little spare space, a man will carry three wives (if he can afford them), dogs, a tent, a few seal carcasses, and endless other impedimenta! I have seen a wife and children and even dogs being ferried along the Coast both on and in a kayak.

The kayak is the most wonderful boat of its size. It can go through breakers off a flat beach, turn over and come up again, go to windward faster than a four-oared row-boat, jump over another boat, ride almost any kind of sea—and the paddler always faces the way he is going. They are so steady that I have shot geese with a double-barrelled eight-bore gun from one. When you land you pick your craft up and take it home with you on your head. If you are caught in ice you jump on to the floe and pull the kayak up after you.

But to return to the subject of cooking. If we had to substitute a stone lamp for a portable stove, seal oil and moss for alcohol, and instead of using matches had to make a fire by holding the vertebra of an animal in our teeth and with a seal's rib bow and deer tendon line had to make fire by rotating a dry stick in a rotted bone cavity, would it be long before we preferred to jerk our walrus meat, sun-dry our fish, and eat them raw? I have watched an Eskimo, who had brought a supply of sun-dried walrus meat on board the hospital ship with him, stripping the dry black strips and chewing them with such relish that I tried them myself. I still prefer ham and eggs. As a matter of fact, however, Eskimo do demonstrate that it is correct to say that man is a "cooking animal." For amongst the very earliest relics of Eskimo life are wonderful stone pots and kettles. Many have been brought to us in Labrador, amazingly hewn out of solid granite blocks, where soft stone has not been available.

Evidence shows that an Eskimo values his large granite kettle as highly as we prize ours of copper or iron. If you or I, with only an Eskimo's tools, had made such a pot, nothing would have induced us to part with it. Even death failed to part it from an Eskimo owner. Being the most valuable thing he possessed, it was always buried with him, a small hole being bored through it so as to set its spirit free also, so that it might accompany him to the land beyond, which he believed in as naturally and as implicitly as in his home here. What better evidence could be afforded of devotion on the part of his ever-needy family! It is surely more unselfish than the custom of the Chinese of burning only tinsel paper effigies of the belongings of the departed, merely as a symbol of freeing the spirits of the possessions. The similarity of these habits suggests the persistence of a common racial custom.

The best evidence of the value placed on these pathetic tributes to the departed is the fact that to-day, if the kettles are to be taken from ancient graves, something else must be substituted. This is equally true of the stone lamps, stone necklaces, stone knives and arrows, and other tokens of their faith and hope. Their intellects, now that they are Christians, would exempt them from such obligations, but their hearts are in the same place as ours. In graves any distance from the Moravian Mission stations I have seen new rifles, good kayaks, and other valuables still laid in stone caches by the bones of the departed loved one. I once sent two Eskimo to get some old stone kettles from a burial cache inland. We had to supply something to put in the place of the things they took, and happened to be in possession of a number of old razors. As Eskimo do not have hair on their faces these implements seemed scarcely appropriate to appease the spirit even of a good-natured Innuit. But my messengers were perfectly satisfied with them.

Similarly nothing would persuade many of my British neighbours on the Labrador Coast that a seventh son, or

43

the seventh son of a seventh son, cannot cure almost anything; exactly as His Britannic Majesty used to heal "The King's Evil" by his touch. Indeed, close to one of our hospitals there dwells now just such a seventh son, who is often called in before sending for the doctor, to stop bleeding or "heal an evil."

On the other hand, in suffering or bereavement, the Eskimo show remarkable fortitude and resignation. On one occasion one of the leading Eskimo at Hopedale had been reloading the cannon with which they welcomed each year the arrival of the Moravian supply-ship *Harmony*, when it exploded and blew off both his arms. Before I saw him he had lain for a fortnight with practically nothing but cold-water dressings on his wounds. The awful pathos of the man's suffering led me to try and sympathize with him. With a bright smile he replied, "It is nothing to what my Saviour suffered for me."

Another time, an Eskimo was showing me the spot where, as he and his brother returned in a very rough sea in their kayaks, his brother capsized and was drowned. "Did you try to rescue him?" I asked. He shrugged his shoulders. "But why not?" "Ajaunamat," he replied with a further shrug. "Ajaunamat" is their equivalent for "kismet."

Like all human beings, the Eskimo had certain men to whom to go in times of sickness and trouble. Before the advent of the Moravian Mission these men, called Angekoks, acted as sorcerers. There were no priests among the Eskimo, for though a deeply religious people they had no kind of worship. To them everything had a spirit, even an iceberg or a tobacco pipe. Their gods were many. The mother of all seals lived in the moon, and when properly invoked by the Angekok (who had to be well paid) would drop a seal in their bay to lure others to that harbour. The father of all caribou lived in the centre of the earth, and could be propitiated in the same way. Tongak was the evil spirit of the sea. The story goes that the mother of storms lived in the ocean, whither she had run away to spite her father. In return he had cut off her fingers, which came to life as great animals of the deep.

Comparing the Eskimo of the South with the old whale-hunting Eskimo of the North suggests an evolution which must have occupied a longer period of time than even our most vivid imagination can picture—possibly ten thousand years. There is evidence that the Eskimo did not always follow the sea, though to-day not one of ours lives a hundred miles from it. A race existed in the Barren Lands of Canada which lived chiefly off the vast herds of caribou which fed on the arctic prairies—a multitude which has never been equalled in the world except by the buffalo of the West. Photographs taken as late as 1890 of Eskimo west of Hudson's Bay, dwelling on these arctic prairies, show them dressed only in skins, without any weapons but flints, living in skin tents, never having had contact with civilization, and apparently unacquainted with anything which could connect them with the world outside.

Polar Eskimo discovered in the present ice cap the "cold-stored" carcase of mammoths which perished in the last glacial period, fully ten thousand years ago. They actually partook of soup made of the flesh, preserved in a manner that is a forerunner of the justly famous Birds-eye Frosted Foods process.

Eskimo clothing has been evolved along thoroughly scientific and utilitarian lines, but the element of beauty has been closely studied. The clothing consists of two pieces, a "kossak" or jumper, without any opening whatever except at the bottom and for the face. The garment is slipped on over the head and arms and comes well down over the second piece, the trousers. These also have no opening except at the top and bottom. Both pieces are made of the skins of reindeer, a material which allows no escape of the heat produced by the body. The Eskimo is doubly insulated by his special layer of fat, and an exceptionally oily skin. In very cold weather a belt can be worn to close any draught, which is additionally checked by a heavy trimming of bear fur, closing all chinks. A similar trimming closes any leaks around the face, while the trouser legs fit into loose, very soft skin moccasins which reach up to the knee. Underclothes are made of softened skins of birds with the feathers next to the body. Only those who have tried to get these birds' skins free enough of fats to be usable can appreciate the cleverness of the Eskimo women, who chew it out with their teeth without injuring the feathers.

The skin of the caribou is undoubtedly the best material for retaining the heat of the body in extreme cold, with the least weight and the most flexibility, enabling exercise to be taken easily and heat thus engendered. With these ends in view we ourselves have substituted a very special material, now called "Grenfell Cloth," which we find more economic and efficient. Those of Admiral

The Pageant of the Eskimo

Byrd's men who used it at the South Pole, and the Admiral himself, commended it highly. Hudson's Bay Company men in the Arctic have used it on long dog trips. Flying men, owing to its extreme lightness, praise it highly. The expedition to climb Mt. Everest has selected it, and Watkins used it on the Greenland Expedition. Captain and Mrs. Mollison wore it on their transatlantic flight.

In the depth of winter an Eskimo will, by the help of his dog, march out onto the frozen sea and detect the hole in the ice which a seal has kept open from below the surface with his breath. The seal may have kept several such holes, and may not come back to any particular one all day. Nevertheless the Eskimo will build a snow wall to fend off the wind, and put a spear of bone through the surface ice, which will move and warn him when the seal is below. Then with his arm resting on a block of ice he holds a harpoon with a detachable head, which is fastened by a rope of seal hide around his leg. He will sit motionless in that position for hours—indeed until the seal *does* return. Then he must plunge with all his might without seeing his victim, which even then, in its violent struggles to escape, may break the man's leg. Surely the ancestors of anyone who can support a family by this industry must have been able to weather a casual ice age!

His courage is such that he will tackle a monster polar bear alone, at a pinch, with only a dog whip. He fastens his keen-bladed knife to the end of the thirty-five-foot lath, and jumping around his enemy like Rikki Tikki Tavi, finally lashes him to death. For ingenuity in small

47

matters also the Eskimo are ahead of many of us "civilized" folk. We sent to the College of Surgeons the evidence of the Eskimo's claim to be the first inventors of the most modern type of surgical needle. It was always skin which they had to sew. The seam had to be waterproof and windproof, whether it was a kayak, a boot, or a kossak they were making. The needles they invented were made of driftwood and were curved to allow sewing to be done on a stretched, flat skin. The needle had to be long to be held even in their supple fingers, for they had no forceps such as we have for a similar purpose. The needles were three-sided as far as the middle, in order to cut easily through the tough skin without lacerating it, and to make it possible to go through only the number of layers required. The back end of the needle was round, exactly as in the most up-to-date surgical model, to leave an easy hole for threading, and one which would not tear and cause leakage.

When sewing a kayak, the skin is stretched over a frame; and the problem often is to put on it a watertight patch. We once sent a kayak to a surgeon at home, because he had appreciated its immense superiority as a light boat in rough water and for hunting birds. When, however, a cut was made by mistake in the skin cover, he was utterly unable to mend it, and we had to send along the Eskimo technique.

The Eskimo are not only clever mechanics but keen observers. I have found them first-class pilots, even though their own boats drew next to no water and mine drew many feet. When they do not know, they say so at once.

48

The Pageant of the Eskimo

The race is vanishing. Why? Because "civilization" is invading its territory. In 1919 a steamer bringing supplies to a Moravian Mission station at Okkak where there lived three hundred and sixty-five Eskimo and eight Europeans, had two seamen aboard her, convalescing from "flu." A few Eskimo went on board during the three days the boat lay in harbour. In three weeks three hundred Eskimo, including every man in the place over twenty-five years old, and one European, were all dead. Two years later I was asked to go and bury in a near-by bay thirteen bodies which had been discovered under the ruins of the isolated fallen cottage of a white trapper. Some of the Okkak Eskimo had fled there for safety in their terror and had been taken in by their white friends. The trapper, his wife and family, and all the refugees had died together. Not one had been left to tell the tale.

Fortunately their claim on humanity as fit to survive does not rest on their resistance to the germs of civilization. I can think of no better illustration of this than the two following accounts taken from the Hudson's Bay Company's interesting little magazine, the *Beaver*.

"No wilder and more desolate region can be imagined than the West Coast of Labrador in Hudson's Bay. Bare, bleak rocks and vast wastes of moss and sand everywhere meet the eye. Of verdure properly speaking there is no more than in the Devonian Ages, except a casual patch of rank grass, a few stunted spruces hiding in hollows only emphasizing the inhospitality and sterile nature of the land. Its only attraction lies in what nature has left undone. Climate and soil produce nothing to reward the agricultural worker or sustain human life. But the land is not uninteresting, for man can live and thrive there, where vegetables cannot exist. From time im-

49

memorial it has been inhabited by numerous bands of Eskimo, amazingly hardy, who feed, clothe and provide for their families without any help from civilization.

"Our camp was at the foot of a great, bleak hill by the swirling waters of the Kasak river. Beyond a few shrubs, scattered far apart in the hollows of the hills, were a few skin tubiks of an Eskimo settlement. Three tiny specks could be seen moving slowly along against the wild, rocky side of the immense hill above us, bending up and down occasionally as if aimlessly seeking for some hidden treasure amidst the chaos of stones. The breeze whistled past, lashing and stinging my face and hands as I climbed up the rocky river bed in search of the forlorn figures. At last, on the other side of a gigantic avalanche of rocks, in a slight depression a few dead willow bushes showed their bleached branches among the stones and moss. There were the three gallant figures. They were an Eskimo great-grandmother and her two little, frail great-granddaughters, gathering one by one the twigs of the precious wood, all three contributing their share to the support of the tribe."

A description of a winter's night on the open frozen sea helps one still further to respect these people.

"The dogs" [so writes this Hudson's Bay Company's clerk], "seeing the lights of a few snow houses, galloped up and stopped at the door of a tunnel several yards long. Having crawled through the tunnel I came to three very small holes. I wriggled through the left-hand one and found myself in a commodious room twelve feet in diameter and eight feet high. It was well lighted by two stone, seal-oil lamps with dried moss wicks. The clean white of the roof, floor and walls reflected the light. A platform two feet high occupied half the room and was covered with deer skins. Against the wall blankets and bedding were rolled. A board on snow blocks made a table; and on a scaffold made of willow sticks over the lamps garments were spread to dry. Sitting on the sleeping bench I removed my outside deerskin garments, which a woman carefully brushed free of snow, folded and put away. She then prepared tea over a special Primus lamp, with bread and hardtack and jam. Others kept crowding in and gladly accepted a biscuit and a cup of tea. She next cut up a raw frozen salmon and gave one piece to everyone. Contrary to my expectation, the taste was not unpleasant; with them it is a favourite article of diet. With so many people the temperature of the room began to rise, with the result that the roof began to drip in places. My host cut a piece of snow from a block that he kept handy and put it on the dripping spot, where it froze on and instantly stopped it. At 11.30 P.M. I indicated that I wanted to sleep. Immediately all our guests took their departure, first prostrating themselves on the ground to get on even terms with the door. A nicely fitting snow block was now placed in the door to keep out draughts and inquisitive dogs who had already paid us a visit. They were now confined to the tunnel.

"The bedding was now spread out, the lamps extinguished, and soon the family and I were in our respective sleeping bags, warm and comfortable. Before dropping off to sleep I pondered over the amazing character and resourcefulness of the people who live this life."

In a recent research, in trying to account for the increase of the Eskimo population in Alaska and Greenland during the past twenty years, it is stated that a physiological weakness was making the birth-rate among the Eskimo lower than their death-rate, until the tide turned, due to a "mixture of European blood." The higher birth-rate in South Greenland was attributed to the admixture of Viking blood—though it is generally admitted that that element was wiped out four hundred years ago.

The real truth is: (1) the Eskimo can compete with nature until he destroys its living animals, but though he is tractable he has so far been incapable of being taught to conserve life. (2) He cannot compete against nature and against predatory man, as the advance northward of the fishermen, though the best-intentioned of people, has demonstrated. His ability to destroy has developed in advance of his ability to construct. The fact of war, the unwillingness to disarm, and the slow advance of co-operative as against competitive systems, all show that "morally civilized" man has not yet solved this problem for himself, either.

In Greenland the problem of the survival of the Eskimo seems to have been solved by the fact of the Danish Government enforcing isolation. There the Eskimo are increasing. In Alaska exactly the same thing has occurred. A paternal Government, together with isolation procured by the introduction of reindeer, have achieved the desired end. The deer have to be herded up on the tundra, which keeps the Eskimo away from the mining camps and more in their natural environment as chronic wanderers. The Canadian Government have endorsed this policy of the United States by placing two thousand reindeer at the mouth of the Mackenzie River for the benefit of their Eskimo—an experiment which will be watched with great interest. Our own reindeer experiment demonstrated conclusively how easily this could be repeated in Labrador, given Government support. We still hope that the Colony of Newfoundland may, before it is too late, give the deer the protection and assistance which they refused me for them at the time of our experiment.

A "closed zone" for Eskimo, with special permits required for all others entering the area, would, we believe, save them yet. The Moravians wisely took up large areas of land, realizing the necessity of segregating their Eskimo. They did not take up nearly enough, as it turned out. But even their measure of success, which was helped by their being a little farther away from outsiders than the more southerly groups, is another proof of the value of the policy. Like birds and other animals, the worthwhile Eskimo needs sanctuaries if he is to survive. Our contention is that if the Eskimo of Labrador is to be saved, an intelligent effort must be made on his behalf at once by a Government which cares for the "Innuit" for their own sakes.

IV: THE PAGEANT OF THE VIKINGS

"Winged Hats and Dragon Ships"

AT LEAST three hundred and twenty books have been written about the Viking voyages to America, most of them since 1837. None of the authors have ever visited these coasts, much less cruised them in small boats as the Vikings used to do. Some attempt to prove that the Norse voyages were mere fables, just as the formerly accepted tales of Antonio Zeno, in 1380, or John Szolny, in 1472, the Polish pilot of Denmark, have been shown to be mere inventions, written for political gains rather than for historical purposes.

The Vikings' visits to North America, however, are proven facts as far as anything outside mathematics is capable of proof. Indeed, in no less than six official vellums in Rome it is stated that in 1121 Bishop Eric Upsi or Gnupsson was appointed by Pope Paschal II as Bishop of Greenland and Vinland *"in partibus infidelium."* Unfortunately he never returned from his very first attempt from Greenland to visit the Vinland end of his See. But that journey of the Bishop was at least one authentic voyage of the Vikings, and it leaves no escape from the conclusion that his parishioners before him must have made voyages. No less than seventeen bishops of Greenland, with their headquarters at Ericsfjord, are on record. Their flocks sent twenty-six hundred pounds of walrus ivory every year to Rome for Peter's Pence.

The skippers of the Dragon Ships kept no logs. They were not able to write. The Sagas were stories handed down from one to another and written, alas, by others. No court of law would dream of accepting their details as evidence. They are almost all songs glorifying the deeds of chiefs, whose greatness lay in their sea genius. The voyages of the great Eric, and of his sons Thorstein, Leif, and Thorvald, of his daughter Freydis, and of his son's widow Gudrid and of her second husband Karlsefni, all concern Labrador. Others, of which there were undoubtedly many, were unrecorded for lack of scribes. The real marvel is that in that age there was anyone to produce the Sagas that do exist, and that during such constant fighting they could have been preserved. There are to-day no real records of even John Cabot's voyages, made five hundred years later. Even the great Dampier's and many others end nowhere.

The writer has cruised along all these coasts many

times during the past forty years, in every kind of small sail and power boat, from Cape Breton to Cape Chidley. At first it was in a boat forty-five feet long and eight feet broad, with a six-foot draught—almost exactly the size of a Dragon Ship. But having a steam engine, it was able to beat any boat propelled by oars on such a coast, even if every rower were a Viking. As one result he does not believe that the Vikings ever got south of the Straits of Belle Isle; and, incidentally, there has never been discovered one single atom of evidence, in remains or otherwise, to prove that they did. In Baffin's Land, yes. For in 1824 there was found in Baffin's Bay, in a region supposedly never visited by a white man before the age of modern exploration, a stone engraved with runic characters, which states "Erling Sighvatson, Bjarni Thorhason, and Eindrid Oddson raised these marks and cleared land here on Saturday before Ascension Week, 1135." In Hudson's Bay? Possibly. For faith in the genuineness of the runic stone discovered in Kensington, Minnesota, is growing in some quarters. It gives an account of Vikings who left their vessel in Hudson's Bay and marched inland, where they were attacked by Indians, "and many perished." No reason has ever been shown why the Vikings would want to fare any farther than our beautifully wooded bays, with their endless berries, salmon, furs, and game, except that most people think of the east coast of Labrador as all barren, forbidding wastes, and forget that no part of it lies north of England and Scotland.

Major Cartwright, in 1786, on arriving in Sandwich Bay, halfway up the Coast, straight from Marnham Hall in Norfolk, described it as Paradise, and settled there. The end of the bay is still so named.

Thorvald, coming from treeless Greenland, would scarcely be less impressed with it. Yet when the statue of Leif was erected in Boston to commemorate his having landed in Back Bay, the argument was used that Labrador was "as destitute as only Newfoundland of trees, meadows, and sandy beaches—at best a scene of desolation, and therefore could not possibly be Vinland." Yet one lumber mill in Hamilton Inlet for some years cut up to three million feet of lumber.

Since Thorvald's day many a man not from Greenland has said of this bay as Thorvald did, "This is a fair land, and here I wish to make my home."

If any apologist for the theory that the Vikings voyaged to New England is honestly seeking the truth, let him cruise our Labrador coast in a similar boat and get some first-hand experience of its immense difficulties, and of the time necessary to travel from Cape Chidley to the Straits of Belle Isle. Let him also remember that Gudrid the Fair took back in her boat to Greenland a cargo of berries and wood and that Freydis made similar journeys later for cargoes of timber. Those who have crossed the Straits of Belle Isle in such boats themselves, even with no load, know very well that her men could not have rowed the said craft loaded from Rhode Island to Greenland. Nor would they have ever met in Rhode Island Skroelings, or Eskimo, using skin boats.

On the other hand, in books like Professor S. E. Dawson's or Professor Fischer's "Discoveries of the Norsemen in America" there is ample proof that the Vikings did land on the American continent. The erudite botanical researches of Professor Fernald leave still less room for any doubt that Helluland, Markland, and Vinland must all have been in Labrador. A manuscript geography of the twelfth century expressly states, "From Markland only a little way on lies Vinland the Good."

Gosling's "Discovery and Exploration of Labrador," the result of years of research, with special privileges in England, Canada, and France to examine charts and records, clinches that fact. Alas, though a Newfoundlander, he also had never cruised the Labrador Coast.

On the other hand, a recent book which takes itself seriously, argues as follows: "Can we imagine these Icelandic broadswordsmen in armour getting ecstatic over the prospect of berry decoctions? One cannot imagine a Norse warrior quaffing fruit syrups. Only real grapes could satisfy these Icelanders and men from Greenland. Consequently Vinland must have been further south than Labrador." Its writer further forgets that neither in Iceland, Greenland, nor Norway do grapes grow! Neither could he have known that the small Labrador cranberry makes an excellent tart wine.

Though these voyages of the Norsemen may appear to have been barren of results, the traditions of Vinland were familiar to Columbus, and authorities have stated that in 1477 he made from Bristol at least one voyage to Iceland. They were therefore not altogether devoid of influence on our own history.

It is written in the Sagas that in the year 986 Eric the Red, a Viking chief, was banished from Iceland for having slain the two sons of Thorgest, another powerful Jarl, in a family argument. Having been banished before for similar indiscretions, he was now outlawed. He knew that Ulf the Crow, over a hundred years before, had been driven west by gales and had been frozen in all winter off the shore of some western land. With twenty-five vessels he sailed away in that direction. Some time later he found land, but only fourteen of his vessels survived. After exploring the west coast for three years he revisited Iceland. Here he again had a fight with Thorgest and was beaten, so he returned once more to Greenland, settling this time at Brattahild, in Ericsfjord on the southwest coast. No trees grew there, and making a living was not easy even for Vikings. So Eric called his section "Greenland," for he felt that "settlers would be more readily persuaded there if the land had a good name." In his actual harbour the delta *was* green. Here two colonies grew up, which, existent ruins suggest, contained at one time five thousand inhabitants. These settlements lasted about four hundred years.

Meanwhile another Viking, a trader from Norway, Bjarni, son of Herjulf, had returned from a cruise before Christmas "to drink the Yuletide ale with his father in Iceland." At that time of year it is dark practically all day in those latitudes, and there the seas are apt to be exceedingly tempestuous. Bjarni's boat was small, only sixteen and a half feet wide and about seventy feet in length. It was primarily a row-boat at that, with fifteen oars on each side, and one mast and a square-sail, which was only of any use when the wind was fair. In bad weather these boats were absolutely at the mercy of the wind and weather. The boat must have been heavily loaded, for besides the crew of thirty-five men it had to carry food and water for an indefinite number of days, and arms and armour into the bargain. More serious was the fact that this cockleshell possessed no compass or sextant, not even an astrolabe, no chart, no sailing directions, so that once you were out of sight of land, it was quite impossible to tell where you were or which way to steer, except by the heavenly bodies when they happened to be visible. The Pleiades were the favourite constellation used.

The frequent fogs and almost Stygian darkness of the Arctic winter and the abundant floating ice might have afforded sufficient excuse for Bjarni to leave his chair empty for once at the Christmas family gathering. His boat had no accommodation, there were no cabins except a cuddy in the bow, and such shelter as narrow sideboards afforded. There was no place to cook, no beds, no toilets. There was not even a rudder, only a huge oar slung through an iron band in the boat's side, called then the "steer," now the starboard side.

Forty years of experience of small boats in these waters makes it certain to the author that without exceptional luck no such craft could, on a long voyage, possibly average two miles an hour. With a head wind and sea they could not have made any progress at all. Thorstein Ericsson himself never got across; and more than one ended up on the wrong side of the Atlantic. That they could row all night as well as all day in icy seas is inconceivable. Supermen as they appear to us softer human beings of to-day, they were human, after all.

Bjarni, finding that his father had left Iceland with Eric, was so annoyed that he decided to sail at once and search for him in the unknown West. He encountered nothing but gales of icy wind and much foggy weather, so that they "sailed many days without seeing either sun or stars." When at length they did see land Bjarni expresses no surprise that he was "in waters of which he had never heard." It was not the land of barren mountains and great glaciers for which he was looking. It had only small heights and was covered with dense forests. He needed wood and water, and many have wondered why he did not land. It was December, and all harbours on the Labrador Coast are frozen up at that time of year. He could not get his boat into safety for the winter. On the other hand, he could get all the fresh water he needed from the pools on the ice.

The mention of ice would be censored by a man like Eric, who wished to suggest fertile lands. Arguing with Eric was unhealthy. Bjarni put to sea again and after a few days' further sail was amazed to again see wooded land. He was now in a hurry to find a harbour, and so once more went straight on without landing. This time he headed north, which, as the "sky now became fair," it was possible to do. Fair weather on the Labrador Coast means a wind between northwest and southwest. After six days Bjarni sighted land on the larboard side. There were high mountains, ice, and glaciers. This must have been the south coast of Greenland. By tacking, and following it along for four more days "before a good wind which arose" he came to Herjulfness, the very place where his father was living. He was still annoyed, for he was too late, after all, to drink the Yuletide ale with him.

Thus was the American continent discovered by Europeans in the year 987. Bjarni must have seen Labrador south of the tree-line.

Trifling incidents often change history. If it had not been for his horse stumbling, the great Eric would himself have been the first white man on record to land on the American continent.

His son, Leif the Lucky, had actually persuaded him to set out at once and look for Bjarni's well-wooded land; but after so bad an omen he decided against the venture. Leif, however, had bought a boat from Bjarni, and with a crew of thirty-five men, at once set sail himself, heading southwest. He came "first to the land Bjarni saw last." He landed and found a low land, with endless flat stones, and behind that mountains with snow on them. Exactly as Eric called his one fjord "Greenland," so Leif said, "I will call this spot Helluland—the Land of Flat Stones." It has always been said no such place can be found in Labrador, since high cliffs face the sea along its whole length.

About a hundred miles south of Cape Chidley lies a bay called Kangalaksiorvik. The mouth is wide and its north side is sandy. On the south side are endless acres of flat stones, reaching away to the snow-capped Torngat Mountains. We have christened this Helluland. Leif sailed on south and landed next, after two days, "where level sand was by the sea," and slopes behind were well wooded. The Kiglapeit, or dog-toothed mountains, two thousand feet high, jut out into the sea about one hun-

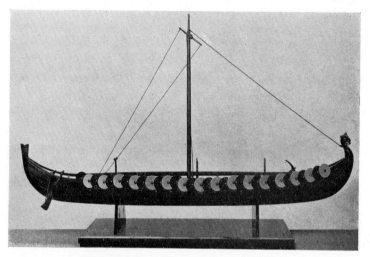

VIKING SHIP (8TH TO 10TH CENTURY)

AS THE VIKINGS SAW IT

"I WILL CALL THIS LAND HELLULAND—THE LAND OF FLAT STONES"

Photograph by F. C. Sears

A PIECE OF HELLULAND

dred and fifty miles south of Helluland. On the north side is a harbour that stands directly in the way of vessels coasting to the southward. The mountain-sides are still covered with forest. The north side consists of miles of level sand dunes, with trees behind. This answers well to the description of the place of which Leif said, "This shall be called Mark, or wood-land, for that which doth most abound here."

Still he was not satisfied and sailed on before a fair wind for two more days and nights. This could have brought him to the outstanding land on the south side of Hamilton Inlet, another two hundred miles. The saga says they sighted land, and then came to an island which lay to the northward of this land. They had passed "the end of the land," which is exactly what the north side of Hamilton Inlet looks like from George's Island—for this Great Bay runs in for a hundred and fifty miles and is twelve miles across at the mouth. The south side has a sandy beach for miles to Cape Porcupine.

After landing they again sailed on "into a certain sound, lying between an island and a cape which jutted out from the land." They passed on between them into broad reaches of shallow water, where it being ebb-tide they ran their ship ashore. As soon as the tide rose, she floated off, and they "conveyed the ship up a river, and so into a lake."

A better description could hardly be written of the high, projecting cape called the Horse Chops, just to the southward of the miles of sandy beach south of Hamilton Inlet. The fishing fleets still pass between that great landmark and Pack's Harbour Island, on which a lighthouse now stands. Within, opens the most beautiful bay in Labrador—Sandwich Bay, the mouth of which is marked on the charts as "The Flats." On this I have myself stranded my small boat no less than four times. It is mostly sand, however, and we have floated off on the rising tide unhurt, and then gone on through what looks like a river-mouth, where a very heavy tide runs, between Earl Island and Caribou Castle. This in turn leads into a lake now known as Cartwright Harbour.

Here the dense woods with the beautiful varying greens of the larches, firs, spruces, and birches, when contrasted with the cold waters of the icy sea outside, make it seem like paradise. Dr. Packard, who visited this coast, claims that it answers exactly to the description of the "wonder-strands." Personally I have little doubt that here is the spot where Leif brought up. Any man would want to stay there. Here Leif built his "booths," or houses. Wood was on every side. "The salmon were larger than they had ever seen." This bay is still the best salmon fishing centre in the country. There is ample fodder for cattle wherever there is any space between the forest and the landwash. The Saga interpreted by the Norse of that date allows at this place, Vinland, seven to eight hours of daylight in winter. Cartwright is about the same latitude as Chester, England, where that is approximately the amount of daylight between dawn and dark on the shortest day.

Leif called this section Vinland, or Wineland, because of the abundant "vinber," which made such excellent wine. Professor Fernald proves conclusively in his monograph entitled "Plants of Wineland the Good" that these

64

were never grapes, but our endless red currants or small red cranberries.

In the fall of the year near Cartwright I have been myself ashamed to walk at times off the beaten path, because of the waste caused by treading on countless cranberries which stained one's moccasins blood-red. These are easily preserved berries. We just fill up any barrel and freeze them for winter. This could not be the case in Nova Scotia; still less farther south. Secondly, the Norsemen found here their own "viti," or wheat. This is a tall grass (*Elymus arenarius*) whose seed was regularly used for flour in Iceland. It is very abundant in Labrador. We use the straw for making baskets. It has no resemblance to either wild rice or Indian corn.

In 1783 one Icelandic writer says that the flour from this "wheat" was much more nutritious and finer than any wheat which they could import; so that no other corn was imported. We call it sea-lime grass. It sows itself abundantly, just as the Sagas describe.

The Vikings also found here the "mosurr" wood. This cannot be the maple, for they also found it growing in Finland, where there have never been maples. Out of the mosurr-wood knobs the Vikings made drinking bowls. These are the hard, round knobs which we find on our birches. Harold Haardrada speaks of them in 1086. They were unique for hardness and highly prized.

It is easy to understand what excitement Leif's return the following year to Greenland afforded. Eric's son Thorstein was at once besieged by his friends to go in search of "Vinland the Good." He needed persuasion, not being much of a sailor. Indeed he never got there, for

65

owing to adverse winds he first sighted Iceland, and then birds off the Irish coast. He finally only arrived back west as far as Greenland, by winter. There he died of an epidemic shortly afterwards.

Thorvald, Eric's third son, by Leif's advice, now also hurried off to Vinland. He found Leif's "booths" and stayed there all winter. His description also of the many islands, sandy coves and shallows, fits Sandwich Bay admirably, as does his spring trip to the east along the Coast, until he "came to a great cape." About sixty miles east of Paradise is just such a cape. It now has a lighthouse on it and is called Cape North. On each side of the cape are beautiful small bays, excellent harbours for boats of light draught. These are still used as sealing stations, since the herds of seals pass north and south round the cape in the spring and fall, forced close to the cape by the large islands that lie off it.

"This is a fair region," said Thorvald, "and here would I like to make my home." Unfortunately on the beach he stumbled across "three mounds." These proved to be three skin boats, under each of which were three "Skroelings" sleeping, exactly as the Eskimo do under their large, skin-covered oomiaks, which just about shelter three men. These men were small and swarthy, and had broad cheeks and great eyes. They were "ill-looking" and their straight, black hair looked ugly to the fair, curly-haired Norsemen. Finding that he could not understand them, Thorvald tried to kill them all. One escaped, however, and told his fellows. They were evidently there hunting seals, on which they lived. Next day hundreds attacked the Norsemen with bows and arrows, and one arrow, coming in between the shield and the boat, pierced Thorvald in the armpit and killed him. Before his death he advised his fellows to return at once, but to bury him on the cape "which seemed to me to offer so pleasant a dwelling place. So it may be the truth fell from my lips when I expressed the wish to abide here. You shall place a Cross at my head and my feet, and call it Crossness forever after."

His companions then returned to their winter camp, and collected vinber and wood for a cargo to take home with them when they returned to Greenland the following spring.

Thorstein's father-in-law now died, and his wife, Gudrid the Fair, went to live with Eric. Shortly afterwards she married a visiting nobleman called Thorfinn Karlsefni. He was a descendant of Kiarval, King of Ireland. Gudrid immediately persuaded him to make a voyage to Vinland. She was regarded as the wisest woman in Greenland. Not only did she go with her husband, but Thorvald, the wealthy husband of Eric's last child and only daughter Freydis, joined their fleet of three ships. After three days and nights they came up to the Land of Flat Stones, and then, still running before a north wind for three days, they came to a woody land, on which they found a bear. One often meets bears on these off-lying islands, earning a living off seals and birds. This was Markland, and lying off it was a big island with a beach, to-day called Beachy Island. They now sailed south again along the land for a long time, where there were long strands just such as still lie along the Adlavik shore to Cape Harrison, then along Byron's Bay to Holton, thence from Hamilton Inlet to Sandwich Bay. Eider-ducks' nests here were in such numbers that they could scarcely help stepping on them, which would be quite natural so long ago on the east Labrador Coast. Even still, farther north, I have known three thousand eggs gathered on one lot of islands at one time, and then there were as many left behind. This was on the Mettek Islands near Helluland. It would not have been the case in Nova Scotia. They also found a stranded whale, which is natural, as there are many whales there, and I have seen a sperm whale run ashore. There was a big Norwegian whaling station on the islands off Cape North.

Karlsefni found a river which "has great bars at the mouth, so that it can be entered only at the height of flood tide." Fifty miles up the sandy shores of Sandwich Bay lies Eagle River, which has exactly such bars and on which I have myself stranded my jolly-boat more than once going into the river to catch salmon, which are innumerable.

The Saga says: "They stood into the bay with their ships. There was an island at the mouth of the bay with strong currents, so they called it Stream Island." Every big basin that is filled and emptied every tide through a narrow channel must have a fierce current at the mouth. In Sandwich Bay, between the south point and the big wooded island, only a stone's throw across, is just such a tide. It twists my steamer almost around, steaming nine knots.

Through this entrance one morning came endless canoes, made of skin, "with Skroelings brandishing

68

staves in the direction of the course of the sun," exactly
as Eskimo in their kayaks appear to do with their double-
ended paddles. A strong trait in the Eskimo is their naïve
curiosity, and the Saga proceeds, "The Skroelings on landing went about marvelling at what they saw, especially
the weapons"—which the Vikings refused to sell them.
That winter Gudrid gave birth to the first white boy
born on American soil, and called him Snorri. They had
already slaughtered some of the Eskimo, who now made
life so unsafe for the settlers that they were forced to go
north again; but only after Thorvald, Eric's son-in-law,
was killed by an arrow.

Passing Markland, they captured two Skroeling boys
whom they took home with them. Karlsefni and Gudrid
reached Brattahild safely and once more went to live
with Eric.

Anyone who still doubts the Viking voyages to Vinland can remember that Adam, canon of Bremen, says
in 1601 that King Sven of Norway wrote of "an island
in the Western Ocean called Vinland," which he says
was so called because "vines grow wild there, and because
the Danes certified that grain grows there also unsown."
The Icelandic historian Ari, earliest and most trust-
worthy of scribes, says that his uncle learned first-hand
from Eric the Red of the Norse voyages. He refers to
Vinland as being well known. Abbot Nicholas of Thin-
gyre, about 1150, mentions Vinland. The Flatey Book,
about 1380, refers to it repeatedly. The manuscript geography of the twelfth century states definitely that
Helluland lies south of Greenland, that then comes
Markland and then Vinland the Good. Unfortunately,

this author adds that he thinks Vinland is joined to Africa! The fact that Leif says there "came no frost there" during the winter is obviously relative. We think there is frost in winter even at Cape Cod.

Karlsefni on his voyage in 1007 took sixty men and five women and all sorts of cattle, including a bull. He bore out to sea and came to Leif's booths. No one can believe a boat so loaded could be rowed to Boston from Greenland.

Many traces of stone houses and stone-protected tombs, such as the Norsemen built and which the Eskimo never did, have been reported on the Labrador Coast. In 1811 two Moravian missionaries describe such ruins on islands off Nain, and especially on Amitok Island, latitude 59° 30', which they visited on their way to Ungava Bay, another in Ryan's Bay in latitude 59°. No such houses have ever been found inside Ungava or Hudson's Bay. In 1831 another Moravian missionary asserts that the visits of the Norsemen to Labrador are proved by the stone houses on the islands. Another, Dr. Rink, in his "Traditions of the Eskimo," says that one Eskimo told him, "in old times the Innuits, or Greenlanders, and our ancestors lived together, but they fled for fear of our people who killed them—they were strong and formidable—huge blocks of stones which they only could move are still to be seen, and ruins of their houses, built of stone, chiefly on islands. These differ from the abodes of our people." Bishop Martin told us of his Eskimo recognizing pictures of Norse stone houses, which he had showed them, as resembling some which they had seen on the Coast. I myself have seen stone mounds, covered with slabs, on the top of a hill, which resembled a look-out. The Eskimo never build such.

Splendid though their physical courage and physique were, after all the Vikings were only human beings and predatory at that. So their settlements came to the usual end, sometime in the fourteenth century. Pestilence and Black Death reached even there. Fights among themselves and more especially with Labrador Eskimo coming via North Greenland, also reduced their numbers. Norway was itself in trouble and neglected them, and they had no wood to build ships, or even boats. The last ship which visited them sailed in 1406. Pope Nicholas V in 1448 and Pope Alexander VII in 1500 wrote sorrowfully of their "dear, lost children." The latter states, "No ship has called there [Greenland] for eighty years," and he sent an expedition to look for the survivors. None were ever found. Of the last tragic days of the great Greenland colonies nothing whatever is known.

V: THE PAGEANT OF THE BIG FOUR

The Kaleidoscope Shifts

"WRITERS forget that the bygone ages of the world were actually filled by living men . . . not by abstractions of men," said Carlyle.

In the long interval of over four hundred years which has elapsed while our curtain was down Vinland has not been forgotten. Iceland and the Pope took care of that. The Vikings had failed to settle the American continent "westward ho." The irony of fate had decided they should settle it via the East. The stepping-stones were to be England, France, and Spain. Thither the Norsemen went and saw and conquered, from the North Cape to the Pillars of Hercules. They laid siege to Paris, William

72

the Norseman captured England, and as early as the ninth century they held the whole Atlantic coast and the Rhine Valley. Here they transmitted their sea genius to those who, with increased facilities, eventually succeeded where their forbears had failed. Incidentally they gave England her "seamen of the sixteenth century," the men who fought the Armada, and her "admirals all"—the Drakes, the Raleighs, and the Grenvilles.

While they held the north Spanish Coast they taught the Basques to hunt the whales, which were there then in great abundance, and no small link in the final chain binding the Old World to the New. For, seeking cold waters, they retired towards the north and west, as the fishermen drove them farther and farther afield.

Myth and fable grow with the lapse of time, but it is easier to distinguish between fact and fiction of the sixteenth century than of the tenth, even if the "archives" are still largely oral. Thus any account of voyages will always have to be regarded in the light of neo-Sagas, with allowances for the points of view of the various "raconteurs." Naturally the best known records are those concerning the "Big Four"—Columbus, Cabot, Cortereal, and Cartier; for it must be remembered that each of these was under the direct ægis of a king, who had better facilities for preserving accurate accounts than even the gentry of that day, for the latter devoted more attention to splitting weasands than to writing and spelling, which were largely relegated to hired varlets or "shaveling priests." Their own records are, however, no reason for accepting as gospel that any of these four was the first to discover America, for that constituted a title

73

to possession. Without disparaging the great Columbus, only imagination pictures him as ignorant of the fact that if one sailed on long enough one must find land and not the edge of the world, off which the ship would drop into an unfathomable abyss. We have always had a sincere sympathy with his crew who, being ignorant of this fact, were anxious to turn back before it was too late.

Paolo Toscanelli, a learned man of science in Florence, had made and given to Columbus two charts, with many details whereby to steer; and another of his friends, Behaim, had actually made a globe. Columbus knew more of what Homer and Herodotus, Solon and Strabo, Pliny and Plato and Horace, and countless others through history, had written of "the land beyond the Pillars of Hercules across the Western Ocean" than any of us ordinary men even to-day, fables, though the stories of St. Brendan and his monks, and of the blessed isles they visited maybe, as well as those of Prince Medoc of Wales and the Welsh colony he founded in Virginia, not to speak of the endless stories of the lost continent of Atlantis. Columbus accepted them seriously and put them on his map. Pliny stated that forty-two days' sail westward from Africa lay a land called "Hesperides." Columbus sighted land forty days out from Palos. When later he discovered that Cuba was not Japan or Cathay, but an island, and remembered that Pliny claimed the Hesperides were guarded by islands, he certainly considered that these "fables" had a basis of fact.

At that time the Old World was seething with wars and troubles till the pressure reached the bursting point. The spirit of unrest at last gave birth to men who had the courage to invite fifteenth-century kings to invest their money in ventures even if they might not be literally "gilt-edged." It was persuading a Tudor Queen to sponsor a similar undertaking in these "new lands" that later cost Sir Walter Raleigh his head.

It so happened that at the time of Columbus, the Pope, who was then the king of kings in Europe, with his inside information had forestalled the westward gold rush by dividing the globe into two parts at the Treaty of Tordescillas, in which he gave half to Portugal and half to Spain. This "officially" delayed France and England to a considerable extent in the race that was frankly for gold, and not for geographical information or for the safety of heathen souls. Indeed the Centuriones, the great bankers of Genoa, with whom Columbus is said to have served, had just succeeded in establishing the gold standard. Everyone who could manage it was racing to the Indies and to Cathay, to stake out claims early and to discover shorter cuts to Eldorado.

From Abraham of Ur to Abraham Lincoln history has hung on human pegs. Such were the Big Four—Columbus, Cabot, Cortereal, and Cartier. Each possessed all the qualities of leadership, and the three latter each visited Labrador.

Without special permits no seamen were allowed to leave their country in the Middle Ages, they being considered too valuable assets of the State to risk losing them. Common seamen and fishermen were then regarded as mere pawns. However, just as even an edict of the Pope could not keep François and Cartier, or Henry VII and Cabot out of this international race, so no law could keep back fishermen, descendants of Vikings, from blazing the trail to their only possible pot of gold, which then meant just as it still does, following the fish wherever it went. A mere embargo forbidding voyages to the New World, we know was regularly observed in the breach by traders, even later on when the presence of men-of-war patrolling the other side meant confiscation of the ship, and death or the galleys for the men. Lescarbot says definitely that Norman, Breton, and Basque fishermen went to the Newlands before Cabot. It is quite possible. He also says that "becailles" is the Basque word for codfish, and that Newfoundland was called Bacalhaos before Cabot went there.

In 1565, Charles IX of France insisted to the Court of Spain that French fishermen had discovered North America over a hundred years previously, while as for the mainland of America, even John Cabot landed on it before Columbus; and Harrisse, whose life was devoted to these early voyages, says that the Portuguese went to America about 1464. A manuscript found in the Royal Library at Versailles says that Basques and Bretons followed the whales to Labrador. Perhaps there was some reason why Columbus employed a Basque pilot for his ship on his first famous voyage. Our fishermen sailed regularly as far as Iceland from the east coast of England round the north of Scotland, and even around the North Cape into the White Sea to catch codfish. That all these years after no records exist, means nothing at all.

This was the "secret de St. Malo" of the fifteenth century. Fish was gold in those days, and the fisheries of the Newlands in actual fact brought in to nations more

wealth than the gold mines of Golconda or the Indies.
An Act of Parliament of 1542 especially records "the
grate wealthe enjoyed by those using and exercizing the
crafts and feate of fishing." It claims also that "many
poure men and women had thereby their convenynt
lyving, to the increasing strengthe and wealthe of this
Realme." But nations, like individuals, had no incentive
to publish the latitude and longitude of their fishing
grounds. They preferred to preserve the "secret."

To the unmusical it is impossible to accept as a fact
that anyone really enjoys classical music. The dry-as-
dust historian, sitting in his library, must have found the
tales of the Vikings hard to swallow; just as the audience
of our drama find it difficult to digest the fact that deep-
sea fishermen are not even conscious of danger in a well-
found sailing boat, however small, especially in deep
waters. A fisherman can be so absorbed in his real quest
that when he strikes grounds as generous in codfish as
those of the New Lands proved to be, he will hardly
glance over the rail at an unexpected island, provided it
does not get up and hit him. An experience of nearly
half a century in small vessels amongst deep-sea fishermen both in the Atlantic and in the North Sea leaves the
author no escape from this conclusion.

The *Squirrel*, in which so long after Sir Humphrey
Gilbert, governor of the "New Lands," was crossing the
Atlantic back to England, was only ten tons burden—
not half the size of the fishing vessels which, year after
year, before the *Santa Maria* ever set sail, crossed each
year to the gold mines of the Grand Banks. True, fishermen then had no accurate navigating instruments, but

77

neither did the Big Four themselves possess them, and they might have cared about such trifles.

In 1887 we sailed our small boat to Iceland. It happened that none of us had ever seen that Coast, so that when land appeared on the horizon, seeing a fishing craft from Grimsby near us, we rowed aboard to ask what part of the Iceland coast it might be.

"Bless your soul, I don't know," said the skipper.

"Couldn't you show me on your chart?" I asked.

"I haven't got a chart, and couldn't read it if I had."

"How long have you been coming to Iceland to fish?"

"Just on forty years," replied the skipper, as he bit off another quid, and invited us to a mug o' tea and a yarn in the cabin.

Columbus himself recorded that in 1484 he met in Portugal a Madeira seaman who swore he saw land every year out to the West.

Alas, as fish was the only gold to fishermen of the fifteenth century, so the flowing bowl was their only pleasure. It followed inevitably that the secret of St. Malo was a more open one than the skippers, returning each year with fat cargoes of Bacalhao, or cod, from Labrador and Newfoundland, to Dieppe, Honfleur, St. Malo, and other Breton and Norman ports, cared to admit when they too were not "in their cups." It helps us to understand the viewpoints of the fishermen of those days, to remember that in 1483, on the 8th of July, the King, Louis XI, thinking that he was suffering from leprosy, dispatched two ships from Honfleur to the coast of Africa, with three hundred men. They towed a barge in which to collect and bring back turtles' blood, as the

King had been told that if he bathed in it he would be cured of his leprosy. When nine years later, Columbus, the first of the Big Four, let the cat out of the bag, there being no longer any possibility of secrecy, the best alternative was to provide some method of registering those who went across the western seas. It is suggestive that as early as the year 1500 many fishing vessels of forty to a hundred tons burden are actually on record as having sailed from that one port of Honfleur.

The English flair for burning French seaports has been no small handicap to the historian. He must therefore look for sidelights to odd references in old legal or ecclesiastical documents, which had a better chance of escape than town archives. Thus in 1624 the Comte de Montmorency brought suit against the "Habitants" of St. Jean de Luz, concerning their right to trade with Terre Neuve. It was accepted as evidence that seamen of that port had discovered Terre Neuve three hundred years previous to that date. In 1560 there were still records of Basques in Newfoundland. Basque tiles were discovered some years ago in Red Bay Harbour, Labrador, which on the oldest maps was styled "Hable de Baleine." Red Bay fishermen of only a generation ago used to shoe their komatiks with the jaw-bones of whales, which they dredged up from the bottom of the harbour. Notwithstanding Ibáñez and others, there is little doubt that Christopher Columbus and John Cabot were both born in Genoa, about 1450. As both were interested in navigation and schools were scarce, they may possibly have met. Both being lovers of adventure, they must have been equally attracted by the same sea tales of Venetian,

Greek, Breton, and Basque heroes, just as Jewish boys enjoyed the stories of Abraham setting out for an un- known Land of Promise, or of Moses and his people ven- turing forth in search of a land "flowing with milk and honey." Like Columbus, Cabot went first to Spain, as did many other unrecorded adventurers. A whole suburb of Dieppe, called Le Pollet, is of Venetian origin, and its fishermen to-day still have distinctive dress and customs.

As a young man Cabot had gone to Venice, where he married. While on a business trip from Venice to Mecca he saw the caravans of the Emperor of Cathay, bringing gems and spices from the East. He knew of Galileo's teaching the world was a globe, and probably also that in 1410 a Cardinal (D'Arthe) had written that the earth was spherical. He was familiar with Marco Polo's ac- count of the sea "which lay to the East of the Great Khan's dominions." He may even have talked it over in Spain with Columbus, where he, too, went first to arouse interest in sending out an expedition into the unknown West. As he was unsuccessful, he left for London and Bristol, where the venturous West Country men already had a regular, rather less than more legitimate, trade with Iceland. Thence they brought back not only good stockfish, but stories of Vinland the Good, and occasion- ally a little plunder. That Cabot made a voyage there in one of these vessels was to be expected, and Columbus also claimed to have sailed a hundred leagues beyond Tile (Iceland) in 1477, and that the tide rose there twenty-six feet. Possibly he also went from Bristol. Bris- tol customs records of the reign of Henry VI give "Thomas Rowley from Iceland with fish," and "Barque

St. John the Evangelist on June 12th." *Ledger* of Edward IV, 1461, "John Fowey with fish." "Master Hugh Davy and two more with fish," all from Iceland—and so through the years.

After 1493, when the story of Columbus' discoveries leaked out, his Excellency, M. de Ayala, Ambassador of Spain to England, was watching Bristol as a cat does a mouse, and was writing home to Spain about the Bristol voyages. Unless more was then known about land across the ocean than we have records of, no one could have induced a Bristol timber merchant and the King of England to venture this money on a voyage to the west.

The Archives of Bristol state, "This year, 1497, on St. John the Baptist's day, the land of America was found by the merchants of Bristow, in a shippe of Bristow called the *Matthew*, the which departed from the port of Bristowe the second day of May and came home again the 6th of August next following."

This same little *Matthew* was still trading with Iceland in 1504. A letter of August 23, 1497, from Lorenzo Pasquaglio to his brother in Venice, written from London, describes Cabot's discovery of land seven hundred leagues to the west, and says "His name is Zuam Talbot and he is called the great admiral. He dresses in silk and the King has promised him ten armed ships and prisoners for crews."

On December 13, 1497, another record reads of a grant "To our well beloved Jean Calbot, annuitie of twenty pounds sterling from the subsidies of the Port of Bristowe."

Another record is "On the Feast of the Annunciation,

81

Henry VIIth, King of England and Fraunce, hath given and graunted to John Caboote XXli yerely during oure pleasur." Again the Bristol Chronicle of Kings of England reads "Feb. 13, 1498, graunte to John Kabboto, Venecian, to take shippes, which departed from the west country in the begynnying of somer, but to this present moneth came never knowledge of their exployt."

Cabot took with him his "gracious letters patentes" obtained in response to his petition. "To the Kyng our souvereigne Lord, Please it your highness of your most noble and Habundant grace, to grant unto John Cabotte, Citizen of Venes, Lewes, Sebastyan and Sancto, his sonnys, your gracious letters patent under your grate seale in due form to be made, according to the tenour hereafter ensuying. And they shall during their lyves pray to God for the prosperous continuance of your most noble and royall astate long to enduer."

The *Matthew* carried a crew of eighteen men, the right to fly the British flag, and to occupy any such places as they were able to conquer. The venture was to be at Cabot's own proper costs and charges, and he was bound to pay the King twenty per cent of all proceeds, in return for the "gracious letters patent."

After fifty-two days' sail he dropped anchor on the other side. We sailed out in seventeen days in a boat the same size; and he would have made the voyage in twenty had he not listened to his pilot who, thinking that Europe was joined by land to the country they sought, insisted on going by way of Cape Farewell in Greenland to keep the land aboard. The exact spot of Cabot's landing is not known.

The first land we sighted after calling at St. John's was a large, lofty island, some five miles from the shore, the land inside falling away in both directions, exactly as Cabot describes. The island is called Round Hill Island, and the land is called Domino Head, on which now stands a lighthouse. It is almost exactly the latitude of Bristol. Sailing as Cabot did first, to the north from Ireland and then westward to Cape Farewell, and thence to the mainland of America, the voyage should occupy about the time that he actually took. Our opinion is that Round Hill Island off Labrador was his first landfall on the western side of the Atlantic. Newfoundland thinks it was Cape Bonavista. Nova Scotians think it was Cape Breton. Nobody can be certain. It certainly was not the Back Bay of Boston.

The *Matthew* was back in Bristol by August 8th, so it is extremely unlikely that he got even as far as Cape Breton. Verrazzano, who sailed from France in 1523 "to look for lands between those found by Cabot and Columbus," and Cortereal, who sailed from Portugal, only twelve years after Cabot, both suggest that Cabot landed about latitude 50°N. The statement that "tides were slacker than in England" best fits the Labrador landing. As for longitude, Champlain a hundred years later, still with only an astrolabe to help him, found correct latitudes but complained, "God seems to have forbidden man any way to find a longitude."

Cortereal states that in Hamilton Inlet he found an old Venetian sword, some gold ear-rings, and other "small truck" which Cabot had very probably traded with the Indians in a brave effort to bring something back to the king, to justify the "gracious letters patent." Robert Fabyan states that Cabot brought to the king three savages taken in "the Terre Neuve." They were "clothed in Beastes skins and did eat raw flesh, but they could not speake to anyone." Two years later he met them in Westminster, but still "they spake not a word." Eskimo means "raw meat eater." No Eskimo lived near Cape Bonavista.

In an amusing letter written by the astute Spanish Ambassador to his master in July, 1498, he tells him that he has "gotten the mappe monde of the Genoese" (Cabot), whom he accuses of making "a false mappe" in order to pretend that he was not stealing the land of the Spanish king.

On May 24, 1498, Cabot sailed once more "from Bristowe" with five ships and three hundred men, including Bristol and Icelandic merchantmen, who took "goodes and sleight merchandise," for though on the previous voyage they had seen but a few "raw meat eaters," as one would expect in Labrador, they had seen also "white bears, and stagges farre larger than ours," and had found snares for catching game and needles for making nets, suggesting possibly a fur trade. Meanwhile the Spanish Ambassador wrote, "news has been received of the five ships. The one in which was Brother Buil put into Ireland because of a great storm." In a Customs Roll for the Port of Bristol, for the years 1496 to 1499, found in Westminster Abbey, is the following entry, which reads in English, "To Johe Calvot was paid twenty pounds for a promissory note, three of which had been granted to him in February, 1498." It was also recorded that he had been paid ten pounds in August, being designated as "him that found the New Lands." There is no more authentic history of John Cabot.

There is a story of the second voyage that this time he hit the east coast of Greenland first, sailed north along it thinking to find the way around it to Cathay, and still believing Davis Straits to be only a bay. When his crew refused to go farther north because of the ice, he went south around Cape Farewell. He then sailed all along the Labrador Coast, and though he entered Fox Channel and was at last on the right way, the ice prevented him finding the Northwest Passage. Sebastian claimed to have made later just such a voyage, but the accepted authority on the Cabots says that Sebastian's word was not worthy of credence. The statement that John Cabot drew his pension of twenty pounds in 1499 would suggest that he returned from the second voyage, but the Bristol date 1499 was very possibly our 1498.

Cabot supports the fishermen's stories by asserting that the codfish "sumtymes stayed his shippes." The real road to Cathay was opened this same year by Vasco de Gama, who doubled the Cape of Good Hope.

Amongst those who were entering the race at this time was the Governor of the Azores. These islands were a great rendezvous for every variety of sailor of that day, including pirates and privateers, to say nothing of fishermen on their way home. Their yarns of a land to the west were corroborated by the legend that two dead bodies of Indians had once been washed ashore on those islands—much like the story in Roman days that the King of the Batavi had presented to the Consul Metellus two live Indian slaves who had drifted across the westward ocean and landed on the coast of the Belgae. More certain, however, was the fact that pieces of wood, evidently carved by men, and large cut bamboos, had been picked up around the rocks, amongst the débris which was always drifting there from the west.

The son of the Governor, Gaspar Cortereal, went over to see King Emmanuel at Lisbon, who at once sent him out on a western voyage to look for a short way to Portugal's half of the globe. That he went and returned is certain, but nothing whatever is known of this, the first voyage of Cortereal. Amongst other Azoreans hurrying over from Terceira, their chief island, was a lavrador, or farmer, João Fernandez. He was seeking to get charge of an expedition of his own, but, having no "pull" or money, when he met John Cabot in Lisbon he immediately signed on as pilot for him.

On his successful return with Cabot, his stock had so gone up that he found no difficulty in interesting this time the new king, Manoel, though it was to Gaspar Cortereal, who had greater social standing, the "letters patent" were granted. There is little doubt that the king ordered them to follow Cabot's route, and claim Bacalhaos and Labrador, and all that Cabot had found, as part of the legitimate property of Portugal. This is exactly what they tried to do.

They sailed in the spring of 1501. They saw high land over heavy ice fields, but were never able to get in near enough to land. Some authorities have claimed that this was Labrador, but an experience of so many years on that Coast convinces me that this could not be true of the whole length of the Labrador Coast in the month of June, whereas it is the normal condition for East Greenland at that time of year, and that would be following Cabot's footsteps. We believe that Cortereal hit the wrong side of Cape Farewell, that he explored only the ice-bound East Greenland coast, which was called "Labrador" presumably after Joao "the Lavrador." Anyhow, for many years Greenland was called on all the maps of that period "Terra Labradore."

The Portuguese urge, however, was so strong that Cortereal started on another voyage the following May. This time he evidently went farther south, and all that is known of this voyage answers well to the description of southern Labrador, which for many years appeared on the maps as Terra Corterealis. There were "plenty of tall trees for masts." We ourselves have seen them cut up to eighty feet long, at Adlavik Bay on the middle Labrador coast. He describes it as adjacent to the land he had seen the year before, and it is only five hundred miles distant. In the north are "precipitous and barren cliffs, with gullies full of snow all the year round and icebergs close to the shore." These characteristics would naturally suggest to Cortereal that the way to the "land of spices" must be farther south; for till eighty years later, when Davis discovered the Straits which bear his name, everyone thought that Greenland was joined to Labrador and that Davis Straits were nothing but a great bay. Cortereal must have been conscious that King Manoel had not been too pleased with his having had no results to show for his first voyage, so he sailed south, all along the Labrador coast, exactly as Leif had done.

Among the many bays that it is said he explored, it is most probable that he went up the alluring Sandwich Bay, or Hamilton Inlet, in either of which he could have captured the ship-load of either Indians or Eskimo which he placed "below hatches" together with a number of samples of spars from the forests, and then sent them home as "douceurs" in two of his three ships. Sixty Indians arrived alive and proved to be most excellent slaves. The king was delighted. It was just what he wanted. He was gracious enough to say that a voyage which could bring timber to Portugal in a month was well worth while and that he realized how valuable the new country would be, as African natives were getting so wary that it was becoming quite difficult to catch them!

Columbus had done exactly this same thing, trying to save his face when his stories of actual gold failed to materialize. He started a slave traffic to Spain.

Cortereal explored the Gilbert and Alexis rivers, and Hawke Bay, a lovely forty-mile inlet. From this inlet we met a trapper one day bringing out nine black bear skins which he had shot in one day. The rich fur prospects of Labrador which Cortereal reported must have added greatly to the satisfaction of King Manoel. But alas for Cortereal, he and his ship were never heard of again. One name, Cape Freels, was originally Cape Frey Louis, which was the name of Cortereal's chaplain. It is now affixed to a cape two hundred miles south of the Straits of Belle Isle. The Straits of Belle Isle were also thought to be a bay until Cartier's voyage in 1534. As Cabot only gave names like St. John and St. Mark, it is quite likely that Cortereal reached as far south as that extraordinarily dangerous region of Cape Freels—far the most perilous on all those coasts, since hidden shoals there run out for many miles from the land.

Manoel did his best. He sent out Miguel, the brother of Cortereal, with three ships to look for the lost captain, on whose family he conferred the whole of South Labrador. Miguel unquestionably crossed farther south, his ships rendezvousing somewhere in Newfoundland. This was probably in Green Bay, near Cape Freels. The ships separated to look for the missing Gaspar, Miguel going north. The other two vessels met at the rendezvous in the fall, but Miguel Cortereal was never heard of again. We cannot but remember that he was searching the Labrador bays for his brother, and that Indians never forget a good turn—or an evil one.

France was slow in entering the international competition, but about this time a fisherman of St. Malo, called Nicholas, talking to another whose name was Jacques Cartier, told him of the silver and gold which he had seen on his last fishing voyage to the New Lands. Cartier somehow let the secret out to the Bishop of Lisieux. Possibly Nicholas also had confessed his sins in going to the New Lands without permission. It happened at the time also that King François made a pilgrimage to the famous monastery of Mont St. Michel, of which the Bishop of Lisieux was also the abbé. One can imagine in some after-dinner conversations with the king, the abbé relating the fishermen's stories. The king was interested immediately and wished to send out an expedition. Even he, however, had to get permission

89

from the Pope, who had already given away the countries.

The bishop's cousin, as it happened, was Cardinal de' Medici, who had the ear of the Pope, and he secured for François the necessary permission. The kings of Portugal and Spain protested violently, but Philippe de Chabot, Lord High Admiral of France, encouraged François to stick to his guns, with the result that the King gave Jacques Cartier command of an expedition. That a king and an admiral should in those days even listen to a fisherman shows that they had little doubt about the familiarity of the Breton fishermen with the land across the Atlantic.

François wrote to the Cardinal of Toledo, as a salve to his conscience, "the sun shines for me as well as for the rest, and I should like to see the will of Father Adam excluding me from my share of the earth."

The other fishermen of St. Malo did everything they could to make it impossible for Cartier to find either men or ships. They did not want their private preserves poached upon. The Procurator of the Courts, however, ordered that no ship should leave until Cartier had got all he wanted, "otherwise the will and undertaking of the said Lord François will be frustrated." The result was that Jacques Cartier left St. Malo on the 20th of April, 1524, with two ships, with the royal commission in his pocket to explore all districts beyond the fishing grounds and "to occupy all regions hitherto unknown to Christians." His send-off must have been magnificent. A great Service was held in the Church, all the bells were ringing and banners flying, and the mitred Bishop led the procession to the ships when the Captain finally went aboard.

François was out for gain. He paid the expenses and he expected the profits. The race he entered was against three other sporting kings, and he managed to secure a fair share of the prize.

Fortunately, the original manuscript of this voyage has been preserved. Cartier reached land on the twentieth day out, and sighting the great cape of Bonavista, ran into the close-by harbour of Catalina. Sailing north from there he passed by the famous "Funk" Islands, which he called appropriately the Isles des Oiseaux. They were one of the large rookeries for the auks, puffins, petrels, and gulls, which have all through the centuries sought refuge in the Far North. Countless numbers of these birds still breed in Labrador. Here on these low, flat, dangerous islands, far from land, the Great Auk made his last stand. It was on this very spot that in 1913 our expedition camped for a week, but only succeeded in digging up the bones of one pathetic bird. In Cartier's time the birds were so numerous that "unless a man did see them, he would consider it incredible, for albeit that they are so numerous, they seem to have been brought there and sowed for the nonce. Yet there are a hundredfold as many hovering about."

Cartier's log shows that "in less than half an hour we filled two boats, so that besides those we did eat fresh, each boat did powder or salt six barrels of them." He goes on, "our men found a bear there as great as any cow and as white as any swan which on seeing us did leap into the sea. We did later meet her swimming to the land as quick as we could sail. We pursued her in our boat, and by main strength took her, whose flesh was as good to be eaten as the flesh of a calf two years old."

Passing the Isle of Demons, they were prevented by ice from getting into Château Bay, and returned to Carpunt on the south side of the Straits of Belle Isle, where they waited for a couple of days while the ice moved offshore. Then they returned to Château, so called because of the great, flat-topped, sombre outcrop of basalt, closely resembling a mediaeval castle.

The horror of the unknown is still very great among seamen, and Devil's Coves and Hell's Mouths are not uncommon in the nomenclature of this coast. One night in a motor boat, which had broken down, we were drifting towards the cliffs close to Carpunt, called "Ha Ha" because of the devils' laughter said to be heard there. On seeing the light of a passing fishing vessel, we raised a white light on a pole and swung it violently as a signal for help. The schooner at once tacked away from us. We coo-eed as loudly as we could to attract their attention, but they would not come back. Next day it happened that we caught them up, and going aboard I asked the skipper why he had so deliberately deserted us. "Deserted you!" he exclaimed. "Why, we thought it was just one of them devils luring us to the rocks."

Cartier's "Isle of Demons" did then deserve the name. Endless wrecks have taken place there, and though it is ten miles long, it is treeless and without one safe harbour anywhere. However, it is now called Belle Isle, and

THE BISHOP'S MITRE

THE CANYON OF THE GRAND FALLS

is a splendid place for cod fishing, with a lighthouse at each end, and a large foghorn.

We sometimes forget that the land road to the domains of the Great Khan had practically been closed at the opening of the fifteenth century, owing to the conquests of the Turks, so that an all-sea route was a matter of immense importance, especially to France, as she had no possessions in the west. No voyage shows so careful a search for the sea-route to Cathay as does this of Cartier's. He visited every inlet on the north shore of the Gulf of St. Lawrence, and when a little later his boats went up the Saguenay River, he was almost as near to finding what he really looked for as was Columbus on his last voyage, when he landed on the Panama coast almost within sight of the Pacific. For the Hudson's Bay Company once had a route up the Saguenay, and then a few miles' portage to a river that brought them into Hudson's Bay, out of which goes the Northwest Passage.

Cartier called at Red Bay, at Blanc Sablon, which, like Carpunt, had been named for a little Breton village, evidently by fishermen. Farther along the Labrador coast he encountered many natives, men of immense size and strength, but untamed and savage. They used birchbark canoes and killed many seals. They must have been Montagnais Indians, whose numerous battles with the Eskimo were largely due to their poaching of those very animals.

At Baie d'Islettes, or Bradore Bay, he found, as he would to-day, many fishermen. Thirty miles farther west he anchored at Brest, in the mouth of St. Paul's River, at that time the easternmost rendezvous for fishermen from across the seas. "Here, being a Saint's day, we did say High Mass." This was entirely a Catholic expedition, for Cartier considered Huguenots as "imitators of Mahomet and sons of the devil." While anchored at Brest, Cartier rowed all along the coast to St. Augustine Bay. His detailed description of this journey makes it easy for us to recognize each place he visited.

One tiny village still bears his name, though now called Shecatica, a corruption of Jacques Cartier.

His conclusions about this journey were "that the harbours are excellent, but the land is barren and fit only for wild beasts. There is not a cartload of earth in the whole country. This must be the land which God gave to Cain." Obviously he did not enter the rivermouth, for Alonzo de Santa Cruz, writing in 1541, says there are many fine waters and the land has a pleasant aspect because of many trees.

From there Cartier cruised the West Coast of Newfoundland, entering the Bay of Islands. Off Cape St. George he describes the fishery as "the best possible in the world. In less than an hour we caught more than a hundred codfish." He then went round Prince Edward's Island and all along the South Shore of the Gulf as far as Gaspé, where the Huron Indians gave him a royal welcome. He presented them with a great many gifts, and in return for their hospitality he set up a great cross thirty feet high, which somehow he made them understand was sacred. On it was a big fleur-de-lis, which claimed all of his hosts' land for François I, "thereby laying the foundations of the French possessions in Canada."

94

By giving red caps and bright-coloured clothing and copper chains for ornaments to two of the chief's sons, · he persuaded them to go back with him to France. Worried by the cross, just before sailing the chief reminded Cartier that the land belonged to the Indians. Cartier assured him the cross was only a guiding mark for their return.

Then he returned by way of Brest and the Straits of Belle Isle. He made a quick voyage for those days—only eighteen days from the mouth of the Straits to St. Malo. We have sailed the same in twelve and a half.

History has never done justice to Jacques Cartier. His first voyage, from every point of view, was far the finest of any made by the Big Four. It is one of the epic sea stories of the world. A simple and very devout man, his truthful, sailor-like report fully justified the great confidence in a fisherman of any King or Admiral. In four months he had covered four thousand miles of open Atlantic in his clumsy boat. He had sailed some two thousand miles around the Gulf of St. Lawrence in spite of its strong currents, fogs, and short seas, so trying to small sailing boats. He had explored almost all the islands, including the Isle of Demons. He had cruised round Anticosti, an island as large as Wales, visited the Magdalen and Prince Edward Islands, the West Coast of Newfoundland, and almost all the harbours on the "North Shore"; even rowing many miles to make sure of not missing any opening that might lead to Cathay, the most single-hearted search for the Northwest Passage ever made. All this he had done without a chart. Yet he did not lose one ship, or one man, or kill one Indian or Eskimo.

To a man who has himself sailed most of this in a small boat also, it seems quite impossible to believe he had never been there before, as a fisherman. On his return he was created Captain and Pilot of the King, and the following May he left again with three ships. This time they had the most adverse gales in the Atlantic, "as much as ever shippes that went to sea had ever suffered." But so good were his selected seamen, so well seen to was the tackle of his ships, and so wisely had he provided duplicate ocean charts that all his fleet safely rendezvoused at Carpunt. Thence they pushed on without any delay, searching again the whole of the Labrador shore of the Gulf, much of it twice, to avoid possible mistakes.

At Quebec, Donnacona, the King of the Algonquins, received Cartier with open arms, the two Indians whom he had brought back safely from France proving very useful as interpreters. They however betrayed Cartier's real intentions, so that naturally the King did all he could to prevent him from going farther up the river. "Medicine men" dressed as devils staged on the shore a drama foreshadowing certain disaster if he did so. The reputation of the savage Iroquois whose villages lay a hundred and fifty miles upstream was bad. The sand bars actually did prove insuperable. But Cartier, leaving his last ship at Lake St. Peter, about halfway up, pushed on in his boats, and was able to make friends with these supposedly most irreconcilable of all savages. Indeed at first they regarded the Frenchmen in

96

their specially gay dresses as gods, and brought their sick to be touched by them.

The great mountain towering over the Iroquois settlement he called "Mount Royal"; for from its top he saw the vast lands stretching along the St. Lawrence and Ottawa River valleys, "the fairest and best that can possibly be seen."

He saw also the Rapids, which once for all put a quietus on the St. Lawrence River as a possible all-sea route to Cathay.

From an Indian, touching a silver chain and a gilded dagger handle and pointing up the Ottawa River, Cartier understood that gold and silver were to be found there, and in this both they and he were perfectly correct, in spite of the many detractors in France.

Cartier's brand of religious faith did not prevent him, after giving the Indians many presents, from again erecting a large cross with a shield and three fleur-de-lis in the middle, claiming their whole country for France. When he again reached Quebec it was too late to return home, and his ships' crews had already built a strong fort on the shore, for they had discovered that the Indians, incited by one interpreter, were planning to destroy them. During the winter, scurvy killed some Indians and many of the French. Cartier fortunately learned from the second of the two interpreters that the leaves of a certain tree cured the disease. Twenty-five of his men were already dead, and all the rest were sick and hopeless. When, after swallowing a decoction made from the leaves and bark of an entire spruce tree they all got

97

well in eight days, Cartier decided it was a miracle for their special benefit.

As the ice broke up, immense numbers of obviously hostile Indians gathered around the ships. Having himself only men enough left to man two ships, Cartier invited King Donnacona and the two Indian interpreters to a feast on board. There he immediately seized them. He then persuaded the King to show himself on deck and to tell the people that he would soon be back. On May 15, 1536, he got out of the ice and dropped down the river, followed by endless canoes still in vain hoping to effect a rescue. With his usual enterprise he returned to St. Malo by an entirely new route, south of Newfoundland.

Cartier's reasonable reports of the fertility of the new country, the rich furs which he brought back, and the suggestion of mines, again satisfied the French King. They were unlike the extravagant claims of Columbus, and were no undue propaganda, merely to lure impoverished chevaliers to hurry west. The reports said that the fields were full of wild corn and peas, "as thick and rank and fair as any that can be seen in Brittany. There is also great store of gooseberries, strawberries and roses, with other very sweet and pleasant herbs." Of the islands Cartier claimed, "they are full of fair trees, goodly meadows and plentiful wild fruit, while the weather in summer there is hot." So the King decided on a third expedition, with a view to the foundation of permanent settlements, which were to be the forerunners of the famous Acadia, the Land of Evangeline and of New France.

Carlos V, King of Spain, had meanwhile gone to war with France, and so greatly delayed things. When the peace of Tours, 1538, made it obvious that he could not forcibly prevent François from sending a third expedition, he used, as in England, his wily ambassador as a spy, persuading the King at least not to put Cartier in charge of it. He used the plausible argument that much of the failure of Columbus' expeditions was caused by the Grandees in his company who, once they were away from Spain, flung in Columbus' face the fact of his humble birth, and flatly refused to accept his orders. So François selected the Sieur de Roberval for chief command, a lordling who had wasted his living, and whose head had been so turned by flattery that François called him "the little King of Picardy." To encourage him to go, the King conferred on him the titles of Lord of Norumbega, Viceroy of New France, Lord of Hochelaga, of Saguenay, of Terre Neuve, of Carpunt, of Belle Isle, of Labrador, of Baie St. Lawrence, and of Bacalhaos, and gave him forty-five thousand livres and many privileges.

As a first result there was much time lost in preparation. The King had promised to send a hundred "volunteers" for the new colony, but all that were procurable were convicts lying in jails under death sentences, and of these he was not allowed to take heretics, traitors, or counterfeiters. Those men, chained together, marched into St. Malo. A girl of eighteen, voluntarily chained to her lover, completed the bargain. But the expedition was delayed all winter, and not till May, 1541, did Cartier get away with his five ships, and then without Roberval.

The ships were scattered by gales on their way out;

but again all met at the old rendezvous of Carpunt (Quirpon). The Sieur de Norumbega was not amongst the number. It subsequently appeared that he had returned to France. Cartier sailed right on to Quebec and though King Donnacona and the interpreters had died in France, he was cordially received by the grateful successor in office. The crews, however, at once built a strong fort and sowed gardens, while he with two boats pushed up again to Montreal.

He very soon discovered that the Iroquois also were only waiting for a chance to attack him, so he dropped hastily down the river and rejoined his ships. After his unusual way of taking counsel with his captains and men, he decided to stay for the winter, in spite of the unfriendly natives.

Again many men died of scurvy, and in the spring of 1542, terribly discouraged, he started home, calling at St. John's, Newfoundland, on his way. To his amazement he found in the harbour five French vessels under Roberval, on his way out as Governor, with two hundred men and women settlers. In spite of his order to Cartier to turn back, that intrepid seaman and his vessels slipped out in the night without saying good-bye. He carried with him what he thought were gold and diamonds, found near Quebec, but the latter turned out to be crystals, and the former to be low-grade gold and copper; so that "Canadian diamonds" became a byword in France.

A Labrador fog hangs over the end of these records. Report says that as Roberval proceeded on his way north a young chevalier was found to have made overtures to the Lady Marguerite, Roberval's niece, so while passing Belle Isle, the gloomy "Isle of Demons," Roberval landed the girl and her nurse with a few provisions. The chevalier, jumping overboard at the last moment, managed to land through the surf, carrying with him two guns and some ammunition. A child was born and died on Belle Isle, as did the nurse and the chevalier, "of persecution by devils," so the saying went. Two years later the girl, quite mad, and therefore of course also said to be "possessed by a devil," was picked up and carried back to France by a Breton fisherman.

Roberval's management of New France was no more of a success than his management of his niece, and the synonym "Land of Cain" became in France no longer limited to the Labrador Coast. Quarrelling, crime, and scurvy lessened their numbers. Two years later Roberval and his men were starving. So it came about that by the irony of fate in 1545 Cartier fitted out a last expedition to go to his rescue. Cartier's own absolute genuineness held the King's friendship to the last, and he was awarded a small pension with the title of Seigneur de Limoilin, the village in which he lived. There he died in peace twelve years later.

VI: THE PAGEANT OF THE FRENCH

"Le coq se trouve dans le nouveau monde"

FOR two hundred and forty years, from the time
Cartier planted his fleur-de-lis at Gaspé until the
Treaty of Paris in 1763 when the French finally handed
over all their possessions in Canada to England as a
result of the victories of Wolfe, the destinies of Labrador lay in the hands of France. During the first seventy
years only a few French settlements, mostly fishing stations, grew up on "the Labrador" as far north as Hamilton Inlet; though some of their most famous explorers
cruised the whole length of the coast into Hudson's Bay.
The trouble was that all "New Lands" were expected to
fling ready-made bars of gold at the first newcomer,

without working for them, and Labrador was a "workman's land."

During the two centuries and over of French occupation, England and Spain especially were constantly making any regular policy she undertook impossible on the seas, as on the Labrador Coast. France, as one answer, early armed the natives—a wise policy only if she was anxious to hasten their extermination. The decline of both the Indians and the Eskimo soon began, helped by habits and diseases contributed by civilization.

Most people have forgotten to-day how anxiously at first the Pilgrims in New England awaited supplies of food from the Old Country; and that the early Californian settlers must have died of starvation if food had not been sent to them from Mexico, while who of us even remembers that what induced a Scotch King to sign the *Mayflower's* Charter to sail to America was not possible gold mines, much less religious freedom, but just Labrador's naturally abundant wealth, viz., "fish." When the application from Leyden for permission for the Pilgrims to go to America was handed to King James, that canny Scotchman asked simply "Why? What profit hath it?" "Fishing, Sire," was the improvised reply. "By God's soul, 'tis an honest calling," he answered. " 'Twas that of the Apostles." And he forthwith signed the charter. Later on, the Pilgrims actually sent home a cargo of dried fish.

That England had not previously profited as she might have done from Cabot's discoveries was due largely to King Henry the Eighth's troubles at home. That France was never left alone to "dig herself in" had

103

much to do with her failure in the New World. In Europe, as in Canada, of which Labrador is but an extension, even their greatest solons never dreamed that "Nova Francia" could one day become, as Canada has, the richest precious metal producing country and one of the greatest timber and agricultural lands in the whole world, besides becoming the home of unquestionably one of the finest people the world has seen. Want of faith and the get-rich-quick spirit was why the New World's silver, nickel, copper, and aluminum, to say nothing of its radioactive rocks, have had to wait so many years for exploitation.

Actually it was "fish," not gold, that kept up the interest of France in the northern parts of the New World. This was the secret of St. Malo, and as soon as voyages became lawful it was recorded that as early as 1504 Dieppois had fish stages in Newfoundland. In the same year an Honfleur man published a chart of Terre Neuve and Labrador, where everywhere small settlements grew up. A Dieppe fisherman founded Brest at the mouth of St. Paul's River. Alas, all the Dieppe annals were burned by the English in 1584. As early as Cartier's second voyage, he met on the Labrador Coast a large Breton fishing boat looking for the town of Brest. From 1541 to 1545 no less than sixty Normandy fishing vessels cleared annually for the "fisheries of the Newlands." Then France was again at war, and until 1560 none are on record as going; but from 1560 to the end of the century, when France again made a serious effort to colonize Canada, French fishing vessels were very numerous, both on the coast of "Terre Neuve" and in the "Grand Bay," or Gulf of St. Lawrence.

At first the westernmost rendezvous for the fishermen was at this Labrador "Brest"—at the zenith of its existence a centre for a couple of thousand people in the summer-time. It eventually fell into disuse as it became safer to settle farther west, and Tadousac, in the mouth of the Saguenay River, partially took its place. The fact that no remains of the wooden houses of Brest exist to-day means nothing. No one, unless he had witnessed it, could believe how rapidly a wooden settlement in Labrador can disappear. Once a place is deserted, houses are not left standing long; every bit goes for fuel for others. Close to the site of old Brest is the Isle de Bois. No one could now believe that it ever deserved its name of "Woody Island," for not even a tree root remains on it to-day; yet forty years ago, when we first visited it, there were important Jersey fishing "rooms" there. The owner was a merchant, a magistrate, and Lloyd's surveyor for the Coast. These "rooms" were abandoned only quite recently. Yet no one looking at it to-day could believe that it had ever been inhabited.

There is therefore nothing strange that on maps after 1626 the name of Brest disappears, though in a map of Lavesour, published in 1601, Brest is marked in large red letters and correctly placed just west of Blanc Sablon. Again in a map of 1625 by John Geratti, Brest is once more correctly marked; while a map published by this same man in 1634 marks Terre Neuve, but fails to mention Brest, doubtless because by that time he had heard of its decline and not because the town had never existed. In 1660 a map published in Amsterdam calls the old harbour "Porte de Quartier"—while the town of St. John's is not even alluded to; but St. John's existed all the same!

On a map of Nova Francia, brought out in 1597, Brest is marked larger than Quebec, quite as we should expect for that date, and a picture of a fortress is drawn beside it. Labrador is called Terra Corterealis on this map, and Anticosti Isle de l'Assumption. Another map of the year 1626, called America, has those known parts in that unknown world described and enlarged. On this again, Brest is placed in exactly the right spot.

Traditional evidence has its value. Lewes Robert's Merchants Map of Commerce, printed in London in 1639, states about this South Labrador Coast, then again styled "Terra Corterealis," that "on the south thereof runs that famous river of Caneda, rising out of the hill Ombredo, running nine hundred miles. The chief Towne thereof is Brest, Cabomarsa, and others of little note." Perhaps this does sound like a page of "Gulliver's Travels"; but the St. Lawrence is a famous river of Canada. It does run south of Terra Corterealis. It is nine hundred miles from Battle Harbour to Montreal, and the river is navigable for eight hundred to Quebec. There is a mountain called Cabrado on the Saguenay River, which river was doubtless thought to be the source of the St. Lawrence in that day.

The site of old Brest is still the most alluring region for small boat work on the south coast, exactly as Cartier found it. For fifty miles of the shore there are networks of channels, which might, after uniting in the

"Great Square" of Cumberland, well be an entrance to a Northwest Passage.

Samuel Robertson, a man born and bred close to old Brest, whose highly respectable descendants still live "in this fringe" at Tabatier, has been branded as a "first-class liar," because in lecturing before the Royal Society of Canada in 1843 he asserted that Brest had, besides stores and other buildings, two hundred houses and a thousand inhabitants. He mixes the location with that of a De Courtemanche at Bradore which also became later a large settlement. He is discredited also for giving De Courtemanche the title of Seigneur, and calling "1704" the seventeenth century. Such mistakes a Labradorman beyond the reach of libraries might easily make, and yet know more about Brest than we do, almost a hundred years later.

Augustin Legardeur, Seigneur de Courtemanche, did come to Labrador in 1704. He was son-in-law to a wealthy tanner called Charest. Only very recently in the courts of France has a separated "de" been declared not to involve a title of nobility, which Mr. Robertson could not have known. Moreover, Legardeur did, as Seigneur, hold a grant, from the Government of New France, of Kegaska to the bottom of Hamilton Inlet for ten years, "for trading with the savages." The fact that De Courtemanche does not mention Brest, which had vanished nearly a hundred years before he came, means nothing whatever. He does not mention Tadoussac, which certainly did exist then.

The more one regards him as the son-in-law of a rich tanner, the less one expects him to be interested in the glories of an old town which had departed a century before his time.

True, Quebec ecclesiastical records have no account of a church in Labrador in those times. However, that no church grew up there was no fault of the priests. It is definitely stated that they were refused permission to go there since "the land was not yet suitable for men of that cloth." The rush from Europe, where everywhere Catholics and Protestants were at daggers drawn, made it inadvisable. A martyrdom of a Jesuit among the Iroquois involved no political aftermath.

In an admirable letter of De Courtemanche, still preserved in the Archives de Marine in Paris, he describes a voyage he made around his whole Labrador domain, giving detailed accounts of all the harbours. He was immensely impressed with the possibilities of the land, especially the caribou, the furs, grouse, and wild birds, salmon and seals—all of which have suffered badly for lack of protection.

In the early nineteenth century the site of old Brest was again a great rendezvous for fishing vessels from Salem, Gloucester, Newburyport, and other New England ports. Into its magnificent harbour a beautiful salmon river enters from a well-wooded valley.

It is still the best stand for the cod fishery; as in those days it was the best for whales and porpoises. The most prominent planter on the Labrador Coast assured me that in a single year he had cleared forty thousand dollars there from the fishery alone. That it was one of the battle-grounds of the Indians and Eskimo is yet another suggestion that they also were well aware of its value, and perhaps accounts for the fact that then, in 1630, "the savage Eskimo, still clinging to this place, were totally extirpated."

Another interesting letter is that of the Sieur de Combes, a gentleman of Poitou, living in Canada. It was published in Lyons in 1808, and describes vividly "the marvels, excellence and wealth of the country, and the hope that there is of Christianizing America." After a most natural expression of love for his family and friends, and of the chagrin which his banishment to a land cut off from communication with them costs him, he writes that he is hoping to see his friend, the Sieur de Dongeon, who is the Governor of and resides normally at Brest—"the principal town of the whole country, large, strongly fortified, peopled by about fifty thousand [!!] and furnished with all that is necessary to enrich a full sized town."

This letter, a printed copy of which is preserved in the Lenox Library in New York, has been dubbed "a fairy tale of the wildest sort." Exaggeration in numbers is not unknown in the Bible. Yet we do not reject the whole of it because of an almost certain copyist's error. The tales brought back to the ship by credulous sailors, who had been landed on an unknown Isle of Camon, are perfectly intelligible in the light of the average mentality of that day. The Sieur de Combes made no pretence of having *been* to Brest.

Brest must unquestionably have had a Governor of some sort, and probably no record office. For in those days fishermen, privateers, and "gentlemen" galore from St. Jean de Luz to Bristol Port, who were glad enough to get their anchors down anywhere in safety, unquestionably swelled the numbers of that far-off town in the summer months, and would resist to the last any attempt to register their whereabouts. For legitimate seamen also it was then far the best place to rendezvous and revictual.

The present Master of Bonne Esperance, the site of old Brest, has an ancient cannon mounted in his fishing "room," which years ago his father dredged up in a fishing-net close to his house.

During the years following the decline of Brest, Bradore, not being dependent on anything but the sealery and fishery, went its even way. As it was only thirty miles to the east, and an excellent harbour, it doubtless profited by the decline of its neighbour. Bradore was then called Baie des Espagnols, and Spanish ruins were described as being still extant there in 1706.

In 1900 there still lived in Bradore a member of a Jones family—a widow over whose head we had had to help to put a roof. Yet only a few short years previously, the Jones family of Bradore not only brought down a pair of horses and a carriage from Quebec, but built a road along which to drive them. We ourselves purchased from an old fisherman on the Coast a box containing ancient Spanish and French silver dollars, all over a hundred years old, which he had dug up under his house. Disaster overtakes the prosperous on our Labrador Coast as it does elsewhere in the world. In the middle of winter in a tiny hut in this village, it was our sad duty to remove the lower limb of one of its last residents.

During these years, the English fishermen from the

Coast had incidentally played their great part in the defeat of Spain and the destruction of the Armada, and a second effort to colonize Canada in 1591 by the French had failed. The ships of the leader, a Marquis de la Roche, were "driven back by storms, he having only succeeded in landing on Sable Island some sixty of his men." For seven years no vessel touched at this island, and then a Norman pilot brought back to France twelve surviving, half-human, hairy bipeds, who had lived on birds, seals, and chance wrecks—and whom on their return, though condemned criminals, the King pardoned "in pitie of their miseries."

Yet another reason for the failure of the French efforts to colonize was now to be illustrated in the St. Lawrence. While Louis XIV and Cardinal Richelieu had been mercilessly persecuting the Huguenots in France, they had also founded "the Company of New France," and the Labrador saw endless French ships, men, and money passing up its shores. Champlain had fortified Quebec. Priests were hard at work "Christianizing" the Indians. New France seemed at last on a solid basis.

But it so happened that an English Calvinist from Yorkshire, called Kirke, had married a woman of Dieppe, and he had settled there and accumulated a moderate fortune. His three sons, David, Thomas, and Lewis, were each trading for their father's London Company as captains of small ships in the Gulf of St. Lawrence. In 1628 they sailed again from London, carrying English letters of marque. At Gaspé they surprised and burnt the French supply fleet, and, creeping up the St. Lawrence, took Tadoussac. David, the oldest, sent Lewis on to Quebec to tell Champlain the news, and demand his surrender. The letter was carried ashore by Basque fishermen whom they had captured. They had destroyed his supplies from France, and the Iroquois had cut off his land supplies, but as he felt it was not decent to surrender so fine a fortress without a fight, the Kirkes decided to wait at Tadoussac till spring. Meanwhile, Richelieu sent out a magnificent supply fleet of eighteen vessels under the Marquis de Roquemont, with cannons, provisions, settlers, and many priests. The three Kirkes fell upon them at anchor in Gaspé Bay, and captured the lot. They rifled and sank ten, and Thomas took the rest of them to Newfoundland, while David went again to Quebec, where Champlain and his men had been living on roots and leaves for many weeks. This time they had to surrender, and David, leaving Lewis in charge, carried his prisoners to England for sale. On his way down the Gulf this modern "giant killer" met two French men-of-war under the Marquis de Caen waiting for him. David captured both ships, and, having burnt them, added the Marquis to his booty. The many priests they had captured were described among the valuables as "not vendible." France then owed Charles I a balance of two hundred and forty thousand pounds on his wife Henrietta's dowry, to get which he gave them back Quebec and everything the Kirkes had captured, including the rich furs. David got little but an empty title, and new letter commissioning him as Admiral Sir David, and entitling him to go and "fight again for his king." For three years the whole French colonizing work had been entirely suspended. It seems that King Louis was furious when he heard of the exploits of the three Kirkes, for he had them burnt publicly in Paris—in effigy.

Now again a peaceful exploitation of the Labrador began. Amongst many other grants, one François Bissot, again a Norman tanner who had made money in the business in Quebec, obtained the Seigneurie of the Isle aux Œufs, a large island, still the home of countless thousands of auks and puffins. Bissot also got the fishing rights over the whole coast from Seven Islands to Bradore. Thereupon a new era for Brest began. Permanent fishing stations were established all along the North Shore. Bissot had a separate post at Mingan and other places as well for fishing, sealing, furring, and trading. He met with great success. His daughters married the *"jeune noblesse,"* one of them being the great Louis Joliet, who with Père Marquette journeyed two thousand five hundred miles in canoes, discovering the Mississippi and cruising nearly to the Mexican Gulf through endless savage Indians, without injuring one. Joliet was a second Cartier.

Perhaps the most remarkable individual in the whole story of Labrador now comes upon our stage. In 1652 Pierre Radisson, aged seventeen, was hunting with two friends, north of Quebec. They were ambushed; the friends were killed and scalped by the Iroquois, but Pierre himself put up such a good fight he was adopted into the tribe. He was later tortured for attempting to escape, but the chief who had adopted him saved his life. Forced to help the Iroquois in their attack on the Dutch at Albany, he at last escaped down the Hudson to New York, and so to Amsterdam, where he joined a fishing vessel and again got back up the St. Lawrence. His marvellous courage and intimate knowledge of the Indians carried him through a thousand hairbreadth escapes all over the whole northwest. With his brother-in-law, Groseillier, he travelled to Hudson's Bay, through endless dangers from Indians. There they found the trade with Eskimo and Indians so lucrative that they returned, and tried to induce the French to form a Hudson's Bay Company—but without success. At last, with introductions to Charles I, they visited London, where the merchant adventurers gave each of them charge of a small vessel to trade in Hudson's Bay. Passing north of Labrador, heavy gales in the bay gave the captain of Radisson's vessel "cold feet" and he returned to England; but Groseillier, in the pinnace *Eaglet,* went on and wintered in James Bay, where he collected an invaluable cargo of furs.

To this Company, with Prince Rupert as Governor, King Charles granted a charter in 1670—that has been one of the wonders of the New World ever since. Our two Frenchmen made several more almost incredibly dangerous but successful expeditions for the Company both by land and by sea. Thus came the strange coincidence that Frenchmen were again largely responsible for holding Canada within the British Empire. Amazing to say, Radisson died in his own house, aged seventy-four. The "Hudson's Bay Company of Gentlemen Adventurers" were calmly given all the land drained by rivers falling into the straits or bay of that name. The grant read: "The whole trade of all these seas, straits and bays, rivers, lakes, creeks and sounds, in whatsoever latitude

114

they shall be, that lie within the entrance of the Straits commonly called Hudson Straits—also all fisheries." This modest document conferred upon them nearly a third of North America, including half Labrador; and they held the monopoly of trading rights for a hundred and ninety years. The company had practically the rights of a modern self-governing colony.

Ten years later from his home in Mingan (where he is buried), Joliet crossed on foot to Hudson's Bay, where he found the English firmly entrenched. He refused all their offers to join them, crossed back through Labrador to Quebec, and reported to Governor Frontenac, who gave him the Seigneurie of Anticosti. There in 1690 Sir William Phipps, on his ill-fated voyage to attack Quebec, took him prisoner and burnt his house. Joliet, after being exchanged, voyaged again as far as Hamilton Inlet, where he tried to establish fishing and trading posts. He also traded with his father-in-law, Bissot, along the South Labrador Coast till he died. Meanwhile Frontenac had sent the son of an innkeeper from Normandy, who had settled in Montreal and been made captain of the city, with a couple of vessels, to drive the English out of Hudson's Bay. This man had been ennobled by Louis XIV for his splendid courage and leadership. Oddly enough, nine of his eleven brothers had also been made nobles for similar reasons. For his marvellous feats he was known best as "The Cid" of Canada, though Sieur d'Iberville was his title. Soldier, administrator, navigator, he was later the founder of Louisiana. On this occasion, in 1687 and 1688 he took every post in Hudson's Bay but one, captured immense booty, at least two

British ships of war, and two large vessels loaded with rich furs. He took Fort Nelson after amazing adventures, called it Fort Bourbon, and wintered there, losing twenty men from scurvy. He practically repeated these adventures in 1695, on one occasion only saving his four ships by tying up to icebergs.

When in 1697 the Treaty of Ryswick was signed it was specified that all possessions which France and England had before the war must be restored to their original owners. Labrador presented a Dutchman's puzzle, and a commission was appointed to draw a line between Rupert's Land and Canada, which had once more to go back to the French. The English proposed a line from Cape Grimmington (probably Cape Uivuk) to Lake Mistassini, S.W. to latitude 49° and then indefinitely west. Needless to say the line was never drawn, and no one knows now which was Cape Grimmington.

From now on seigneuries along the Gulf of St. Lawrence were showered upon young French gentlemen, who sought to retrieve their fortunes after the wars. Amongst them was Amador de St. Paul, for whom the seigneuries of that river were then created; and our friend the Sieur de Courtemanche, who built Fort Chartrain as his headquarters at Bradore, of which place he could not speak too highly. He had "a beautiful background of hills and trees, rivers and lakes full of salmon and trout, abundant game to support all his dependants, and endless codfish." He found also a new and gentler race of Indians, "easy to convert to Christianity," probably Nascopies, who had always been friendly to the French. These both traded with and worked for him.

116

In the harbour they discovered, and describe, endless remains of whales, which were accounted for by the Basques, who had been there "from time immemorial" but had been eventually driven out by "bloodthirsty Eskimo," who destroyed all their properties during the winters, when they themselves returned to Spain.

The truth of De Courtemanche's stories is best endorsed by the fact that ten years later, when he was in Paris, the King, who was then at Marly, granted him in fee simple all the land around Bradore, and the sole right to fish for seals and to trade with the savages, together with the renewal of his former grant. He also created him "Commandant of the Coast of Labrador," where he was to rule and settle all disputes as a military officer, he being a captain of "a company of New France."

A letter of great interest, written by a priest who spent the summer on the coast, supported all De Courtemanche had claimed regarding the glories of the short summer and the abundance of wild life. He wanted France to make it her "Peru," "for its fisheries alone offer greater wealth at less expense than the gold mines of that country." After describing the unequalled furs and their abundance, he remarks quaintly that the caribou skins, which are innumerable, dye scarlet better than any fur. His reports of the plentiful salmon, seals, walrus, whales, oil, ivory, and eiderdown, and the possibilities of copper and iron, were all facts—as were the "prodigious numbers of Moyeis (auks) which furnish quantities of down and eggs good to eat." The King, he continues, has given this grant to M. de Courtemanche for his life. He describes the large garden with peas, beans, herbs, roots, salads, and remarks that the barley and oats which they sowed have grown well. He says that they keep "horses, cows, sheep, and pigs, but that they have to send the horses and carts for wood across the plain [still very noticeable] about four leagues long, or else fetch it by boat from Eskimo River." He recounts how De Courtemanche employs thirty families of Montagnais Indians for the fishery, the chase, and to work for him. He suggests that France create three main settlements to begin with so as to develop the whole of the Labrador, at strategic points, like Hamilton Inlet, Ste. Barbe, and Château. He estimates that there are thirty thousand Eskimo in the country, but claims that their decline is entirely the fault of the foreigner, who has maltreated them atrociously. He affirms that the Eskimo are more timid than savage, and agrees with De Courtemanche, Joliet, and others that they are civil, gay, warm-hearted and gentle, and their women chaste.

He wants French fishermen to be forbidden to kill them, or to give or sell them intoxicants. He thinks the fishermen should be forced to try to win the confidence of the Eskimo, and wishes a Jesuit priest sent among them "as they have a great talent for humanizing the most ferocious savages." The Eskimo are to be urged to take up their abode near the French. The Moravian experiments show how absolutely right this priest was.

He continues wisely: "Those who always see difficulties and have not the courage to undertake large enterprises say that Labrador is a place cold and sterile, where nothing that is necessary to life can be found. . . .

". . . Only by cultivation have Sweden, Norway, Rus-

118

sia, Scotland, which are all as far, or further North, become fertile and capable of supporting their large populations."

This astute visitor advises that the interior and the coast be surveyed, suitable cattle be introduced (he suggested from the Faroe Islands or North Canada) the caribou should be domesticated as in Lapland, plants and birds should be adapted and protected. He suggests that if plants will not grow, salt should be used in the cold, acid soil, as in Poland. Large hostels or inns for seamen should be built at each of the three suggested centres; also there should be "a curé, an honest one," with a "church well and properly adorned." The curé could be a St. Sulpician if a Jesuit is not available. Plans for solid houses should be furnished. "Lime, bricks, tiles and pottery can be made in the country. Bees such as are kept in Muscovy and Poland should be tried."

Altogether this letter of recommendations was an extraordinarily far-seeing one. Had his advice been carried out, Labrador would have long ago entered upon an era worthy of her possibilities.

De Courtemanche died in 1717, and his son-in-law, De Brouage, ruled in his stead. For forty years the latter wrote regularly a letter to the Archives de Marine in Paris. During those years new industries opened and much money was made on the Coast. A regular trade sprang up with the Eskimo, especially in Hamilton Inlet.

Salted salmon now became a regular industry, and with porpoise and other oils they furnished the whole lighting of Canada. One year a thousand barrels of oil were shipped to Paris alone. Bradore became a small town

119

with some two hundred houses, a safe place to leave boats and stores when the fishermen returned to Europe each winter. For, alas, they all carried guns, and killed not a few of the Eskimo every year, who made such reprisals as they could.

In 1760 not even prophets dreamed that the vision of a great and prosperous New France was shortly to be forever extinguished. The end was suitably dramatic. France was beaten in Europe, but Montcalm still reigned supreme in Quebec, when in 1763 there came once more, creeping up the St. Lawrence along the Coast of Labrador, a British fleet. From these vessels, now anchored off the Isle d'Orléans, which had witnessed so many classic struggles, British soldiers in the darkness of night rowed their boats up on the tide beyond the great cliffs on which once stood Champlain's fortress, and was still the capital of France's great empire in the New World.

Stealthily the boats crossed the river. Silently they drifted down with the current, invisible under the great cliffs. Landing in a little cove, under cover of darkness, they scaled the heights and gained the Plains of Abraham above. The French troops issued to resist them. Wolfe, the gallant leader, fell on the field. The battle was fierce but short. Its close marked the fall of the city and with it forever the rule of France in Canada. But what "le coq" lost by war it achieved by peaceful penetration —visibly, a permanent place *"dans le nouveau monde."* Their very language has again become the language of the Labrador coast of the St. Lawrence, for as Canada opened up there was a continuous leak from its population. The English kept leaving Labrador for the south

120

side of the Gulf, where the climate was less rigorous and
trees and soil more generous. The remaining French,
with larger families and close religious affiliations, once
more took their places "de facto." To-day the French
hold that western section of the coast, but now as good
fellow-subjects of Canada with the British, under the
honourable title by which they have become so well
known, "Les Habitants Canadiens," while the English
and Scotch, further east and north on the coast, are
now known by their own synonym, "the Livyeres of
the Labrador."

VII: THE PAGEANT OF THE ENGLISH OCCUPATION

The Lion's Share

THE curtain went down with the Tricolour in the last pageant, and now the Union Jack flies over the Labrador stage. This time there is no interval; the curtain flies up again almost before it has fallen. Annexation by the British worked so rapid a revolution on the Labrador Coast that her statesmen and politicians were left mouldering in their stolid precautions for shaping its future. That the famous Captain Cook was at work surveying the Coast afforded a sufficient anodyne for any who were infected by belief in haste. Scotchmen and even English flocked into the country and bought out the concessions of the French settlers. Many of these latter returned to France, in spite of the fact that the terms of the treaty were quite unusual in allowing them to retain their religion, their language, and practically all that would induce them to remain.

The first Governor describes the British immigrants as "contemptible suttlers and traders, who wantonly abused the natives." By 1800 they had practically the whole coast east of Mingan; and by 1806 a Labrador Company led by a certain Mathew Lymburner did a lucrative trade in fish and hides, furs, and porpoise oil as far north as Rigolet. Mathew was no mere fortune-seeker out of work. He was a man of no small parts, going to London in 1791 to make an impassioned speech against the Constitutional Act.

The western boundary of Labrador was now the river St. John, and the whole territory, with Anticosti and the Magdalen Islands, was given to Newfoundland. This time the lure was "gold." We ourselves witnessed just such a rush when the discovery of gold north of Cape Harrison was broadcast. We were not surprised that the very first reply of the Government was to build a jail with iron-covered doors and windows in the then absolutely uninhabited river basin. This early rush was for the gold of the sea, however, even then known to be more generous in riches than Golconda or Peru.

The average value of a whale was about fifteen hundred pounds, no small sum in 1763. One American record states that a New England crew had killed thirty whales within thirty square miles. There was no electric light in those days; all lights were from oil. A pious naval officer says in a letter that he is so glad to see the Labrador settlers increasingly acquiring lamps. He hopes that this laudable advance will not be discouraged by shortage of oil. This observation helps us to understand the Mathew Lymburners of that period.

Such a development across the Western Ocean was not the intention of British statesmen, however. Slowly they were beginning to sense—as the great Queen Bess partially recognized—that the wealth and prosperity of England depended not on mere dead material, but on men. It was seamen especially which England needed at that time. The experience of the Spanish Armada, when her fishermen saved England, had made the blind see that the best gift of even the rich fisheries of the New Lands was the splendid seamen which they developed. Only the press-gang filled the quota of His Majesty's ships in those days when war was practically continuous; and even a Nelson needed fishermen to hold the mastery of the seas. Brute force and slavery have never laid permanent foundations in human affairs.

England sent out as first Governor for her new possessions a splendid personality, Sir Hugh Pallisier. If any individual in that era could have done so, he would have made it possible to say of this pageant, "And they lived happily ever after." But his orders were absolute. "It is the King's intention to reserve the whole of the new possessions for English adventurers. No one must live in Labrador at all. All who on any pretence whatsoever are living there must be turned out. Any Newfoundlander even going to Labrador to fish will be flogged for a first offence, and his possessions confiscated for a second."

Armed with this monopoly, were there no wire-pull-ers in those days? Bristol and other merchants from the south-west of England undertook to send out fishing vessels, and submitted to the bonding of their skippers on each ship for one hundred pounds for every man whom they failed to bring back to England at the close of each voyage.

So Sir Hugh set out to do his best by personally visiting the Labrador Coast. How far he expected what he found, who can say? Alas, there were no kodaks to immortalize his discoveries. His records show that not only had every settler not disappeared as he had ordered, when he had even sent His Most Gracious Majesty's gunboats to speed the parting guests, but "about five thousand of the most disorderly and the very scum of the Colonies have come in." By the same urge which has repeated itself in the Al Capones of the twentieth century "civilization," New England and Canada had contributed not a few disturbers of the peace. Disgruntled at being dispossessed of a fine living, the "obedient ones" had not returned to England to serve as food for the press-gang, but had skipped off to New England to be near at hand and able to continue to reap a share of the wealth. After all, they had been sacrificed without being asked, and without any compensation had been deprived of undoubted rights.

Sir Hugh wrote bitterly about the whole situation to his colleague, Sir Francis Bernard, the Governor of Boston: "The great trouble and difficulty met with on Labrador is occasioned by disorderly people from your Province. The last year, whilst a tribe of four to five hundred Eskimo savages were with me at Pitt's Harbour, I made

125

a peace with them and sent them away exceedingly satisfied, without the least offensive thing happening. I am
well informed that New England vessels, contrary to the
orders published, went to the northward, robbed, plundered and murdered some of their old men, women
and children, whom they had left at home. So I expect
some mischief will happen this year, revenge being their
declared principle. If you prefer to take any other
method for the reformation of those concerned I shall
be extremely obliged to you. For the complaints I have
of mischief committed by others are many, great and
barbarous."

He also found that he had endless further troubles to
cope with in connection with the holders of the old
French grants. He applied at once to England for further naval reinforcements, built a fort in Pitt's Arm in
Chateaux Bay and called it Fort York, garrisoning it
with an officer, twenty men, and cannon. He arranged
for the policing of and dispensing justice in Labrador by
appointing the skippers of the first three fishing vessels
arriving from England in the spring as admiral, vice-
admiral, and rear-admiral respectively. He gave them
the sole right to trade in any way whatever with the
natives, and permitted each of them to leave twelve men
during the winter to prosecute the valuable seal fishery.
Not a soul else was allowed to remain in the country.
However much the skippers got out of the arrangement,
it certainly hustled their dilatory masters and benefited
the Adventurers of Bristol thereby. That the men would
have benefited is very improbable had not Sir Hugh provided also for that possible weak point in his effort. For

in spite of the great unpopularity which it brought him in St. John's he passed a law that merchants must pay in cash to their men at least half the wages to which they had agreed. Though, like all of his other laws, this might be observed largely in the breach (owing to the power-lessness of the men to get it enforced), it at least looked well on the face of such "accounts rendered" as the following, which is only too average a specimen of the dealings of those days:

Tom Bouling to Messrs. Fleecem and Co., Dr.

October	Rum, brandy, and gin, 27 qts.	£1.13.6
	Tea, 1 lb. 5/ Sugar, 1 lb. 1/	
November	Molasses, 4 qts.	5.0
	Ribbon, ½ yd. 1/	
	Soap, 1 lb. 2/3	3.3
	Tobacco, 10 lbs.	1.0.0
	Washing	1.0.0
	Shoes, 9/ Pepper 1 lb. 5/	14.0
	Doctor, 10/ two cotton shirts 8/6	18.6
		£5.16.3
For encouraging two servants in debt to run away		20.8.0
		26.9.3
Due Tom Bouling for summer wages		26.0.0
less by debts		26.9.3
Due Messrs. Fleecem and Co.		0.9.3

Mercifully for this particular Tom, Sir Hugh's law got him £13.0.0.

The admirals were also empowered to seize and destroy any fishing stages or houses which anyone had dared to erect and leave in Labrador. As practically none of the admirals could either read or write, and any who could knew nothing about law and cared less, as their own records show, endless fights resulted between the summer immigrants and settlers, who continued to exist "de facto" and whom it was physically impossible to dislodge—the Labrador of that day not being Arcady. Moreover, the records clearly pointed out that the admirals were themselves the chief law-breakers—the "servant when he reigneth" having a chance for a good fling. Might had become right. But though dictatorship by the unfit was a failure, we ourselves must admit to having used that same principle of "might is right" on the Labrador in securing cheap, effective, and remedial justice when otherwise it would have been impossible, since the wronged parties were far too poor to pay for justice and far too dependent to dare even to ask for it. A gold standard seems to have some disadvantages, but Sir Hugh rightly judged a peonage system to be worse. Meanwhile British settlements grew up as far north as Hamilton Inlet, in spite of "His Gracious Majesty"!

Another activity of Sir Hugh's had a more permanent effect, however. He gave a hearty and helpful hand to the Moravian Missionaries, who, actuated by love for their fellow-men—the one impulse which never fails—in 1770 were starting work on the Coast "among the savage Eskimo in the North." Though the embittered men whom they first encountered murdered the pioneer little company, they shortly demonstrated that in reality the Eskimo were gentle, docile, hospitable, and an extremely capable people; as did later the famous Major Cartwright, and indeed everyone else who dealt honourably with "The Innuit."

After the cession of Canada, unpractical British politicians airily gave to France the right for all time to fish

128

on the shores of a British colony. This naturally added greatly to the Governor's difficulties. The French made desperate efforts to get back some share in the rich fisheries which they had prosecuted for centuries; and out of the small "rights" which they both possessed—now called "privileges"—they made the most possible, until finally they construed their privileges in Newfoundland to mean that an Englishman might not fish on the beach in front of his own doorstep. They even seized on Belle Isle at the mouth of the Straits of that name, still to-day the richest "stand" for fish anywhere in the North, landed a thousand men from two hundred boats, built stages, and for several years reaped rich harvests of codfish, until His Majesty's ships succeeded in driving them out. As late as 1856 Newfoundland learned with horror one day that English politicians were considering giving to the French equal rights on the Labrador Coast. Such an uproar was raised, however, that the matter was dropped like a hot potato and a promise given that His Majesty's Government would not again interfere with the internal affairs of her colonies—a policy which, it will be remembered, had cost them a long war and the loss of their American colonies. As late as 1904 they had still to pay for the actions of their predecessors; for when a British admiral gave judgment against English fishermen for catching fish out of a boat on their own beach England had to settle the dispute by mildly making some land concessions in Africa, in return for whatever possible rights existed.

If we could believe that the return of Miquelon and St. Pierre and the "French Shore" rights were merely the result of folly, we could forget it, knowing that hindsight is easier than foresight. The ugliest spot in this whole pageant is the real cause of so many troubles which have arisen since. The responsibility for the terms of that treaty was entrusted to the Duke of Bedford and Lord Bute. When the terms were declared in the House of Commons Lord Chatham rose and openly accused them both of having accepted large bribes from the French— some three hundred thousand pounds apiece—for making these absolutely unnecessary concessions.

The "open letters" of the famous "Junius" to his colleague were never answered. He wrote to the Duke of Bedford: "The Treaty is a glorious monument of Your Grace's talents in negotiation. We are, My Lord, too well acquainted with your pecuniary character to think it possible that so many public sacrifices should have been made without some private compensation. Your conduct carries with it an internal evidence beyond all legal proofs of a Court of Justice."

Aggressions of French privateers added materially to the troubles of the English. In 1796 Admiral Richerey, who was destroying fishing craft on the Grand Banks, sent Commodore Allemand with three ships to harry the Labrador Coast. Fortunately fog and bad weather delayed him until most of the English fishermen had gone home. However, it is said that he returned and summoned the little fort at Chateaux Bay, which Sir Hugh Pallisier had built, to surrender. When the garrison refused, he proceeded to blow it to pieces. The English had burned everything in the fort and then escaped to the woods where the French failed to catch them. They did, however, secure a rich convoy of furs belonging to the Hudson's Bay Company; and after burning the ships which they did not want, took the rest with them. The Bristol firm of Noble and Pinson claimed afterwards that they had themselves destroyed twenty thousand pounds' worth of supplies in their stores to save them from falling into the hands of the French. Their claims were never allowed!

Sir Hugh Pallisier's difficulties with the New Englanders proved insurmountable. They were nearer than the English to their "gold field of the ocean" where many of them had fished for years. Their supplies and outfits were much cheaper. They were able to do quite a bit of illicit trading with the natives and other fishermen. Indeed Lieutenant (afterwards Admiral) Roger Curtis left it on record that they were "a lawless banditti, swarming on the Coast and in the Gulf like locusts, committing every kind of offence with malignant wantonness and were the cause of every trouble with the Eskimo." Their numbers from year to year are more or less recorded, the estimates running to many hundreds of vessels, and fifteen to twenty thousand men, following for the most part the cod fishery, the whale fishery, and occasionally the rich herring fishery. Nine hundred and thirty-five vessels were reported as passing the Gut of Canso in 1800.

As early as 1765 they brought back nine thousand barrels of oil to Boston. To this trade they added smuggling, chiefly rum and tobacco, as a side-line. To thicken the plot, more Jersey firms, Norsemen to the backbone who still insist that the King is Duke of Normandy, now began to come out and make settlements at Forteau, Blanc Sablon, Isle de Bois, Henley Harbour, and Battle Harbour. Such were the De Quetvilles, Fallé Frères, Boucher Frères, and Lucas and Robin.

The war of the Revolution came in the midst of these troubles, and American privateers swarmed on the Coast, many of them only too eager to pay off the grudge they had for having been driven off the shore previously. This was possibly one more tiny factor in swaying public sentiment in the American colonies against the English.

No one can deny that these New England fishermen displayed physical courage and good seamanship. Fishing for whales with hand harpoons from small boats was only one of the endless dangers to be encountered. Some seasons they made heavy losses. About 1775 many for this reason were fishing for cod inside the Isle de Bois in the Straits, taking their catch home to settlements in their own country, as they dared not carry it to Europe for fear of Barbary rovers. Many, too, fell victims to the watchful frigates of the British Navy.

In spite of all this, even after the Revolution, they were catching forty thousand quintals of cod more per annum than were the English. In the War of 1812 their fishermen led privateers in many depredations. Report has it that at one time a man could walk across St. John's Harbour on the decks of those captured and brought to that port.

After 1818 pre-Revolution rights to fish on the Labrador were returned to the Americans. Large numbers of boats from Gloucester, Newburyport, Salem, Eastport, and the Maine coast came to the fisheries. When

132

we went on the Labrador in 1892 we found these New Englanders fine men in well-equipped vessels, and regarded as welcome visitors. One fancies that the criticisms of their predecessors were not unduly generous. Nowadays they have larger and better found ships, and also power, and so venture further on the Grand Banks, where fish are bigger as well as available much nearer home.

In the old days, besides the French and the New Englanders, the English added greatly to the difficulties of the local authorities. The members of the crews were not only very poor men, but under the merchants were little better than serfs, so that almost any change for them would be for the better. Moreover, the New Englanders really sympathized with and needed them, and were able to offer them far better terms for their catches. France was openly giving bounties on all fish brought home. New England followed suit with special privileges to her fishermen. Besides being able to give cheaper supplies they offered higher wages, no truck trade, and a feeling of freedom which a fisherman naturally coveted. The fact is that every inducement was offered to English fishermen to desert. I would be the last to impeach the loyalty of our fishermen, but the remark of an Irishman sticks in my memory: "Sure, sir, I can resist anything except one." "And that is what, Pat?" " 'Tis temptation, your Honour!"

One plan of escape was openly winked at in Newfoundland. When a vessel was leaving for England a number of fishermen would take passage on her, and when well outside the three-mile limit, seize the ship by agreement and take her to Boston. There the rightful skipper was set free on his protest. One year from one bay alone, several hundred fishermen found their way to New England. A skipper, one Stout of the ship *Good Intent,* was said to have carried six hundred men there in one year, by heading them up separately in casks while the ship was being cleared for sea. Another case of real piracy is on record. While their vessel was anchored in Chateaux Bay, a crew seized an English ship and carried her off to Boston—when, in spite of Government protests, there is no record of her being deported!

"L'homme propose et Dieu dispose." English politicians at last awoke to the cataclysmic error to which Soviet Russia is to-day still blind. Man is not a Robot. He cannot be driven by force forever. So as early as 1774 it began to be recognized that the policies of the British Government dictated to Sir Hugh to be carried out on the Coast were impossible. They were reversed by the "Quebec Act," and the whole of the control of Labrador was once more handed over to Canada. In those slow-moving days, however, she proved as unable as Boston had been to see that law was upheld on the "lonely Labrador"; and returned to Newfoundland the jurisdiction in 1804, when the shuttle shot back. This time the western boundary was fixed at St. Johns River. Now it is at Blanc Sablon.

Governor Hamilton estimated the number of vessels on the Labrador in 1802 as one thousand, the value of codfish being exported annually as already a million dollars, that of furs ten thousand dollars and of seal and salmon and cod oil as nearly three hundred thousand dollars. In

1863 the Labrador salmon trade alone amounted to a million dollars; and in that same year in Blanc Sablon harbour were anchored no less than eighty Nova Scotia vessels and ten from Jersey. As late as 1900 Halifax schooners traded in Hamilton Inlet and along the northeast coast.

Meanwhile courageous business men kept founding stations in Labrador. Such were the Slades of St. Francis Bight and Venison Tickle, Baine Johnson at Battle Harbour, Warren at Indian Tickle, and so many others that by 1900 rooms had been built all the way to the Moravian Mission station at Hopedale. The Hudson's Bay Company had posts at Cartwright, Northwest River, Rigolet, Davis Inlet, and Nakvak, on eastern Labrador, besides Romaine, Mingan, St. Augustine, and other points on the South Shore.

In 1770 a new firm, organized this time by a soldier instead of a king, sprang up on the Labrador. The family of this Captain George Cartwright were kinsmen of Archbishop Cranmer. The captain had fought through the Seven Years' War as aide to the Marquis of Granby, with little profit to himself, and being unable to secure promotion (a matter of paying for it at that time) he had resigned. As his brother was lieutenant on Sir Hugh Pallisier's ship, he joined him on a Labrador cruise, and seeing the possibilities for trade and sport in that country, he persuaded another lieutenant on board, who spoke Eskimo, to embark with him on the venture. A Bristol firm operating in Newfoundland financed them; and in spite of the then existing laws, the Governor actually sent

His Majesty's ship under Lieutenant John Cartwright to help him build up his premises.

Cartwright has left us three volumes called "Transactions and Events During a Residence of Sixteen Years on the Labrador." It is a diary which for vividness in describing the life of the day is second only to Pepys'. Both Southey and Coleridge declared it deeply interesting. As one might expect among semi-slaves, which men were in those days, "debauchery and drunkenness was the custom." Cartwright describes the Irish revels every Christmas as "intolerable but bound to be submitted to." A prodigious fire having been built in the house, a gun was loaded with powder only. As it was fired everyone drank a dram of rum, a ceremony which concluded with three cheers. Then all hands went into the house and got as drunk as they could, "spending the whole night drinking, quarrelling and fighting." Like an officer of those times, Cartwright ruled over his eighty Irishmen and Dutchmen "of the lowest types," as well as over the Eskimo, with a rod of iron. The Diary abounds in such items as, "I gave McCarthy twenty-seven lashes with a small dog-whip on his bare back to-day, and intended to have given him thirty-nine; but as he then fainted, I stopped and released him, when he thanked me on his knees for my leniency."

When an Eskimo stole a skein of thread in the shop he immediately made him return it and then gave him a thrashing. When the man put up a fight, Cartwright "threw him out of the tent by a cross-buttock, whereupon he pitched on his head with great force."

His trade with the Eskimo and Indians became lucrative. He writes: "One afternoon I got 3 cwt. whalebone, one wolf and one black bear skin, ten seal skins, nineteen fox skins, twelve deer, four otter, two marten (sables) for a few beads and trifles of no commercial value." Another frank entry reads, "Bought a silver fox skin to-day for a twopenny comb." It is not to be wondered at that for some years he made a hundred per cent profit.

Three years before his arrival the Eskimo had killed three of a certain Captain Darby's men at Cape Charles. Yet the Eskimo trusted the major; and when he was ill, much to his annoyance, their Angekoks, or medicine-men, and other well-wishers came and made incantations outside his window all night long. To the end of his stay their friendship was unbroken, for he tried always to satisfy them, though he was invariably firm and attempted to execute justice as well as win their affection.

One year he took five Eskimo back with him to England, where naturally they caused great interest. Among others, the famous surgeon, John Hunter, invited them to dinner. Wandering in the house, they came across a skeleton in a glass case and were terribly frightened for fear they were going to be killed and eaten. On another occasion they went to see the caged animals in the park and enquired whether the monkeys were Eskimo. They were later annoyed that they had recognized them as more like the Innuit than the Kablunaks. Cartwright took them also to his home, Marnham Hall (where the family still lives), and the Eskimo were not only put on horseback at a meet of the hounds, but even were in at the death. However, they got tired of London and its many people and noises and smoke and wanted to return to Labrador, "which is good and where seals are plentiful." On the voyage out all but one unfortunately died of small-pox; but though expressing great grief, their families never blamed Cartwright.

With regard to women he was frankly immoral. Thus he records borrowing the wife of a native Eskimo for the winter, and returning the children, which the over-generous owner had included free! Yet he was religious after the fashion of that time. On Easter Sunday he writes: "I read Prayers to my family both forenoon and afternoon." After escape from a special danger he notes: "We could attribute all these things to nothing but the effect of the immediate interposition of the Divinity, who had been graciously pleased to hear our prayers and grant our petition."

In financial matters he was a man of strict honour; and when later he was ruined by circumstances over which he had no control, he refused to go into bankruptcy, preferring to carry the burden of debt in the hope of paying it off.

Still at the village of Cartwright on the Labrador is a tomb in his memory, but as his bones are buried in England for many years there was deposited in the tomb a large demijohn of rum as the most appropriate memorial! We ourselves have recently built a hospital, school, and orphanage at Cartwright, and hope to make it the capital of the new Labrador.

He was the only man we ever heard of running down foxes with his greyhounds in Labrador; and an excellent picture of him with a couple of hooded hounds is still extant. He used to build corrals to catch wild caribou in.

He also caught many in nooses slung under trees, proving how much more numerous those animals were then than they are to-day. His skill as a trapper was phenomenal.

In peace-time he suffered most from his Christian neighbours, the trading firm of Noble and Pinson, "who have been my inveterate enemies ever since I came to the Coast." They forcibly seized his salmon rivers, involving him in an expensive lawsuit in England. Several of his buildings were destroyed by fire.

In the War of Independence he suffered terribly from privateers piloted by disgruntled New England fishermen. On August 27, 1778, at one o'clock in the morning Cartwright was awakened by a body of armed men from the *Minerva* of Boston, commanded by John Grimes, "son of a superannuated boatswain of Portsmouth, England." They carried the unlucky Cartwright on board as a prisoner, where he met the surgeon and first lieutenant, "two of as great villains as any unhanged." They had already plundered his southern settlements and now proceeded to sack Caribou Castle, a station close by. The remains are still extant. They would have plundered two more of his posts about thirty miles up the bays, Paradise and White Bear River, had he not mentioned that he was momentarily expecting the arrival of the English frigate. They robbed him of practically everything and lured away half of his men, as the *Minerva* chanced to be short-handed and Grimes offered a share of the booty to anyone who would enter his service. Thirty-five of the Irish and Dutch in the major's employ accepted this proposal; but needless to say on reaching Boston they never got a penny but were thrown ignominiously into prison, where they languished for many months. Grimes also stole Cartwright's brig, *The Countess of Effingham*, loaded with salt and food; but she was re-taken on the passage by five of his men who were aboard her and restored to his agent in England.

Cartwright reckoned his losses of that day at fourteen thousand pounds, a large sum in 1779. In his inimitable Diary, however, he did not forget to enter the temperature, direction of the wind, and nature of the clouds the same night. It may have been some consolation to him to know that at the same time Noble and Pinson lost three vessels and all their stores, while Slade and Seydes at Cape Charles lost one vessel each.

The next year another privateer entered Battle Harbour, captured a sloop, and again destroyed Slade's stores. Everyone had to go on short rations. Indeed everybody north of Trinity was in the utmost distress for provisions, due to similar depredations, since no relief vessels arrived from England.

Cartwright's description of the salmon in the rivers at the head of Sandwich Bay bears out old Leif's estimate of that region: "In White Bear River you could not fire a bullet into the stream without killing one." The shores there and in Eagle River were strewn with the remains of thousands, partly consumed by bears. He counted thirty-two bears in sight at one time, and there were many more in the woods. Several of these were white bears, which were fishing for salmon. He shot six. It is not to be wondered at that with cod, salmon, and seals, he continued to do well.

He planted a fine garden. His mine, however, turned out to be worthless, and neighbours to whom he had lent money failed to repay him. He became involved in more lawsuits, and so was forced to leave his "beloved Labrador."

"Where the Eskimo from ice and snow now free
In shallops and whale-boats do go to sea.
In Peace they rove along this pleasant shore,
In plenty live, nor do they wish for more.
Thrice happy race! Strong drink nor gold they know;
What in their hearts they think, their faces show.
Of manners gentle, and their dealings just—
Their plighted promise you may safely trust.

. . . . . .

With these I frequent pass the social day.
No broils, no feuds, but all is spent in play.
My will, their law; and justice is my will.
Their friends we always were, and friends are still."

One other incident, that of the brave young doctor at Fort York, should not be forgotten in this story. Hearing that he was badly needed at Cartwright he started to walk there on snowshoes, a distance of not less than three hundred miles. Alas, he lost his way and was frozen to death. He was found a few days later with his faithful Newfoundland dog, which remained by his side in spite of all persuasions.

But to return to the fortunes of the Labrador. It was only fifteen years after she had been once again tossed back to Newfoundland to manage, that the whole Côte

141

du Nord was once again returned to Canada. In the light of to-day there are not a few who feel that the Labrador Coast should naturally have remained a part of Canada, as should also the Alaskan Coast. Meanwhile an utterly indefinite treaty gave to Newfoundland the fisheries of northeast Labrador "and the Coasts thereof," with all the land to the east of a line from Blanc Sablon to the fifty-second parallel of latitude, but with no defined western boundary. Indeed, I once heard an impassioned preacher praying for Labrador as follows: "Thou knowest, Lord, this great and needy land—bounded on the East by the Arctic Ocean, on the South by the mighty St. Lawrence, on the North by the frigid waters of Hudson's Straits, and on the West by—O Lord, Thou knowest!"

The final settlement as it stands to-day was only arrived at in 1927, when the world was beginning to suspect that, after all, Labrador had a real value; and Newfoundland and Canada were willing to spend two million dollars fighting for it. Most of the legal trouble lay in the wording, "and the Coasts thereof." Were they bounded by the three-mile limit, or by the height of land, or by the territorial waters of the sea? Newfoundland tried to make it the height of land. The original treaty was written in the English of the King James version of the Bible. It was argued that there Christ is described as "walking in the Coasts of Tyre and Sidon," and that it is absurd to suppose that it was meant that He limited Himself to the three-mile limit! So Newfoundland, to her amazement and gratification, was given "all the land drained by rivers running out on the East Coast." As the Hamilton River runs into the coun-

142

try for at least four hundred miles, cutting right through the height of land, this grant involved a serious slice cut out of the hinterland of Quebec; and that was definitely never intended by the original makers of the treaty. It seems pertinent to repeat here that forty years ago Newfoundland offered Labrador to Canada for nine million dollars and the offer was refused. Recently the Government of Newfoundland tried to sell Labrador to Canada for a hundred and ten million dollars—a mere bagatelle to what it is worth, or to what will probably be asked for it fifty years hence. Moreover, this time Newfoundland proposed to retain the sovereignty and fishing rights. Canada has at present refused. Labrador should profit greatly by union with a large country which can afford, and does at present exert, such excellent supervision over the fisheries and other interests of the Côte du Nord.

In 1811 a Surrogate Court was authorized for Labrador and given effect in 1826 by Sir Thomas Cochrane, the Governor of Newfoundland. The court consisted of a judge, a clerk, a sheriff, and five soldiers, with a special boat and two constables, the whole costing the Colony approximately seventy-five thousand a year. In 1832 it cost also the lives of three of the sailors from the judge's own vessel, the *Belinda,* since they were drowned near Seal Islands.

To anyone who knows Labrador and has a sense of humour the records of that court while it lasted are amusing reading. To begin with, owing to the law-abiding nature of the people, "the work of the court was so easy as to be without precedent in any part of the world." The records of the closing year, 1833, after giving the names of the eleven places visited along over two hundred miles of coast-line from Blanc Sablon to Gready Harbour, read tersely, "No business came before the Court." Yet the very first official act of this "expense on our cod fishery," as the court was shrewdly dubbed, was to grant "licenses to sell by retail malt, wines and spirituous liquors, both at Rigolet and Mullins Cove." For this the court received the impressive sum of three pounds, fifteen shillings, and seven and a quarter pence towards its expenses. The nature of the blessings conferred is felt in the musty records of twenty years later, by which time all the members of the various stations of the Moravian Mission, trying to develop the country and people by methods exactly the reverse, were driven to humbly petition the Colonial Secretary in London for the first time to protect their "congregations on the Coast of Labrador from the selling or handing to them rum or other intoxicating spirits."

In a former chapter we have seen how in 1670 Charles II granted to that renowned cavalry leader, Prince Rupert, and to some gentlemen adventurers, all the rights to trade and commerce within the entrance to Hudson's Bay. As we saw, the French disputed his right to do this, and that famous gallant Joliet, with D'Iberville and De Troyes, made an expedition north and drove the company from all their stations except one (Albany).

In 1697 and 1713, the Treaties of Ryswick and Utrecht forced the French to relinquish all claims to the Bay. In 1792 the British Crown again pronounced valid the claims of the Hudson's Bay Company "to all lands on the Coasts and confines of Hudson's Straits." In the same year the Company established their territorial rights on the Labrador peninsula; but these were not exercised until 1831, when a post was founded at Fort Chimo in Ungava Bay, and again in 1833 a station at Rigolet in Hamilton Inlet. John McLean, the first factor at Fort Chimo, made a wonderful journey across country to establish communications, and has left an account of it and of his twenty-five years' service in the Hudson's Bay territories.

It was in 1869 that the Company sold all their sovereign rights in British North America to Canada for one and a half million dollars, reserving the right to carry on their trade in their corporate capacity, and much land in various sections of the coast. Not only do their ships still carry home to London furs and products of the North, sables and ermines and silver foxes for kings and queens and until recently for tzars, but their trade has grown enormously, and amongst other places, they have posts all along the Labrador, most of them founded in quite recent years. Few realize that every year their trading steamers, starting from Montreal on the east and Vancouver on the west, so nearly meet by the famous Northwest Passage that the officers are able actually to do so with only a hundred-mile land journey, and so complete their "chain-store" system right across the whole continent of North America. Amundsen found the Northwest Passage, but the great Company alone have used it.

The Hudson's Bay Company have played an important part in the development of Canada and Labrador, forming a monument for all time to come of the courage, venture, ability, and devotion of their employees, even if in early days their policies were dictated by the spirit of the times.

Revillon Frères, the great Parisian and Canadian fur company, went into serious competition with the Hudson's Bay Company early in the twentieth century. They built a post of their own in the Company's back yard at their chief trading centre in Hamilton Inlet, and another in Sandwich Bay. They competed with them by sending regular buyers all along the Coast in winter. This policy paid the trappers better than it did the rival companies. To-day these posts of Revillon Frères are both closed. Fur buyers continue to come along the Coast in winter by dog-team and in summer in boats. These buyers made it exceedingly difficult for a company which is trying to maintain all-year-round posts, thus assuming no small responsibility for the people. When the rivals have passed on, often taking with them the cream of the catch, their responsibility ceases; but not so that of the Company. This fact accounts for the higher prices which the Company have to charge for their goods, which naturally disgruntles the local dealers.

The recent fall in prices of fur and fish greatly hurt the Company, as well as the people. Their splendid effort to raise the value of our salmon and other products by improved methods of preservation, handling, and marketing has laid Labrador under a real debt to them. Their recent constructive work, carried on at great expense, is one of the redeeming features in the story of the English occupation.

Amongst those who have been most intimately associated with Labrador during the last century are some

RAPID TRANSIT

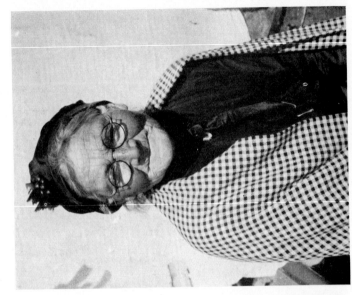

A MOTHER IN ISRAEL

ABE, THE MATE OF SIR WILFRED'S HOSPITAL BOAT

of the well-known firms whose head offices are in St. John's. Job Brothers & Company for over a hundred years have carried on an extensive fishery all along the Coast, and especially near Blanc Sablon—close to old Brest—and the neighbouring villages. Their experimental work of making fish fertilizer in great quantities at Salmon Bay failed only after a most laudable attempt, due to difficulties in transporting the offal to the factory. Their whaling station at L'Anse au Loup came into the field too late. Baine, Johnson & Company, an old Greenock firm, still carry on business at Battle Harbour, Henley, and places near by. They have been the backbone of the fishery in that neighbourhood for nearly a hundred years. A fire that destroyed their buildings two years ago and spread to, and destroyed, our hospital at Battle Harbour was a great setback to the progress of the local fishermen. Bowring Brothers, the great firm from Liverpool, have also done much to develop Labrador. Their whaling station at Cape Charles was a success for many years, until the large one of Messrs. Rorke farther north rather cut off their catch. Perhaps Bowring's most important piece of developmental work was their coastal mail steamers, *Portia* and *Prospero,* which for many years have infinitely improved the passenger and mail services of the Coast, to the great blessing of thousands of poor people.

Many unique men and great sailors have passed across the Labrador stage, yeoman fishing families from Devon, Dorset, and the West Country. Among the outstanding names have been the Blandfords, Whiteleys, Grants, Bartletts—so well known the world over for their Arc-

147

tic work—Barbours, Keans, Whites, and many another, brave in venture, self-reliant in danger, quick in action, of high moral character and deep religious spirit. They have been men gifted with the sea genius of their race, strong and gentle, stories of whose resourcefulness and self-effacement would fill volumes. Heredity and environment alike have combined to make them what they are; danger and constant responsibility have imbued them with a spirit that even when purposely masked by an apparently rough exterior, only impresses landsmen the more. If Labrador had never made any other contribution to the world than her great fishing captains, any real man would wisely take off his hat to it.

The story of Labrador has always been like that of the sea, succeeding waves with high crests, and in between deep hollows. To-day it is just emerging from the bottom of a hollow. Some might say it is still crawling along the bottom, as Europe is doing in matters of finance; but in time Labrador, like Europe, if rightly handled, is bound to rise again to the crest of the wave.

VIII: THE PAGEANT OF THE UNITAS FRATRUM

Peaceful Penetration

ONCE more the curtain rises, again without an interval. France had not yet handed her New World to the English when this scene opened. Thanks be to God, concurrent with the lust for power, gold, and self, which makes so much history, other impulses also achieve results and leave a visible track on the sands of time.

A young nobleman, driving to Paris to complete his education, stopped to bait his horses at Düsseldorf. While waiting, he strolled into the ancient Town Hall to see the pictures. The horses were ready, the grooms waiting, time was passing, and messengers were searching for the missing Count. In the half light of evening he was found standing in front of a large and speaking painting of "Christ Crowned with Thorns" by Domenico Feti. He was wrapped, apparently, in utter forgetfulness. Beneath the painting was written:

"This have I done for thee.
What hast thou done for Me?"

When at last the Count von Zinzendorf rejoined his equipage, to the amazement of his lackeys he ordered his horses' heads turned homewards. A new motif—to give, not to get—had become the impulse which dominated his entire life.

Thus was renewed the truly Christian Society of the Unitas Fratrum, the Moravian Church which had existed since 1457, in blood and persecution.

The next scene is in the fo'castle of a Dutch whaling-vessel, pursuing the "Moby Dicks" of that day and using the harbours of Greenland, like a second Brest, to render their oil and re-victual their ships. In this work even common sailors learned to talk intelligently with the Eskimo. A sailor, Jan Erhardt, is writing a letter home to a friend, Johannes de Watteville, now the bishop of the young Moravian Church. Year after year he had seen the marvels achieved by humble men sent out and endowed only with the same human assets as he had himself.

The vicissitudes of the cause had, no doubt, often taken them to the Labrador Coast, and the terrible contrast of the conditions of the Eskimo natives there to the Greenland ones once again sounded a call more potent than that of any other motive in history. Once again he writes: "Now, dear Johannes, thou knowest that I have an amazing love for these barbarians and it would be a source of greatest joy if the Saviour would make me fit for this service." Sorrowfully, Count Zinzendorf advised that as yet the task was too great for their resources.

However, two years later Jan's chance came. Three London merchants, Nisbet, Grace, and Bell, all members of the Moravian Church, were fitting out a trading vessel, the *Hope,* for Labrador, and needed an interpreter and pilot. The owners closed the bargain to take Jan for the post and to give passage to three others of the Brethren "willing to stay among the savages." On arrival, Nisbet's Harbour was chosen for the winter stopping-place, and they went to work with a will to build a house, while Jan piloted the vessel around trading.

The latitude was about 55.30° and corresponds roughly with Arvertok, north of Hopedale. Some weeks later, the forlorn *Hope* returned with her flags half-masted. A week earlier, Jan, the captain, and five men had gone ashore with their only boat and never returned. So the mate brought all hands back to London. The following spring a whaler from Newfoundland found the remains of the seven men murdered on an island. The new apostle had paid the full measure for his faith.

But the quest had only become more chivalrous, and this time, as once before, a carpenter was to be the knight "sans peur." This humble, unlearned landsman, with no equipment but his faith, Jens Haven, was six years later serving in Greenland to learn the Eskimo language. Four years afterwards, alone and at his own expense, he had

151

worked his way through London to St. John's, Newfoundland. There he found the new Governor, our friend Sir Hugh Pallisier, sincerely anxious to help him. Having shipped on a fishing shallop bound for the Labrador, we see him in company with ten other of the quaint little craft bound north and already halfway across the Straits of Belle Isle, when four more shallops, flying to the south'ard, brought them news that the English had just been driven from Chateaux by hundreds of Eskimo. Fearing to proceed, they sailed back for old Carpunt Harbour.

Marvel of marvels, right in the harbour there lay at anchor the war frigate of the famous Captain Cook, who at once sent the Protestant carpenter in an Irish Catholic vessel over to Chateaux. Jens' first meeting with the savages was as dramatic and as joyous as that of Nansen at Etah when he returned from the ice. We quote Jens' own words:

"I called out to him in his kayak to come to me, that I was his good friend and had good news for him. He answered in broken French. But I begged him to speak to me in his own language and to bring his friends—on which he went to them and cried with a loud voice, 'Our friend is come.' I put on my Greenland clothes and when they came back they said, 'Here is an Innuit.' Our captain was afraid to let so many come alongside, so I went out to sea to meet them. They invited me to come to an island, an hour's row distant, to see their families. Conceiving it essential to Our Saviour's cause that I should venture my life I said 'I will go. If they kill me then is my work done.' The men who put me ashore rowed off and waited to see what happened to me. I was immediately surrounded. Everyone wished to show me his family. I gave them some needles and fishhooks, and after two hours left them, promising to return.

"Later when I begged them not to steal they said, 'But the Europeans do also.' When I spoke to them of the Saviour's death they were struck with terror, supposing that they were being upbraided for some of their former murders. They insisted afterwards on my being present at all their trading transactions (not an enviable position), for they said, 'You are our friend.'"

The carpenter was later carried home safely by the man-of-war. So pleased was Sir Hugh that the next spring Jens, together with three more of the Brethren, was sent straight to the Labrador. Another shift in the scene shows us His Majesty's man-of-war, and the *Hope* at that, carrying men whose sole weapons were faith and love as material factors for Labrador's good!

Success beyond their expectations was achieved. A real friendship was developed with the Eskimo through the trust in them and real love for them which the Brethren showed. When Sir Hugh's ship next sailed into Chateaux he was able to meet the Eskimo freely and conclude a peace with them from which he rightly expected great results.

Little wonder at the bitterness of his letter to the Governor of Boston, when he found that the New Englanders on the Coast had so barbarously broken up all he had accomplished. The reconnaissance of the Unitas Fratrum was over. They once again returned home to make further preparations for coming back to the Coast. But besides their discovery of the trustworthiness and lovableness of the Eskimo, they saw the terrible danger which this new confidence in Europeans entailed for the Innuit. The curtain drops momentarily to denote a lapse of several years.

To the practical, up-to-date man the word "mission" often connotes inefficiency, but they are shallow thinkers who confound Christianity with mere words, or mere creeds. The new motif was efficient and business-like; and the Moravian Church at home refused to carry on the work among the Labrador Eskimo at all until a land grant sufficiently large to protect the people, who would certainly settle around their stations, from unscrupulous traders and settlers had been given them. "It would be better to leave them ignorant of the Gospel altogether than to expose them to the dangers that would otherwise be involved."

At the beginning of the eighteenth century the Eskimo in Labrador were estimated at thirty thousand. When the English took possession there were only five to eight thousand. To-day, over a hundred and fifty years later, the only Eskimo left alive on the whole Labrador are about a thousand, all of whom are on the reservations of the Moravian Brethren. What further comment is needed? For the first of these reservations the Moravians had to wait years before obtaining the grant from His Gracious Majesty. Even Sir Hugh Pallisier was not far-sighted enough to advise the grant being made; though each time the Brethren sailed north he sent them off well fortified with "scraps of paper." That grant, finally given, is dated "Court of St. James', the third day of May, 1769." It was for twelve miles square, only a hundred thousand acres. Had it been ten times as large no one would have suffered, and endless lives might have been saved.

These real prophets were meticulously careful about baptizing any mere "professor of faith." The applicants must prove their fitness far more conclusively than we are asked to do to-day. Consequently, the first ceremony was not until 1776, when characteristically the first fisherman member of the new church was christened Peter. The service was so impressive that the whole audience was deeply moved. They were perhaps only more candid than we are, when one exclaimed that he, too, believed very much, but what he wanted most just then was a knife! It must be remembered that Eskimo are only human beings and that the battle of life is as difficult in their country as in ours. It was a member of a church who in a Scripture examination when asked, "What is a deacon?" replied, "A deacon is the lowest form of Christian."

Our friend Roger Curtis, the budding admiral, was now sent north to report his own personal impression of the work of the Brethren. He was a man whose report, as we have seen in the case of the New Englanders, would sometimes make a brass statue blush. Yet his estimate of the Moravians reads:

"They chose for their residence a place called by the Eskimo, Nonyoke, but to which they gave the name of Unity Bay. Their house was called Nain. It is a good situation and well contrived. There is a sawmill there already, worked by a small stream which is conducted there by their industry from the mountains. They have a garden and they raise salads in tolerable perfection. The natives love and respect them. No bolt is necessary to prevent their intrusion without permission into the palissades. The natives are beginning to abandon their sloth and do work which before they despised. The Eskimo appeal to the missionaries in their quarrels and obey them. A herd of barbarous savages are in a fair way to become useful subjects."

Doubtless to please Sir Hugh he adds, "The adventurers on the Coast will now prosecute their business with greater security."

Cartwright only exposed himself by saying that "the Eskimo dislike the missionaries and would not live near them or trade with them any more." He suggests that they were out merely to make money.

"Still as of old man by himself is priced.
For thirty pieces Judas sold himself, not Christ."

The fact that the Eskimo helped the Moravians to establish four more stations after this, and that His Majesty granted them land for each, permits us to "ha' oor ain opeenions."

The answer of the traders to the Moravians was to carry cheap, flashy goods and plenty of ardent spirits, and to entice the still foolish Eskimo south in summer, into which trap too many even of the baptized regrettably fell.

At this moment two actors cross the stage. An American of marked personality, Nicholas Darby, had come to trade at Cape Charles. He was well known as the father of the famous beauty Perdita, whom Romney, Lawrence, and Sir Joshua Reynolds have immortalized. In revenge for previous atrocities, the Eskimo killed some of Darby's men. In the general fight which followed many Eskimo were killed, and four of their women, two boys, and three girls were taken prisoners. Darby's partner took to England one of the women, Mikak, and one boy, Karpik. Karpik did not get back to Labrador. He died at Fulneck in Yorkshire, where his grave is still to be seen. The rest finally returned safely home, however. Mikak and her husband were of great help to Haven, when first he found himself preaching at Nain to eight hundred Eskimo. Both later fell victims to the wiles of some traders, were lured south and "went to the dogs." Two years subsequently Mikak returned to Nain to die. Her husband, who was known to have committed many murders, returned also. Both were terribly repentant. The mission diaries assure us that they both died convinced of forgiveness and in peace.

Meanwhile poor Nicholas Darby had lost all his money through privateers and the malice of his enemies. The lovely Perdita had to go on the stage in London, for which career David Garrick himself trained her. Later she became only one more discarded victim of that utter villain, His Royal Highness, the then Prince of Wales.

The Moravian Records state that the real results of their work did not begin to any large extent until 1804, "when a fire from the Lord was kindled among the Eskimo." Before they erected any permanent buildings they laboriously obtained the consent of the Eskimo by explaining fully to them why the Brethren had come, giving them gifts and getting from them a signed document of consent. For the first time the original owners of land were consulted.

As when Cartier left St. Malo for his first voyage, a great gathering had been held to wish "god-speed" to these new adventurers—this time in the old church in Fetter Lane, London. If Denmark sent Jens Haven, England did more, for his better half was an English girl. The leader of the expedition was Dr. Brasen. The little company totalled fourteen, at least half of whom were Danish or English. They packed their belongings into the boat with German precaution, even their building being all ready to erect. Captain Mugford took them safely to Nain, Cape Mugford; the great cliff, three thousand two hundred feet high and one of the finest on our coast, is named after him.

Through the intervening years the Moravian workers have been largely Germans. Many have been of the artisan class, satisfied with very little and content to remain at their posts for life, only visiting their home country very occasionally. Until quite recently they lived in common, each family having a sitting-room and a bedroom, and all sharing the common dining-room and kitchen. The expenses were defrayed by the Moravian Society, with headquarters in London. In early days the pay of a single man was twenty-two pounds sterling a year. At seven years of age the children were sent home, to be cared for and educated by the Society. Wives often enough were sent out, having been chosen by lot from among the Sisters willing to go on those terms. Yet the marriages seemed happy and have never been known to end in divorce. That the individuals have been satisfied with their life-work is suggested by the fact that four hundred and twenty-seven years of service have been given to this work by members of one family.

The Unitas Fratrum have shown their wisdom also in preserving the trees wherever possible; and to-day their hospitable centres are in every way oases in the desert to the traveller. To go into their trim, neat little gardens is delightful. Their settlement plan for the Innuit was of great value, but making them forsake their former nomadic life, when sanitation was unnecessary, has proved a danger. Even land-grants are unable to keep out the minute germs of epidemic diseases. Carefully kept statistics showed, however, that up to 1890 the Eskimo around the stations were on the increase.

A heavy toll has been exacted by exploiting the Eskimo in Exhibitions. Even Hagenbeck, the famous wild animal merchant of Hamburg, collected a cageful of eight men, women, and children, who insisted on going in spite of all protests of the Moravians. They were first exhibited in the Zoölogical Gardens in Berlin, then went on to Spain and on to Paris, where they all perished. The bright side of this cloud was that none lived to bring back disease to his own country. Fifty-seven were taken later to the Coast as best they could, bringing with them in lieu of their pay a severe typhoid infection, from which ninety-seven died at Nain the winter following. Thirty-three more were taken on tour through Europe in 1898 against everyone's warning. They ended up at the Buffalo Exposition. This time the six survivors brought home with them a social disease which spread through the whole of the largest settlement, and from which in turn many died.

In 1904 a large percentage of the Eskimo died of influenza. Thirty-six were buried in one grave alone. The Europeans on the Coast were evidently practically immune, for we had only high temperatures. At Okkak and Nain, again in 1911, some five hundred Eskimo died of influenza. It is well known that the danger from epidemics to native populations is great. John Paton describes how traders desiring one of the South Sea Islands would land a man with measles on it, whereupon every native would perish.

In 1890 the beautiful little Moravian station at Zoar was open. It was situated at the head of a deep fjord. Five years later the Eskimo had moved away and it was closed. As late as 1900, however, we found rhubarb and cultivated plants flourishing in the old garden, so having shot some ducks on our way up the Bay, we held a memorial feast on the abandoned site. Hopedale, the second station in importance after Nain, has now about one hundred and twenty Eskimo. Ramah and Cape Chidley stations have, like Zoar, been closed as the surrounding Eskimo died or moved away. Hebron, one of their oldest stations, still functions, as does Makkovik. In 1921 a new church was built at Nain and many new supplies sent out to celebrate the one hundred and fiftieth anniversary of the Moravian Mission on the Labrador. Their store caught fire, through someone dropping a lighted cigarette butt, it is thought, and all the buildings of the station—house, store, and church—were completely destroyed. The head of the Mission on the Coast is practically always a bishop who ranks and is paid exactly like the others. The superintendent lives at

Nain, where also a brother, trained at Livingstone College in London to a rudimentary knowledge of medicine and surgery, often saves a life, a limb, or a function. For some years recently a hospital was maintained at Okkak, with a qualified doctor in charge.

The early policy of the Moravians was to run a regular trade for the Eskimo and not encourage them to learn English, thus hoping to keep them away from trading with the whites. The Mission bought all furs, ivory, fish, and oil, and every year a ship from England brought out all supplies and took home the products. For a century, the *Harmony* and her successors of the same name sailed out year after year without accident. Even in the times of French and Spanish wars and Barbary rovers, she was never captured and never wrecked. As the Moravians possessed free trading rights before Newfoundland was a sovereign colony, that privilege was lately extended to the Hudson's Bay Company at their stations, when they bought out the Moravian trade. In return they are responsible, as were the Moravians, that the indigent natives are not left to starve.

We have always regarded the man who supplies your food as possessing every whit as much capacity for preaching the gospel of love effectively as does the man who acts as your carpenter, or supplies you with medicine or with theology. We still hold strongly that a Unitas Fratrum should be able to do better for such a unity as they and their congregation form than any individualistic "unitas" or company without necessarily any interest to serve but their own.

Shortly after the coming of the Moravians, Sir Hugh

Pallisier, seeing the results which they obtained, artlessly assumed that it was he who had been wholly responsible for Jens Haven. In 1774 the Governor ordered the Brethren, who had arrived only two years previous, to prevent the Eskimo from coming south each summer to their undoing. As he sent no police or soldiers, he must rightly have rated the constraint of love as against fear. On the other hand, when the Society's manager in London, after the first little band had been murdered, appealed to His Gracious Majesty for a blockhouse and arms, a different appraisal of relative values was suggested. The enigmatical reply of our Aberdonian Defender of the Faith of that day was fifty old muskets and some rounds of ammunition. One remembers again the dictum of Roger Curtis, that very candid critic, "Shielded by virtue, the Brethren find the protection of arms unnecessary."

To-day the natives are gentle, always cheerful, honest, and law-abiding. They are entirely Christianized, and in their daily lives and worship set excellent examples to all comers. They are musical and not only do good part singing, but play tunefully on many instruments, including the organ. Perhaps they do not catch as much codfish as do their competitors, but they "make" it better and it always fetches a higher price. The Eskimo are naturally fatalists and very easy-going. Their houses are made of wood; and unfortunately, but unavoidably, they have been taught to use European food and clothing. They can still beat the whites at making snowhouses, and at hunting seals in their skin kayaks. In winter they hunt fur-bearing animals. Until recently they

Photograph by F. C. Sears

"THE LAND GOD GAVE TO CAIN"

"HOPEDALE"

MORAVIAN MISSION STATION AMONG THE ESKIMO

have each Easter had a great caribou hunt; and again departing from ancient custom they go trapping far into the country. Seven hundred caribou have been known to be killed at one hunt, the meat being taken off the bones where the animals were killed, to enable it to be carried home out of the country more easily. To-day the deer-hunting is restricted by the Newfoundland Game Laws.

The Eskimo dies in heat and hates to be shut indoors. In the epidemic of typhoid of 1896 which we were trying to help to check, we had persuaded some of the patients to remain in their tents, as they had high temperatures. In one case we thought wise to enforce our ruling by removing the patient's clothing, including his trousers, and so keeping him in his sleeping-bag. However, he failed to understand our laudable designs and when we returned the next morning he was sitting outside stark naked waiting for the family physician and the purloined clothing. The Roman Catholic Bishop of the Arctic, whose sacrificial life among the snow-houses and within the Arctic Circle for thirty years is almost unparalleled, says that those very Northern men always die the second year they spend in the south.

When the exploring steamer *Polaris* was lost in the heavy ice, nineteen Americans with two Eskimo men and one woman were left adrift on the floe. For three months they drifted south, first on one pan and then on another as the pans broke up or turned over in the seas. The Eskimo men fed the whole party by hunting seals in their kayaks, which had been rescued before the ship sank. The Eskimo woman gave birth to a healthy baby

163

on the ice. After over a thousand-mile voyage on the floes, occupying three months, they were all picked up by the Newfoundland sealing steamer *Tigress*. The Eskimo in gratitude were taken to America, where they were given houses and everything they needed. However they died very shortly thereafter, unable to acclimatize themselves.

There could be no more fitting close to this pageant than a reference to the official report of the late Sir William Macgregor, former Governor of Newfoundland, Doctor and Gold Medallist in Medicine, scientific expert, Gold Medallist of the Royal Geographical Society, and holder of the highest Gold Medal obtainable in the Empire for saving life with great personal courage. The report was written after a summer spent in personal inspection of the entire Labrador Coast and its problems.

This entry reads:

"We arrived on Sunday at the Eskimo island about six in the morning. There were a hundred and twenty natives in the little harbour. I was curious to see how these people would conduct themselves on a Sunday when completely beyond the control of the Moravian Missionaries. It is purely a fishing station, occupied only during the fishing season. The whole community was at rest, including three fishing vessels lying at anchor. We proceeded to the little church where they had all assembled on the ringing of a bell. They had built the church themselves. A native, a chapel helper, conducted a brief morning service. There could have been no better opportunity than this surprise visit to test the efficiency of the work of the Brethren. Without supervision, control, or prompting, left entirely to their own guidance for weeks, and at perfect liberty to live as they pleased, these 'savage' natives were

164

found to keep Sunday as strictly as do any people in the world. Few communities, just for a few weeks in summer and those the busiest of the year, would build a church; but these poor men had done so and also bought a serviceable harmonium with which they accompanied the singing. The church is well provided with seats, is lined inside with dressed lumber and has a small pulpit."

"Some of them already had forty quintals of fish, and the Honourable Captain Dawe, who accompanied us, inspected it next morning and declared it excellently made. There was an entire absence of intoxicants from the island."

"Nothing that I have seen on North Labrador was so impressive as the condition of that populous little harbour on that Sunday morning. The peaceful rest and quietness, the stillness, the complete lull from the busy labours of the week, in such a community and in such a neglected and isolated spot, in such desolate and hopeless-looking surroundings, gave one at a glance, as it were, a telescopic view of the practical results of the devoted and unselfish labour of generations of Moravian Missionary men and women."

IX: THE UNDERSEA PAGEANT

"Oh, Ye Whales and all that Move in the Waters"

THE very essence of a pageant is that its beauty and its order do not depend wholly on the star actors. A pageant is a democratic institution, and to neglect the supernumeraries would be inexcusable. So our drama swings now from Homo Bimana to some of the humbler of the "brothers of St. Francis," hoping that a modern audience will find in them more of interest than did our early fathers. They permitted two thousand years to slip away between the time of the modest list of one hundred and fifteen denizens of the deep, recorded by the great Aristotle in the fourth century, B.C., and that of Belum in the sixteenth century, which totalled only

166

one hundred and ten. A hundred years later, Willoughby at Oxford increased the number to four hundred. The real study of the submarine pageant was begun by a Dutchman, Peter Artedi, who, alas, at the age of twenty-nine, in his extreme zeal, fell into a canal, and, having neglected the science of swimming, was ignominiously drowned.

This neglect of the undersea actors is less intelligible, seeing of what untold value they are to man, and also how absorbingly interesting are the endless methods they adopted for their survival. Early even in geological times, the Mosasaurus, with a neck eighty feet long, became amphibious, having realized the mistake of trying to live off the land, and to rely for safety on mere size. Whales, now the largest mammals on this planet, showed their wisdom also in abandoning companionship of the dinosaurs, who were still vainly trying to eke out a living on the land, and tucking up their hind legs under their skin, where they now lie hidden like an umbrella in a walking-stick, the whales frankly joined the submarine actors, retaining only enough of their front legs to balance with or hold their babies while suckling. They now swim automatically onwards day and night, with their mouths ever getting larger, and eternally open, so that tiny living animals of the sea, which multiply in endless billions, pour ceaselessly through their mouths. These "shrimps" are sieved out as they pass by what is called "whalebone" or plates, some three hundred of which, up to four feet long, with frayed edges for the sieve, were in one Labradorian, spread over jaws eighteen feet long. They weighed eight hundred pounds, and then were

The Romance of Labrador

about half those of Cousin Rorqual, or Right Whale, who, being of great value before steel replaced whalebone in ladies' corsets, had to fly north for safety to the eternal ice edge. There "shrimps" were scarcer, and sieves had to be larger, reaching over ten feet. In 1720, Captain Atkins of Boston records, "I bought a lot of whalebone, fourteen feet long, from the Eskimo, for ten shillings' worth of goods, and sold them for one hundred and twenty pounds sterling." To automatically keep emptying his mouth, as soon as about a puncheon-full of shrimps accumulates, his enormous tongue swells up and forces it all down his throat like a piston. This enables him to need a gullet only eighteen inches wide.

Once when we needed whalebone to supply runners for our sledges, four men with ropes pulled open a dead whale's mouth for me, and armed with a sword lashed to a long handle we walked in and dislocated the lower jaw. The joint was so far down it felt as if one were following in the footsteps of Jonah; and the operation altogether took four hours. All this bone makes whales' heads very heavy. So the sperm-whale has developed a large oil-tank in his to help float it. We saw some fishermen take fourteen gallons of oil from the head of one which had rammed it against the Labrador cliffs at Battle Harbour. Even a blind whale has never been known to starve, and blind whales are by no means rare. If a big whale runs ashore he does not really die of suffocation like a fish; he starves to death.

We measured a yellow or sulphur-bottomed whale, which is the largest of them all. He was one hundred and five feet long, with a waist forty feet round, and he

168

weighed about one hundred and fifty tons. A couple of these, having to roam round the country-side for a living, would be as destructive as an invading army.

The sperm-whale has kept great teeth with which he can bite a boat in half, in a mouth large enough to take one in, teeth as large as one's wrist, which never decay because they are a foot or more apart and no food can lodge between them. In the stomach of one sperm-whale were thirteen porpoises and fourteen seals. Sperms will even eat a white whale twenty feet long. Being now forced to feed largely on octopuses, which live at great depths, he has practically no division between his mouth and his ears; so he literally listens "open-mouthed" as he swims along. He has an automatic bag, which expands and shuts the water off from his nose when he "sounds." He has also a marvellous elastic skin, which compresses equally, and protects his "internal workings" from undue pressure at almost any depth.

A good octopus is a "bonne bouche" for him. The tentacles of one in St. John's are nineteen feet long. Those of one found in a sperm's mouth were twenty-seven feet long. Jules Verne did not unduly exaggerate when he pictured the terrible tentacles covered with deadly suckers coming down the cabin-stairs in search of the occupant.

The whale's venture into the sea has been a success. Indeed, whales are much larger than they used to be. If they go on eating at the present rate, they may hope in time to equal the one which Pliny describes as living in the Indian Sea, as "a large fish called Baleina, so long and broad as to occupy two acres of ground." Another witness of that period, not to be outdone, declares, "they are nine hundred feet long"; while Olus Magnus puts their length at "nine hundred and sixty feet."

It helped us to imagine the gargantuan muscle power of a large whale, when we saw a couple of his cousins called "gladiator" or "thresher whales" chasing one, and watched their victim throwing his immense bulk clean out of water in his endeavours to escape. He fell back each time with a crash of a waterfall and the noise of a thunder-clap, but only to be speared by swordfish waiting to prevent his "sounding" for safety.

Sperms were so numerous in 1930 that the orders to harpooneers of the Gready Whale Station were not to kill sperm-whales, as it was easier to extract the oil from the other kinds. When not at meals, a sperm is a thoroughly domestic member of the submarine society. Indeed, the old bulls may have several wives until some bigger and better whale comes along. They travel in shoals, the youngsters being always in charge of a couple of old folk.

They have eyes which are now of little value, and are small and at the side of the head, so that they can see neither forward nor backward, and the little used muscles that move them, which are as big as a good beefsteak, are the tenderest part to cook for dinner. They still need ears, however, to warn them of the approach of their cousins. These threshers are small and rely on their speed and terrible teeth. You can often see, off the Labrador, the back fins of these piratical cannibals sticking six feet out of water. They hunt in companies like all gangsters. A whaling skipper describes two that he saw attack a huge sperm mother with her baby. The mother dived with the baby to the bottom for safety, but the water was shallow, and her cousins could follow her. They bit huge mouthfuls out of her, till she was forced to give up the fight, when they incontinently ate the baby.

So marvellous are the adaptations of these remnants of a fossil age that a visit to a whale factory, even allowing for its olfactory drawbacks, is well worth while.

Truly marvellous are the "make-ups" of our other actors, the real fishes. Sunlight only penetrates the sea for two hundred fathoms. Fishes above that have developed large "glad" eyes. Below this some have developed "side-lights" through their skin, others have grown feelers from their foreheads, on which they hang phosphorescent lights, others put their eyes well ahead on these poles, like our lookouts on the bowsprit end.

Undersea performers use mostly their jaws for fighting, especially developed often, like Father William's, who adapted his by "arguing each case with his wife." Long before man recognized the value of a screw to drive ships along, fishes developed a form of propeller in their tails and back fins. To balance, they developed chest and back fins, without which they float belly up. Others, like the Blenies, have developed their chest fins even further so as to be able to take a stroll along the bottom. Others, "on the road to Mandalay," have developed partial wings, and use the chest fins for parachuting. One of our commonest has turned his into a sucker, and, sticking to anything that floats, drifts about upside down and swallows whatever comes along.

171

Many fish are still ahead of those who profess that there is no such thing as pain. A pike with his lips torn to rags by swallowing a hook, will return almost immediately and take another hook. A shark, feeding on a whale, will allow himself to be repeatedly stabbed in the head, and not let go. A shark caught on a hook and cut open, and his liver taken out for its valuable oil, has been thrown overboard, only to return again and take another bait.

"Eat or be eaten" is the motto of to-day's actors. They sleep and take rest at times, but life is largely devoted to the pursuit of food. Survival depends largely on their teeth, as they have no other organ with which to seize and hold prey. Again they are ahead of us, as they grow new teeth when others are lost. Some have them on hinges so as to be able to tuck them away. Salt-water fish are the most voracious, and many "live on their family."

Not even Eskimo or Negroes can equal to-day's actors in their capacity to adapt themselves against emergencies for heat or cold. Carp can survive in solid ice, and swim away when it melts out. The eggs of salmon and trout have been carried in ice from England to Tasmania and New Zealand, and then successfully hatched. Many a cargo of turbot and plaice I have seen kept in ice in the lockers of a fishing vessel, and, a week or more later, come out "all alive" at the fish-market. On the other hand, some fish can live on in solid mud. The lung-fish, when he senses the approach of drought, wraps himself up in a nice coat of mud, leaving only a tiny hole to breathe through. He has developed a lung specially for

172

such emergencies, and so he can await the rain, which when it comes makes the desert suddenly alive with fish! They can easily beat even Gandhi at going without food, and make hibernating bears and woodchucks look to their laurels. Carp and gold-fish go months without eating or losing weight. Many fish do not eat during winter. Some hibernate in dry ponds over a period of years. Pike scarcely eat anything in the summer. Salmon have gone a year and a half without food.

Some fish, like some toadstools, have developed power to poison their hosts, and others the power to give fatal electric shocks, long ages before Franklin, Faraday, or Edison ever saw daylight.

Some of our fishes are caught under the ice north of eighty-three degrees, where it becomes difficult to follow them; but they can live a thousand fathoms down where the temperature is below freezing, and the pressure a ton to the square inch. When brought up, these fish practically burst, even their flesh becoming very fragile and soft.

Rolling along, like "Old Man River" in many Labrador inlets, you will see Grampus, a whale about thirty feet long. He and the many porpoises destroy a host of fish. We hunt both, as their flesh is among our best meats. The "greyhound of the sea," the finback whale, about sixty or seventy feet long, is common on the Coast. Like the Humpback, which is some ten feet longer, he is too rapid and too good a fighter for the old rowboat and hand harpoon. They fall an easy prey to the small modern steamers with their gun harpoon, which travel much faster than whales, unless they are frightened. The harpooneer's job is worth up to ten thousand dollars a year and is often hereditary. Every time he fires the gun there is fifteen hundred dollars on the end of the line—or there is not.

Every year in order to give our convalescent patients a chance to earn a dollar to carry home, we buy a number of narwhal tusks. They are solid ivory, six to eight feet long, and are the two front teeth of this small whale twisted round each other, and then fused together. He uses them to dig up clams out of heavy mud.

Even when wounded, a whale is unconscious of his powers against a boat which is no larger than himself. Once a whale in his final flurry put his head through into the engine-room of the little whaling steamer. Another time, the man in the maintop, thinking that the harpooneer had "missed his fish," did not order the line to be given, and the fish rammed his head through the boat's bow. Even then, canting the hole out of water by tricing up the monster on the other side and by keeping the pumps going full speed, the skipper brought home safely both his ship and the whale. By tricing a killed whale's tail high up the rigging, three whales can be brought in at once.

A full-grown whale can remain under water for an hour. This is made possible for him by a huge reservoir of blood in front of the spouting apparatus; this is over-oxygenated. A good harpooneer can tell by the number of spoutings how long the whale which he is chasing can remain submerged. To aërate the blood thoroughly, a sperm-whale blows about sixty times, once every ten seconds. Whale meat is perfectly suitable to eat. When served as "Newfoundland beef" everyone likes it. Who can predict what a baby reared on the milk, meat, and hormones of a whale might develop into? In London, in the College of Surgeons, a skeleton of a six foot man sits easily inside the chest of another, one O'Brien, who did not stop growing until he was nine feet six inches tall!

As early as the eleventh century, a big "corporation of whalemen" operated from Caen in Normandy. Down through the centuries the story has been the same. In 1904, two companies on the Labrador killed a hundred and fifty-three whales, valued at seventy-three thousand, four hundred and forty pounds. In 1905, three sulphurs, and one hundred and nine finbacks, valued at forty-two thousand, three hundred and eighteen dollars, were destroyed. In 1906, two companies killed eighty-five whales; in 1907, ninety-four. Yet these numbers are bagatelles in comparison to those killed by the New Englanders when England first owned the Gulf, and when whalebone was fetching four hundred and fifty pounds sterling per ton.

White whales weigh about twenty-five hundred pounds. Their skin sells as porpoise-hide leather, and in the old days, the hundred or more gallons of oil which one yields fetched a high price for illumination. They eat many fish and seals. They leap in the air like porpoises. Sixty were taken in nets at Cape Chidley in one day. Their outside gelatinous skin is valued by the Eskimo, who will cut off long strips and eat them as a pigmy in Africa devours raw hippopotamus flesh. The Canadian Government recently sponsored the bombing of schools of these whales in the St. Lawrence, because of their supposed damage to the cod fishery. In 1834 New Bedford whalers landed twelve million gallons of blubber. In 1931 Norwegians took home seventy million gallons.

Without protection, not even a yellow-fever mosquito in Panama, or ague-giving ones in Africa, can resist modern man. "Every wild terrestrial mammal to-day is being killed faster than it breeds." So claims the greatest American authority on the subject. We would add that the same holds true of our whales and seals as it does of our trees. Without protection, it is a losing battle for them all against modern man.

Sea-cows, or walrus, were once plentiful in the Gulf of St. Lawrence, and great herds came to the Magdalen Islands. In 1641, a vessel hunting them off Sable Island secured four hundred pairs of tusks. To-day, walrus are practically extinct along the whole Labrador coast. The Eskimo and northern natives, armed with repeating rifles and explosive bullets by trading companies desiring skins, are proving fatal to the walrus. Though it is now so easy to shoot them at a distance, still most escape wounded, and perish. Whole communities of Eskimo have perished of starvation as a result of having destroyed their own natural food supply with these deadly modern weapons, given them only to gain a few dollars for strangers. As soon as it ceased to pay to give them ammunition, these Eskimo starved, as they had become unable to use their old simple harpoons and bows and arrows.

I have seen sick Eskimo grow strong when fed on raw walrus meat, dried somewhat in the sun. These same men soon died when sent south and fed on civilized diet. No walrus should be shot at any point west of the entrance of Hudson's Bay Straits except by the natives, and only for their own use. The animal is of very little value to the white man; but if the walrus goes, the Eskimo will have to follow. Nearly everything which an Eskimo needs can be secured from a walrus—his clothing, boat, house, weapons, lines, food, and firing.

Walrus are not migratory. They are ungainly, harmless, and even shy, hardly willing to get out of their own way. Great, good-natured fellows, they will let succeeding waves wash them ashore, and practically roll them up on the beach, rather than scramble up themselves. They would even lie on top of one another, when there were a thousand or more together, being too lazy to move. An observer describes how he watched a herd of them basking on the Alaskan beach. Before one dozed off to sleep it poked the one next to it and woke it up, so as to have one always on the alert. They use their tusks to help them climb out onto the ice, or to dig up the bottom for clams. Only when wounded or defending their young will they attack a boat.

Closely resembling these genial personalities of the undersea pageant come the seals. Anyone who has seen the human qualities of performing seals in a circus, and has any love for animals, must most deeply desire that they should be protected. The splendid results of the co-operation of America, England, Canada, and Japan in preserving the seals in the Pacific have met not only with the approval, but with the sincere gratitude, of all right-thinking people. For there, those marvellous friends of man were threatened with extinction. To-day

177

the herds are once again as numerous as ever, showing that not only on the land—as in the case of the buffalo—but in the sea, man can, if he will be unselfish enough, use without abuse the creatures which have been placed in this world to help make it worth living in.

Pacific seals have not joined the undersea pageant as whole-heartedly as the whales or the Atlantic seals. They prefer solid ground to bear and nurse their babies. All other seals have gone as far as to make their nurseries on the solid ice-floe, and to give up their fine fur coats for safety's sake; so that the seal with the best fur coat patronizes only warmer waters. The warm water, by never freezing, has enabled him to retain his outside ears. The polar seals, like the whales, have had theirs clipped off. For this reason, the fur seals are called Otariidae (or eared) and really are sea bears. There are eight varieties of them. The polar seals are called Phocidae. Of these there are seventeen varieties.

Of the cold-water seals, the ones with which Labrador is concerned are the Harps—large, yellowish fellows, with black, harp-shaped patches over their shoulders—and the Hoods, the males of which have developed a big hood or bag on their noses, which they can blow up at will. It makes them look very ferocious in a fight, and also protects them materially from blows over their most vital spot. Both these varieties of seals are still socially minded and all get together at the breeding-time. It is a fatal habit, for this is the time when, to his shame, man attacks them. Large steamers, sheathed to resist ice, carrying hundreds of men armed with repeating rifles and dogwood poles with heavy, iron pikes, leave for the seal hunt. On the tenth of every March, at one o'clock, they set forth from St. John's, Newfoundland, so that all may have the same chance. To make the hunt surer, of late years these ships have been guided by airplanes and wireless messages to the spot where the poor seals have located their nurseries.

The baby Harp seals are very beautiful, being "kotiks" or "white coats." The baby Hood is blue. Alas, each mother has only one. They are practically all born on the same night, March the fifth. In a large steamer, the *Neptune*, we were marooned in the ice-field one March. When we turned in at night not a seal, old or young, was to be seen in the moonlight. We were lying in the smooth, or "whelping" ice. There was much disturbance in the night, and the "bawling" as we got up after daylight was prodigious. That morning we counted over three thousand babies. The milk, rich like that of whales, helps them to grow very rapidly, almost as a butterfly's wings grow when first he emerges from the chrysalis. When born, these seals weigh eight to ten pounds. In two days they weigh twenty; in three weeks, forty to fifty pounds. One baby thirty-eight inches long was thirty-four inches around the waist. They grow so fat that you can see them lying on their backs in a fluffy bed of snow, fanning themselves with their flippers in the sun, looking like large butterballs dressed in down, with their noses a tiny black dot at the top. At three weeks old, the mothers pull them off the ice by the tail if they are afraid and refuse to go into the water; but once they are in they swim like young ducks. The aristocratic baby fur seal, though born near warm water, makes much more fuss, and has to be regularly taught to swim. Our Kotik soon loses his baby fur in patches, becoming a "ragged coat" before, at three weeks old, he leaves the ice.

The waste in our seal industry is appalling; and now the catch scarcely pays for the outlay. The men love the adventure, but get little monetary return. On the occasion described we waited for a few days watching the little animals grow, and then—well, the slaughter of the innocents in Herod's day was as child's play compared to the massacre which ensued. Many young seals are killed too far from the ship to haul them back, so their skins and fat, called "pelts," are left in great heaps on floating ice-pans, with the special ship's flag on the top. Thousands of these piles get lost. Moreover, all the meat and with it much fat is always wasted, and the pitiable skinned bodies are simply left on the ice, prey for countless sharks.

The babies, once in the water, are sent north by their mothers. Some marvellous magnetic sense enables them to go straight. Alas, great submerged rooms of nets running out from the headlands waylay many of them, especially the yearlings; while the babies, now risen to the dignity of "young Harps," as they beat down north must come up between the pans of ice occasionally to breathe. Once up, childlike, they are very apt to loiter and play. So all along the hundreds of miles which they must travel hunters run out onto the floe, build ice walls called "gazes" on the edges of the cracks, or "swatches," in the ice, and await the unfortunate youngsters with a rifle. At this time the seal is fat and floats when dead. In the fall of the year it sinks. Two of the dogs in a team I once had, learned to dive off the ice edge and swim to the bottom in eighteen feet of water to bring up a seal for me.

The Harp seals are found in both the North Pacific and North Atlantic, but chiefly off the Labrador and Newfoundland coasts. They practically never leave floating ice if they can help it. They never climb out on the land. One might imagine that they lived in constant fear of spontaneous combustion. To make the rich milk the mothers have to leave their offspring both in fair weather and foul, lying on the ice which has moved in the meanwhile, and return to find their one particular baby among all the other thousands. Yet no man could tell two baby seals apart. Moreover, in maternity hospitals, with only a few dozen human babies at most, each has to have a little brass tag chained to his arm, for fear that their mothers will not know which is which.

It is good to know that it is warmer under water than it is in the air. The northern Eskimo, when taking fish out of their nets in winter, must keep their hands and net and everything under water or their hands would be frozen solid in two minutes. In 1931, a tidal wave swept over three families of Eskimo and soaked them all. In a few minutes they were all frozen into solid blocks of ice, and were better preserved than an Egyptian mummy in his case.

The Hood seal is much larger than a Harp seal. He is a fierce fellow at close quarters, but holds a fine domestic reputation. I saw one snatch in his teeth a heavy gaff from one of four men who were attacking him on a small floating ice-pan. Whirling it around like an Irishman, he soon put them all to flight. Both he and his family, however, were all slain on the pan at last. As he was being hauled aboard, his immense weight, of approximately a ton, broke the line and he fell into the cold water. Apparently it brought him back to life, for with one final leap he jumped right back onto the same piece of ice where the tragedy had taken place, still glad to risk his own life in the endeavour to save that of his family.

Old seals, for all their large eyes and gentle looks, eat their prey alive. They will bite a piece out of a fish and leave it to swim away if it can. They will eat live birds swimming in the water. They are great fighters.

Hunting of the great herds of Hood seals—one of the largest species, which used to flourish off East Greenland —only began in 1751. Then there were about a million of them. Yet by 1884 the animal had practically disappeared in that locality. Large numbers of Hood seals are still being destroyed each year off Newfoundland by the steamers of our seal fishery. Five hundred thousand baby seals have been killed in one year. Forty years ago these seals were the mainstay of the Labrador. Everyone then had seal nets with huge, eight-inch meshes in which the animals were caught. Fleets of these nets were set all along the Coast in the fall of the year; for the fat meat and skins of the seals were invaluable to the settlers. To-day it scarcely pays to set a net except in the Far North. There is no question that the seals are diminishing in number, and that unless they are protected or other industries substituted, the white population on the Coast, as well as the northern Eskimo, must disappear.

The Undersea Pageant

Fortunately seals, exactly like men, have not all cared to join the "madding crowd," some preferring to loaf along in the calm fjords and river mouths, where salmon and sea trout are plentiful. One such is our common bay seal. He is a clever fellow, and never goes south into the danger zone to breed. As a youth he affects a beautiful, silvery coat, with a "plus-four" effect at the first moult. He keeps near shore and utterly spurns ice-floes. He can stand heat or cold, salt or fresh water, and is equally at home in the Atlantic and the Pacific, off Europe, Asia, and America, on sea and land. He has all the wits of a fur seal when it comes to learning tricks. The meat is invaluable to our scattered settlers. These seals will outlast the rest, just because they never go in herds. They are mischievous fellows and love clearing the fish out of the fishermen's nets. I have known a fisherman to have to hang on to his nets all day long, just because some roguish bay seals were eating a bit out of every trout or salmon he entangled. Even then he had to be quick, for the seals had a playful way of appearing from nowhere and snapping the fish right out of his hand.

The bay seal can travel quite long distances over land, and stay for hours out of water. One of his cousins seems to be cultivating the back-to-the-land habit, for he has chosen to reside permanently in a Labrador lake, which is at least a hundred miles inland, and five hundred feet above sea level. As a hobbledehoy, the bay seal is appropriately known as a "ranger." He is easily lured to the decoy of a man lying out on a rock in a bag of sealskin, who now and again flaps his legs about. One hunter, however, while doing this was descried by a stranger coming along the shore, who promptly put a bullet through him.

The bearded seal is our largest. He measures from ten to twelve feet long and maybe eight feet in girth—a veritable aldermanic waistline! He weighs half a ton. His coat is very thick grey, and, practically hairless, is all ready for water-tight boots or kayak covers. He is wise enough to keep off the land, but he often gets tangled up in sunken nets, presumably because of the curiosity of the hermit that he is. We know him as the square flipper, and owe him many debts.

Subsidiary actors, we call these denizens of the seas. But they discovered the New Lands long before Winged Hats were heard of, and had developed fur coats ages before man had even learned to cover himself with fig leaves. They have their rights, not merely of priority of discovery, but because even now, with all our superiority, we cannot do without them. For centuries our actors depended on them for life and light. Without these humble creatures the whole fabric of this romance must have collapsed, and the curtain fallen, never to rise again.

In the Great Basin there are innumerable other actors invaluable also to the whole cast. A grateful skipper sent us one day to hospital a huge halibut borne on the shoulders of four stalwart fishermen. The remains of the above-mentioned tribute, after the hospital had toyed with it for a week, were with due solemnity committed to the cabbage-garden, to its no small profit.

A halibut bank, covering many hundreds of miles, has been discovered all along the middle Labrador Coast. Halibut liver is now known to give oil with five times the vitamin content of cod-liver oil; so there should be terror in the strongholds of the tubercle bacillus. A properly smoked halibut steak is an excellent substitute for a Yorkshire ham.

Cold does not bother a halibut. He flourishes most abundantly off Greenland. He is virile to a degree and well calculated to survive. He has an all-embracing appetite and the teeth of an ogre. Woe to the family if it gets in the way when papa is hungry. Half a barrel of flat-fish is only a snack to one of these "real fellows." He lives to a ripe old age, as the barnacles on his back testify.

Our fishermen will have no dealings with the endless flat-fish of the Coast unless forced to do so, nor with the ubiquitous mussel, though to both of these many poor folk owe their lives. In the spring, when the winter food supplies have run out and before vessels from the south can force their way north through the ice, it is to the numerous but despised flat-fish or mussel that the hungry turn.

Fashion and convention are not limited to civilization. Through being dubbed a "dab" and a "mud-dab" at that, a strong prejudice has been aroused against this valuable and versatile friend. Properly disguised, he has secured considerable popularity in New York as an "American sole." As a youngster he is still a free swimming, upright fish. But having found it both easier and safer to lie hidden in the mud, he adopted that mode of life. Not only is mud an excellent ambush, but the slightest move obscures him entirely in a smoke screen, and makes even spearing him an art. He is the trump-card in the argument for adaptation; for, lying in the mud, his under eye became useless, so it travelled round his head, till now both are on one side. Legend attributes his ugly jaw to his smile of disdain when he heard the reception was over. His jaw is also said to account for his being brown on one side, for when Moses had caught him in crossing the Red Sea, after browning him on one side, he caught sight of his face, and hastily threw him back into the deep.

Everywhere, everywhere are the unique and unquestionable monarchs of the scavenger world, the sculpins. Their adaptation for and devotion to their job is almost incredible. They have become an indefinitely distensible sack behind with an enormous hard, round jaw, and an insatiable, omnivorous attention to business. The sculpin is protected by an array of poisonous spikes which prevent even his most ardent friend from making any mistakes. His unequalled zeal for service is best illustrated by the fact that he is always waiting to absorb anything on your hook; and though the barb may have penetrated any part of his anatomy, he will immediately return to his job when you throw him back overboard. To avoid hauling in endless line to no purpose, it is best to oblige him by leaving him temporarily on deck. He, too, however, has many times sustained human life. One winter when influenza had killed every bread-winner in a lonely family and a helpless mother was left, she was able to avail herself of this assiduous fish till help arrived.

Another of our "Chamber-of-Horrors face" group is the lump-fish. He is runner-up to the clam in the idleness championship. Being too lazy to swim about, he has developed a large sucker by which he fastens himself upside down to anything floating about. There by merely opening his mouth he can secure his meals without even having to get up for them. Like the clam he is a model professor of psychology in times of depression.

> *"If jarring tempests beat upon my bed*
> *Or summer peace there be,*
> *I do not care; as I have said,*
> *All's one to me.*
> *A clam,*
> *I am."*

Yet both these maligned creatures have the virtue of contributing their quota to the food-locker when needed.

Haddocks are distinguished by a large black finger-mark on each side of their bodies. This is irreverently attributed to St. Peter's fingers, when he was extracting the tribute-money from the animal's mouth. On our coast local tradition claims that if you are quick enough to pick a haddock out from among the cod in the net, and extract his fin-bone without letting him touch the gunwale of the boat, you will be safe from rheumatism as long as you wear the said fin-bone around your neck.

After the trout, the rock-cod is our best winter fish. Both these are abundant and easily procured. The sleeper shark also remains with us, and makes a valuable contribution. His liver yields thirty gallons of oil of unique value. Mixed with seal oil it is admirable for lamps. His rough skin is used "as is" for scrubbing cabin floors. Tanned, it makes good leather. The rest of him, if soaked and dried to extract a poison, is a most sustaining food for sledge-dogs. He is the embodiment of lethargy. I have hauled more than one out onto the ice with a boat-hook, with scarcely any resistance on their part, though some were larger than I. Yet he has teeth which will peel the skin and fat off a large seal, when caught in a net, so that he can swallow it in one long piece.

"Believe it or not," human beings have regarded a shark's stomach as the surest gate to heaven, and have cast their children to them to make certain of meeting them in paradise.

There is no space to tell of the extraordinary capelin, literally invaluable for food and for bait, or the service-able shell-fish, or cockles and scallops and whelks. The abundance of old shells has made a trade in them remu-nerative. Moreover, mixed with our acid soil they make a fine dressing for the garden. Cleverly they make the mud serve as their fur coat, thicker or thinner as need dictates, by the simple process of boring, and leaving a longer siphon to the surface by which to breathe. It is a dull life, perhaps, but purposeful. What more can be said of any life?

Probably the most valuable of all are the minutest, the tiny crustacea, diatoms, and all that go to form the food of whales and herrings. They are the oil which lubricates the whole machinery of the undersea pageant, and with-out them the whole would be utterly ruined. This is equally true of the many seaweeds, which elsewhere sup-ply food and medicines to mankind, down to the tiny algae that can build up food out of sunlight and the ele-ments themselves.

But what of the human actors in the undersea pageant? Occasional failures of the fishery on the Banks and the competition with better fitted vessels from wealthier countries, drove the poor Newfoundlanders to Labrador. Those having no schooners of their own took passage down with the more fortunate. Once on the Labrador they built mud and board shacks in some cove or harbour and paid freight for carrying back their cured fish to the south. The custom of freighting in steamers and square-rigged ships for Europe has made it common of late to ship direct from Labrador to the Spanish, Greek, and other European markets. The development of mines and paper-mills in Newfoundland has helped out also by giving work to those who have made bad voyages. Their small farms are tended by the aged, the women not needed on the Labrador, and the incapacitated. Many women, however, do go "down north," and enjoy it. Quite a number form part of the crews of schooners.

So "handy" are the men, even when unable to read and write, that they will go into the virgin forest in the fall of the year and come out with a schooner in the spring. What struck us first, coming from the North Sea fisheries in one of our own vessels, were the great risks which these fellow-subjects undergo. Owing to their poverty all running rigging was poor and even their anchors were far too light, their chains were old and untrustworthy and not long enough to hold in the cyclonic storms of the North. They were a great contrast to the Gloucester and Nova Scotian boats which were splendidly equipped, and whose hawsers were the cynosure of all eyes. While towing one of these vessels which we picked up disabled, her hawser alone was all we could handle; and if we stopped steaming full speed ahead, the dead weight of the hawser dragged us astern. Per contra, on one occasion, when caught with seven Newfoundland schooners in fog and sea and obliged to anchor in the open for the night, every one of the seven dragged its anchors or broke its moorings. They were all lost on the rocks, though there was no loss of life. Our chains, however, held splendidly, and so we were able to ride out the storm.

The local schooners were also very small for carrying the big nets, a cargo of salt, puncheons, and barrels for oil, at least two boats and generally a trap-boat in tow behind, as it was too large to put on board. As years went by a few schooners were fitted with motor engines, which added oil and gasoline tanks to be carried. Space had to be found for splitting tables, shields, spare canvas, gear, oars, instruments, food for the crew for three months, fuel and spare clothing. When sailing day came and there were perhaps twenty, thirty, and sometimes more men, women, and children, and all their personal belongings to be accommodated, it is little wonder that the danger and difficulties of the voyage were enormously increased. Water, except for drinking, was an exceedingly scarce article, sanitary arrangements were practically non-existent. Often, when taking a passage on a schooner, the cooking had to be done on deck over a fire in an iron pot filled with sand—a very healthy arrangement.

Of late years, the fishermen freighters, aided by the Government, have taken passages north on the mail

190

steamers; but they have no money to spare and their accommodation even then is so terribly crowded that nothing but the natural, simple-hearted kindness of men of the sea would put up with it at any price.

In the early days I have many times attended patients by crawling through the hatch on deck, momentarily lifted to allow the "doctor" to slip down between the waves flying over the heavily laden vessel. No one who has not seen these schooners loaded for their long voyage will believe that the actual main-deck is sometimes literally under water, the salt water rolling in over the deck through the scuppers even in harbour. Then the poop, quarter-decks, and coamings alone keep the water out, and when under way hatches must be practically air- and water-tight, since any water going below will spoil the precious and perishable cargo for which all the risks are taken.

In these crowded holds, where separations for families have been marked only by chalked lines on the beams, I have attended confinement cases, tubercular patients, and every kind of ailment. Only the sterling character of the fishermen, their real sea genius, their true generosity to one another, and their deep religious sense redeem the situation. Never have I gone aboard a perfectly strange craft without being kindly received. College boys returning home from our work often ask for passages, and invariably the skipper, having no other cabin to offer, has given up his own and been willing to "sleep on the settle." How many of us who read this book would dream of such a courtesy? Poor though they may be in dollars, our fishermen would feel it an insult to be offered payment for their kindness.

Heavy tides, rising and falling up to thirty feet and abounding with swirling eddies and whirlpools at Cape Chidley, add greatly to the danger in that vicinity. Fortunately, on the east Atlantic coast there is only a six to eight foot rise even on "springs." Sudden storms of great violence on our Coast are sometimes accompanied by fog. There are numberless reefs and shoals, still uncharted. In spring, the schooners must not wait for the ice-fields to depart or for storms to abate in their race north to secure headlands or "berths" which are regarded as "prime"—that is, where most fish aggregate. This race is necessary, because often they have left their hut with nets, salt, and gear near the spot, which the first crew arriving will seize for the summer. Many a dispute about "trap berths" it has been my misfortune to adjudicate upon. On the Canadian coast a small fee protects these berths and saves the necessity for rushing north so early in the season.

We are proud of our yeoman fishermen, proud of their physical courage, their self-reliant resourcefulness, and their big hearts, which make them willing, year after year, as soon as the ice-fields begin to leave the shore, once more to fare forth on the venturesome voyages. We once picked up a dory which had been adrift for five days. The men told me that they were "beginning to be hungry." They had the insouciance not to say one word of complaint, as "it was the fault of no one but ourselves." All the same, the losses of the big nets, of boats, and of lives are frequent; and he is indeed a lucky fisherman who can put by a sufficiency for his old age.

The merchant who provides the big net and "grub-stakes" the crew also has his losses. Under the old barter system, if there was any profit at all, the merchant got it first. Now, when the balances owing the fishermen must be paid in cash, the merchant is often so heavily the loser that many firms have broken and gone out of business.

What human laws can do to prevent prosperity we noted recently when leaving Labrador and saw hundreds of tons of good fish lying unsold in the stores, wharves, and vessels' holds, belonging to men who needed wheat above all things; while a week later in New York we saw thousands of hungry men line up for a bite to eat, with thousands of tons of wheat rotting in Government stores. Prosperity must increasingly be as much a result of *international* co-operation and camaraderie as it is of scientific adaptation and technical skill. To make matters worse, there were hundreds of steamers lying in dock doing nothing, while their crews were idle on the wharves and living on doles. They might easily have been exchanging the fish for the wheat. None can escape the ripples of war's aftermath.

X: THE PAGEANT OF THE THREE KINGS

(Of *Sub-Arctic Waters*)

IF ROYALTY is assessed by what a family does for a country, then the rightful heirs to the Labrador throne are denizens of the undersea kingdom. First in his resemblance to the conventional idea of royalty comes His Majesty Salmo Salar, the Atlantic salmon, clad in his flashing armour of silver. He stands unquestionably in the front rank of game fishes; and the two varieties of landlocked salmon of Labrador in all respects rank worthily as kinsmen of the royal blood.

The old story that the North Pacific coast of America was left to any country which wanted it because England had no use for lands where salmon would not take a fly, suggests the claim to princely rank of youngsters which, as mere stripling grilse of a couple of pounds, cannot be landed on a six-ounce rod in less than ten minutes, and which at four pounds will keep an expert at bay for an hour. The salmon's savage strike, his spirited runs, his gallant leaps, and his incomparable endurance and beauty entitle him to claims that all aristocrats will acknowledge.

Leif the Lucky and his Viking followers record his challenge to them. All through the early centuries it was he who secured the first following, only too zealously for his good, of all new arrivals from the earlier Red Indians to the blond British of to-day.

Stability is an economic asset of a royal line, if guaranteed only by its obedience to the scriptural injunction to "be fruitful and multiply." The values of this family to humanity in dollars alone will be referred to shortly.

Our salmon lives nobly, with a summer home in the river and a winter one in the sea. We admire him for his strong love of home, a love which is royally intense, for when he has made up his mind to return there nothing but death can stop him. In one phenomenal storm a complete barrier of sand and gravel was thrown up by the sea across the mouth of an Alaskan river. During the "spring run" young bloods and elders alike flung themselves out of the water onto the offender, and by wriggling and jumping over the pebbles some at least succeeded in reaching the other side. Three things only will keep them from their home—pollution of the water, man's rapacity, and an insuperable barrier, all of which alike spell "death or glory." The second, or "fall run," is more casual and probably for food or a "joy ride." The first venture is led by the old fish, who are guided by experience and by the temperature of the water. They time their arrival in a leisurely way from June to July. They may take a turn back to the sea if the rivers are still too cold when they first arrive. They may run in and out a bit to accustom themselves to the change to fresh water. They can "bide" if they want to.

Most obstacles are things to be overcome. As Nietzsche said, "Everything worth while is accomplished *notwithstanding*." The salmon will leap a twelve-foot cataract, will light in the water of a thirty-foot fall and shoot right up on it. I have watched them, when the water channels have been narrow, many times in error hit the rock-face at the top of their leap, and yet go on trying until, "bruised and dying, they float down on the bosom of the river they loved, to a tomb in the great deep out of which they came." The zeal of the old Lama and Kim for the River of the Arrow was no greater than that of this kingly-spirited fish.

He is more wary than the sea-trout, but like the trout his convictions still lead him into trouble. He sees twine in the daylight but is not willing to accept a check. He will range along until he is surrounded in the pound at the water end of the net, where, confused and angry, he charges it, knows no surrender, and is not satisfied till he has forced the tough twine over his head and gills, when it is too late to save himself.

Once in her own pool, mother salmon finds a suitable sandy spot in shallow water, where the ground is soft and deep and the current gentle. If it happens to be the nest of a sea-trout Her Majesty overlooks the intrusion, and lying on one side scoops out a "redd" or nest with her tail. In this she deposits eggs every day for eight or ten days until she has about five hundred for every pound she weighs. Each time, her partner accompanies her spreading the milt which is necessary to fertilize the eggs. Hungry trout waiting just below swallow a few, but woe betide them if the watchful king spies them. Three to five out of every thousand eggs reach maturity, possibly five hundred to every mother.

Outside in the sea the salmon have grown fat on the rich diet obtainable, on capelin, herring, sprats, lance, and sand eels. The many crustaceans there give their flesh the beautiful pink colour, pinker in warmer water where more of these small animals thrive. But in the river, salmon avoid much danger by taking no food at all, due to which "Banting" they lose about half their weight. A salmon fly is not like any food which a salmon knows. But they "sleep with their eyes open," can tell colours apparently, and it is supposed that some colours just irritate them, while others attract. The same is the case with butterflies and birds and humans. A salmon has been timed to go seventeen months without eating. So the king becomes tough and wiry and his jaw becomes hard. This toughness is a great help to the salmon in his many jousts with his enemies.

When the spawning is all over the spent fish are called "kelts." The tired mother turns black, the males red, black and yellow, and vast numbers die. Some say that they are poisonous to eat, but as the poacher remarked, "Them's not bad kippered." The farthest north fish are

197

apt to live longer and have more families. The championship of the Atlantic is held at present by a Newfoundland fish, which was fourteen years old and had five families.

Salmon eggs are round, pink, and so elastic that they will bound off a board like a rubber ball. At the right temperature they hatch out in a month, but they can wait if it is not to their liking. Stored in ice they have been carried safely to India, Australia, and New Zealand, where in the perfect climate they have developed such love for their new home that they never leave the fresh water. Yet they can, as adults, range from thirty-seven degrees north latitude to seventy degrees.

The babies are always called Alevins for about three weeks, while they live on the large umbilical sacks which hamper their movements, so that they hide away among stones. But beetles, insect larvae, shellfish, trout, rats, and diving birds all love babies enough to take them in. If they survive they become Parrs, and in the South remain some two years in the river. Farther north they stay four or even six years. Anyhow, they throw their parents' scruples to the winds and eat voraciously. As Parrs they may grow to a couple of pounds, but the full glory does not appear until the third spring, when they assume their glittering silver armour, and take the title of Smolt. They may then remain another year or even two in the river, but usually fare forth with many comrades of their own age into the immense, unknown ocean.

Like real rovers they can travel anywhere. We caught a ten-pound salmon near Belle Isle, with a tag in his fin to show that he was a five-year-old Nova Scotian "Blue

SALMON FOUR YEARS IN RIVER

Photograph by F. C. Sears

ONE OF THE THREE KINGS

SALMON SEEN JUMPING UP FALLS

Nose." Once out in the sea they take the name of Grilse, and may not return to their river for two, three or even four years. In the sea they grow rapidly and usually become large fish. Nor do they always return to the same river, though they appear to make efforts to do so. On their first visit home they do not generally have a family, but loaf around in pool and lake, and enjoy a more unhampered trip—at least until they are from five to six years old and weigh about ten pounds.

It is easy to tell the story of a salmon's life by his scales. These, like our nails, grow from the surface; and the rings of greater or lesser width apart on them show by the speed of growth whether the fish was feeding in the sea or starving in the river.

Hundreds of Labrador rivers are stocked with salmon, sea trout, and river trout. As they have taken a fly in every river we have ever fished, it is doubtless true to say that they will do so in all its rivers at the right time of year. The chief authority, Dr. Thomson, of the Newfoundland Fishery Research Bureau, said in 1931, "Up to the present there is no serious evidence that the stock has suffered depletion." For fighting, the Atlantic Labrador salmon is the gamest fish anywhere in the world. No Labrador rivers are reserved. A simple license makes a visitor free of all of them. In these days the flies are an unsurmountable difficulty only to the unprepared. No rivers are netted. No nets are allowed within two hundred yards of the outside entrance. The legal width of mesh for a salmon net is seven inches, so most grilse go right through. It has been shown statistically that it is a valuable precaution to prevent fishing in a salmon river on one day in seven. Labrador fishermen invariably obey that law, because they consider it a divine one.

Very large trout up to twenty pounds, game whitefish, and ouananiche, or land-locked salmon, afford excellent sport in all the higher reaches of our big rivers. In July, 1775, Major Cartwright wrote, "In Eagle River we have a hundred and forty tierce (three hundred pounds each) ashore, but have had to take up two nets as fish get in too fast. The big pool is so full of fish that you could not fire a ball into it without injuring some. On the banks are remains of thousands of salmon killed by white bear around the pool." In 1779 he writes, "We are killing seven hundred and fifty salmon a day in Eagle River. We should have had a thousand tierce by now at Paradise if I had more nets. At Sandhill Cove two men have two hundred and forty tierce ashore, and could have more, but they have no more salt." Waxing poetical, he adds, "Salmon up fresh rivers take their way. For them the stream is carefully beset; few fish escape!" This was caused by ten nets, each forty fathoms long, end to end, stretching right across the stream.

In 1921 Mr. John Clouston shipped to London nearly nine thousand pounds of frozen salmon. Owing to the Birdseye Instantaneous Freezing Process, salmon is shipped to-day to any part of the world, and can be put on the table so that an epicure cannot tell it from a salmon caught the same day. Fresh salmon, frozen by this process, are shown to be sterile of all bacteria, a statement which cannot be made of any other method of curing it, except by tinning.

Our cold-water salmon are crisper, flakier, fatter, and

more succulent than any others, and much more so since all are caught in the sea. Twenty fishmongers, at a dinner given in the Fishmongers Hall, were asked to pick out the fish that they liked best from the three varieties —fresh fish from England, from Scotland, and the instantaneously frozen ones from Labrador. Sixteen chose the Labrador fish. When salesmen are willing to make salmon a poor man's food instead of a luxury, tens of thousands who have never had the chance to taste this delightful and nutritious king of fish will be able to add it to their ordinary food staples. Amongst others, Her Majesty Queen Mary has given her unqualified approval of it.

2

King or no king, one thing is certain, the great Atlantic basin with all its infinite wealth has produced through the ages no greater blessing to mankind than the humble herring. As neither the Mediterranean nor the Pacific has yet succeeded in evolving him, he has almost a monopoly as a source of wealth to the Norse blood in the struggle of that race for existence. Anglo-Saxons, Bretons, and Basques have owed far more to the herring than has been realized. Men have wondered that the small islands known as "Britain" could feed their relatively large population, and without great farm-lands and prairies raise such well-fed generations. On a potato alone a man starves to death; if he can add a herring to it he has an ideal diet.

King Herring is the fattest of fish, in spite of the untold numbers of its vast hordes that travel together, which make it so easy to catch in paying quantities, and in spite of the fact that it comes close to the shore to be caught, year after year, at about the same time and in the same places. Thus man may be prepared for it and the fleets of small fishing vessels have time to come leisurely to the rendezvous.

Fat is a prime essential of all food-stuffs, and the most expensive. Many a time I have taken a herring out of the net, and while grilling him over the fire-pot on the boat's stern, seen him catch fire just from his own fat. Many times, too, I have sailed in fleets of boats being brought in by a spanking breeze of wind, and the herring oil had so covered the ocean surface that even old Boreas could not ruffle its contentment.

Professor Huxley calculated that this monopoly of our great food basin of the Atlantic gave us every year an average of not less than some millions of tons of fat and protein—man's most costly food necessities. What king has ever contributed more royally to the betterment of nations than King Herring? Even the war debts sink into insignificance, for since history began and until history ends, without complaints, without quarrelling, without fears or defaulting, he has paid, and can perennially pay, this tribute.

Labrador's pride is that, of all herrings, her herring is king of kings. Only Icelandic and Shetland herring can begin to compare with him in size. He is nearly twice as large and weighs three times as much as any others, even from Cape Hatteras to Cape Farewell in Greenland. He yields twice as much fat as other herring. Some of these characteristics Scripture has recorded as royal attributes in the selection of the first king of Israel.

Wise human kings and queens have actually worshipped at the shrine of King. Herring. In 1300 one William Berkelzen of Flanders made an epochal discovery. He not only found out new ways to preserve herring for better food for humans, but became forever famous by this gift to humanity, for he made no selfish patent of it—the first "red herring," the trail of which ever since has been dragged around the whole world. Exploits in preserving kings were well rewarded, no doubt, in the days of Tutankhamen; but on the death of this "mortician," the great Charles the Fifth erected a monument to William's memory, visited his grave, and there prayed for his soul. Mary, Queen of Hungary, paid an even more royal tribute to this benefactor not only by personally visiting William's tomb, but by sitting upon it while she ate a red herring! At least we may regard this as a symbolic coronation of our second king, paralleled by the knighting of the loin of beef by King Charles the Second. If Napoleon was right in saying "men fight on their stomachs," he, too, must have recognized the necessity for loyalty to King Herring on behalf of the armies.

The fact is, the world can afford to lose any other royal family better than this one. Beyond argument, this is being recognized by the immense amount of time and intellect and money spent every year in scientific research, study, and legislation by the nations, in order to secure the persistence of the herring family for all nations for all time. Whether the success hitherto noted has been due to their efforts or not is very doubtful.

Unfortunately, in the cold water the herring has been classed by some with undue severity with King Henry, the Merrie Monarch, as "royal in his inconsistency." On the surface this seems a justifiable criticism; for herrings which for years paid a million dollars annual tribute to the colony of Newfoundland, suddenly dwindled to a few paltry barrels a year. History shows that cycles occur with herrings as with everything else, including history itself. 1020, 1260, 1550, 1660, 1750, 1850, and 1900 were pivotal years of great abundance. The failure is not a moral one this time, but some irresistible physical cause which one day man will discover and remedy if he can.

There seems every prospect of the herring returning to Labrador. Of late years we have frequently steamed through shoals of these fishes, and in the dark been dazzled by the fireworks of their silver sides flashing in the brilliant phosphorescence of the tiny marine creatures which they disturb in their acrobatic flight. Herring have been seen north of Cape Mugford on the Labrador Coast so thick that the sea was like glass for the oil which they were exuding.

With salmon they share the delightful homing instinct, and separate families seek the same banks twice a year in the shallower ocean depths. The individual herring has his first family when he is eighteen months old, and one family annually afterwards. The solution of the puzzle of their choice of location is doubtless a matter of temperature. Fifty-five degrees Fahrenheit is the optimum selected for the family. This may account for the fact that herrings are not known to breed north of the Magdalen Islands. In its earliest stages, every form of life in the ocean is exceedingly sensitive to changes in temperature; so Father Neptune, long before man, had a thermometer at his disposal which was not dependent on the free, inconstant will of the particular instrument any more than is the rise and fall of the mercury a matter of free will or predestination.

We may consider it unwise, but the mother herrings no doubt know better, when they regard it as a necessity to keep their eggs together in the vast ocean water for the purpose of fertilization. They are anchored in a great mass, each mother contributing from thirty to forty thousand eggs. The whole sinks and becomes attached to stones and other fixed objects, while over it floats freely the fertilizing milt. There, alas, it is all too dangerously possible for the endless dogfish and other lovers of these pledges to posterity to scoop them up by the thousand in a mouthful. Moreover, they can be destroyed by endless larvae, crustaceans, and sea-worms. But if every egg of every herring except two were destroyed, says Huxley, the herring would still maintain their vast numbers.

Were it not for one special provision, however, the world would probably long ago have been robbed of this best of friends. While it is true that these babies must worry over how not to be eaten, they are spared the trouble of worrying over what they shall get to eat. Not being predatory, they are spared the eternal query whether you will eat your breakfast or your breakfast will eat you. It is true that herring have teeth both on their tongue and the roof of their mouth; but these are mostly used to guide the water containing diatoms and every kind of living plankton to the fine spines across their gills, where the water that enters it is sieved out, and the food passes on quite naturally down the throat. The food-supply of the vast ocean is so indestructible, so universal, and so nourishing that it can satisfy these vast multitudes of herring, just as it does the whales.

The old fish run great risks in shallow waters, but being very fast swimmers, like modern gangsters, they can make a "quick get-away." Does man's assault make any real difference to the herring? A million tons a year—that is, some three billion fish—are registered as being taken. It has been calculated that stretching nets right across rivers is fatal to salmon; but herring nets are set night after night long enough to reach from England to New York and back again. Moreover, numbers of these drift-nets catch so many fish that they sink to the bottom, and before they can be recovered the victims have been drowned and swollen up in the meshes, so that it causes infinite trouble to get them out and so save the twine—and then they are wasted. Yet Huxley claims that all that men take put together would not compromise one school or family of twelve square miles—and hundreds of such schools exist. History shows that man is only one of the countless enemies of the herring, and that the tribute he exacts does not leave appreciably fewer herring for any of his competitors or for himself.

King Herring has even foregone for his own defence King Salmon's armour and King Cod's spikes. His delicate flesh is due to his having given up eating refuse in the contaminated sea-floor and restricted his diet entirely to bacteria-free live creatures swimming in the all-cleansing deeps. So herring is served in some of the best restaurants, quite raw on ice. He is an ideal food, including the butter and salt which the canny Irishman has to add to his baked "spuds." He is the most easily preserved proteid food possible. Herring can be preserved "round" bones and all, for when rightly served in vinegar the bones only add to the satisfaction of eating him. They are as welcome guests in royal households as in the humblest homes. The suspicion of their being "bourgeois" and *outré* makes them even modern enough for the menu of the most fastidious liner's first-class saloon, where they auspiciously open the day at breakfast, and close it as a final night-cap. At great seats of learning when dinner is over and scholarly and scientific dons are flicking the auricular branch of the nerve of the stomach with the corner of the dinner napkin steeped in rose-water to speed the parting guest, an age-old custom brings round the High Table King Herring, in all the glory of his academic robe of red, decked with brilliant salt crystals, to add to the pleasures of the passing bottles, as the men of wisdom repair to the Common Room for dessert. There is no measure of the herring's adaptability to man's service. As an egg he makes an excellent caviar, as a child he delights thousands as whitebait, as a hobbledehoy he reaches the tables of princes the world over as sardines, and in adult life he is prepared to substitute for almost any finny comrade, rightly spiced, even posing successfully as that stay-at-home but highly respectable Puritan, the brook trout.

In the war herring served well those at home who "stood by the stuff" as well as those who went down to battle; for American vessels swarmed to our shores and paid ten dollars a barrel for herring direct from the net. I saw one man make a hundred and sixty dollars before breakfast. As many as two thousand barrels of herring have been taken at one haul. The importance of his annual visit is therefore easy to visualize. Those with understanding hearts leave no stone unturned to insure his arrival.

Only the very occasional indiscretion of feeding on crustaceans leaves the herring indisposed for immediate service; and even then, by barring in the school with nets and so "confining them to gates" for a couple of days, they are purified and ready for use again. Europe preserves the herring round, America splits him flat, the Dutch clip off his belly with scissors. The branch industries of barrels, canning, transport, fertilizer, are all of importance, especially in Labrador where all the people have access to free wood of the best kind, and still know how to make the finest hand-made barrels.

Faith in the material value of psychology has been greatly increased by oracles like Coué. It is to fishermen that the world owes in large measure its knowledge of the importance of faith in mental and psychic impulses. These modern philosophies may be only momentary and distorted recrudescences of that eternal truth. Seeing the vast importance of the result, endless remedies have been tried "to change luck." In the scientific world, Ehrlich tried six hundred and six remedies before he discovered one of the most important resources known to man. Just so in Labrador, the empirical method is in vogue. Rumour has it that to pick one of those rare herrings, which have red fins, from a school without allowing it to touch wood, and then pass it round and round and round the scudding pole as many times as the number of lasts of herring (one thousand three hundred and twenty fish) you hope to capture, brings certain success. It sounds somewhat like the Bible story of the King of Israel, who was blamed by a seer, certified as a prophet, for shooting only three arrows out of the window instead of a dozen, since each arrow insured one victory over the king's most dangerous enemy. Anyhow, this "old saw" being of Aberdonian origin, costs less than a ticket in an Irish Sweepstake and the prizes are far more numerous. One amusing Scotch "charm" was to dress a fisherman in a shirt as much as possible like a herring, and wheel him right round the town in a wheelbarrow, before starting on the voyage. Charms have varied through all grades of pleasantry to the burning alive as witches, only a couple of centuries ago, of men and women accused of bringing a curse on the fishery. Tinged with the same idea was an absolute prohibition in Ireland of setting a net from sundown Saturday till sunrise Monday, even if it meant enforcing idleness on half-crazed men who, awaiting the arrival of the shoal long over-due, had to watch the few days slip by in which experience taught them they could expect the fish to remain. On the other hand, if the law were a voluntary one imposed by each individual on himself, as our Labrador fishermen make it, who shall say that the character evolved is not worth, even in hard cash, the freely foregone "scoop" which lay within their reach?

3

When the world becomes wise enough to beat its swords into fish-hooks and ploughshares, England may have to seek a new national emblem to replace her Lion Rampant. If, in a millennium of peace, she has to select some substitute for that rapacious and war-like beast, what more appropriate emblem could she adopt than "Three Codfish Natant," seeing that she owed her empire largely to King Cod?

The difficulty of appraising the real value to human life of any very humble thing lies in trying to get far enough away. For four hundred years at least Europe has been catching cod off the American coast, and still the codfish is there, paying a yearly tribute of many millions of dollars. To-day France still pays bounties to every member of a crew catching and drying fish away from France, and on the other hand she, like America, places prohibitive duties on every quintal brought in from other countries. If Labrador fishermen got similar privileges they could almost afford to catch cod and give it away.

When the cod fisheries of England were discovered, there were no potatoes in England, and the poor never got meat in winter. In fostering the fisheries, however, the nations were far from being concerned primarily with providing their people with cheap food. The humble cod had something of even more value than his carcase to confer upon humanity, and that asset was the human character created in catching him. All nations wanted to train men to do their fighting on the sea for them. Spain, Portugal, and the United States have all of them, by their tariff walls, subscribed to this same idea. If the first value of an industry were its return in cash to the public exchequer, ethyl alcohol would be "top dog," for the traffic in intoxicating drinks would be far the most important, though it is a trade utterly destructive of character, of human capacities, and of material. On the other hand, cod-fishing is both productive and constructive. For sea power it has always been the finest man-making environment. To England it has meant freedom and eventually world power.

As a food-supply cod has been the poor man's stand-by on both sides the Atlantic. The palate does not tire of plump, polar-current codfish, cooked in a dozen different ways, while the fat or oil even in these days, when we can make almost everything in a chemical laboratory, still holds the world's championship for nutritional and medical values, even if halibut livers and synthetic vitamins are competing.

Every particle of cod is useful to man. His flesh is rich and gelatinous without being fatty. The skin and bones make fine glue. The tongue and swimming bladder are rare delicacies, and have also been used in the manufacture of isinglass. The second-grade oil is used for tanning. The offal makes a most excellent manure. In Iceland the dried heads are used to feed cattle. The roe makes fine bait. The bones not only carry phosphates for manure, but in the Arctic have even been used for fuel. Being a thin-skinned fish, he can be split rapidly and without danger to the hands. I have timed a man removing the spine at the rate of fourteen fish per minute. Compared with beef, the nutritive value of cod is nine to ten, and the cost less than one third. In England cod are best in winter. In Labrador the cod is always enjoying winter!

Labrador almost suggests a cod standard instead of a gold standard. As long ago as 1386 kings granted as a special privilege the right to fish for cod. It was landlubbers, who, ignorant of the value of those northern seas, tossed Labrador lightly to and fro between New England, Canada, and Newfoundland, like a shuttlecock. It was utter disregard for the rights of fishermen which made King Cod play a distinct part even in the quarrel which lost America to England. It was the cupidity of politicians alone which tossed Miquelon and St. Pierre back to France in 1763, and with them the rights to fish on the French Shore, for which both England and America have since had to pay dearly.

At the time of the Spanish Armada the cod fishery saved England's freedom. Bideford kept back seven vessels from the Terre Neuve fisheries that year, Yarmouth, Plymouth, Exmouth, Poole, and other seaports did the same. In 1585 there were six hundred Spanish fishermen prisoners detained in Newfoundland—a coup played by Sir John Hawkins, which the next year prevented their fishing fleet from sailing at all. Never again was there a big Spanish fishing fleet.

England's possessions in America, Africa, India, and Australia were won a century before the *Mayflower* sailed, and won by these men, unknown and unsung. She

Photograph by F. C. Sears

A MODERN APOSTLE

A NORTHERN NEIGHBOR

was not saved by wealth, or politics or unusual wisdom of rulers, but by the sea-genius of these humble seafaring men. Pitt said that he would not give up England's ownership of the fisheries "if the enemy were in the Tower of London."

Countless family circles owe the cod debts for his unique ability in passing muster as permissible for an article of diet on Fridays and in Lent, before an ecclesiastical council, which put its ban on most articles of protein food. Both fishermen and nations owe a larger debt to the Church for thus encouraging the fisheries than they are aware of.

Moreover, King Cod has given victories to more human individuals fighting with their backs to the wall against an enemy which has destroyed more human lives even than war—the invisible, resistless tubercle bacillus. All the brains of the scientists, all the wealth of the nations, all the prayers of churches have not been successful in displacing cod-liver oil from that pedestal. The cod has not only bred a healthy race; he has invigorated a weak one. Even the transporting of codfish has helped to breed men.

Every year many little sailing vessels direct from Cadiz bring Spanish salt to Labrador and wait all summer for a return cargo of codfish in the fall. Many have been the exciting adventures of these trips, and some very fast voyages were made. The racing has greatly encouraged the invaluable sporting spirit. One square-rigger, the *William*, ran from Labrador to Patras in Greece in twenty-three days. The *Red Rose* reached Genoa in seventeen days, the *Clara*, a fore-and-after, reached Gibraltar from Holton, Labrador, in sixteen days. Our own boat, a ninety-nine ton fore-and-aft ketch, went from St. John's to Yarmouth in twelve and a half days at an average of eight and a half land miles per hour. These are not records, only incidents taken at random. One square-rigger at Bonne Esperance was deserted late in the fall by her crew of five men, leaving only the captain. So he alone took her across to England with his cargo of fish, where he was arrested for being a menace to traffic!

Labrador's arctic-current cod is the best in the world, and the shame is that it does not yet dominate all markets. The Colony's journals blame this on the carelessness of the fishermen in preserving it; but that is only shifting responsibility. What is needed is an efficient Civil Service inspection to protect the patriotic worker from the slacker who gets "the same price anyhow." A good comment is that the codfish cured by the northern Eskimo has long commanded the highest price paid for Labrador fish—suggestive as coming from the buyers, who are the least answerable critics. Those responsible are not the Eskimo, however, but the honest Moravian Brethren, who refuse to accept from a naturally careless and not-too-careful-about-cleanliness people any inferior products. This is also true of a co-operative store where the members sell their fish directly for cash, and the actual value of his fish is paid each man.

One might not suppose that a codfish can be improved by manhandling, but from time immemorial the flesh has been known to be made more tender by beating it with a rod while drying, as its synonyms indicate. For in

Norwegian it is Stockfish (stick), in Portuguese it is Bacalhao (baculum, a stick), in Gaelic Gad (a rod), in Greek Bacchi (rods). Labrador cod smokes beautifully, like a haddock—a secret which the world has yet to learn.

Each mother cod has from three to nine million babies a year, the eggs being protected by each floating freely and singly in the ocean, so that it is not possible for voracious neighbours to destroy all of them. Inestimable quantities of milt make certain of fertilizing the eggs in the open water, and success is made more sure by immense numbers of cod meeting in shoal water at the spawning season. Cod seek warmer localities like the Westman Islands off South Iceland to have their young. The fry drift away with the ocean currents, and instinct probably tells the mothers to have their families where they will be carried in the best directions for food and safety.

Many codlings are eaten in youth by their relatives and friends. Only a few achieve their destiny of a humble corner in a fishmonger's stall. The children have few sicknesses, though oddly enough they are subject to rickets and eye trouble.

The Labrador record cod was a hundred and two pounds in weight and five feet six inches long. The English record is a poor second. He was seventy-eight pounds in weight and five feet eight inches long. He was caught in 1755 and sold for one shilling. The largest cod recorded from the Newfoundland Banks was one hundred and thirty-six pounds. In the international competition the honours go to America with a Bank cod of one hundred and sixty pounds. An Aberdeen man hooked a larger one, but unfortunately it broke the line and escaped. When the Englishman suggested to him that it was a whale, he replied that he was using a whale for bait at the time.

The average Labrador cod weighs from three to four pounds. His is a chequered career. Even age does not secure him from becoming a mouthful for a whale, a seal, or a shark. A mother cod "tagged" off the Iceland coast was found in the stomach of a shark off the coast of Greenland. Death from natural causes is rare amongst the codfish. King Cod is himself a true Catholic in the matter of food, though he prefers herring, squid, or capelin. We have watched them by hundreds jumping into huge shoals of live capelin and gorging until they could jump no more.

A book in three volumes was taken from the stomach of a cod caught off Lynn in England, and presented to the Vice-Chancellor of Cambridge University. Scissors, oil cans, and old boots have been found in them. One skipper who lost his keys overboard in the North Sea got them in the stomach of a codfish. Two full-grown ducks, feathers and all, were found in another, apparently having been swallowed alive. Candles, guillemots (beaks, claws, and all), a whole hare, dogfish, turnips, all show the breadth of his appetite. His attention to business is evidenced by his swallowing large stones for the sake of the corallines on them. A cod's digestion needs no artificial aid to handle the problems of his day in the form of a live lobster, a crab, or whelks—shells and all—"au naturel." A Newfoundland fisherman returned the wedding-ring of a lady on the S. S. *Anglo-Saxon,* which she had lost overboard. Cod are so addicted to a diet of sea-scorpions that off the Greenland coast they have almost obliterated that prolific creature.

Why codfish appear to have decreased is not known. It seems impossible that man could make any inroads on their numbers. The best places for catching cod remain the best to the last, which seems to negative the idea. There are no data on which to formulate the law governing the age-to-age increase or diminution in numbers of these finny floods.

Slight variations in temperature affect all fish. Oddly enough, cod loses his appetite in water under thirty-four degrees Fahrenheit. He is not a fussy king, but he prefers temperatures from thirty-five to forty-three degrees Fahrenheit. Warm years have been bad years for the cod. A few icebergs arriving and cooling the bottom water bring the cod to the spot. In Labrador fjords the water twenty fathoms down is practically never above thirty-two degrees Fahrenheit.

It was thought that the cod never wandered far; but tagging has shown that they go regularly at any rate from Greenland to Iceland and back again—distances of over five hundred miles, and often at considerable speed. Ten miles a day for a number of days is no mean accomplishment for so indolent fish on such a diet. They go up Davis Straits and all around Greenland.

Cod may be caught in fresh or salt water, or in depths of five to a hundred fathoms. He comes close to the land each spring for food—one week later for each degree of northerly latitude. Our Labrador fishery begins about the middle of June, when the ice is blown off the coast. It ends about the last of September, not because the fish are gone, but because after that the fishermen cannot get sun enough to dry it. For in November, the settlers capture large cod to freeze up for their winter consumption.

None merit more than do our Three Kings the legend for their coat-of-arms which our royal Prince to-day carries under three feathers. They, too, carry under their scales the motto "Ich Dien."

Order and purpose characterize the whole of nature, and suggest inescapably the intelligent Mind behind it all. In the early days, long gone by, there lived fishermen to whom the world has paid more honour than to any hundred human kings. At that time "fish" was the most precious word in their language. It was a secret of imperial Rome, which far over-shadowed the "secret de St. Malo," in the centuries to follow. It was not only the password of men threatened with torture and death if its meaning were discovered by the powers of the day, but the outline of a fish, scratched negligently in the dust with a bare toe, might either save a brother, or cost the lives of a community. ΙΧΘΥΣ. Ichthus meant "fish" in the Greek language, which they spoke. Each letter of it stood for a word: ΙΗΣΟΥΣ ΧΡΙΣΤΟΣ ΘΕΟΥ ΥΙΟΣ ΣΩΤΗΡ. (Jesus Christ, Son of God, Saviour.) Ichthus thus symbolized their faith in the King of kings.

LABRADOR SUMMER FISHING SHACK

Photograph by F. C. Sears

WILD COTTON

XI: THE PAGEANT OF THE SOIL

Flowering Plants and Ferns

"ARE you not surprised at the number of our flowers?" I asked my companion after a long walk
through the forest.

"Can't say I noticed any," he replied. Some eyes never
do see fairies.

The actors of to-day's pageant may be relatively small,
but their number, their brilliant costumes, and their
cunning devices for outwitting difficulties have the special charm which marionettes afford us when we see
them for the first time. Moreover, they alone supply to
the chief actors the very essentials of life. Nowhere else

219

in the world is there such a stage—so southern a country kept in a refrigerator all the year through.

We shall not introduce the cast by their Latin names. Their S. O. S. reads: "Spare us from anything but good English names, or no one will want to know us. One word of Latin and our goose is cooked!"

"Why call me Lecidia Albocoerulescens Schoerflavo Coerulesens?" piped up a sterile, midget lichen. "If you call me Cladiabelladiflora Schoerochropallida," wept another, "I shall drop out of the play altogether. All we want is to be 'understood.'"

The carpet of the Labrador coast-line is a generous one, even where the soil is shallow. The plants are dense and vigorous. The hours of summer daylight are long, so that the leaves which create their food and do their breathing have the same chance to grow by night as did Jonah's famous gourd; while the flowers which are responsible for reproduction and the survival of the race must sport brighter colours than elsewhere because there are fewer insects to attract. Just so those which multiply by spores in Labrador always have abundance of water.

Few, until they have seen the plants of Labrador for themselves, will believe in the great hillsides red with fireweeds, or in the fields azure with bluebells (I almost said campanulae) or marshes covered with purple azaleas, and the sweet ladies-smell-bottle, the Labrador tea, or the yellow goldenrods and Arctic poppies, or in the lovely red autumn carpets of curlew-berry leaves, the scarlet bunch-berries and the bear-berries. This important gift of beauty to landscape is only one of the contributions of our wild plants. To man's food supply they afford "without toil or spinning" as important a factor to life as do the fowls or fishes. For not only can we grow practically any vegetable we need by starting the seed under glass a few weeks before the frost leaves the ground, but in few other places outside the tropics can sufficient natural fruits of the earth be obtained for no cost except the labour of gathering them. Where else can berries be preserved merely by heading them up in water in old flour barrels and letting them freeze, without the expense of either sugar or a cold-storage plant?

Of the list of the "first four hundred" in the Labrador Pageant of Plants half have visible seeds (phanerogams) and half have hidden seeds (cryptogams). The author who compiled it says it is imperfect, but no botanical list can escape this penalty of mortality. The fact that all the actors have not found their way into "Who's Who" of the plant world is one of Labrador's greatest lures to the visitor. On the other hand, the list is an excellent basis to build on. There is a second list, alas, without their English names, of the plants of the seashore only; and a third, of those twelve miles from the landwash, fills in many gaps. A collection of our plants, in Toronto University, is mostly from the north end of the country. The list is interestingly classified under Common, Arctic, and Barren Land plants. Like the Eskimo, once people of a warm country, many old floral friends have entered with success the "Farthest North" competition.

Away north of the tree-line on our Coast you will find the sweet-smelling Labrador tea, the mountain tobacco, the familiar goldenrod, the antiscorbutic dandelion, the oyster plant, the bog blue-berry, the alluring lambkill or swamp laurel, the mountain heath, the blazing fireweed, the Alpine violet, the purple pyrola, the yellow cloud-berry, the red Arctic bramble, the luscious field vetch, the cinquefoil, the indestructible pink sedum, the Iceland poppy, the pigmy buttercup, the insidious chick-weed, the aromatic wintergreen, the mountain sorrel, the dark red bear-berry, the creeping birch, several willows, the holy-grass, the spear grass, the red campion (ragged robin), the sandbine grass (which we use so largely for basketry and the seed of which the Vikings used for wheat), the moon fern, the brittle fern, the eye-bright, and its lance-shaped sister, and many more, not forgetting the ubiquitous bluebell of Scotland.

I have conceded this partial list in order to prove better than in any other way that even in the extreme North, on the outer seacoast, right in the polar current, to the seeing eye, Labrador is far from a sterile, barren mass of gloomy rocks.

To those desiring to dig deeper I would suggest the following:

1. Report of Brown-Harvard Expedition, 1902; page 177, Preston & Rounds; "Providence, R. I., to Labrador," by E. B. Delabarre.
2. Professor E. M. Kindle, "Geological Survey of Canada." Memoir 141, 1924.
3. Dr. A. P. Coleman, Geological Survey of Canada, Memoir 124, No. 106.

4. Dr. A. P. Low's American Reference Geological Survey of Canada, Part IV, Vol. VIII, 1896.

Inland a warm summer climate replaces that of the ice-chilled coast, and forests cover both mountains and valleys. In the inlets the sides of most valleys are flanked with trees, usually black spruces. As they get nearer the polar current they are so dense and stunted that we call them tuckamore. It is almost impossible to force one's way through. In winter, when the first snow covers all the landscape, there is considerable risk in walking out of the pathway over the tops of these thickets. I have suddenly fallen through and then found it extraordinarily difficult to get out. One cannot climb back on the top, as the snow edge breaks down all the while, and as one cannot force one's way through by walking, the tenderfoot finds no way of getting out at all.

Some of to-day's actors appeared as witnesses in our Pageant of the Vikings, telling us where the Norsemen landed. More were summoned in the great dispute between Canada and Newfoundland, as to who owned Labrador, testifying where salt-water land ends. Thus the beautiful bunch-berry frequently makes an almost complete covering cloth for the land, white in summer and red in the fall of the year, but it must have a fresh-water floor beneath it. In places the sandbine does the same, but now the floor beneath it must be salty or brackish. These very witnesses were called to show the jury in the dispute which could properly be called "the Coast of Labrador" and which could not.

In the "tundra" of the interior fewer of our friends

223

have yet successfully established a footing, and even the hardy trees are only stunted and wizened wraiths of themselves. On the weathered mountain-tops and highest plateaux, where there is a "mer de glace," only actors of the humblest varieties still cling; and yet on just such the famous Sir John Franklin and his men managed to sustain life for over three months. What better argument can there be for our making friends with these puppets of "the soyle"?

Many a lonely journey has been enlivened by the companionship of the little actors. On one occasion in midwinter we were storm-bound in a grove of spruces. In our idle time our thoughts turned to them and we decided to dig down with our snow-shoes to see what they were doing. After ourselves disappearing in the hole over ten feet deep we came upon the unfrozen ground. There we met some green sorrels which we joyfully invited to supper. Two men taking a constitutional were satisfying the hunting instinct by grabbing at random promising bunches of lichens, witnesses again for a friend who was studying the limits of the ancient icecaps of Labrador, which he was locating by the distribution limits of certain plants. The friend's comment on receiving the specimens showed that unwittingly a new discovery had been made, and the amateur is to go down to posterity on the shoulders of something like Taraxacum densleonis Hiramsmithiae.

Who will believe that not cold but dryness is the chief enemy of most of the personnel of this Pageant? Here the abundance of humic acid in the soil, there the quantity of soluble salt in a cold ground, prevents the drinking of water by roots far more successfully than the Eighteenth Amendment does alcohol, while the exposure to drying winds makes matters worse. The greatest sufferers have developed protective devices quite unlike those of their high Alpine comrades. They have a special system of rooms to gather water. They diminish their height to escape the winds—the willow, the alder, and the birch sometimes actually creeping along the ground. The size of their leaves is reduced, as in the pinkish-purple Andromeda, the curlew-berry, and the bearberry, or their leaves are crumpled up as in the bake-apples, or in the narrow spikes like the grasses. Some, like the sedum, fold back their leaves, some use a varnish on one or both faces of the leaf, as in the pyrola or the blueberry. Others develop storage cells for holding water, or the stomata (breathing mouths) which are hidden away underneath the leaf, as in the azaleas, of which one is called Andromeda, because her feet are always in the water.

Some protect the stem and leaf on one side with dense hairs like the poppies and the daisies; others cover themselves with short hairs like felt, or put on a mere dusty-looking coat as if they were powdered. In some cases the result, which is also a remedy, reminds one of the midget trees developed for table landscapes in Japan. Thus, a larch, thirty-two years old, was with us only nine inches tall and three quarters of an inch in diameter, while a balsam fir, fifty-seven years old, was thirteen inches high and two inches across. Still other varieties of plants developed a cup to hold water and devices to trap and swallow insects—like the pitcher plant and the sundew plant. While this dryness is a handicap to feeding and growth it helps reproduction, so that proportionately there are really very numerous flowers, and they appear even more so, since they must all bloom at once in our short season.

Besides these "drys" Labrador has some "wets." Some of them even float in water, having small roots but large vegetal growths like the water-lilies. Yet another kind are "wets" in summer and "drys" in winter. They either drop their wet leaves in winter or cultivate leaves which are wet as youngsters, only becoming dry with the wisdom of old age. On the other hand, our almost constant winds favour transpiration, and also devices for carrying pollen and seeds by air.

Fertilization by wind is a wasteful way at best, but many flowers which are usually dependent on insects cannot trust to the scanty supply of them in Labrador. Long daylight and short seasons tend to make plants smaller. Fortunately, therefore, the devices which protect against too much dryness help against too much light. The shortness of the whole summer season and the consequent imperious need of the plant for haste produces one of Labrador's most impressive experiences. Few people know how much the relative length of daylight and darkness means to plants. A potato tells when to begin to make tubers instead of flowers by the nights beginning to be longer than the days. It is easy to fool a potato with electric light. The heavy accumulation of snow and the long time it takes to melt sometimes suggest that there will be no flowers, when lo! a sudden wand of sunshine, and banished is the last white cover-

ing of frozen water, and the flowers rush out like school-
boys when the bell goes for lunch. Our plants have
learned by age-long experience that as their season for
growing is so short their one chance to survive is to make
the most of it. So they get ready a year ahead all the
embryonic leaves and flowers on which their lives depend. This accounts for the magical way in which apparently ready-made plants can leap out into being the
day the snow goes.

When one remembers the dignified procession of the
same plants farther south, spring, summer, and autumn
in Labrador appear to roll over one another in one quick
coming and quick going—all packed into a brief and
brilliant summer. As the Labrador stretches its long strip
due north and south, the slow movers get left out in the
race and only those of the "quick or dead" type survive.
So our players have done us another good turn by teaching us to start cabbage and other plants two months
ahead of "polar current time."

Among the essentials for life itself are vegetable salts
in food. Scurvy and beri-beri and rickets were as fatal
formerly in Labrador as was the blackleg scurvy on the
ships of our forefathers. This spring we had at one of our
hospital stations twenty thousand fine baby cabbage
plants six weeks old when the frost went from the
ground, all eager for a "place in the sun." Formerly all
we could count on growing on the outside coast were
turnip tops and scraggy leaves. Now we can grow eight-
een-pound cabbages and large fat turnips.

With plants as with men—some relatively unfitted
live on, but they increasingly lose their old characteristics

227

as they get farther north and the season shortens. Thus our main wild food berry, the yellow bakeapple, and its cousin, the red Arctic raspberry, abundant in Newfoundland, get more leaves and fewer flowers, and therefore less fruit, as they go north in Labrador. Finally the yellow bakeapple loses its fruit altogether, though the plant persists.

Meantime some of our actors seem to merely devote their energies to "stunts." Knowing that these are not purposeless, the discovery of the motive behind them challenges our detective abilities. Just at present the joyous bakeapple is breaking all the canon laws by having at will four, five, or six white petals, odd-shaped calyx lobes, and even royal purple leaves, which is as irregular as if a registered criminal were to change his fingerprints. Our glorious fire-weeds show a growing tendency to vary the number of stamens, a most vital piece of their anatomy. In some of our lovely sedums there is going on a veritable riot of variations, stamens having gone up to thirteen in number and pistils from two to nine, as if in some championship competition. The beloved bunch-berry, in his exquisite spring garment of black and white and green colourings, and again in his fall fashion show of glorious reds, has again deliberately started new modes and colours. One wore six upper leaves in a whorl, quite a departure in dresses for her, and with them four gores up the sides and greenish white petals—prototypes of bodice and pleats. Another sister is affecting dark purple or maroon flounces, and not only petals but sepals as well. She is more restrained in her side pleats, having only two, but she had added three pairs of opposite leaves. Wood betony, a common yellow, tously-headed swain of which there are several kinds, is also experimenting in varieties.

The spreading of our fruits depends largely in predacious animals and birds. Mosses, grasses, composite flowers, and other plants like the mustard family, sturdy "drys" like chickweed, and thistles rely on the wind to blow their seed around, an element which in Labrador never goes back on them. The large floating pods, or bladders, of the milk vetches—beloved by cows—seem also to be very effectual. In Labrador, seeds borne by wind or in the stomachs of small animals survive best. How can we despise the humble lichen, who still produces a family if a bit of one leaf finds its way to a wet spot, or even if a whole leaf is impaled on a dry wall? In the actual Arctic zone, the plants are much the same as in the more temperate parts of the sub-Arctic, but relatively fewer.

Our trees have fought their way north and made a good covering for Labrador as far as the latitude of Yorkshire. They have not yet conquered the hill-tops north of that, and half the country is "barrens" in the latitude of the Scotch border. To the west they have reached the shores of Ungava Bay, and on the coast their pickets reach to a parallel north of Edinburgh, to Hebron and the head of Okkak Bay on the Labrador Coast.

Numerous ancient stumps suggest that the whole interior was once wooded over. In 1785 and 1814 the air was so full of smoke all over East Canada that ever since they have been known as the "dark days." Generous folk attributed them to volcanoes in Labrador, though no volcanoes have been known there since pre-Cambrian days half a billion years ago. Something, anyhow, wrought infinite havoc among the Labrador trees about that time; whether it was lightning, or Indians signalling, or careless white men is only of academic interest now. One thing is certain, Labrador could be largely reforested. The commercial value of her forests is greatly enhanced by her being the nearest part of the North American continent to Europe, and by her long inlets providing water-ways right into the interior.

Inland from the coast the summer climate permits forests to cover both mountains and valleys. The forest region contributes to to-day's cast eleven good trees. The nearer to the polar current and the higher the altitude, the smaller the trees, is a fair rule. Ability to hold on against wind-storms has a great deal to do with this. The shallow soil does not give an easy hold, and it is common where the soil is thin to see swaths cut through the forests, as a tornado cuts through the houses in the Middle West. This accounts for the endless fallen trunks which make walking through even our larger woods difficult, and driving dogs impossible, without a cut trail.

To ease the top pressure our trees have learned to taper rapidly, so that a spar, thick enough at the base, must be much taller than elsewhere to give sufficient size to the top. Moreover, to prevent breaking, the conifers grow exceedingly tough and fibrous and so make good planking. One spar cut at Kippikok Bay carried ten inches to sixty-five feet, and made a good spar at eighty feet. One of the "ways" at Rigolet, on which the Hudson's Bay Company's schooner was hauled out, measured fifty-nine feet long and was squared sixteen by nine inches at the bottom, with nine and a half by six and a half at the top. One in Adlavik squared ten inches at eighty feet.

Among our principal trees are:

White Birch, an invaluable friend. With his bark you can start a fire when nothing else will catch. You can write a letter on it, cover your canoe or your house and fish-stage with it or even yourself, if you can peel it thin enough and put it on under a garment. It makes excellent "straw" hats. It is waterproof, and you can tan leather with it. The wood is hard and tough. It grows very far north, and replaces conifers so quickly when a forest is burned that there is little chance for the latter ever to come back. For firing, charcoal, building furniture, for snow-shoe bows, ribs for kayaks, it is the best we have. They will grow in poor soil where nothing else will. I saw a white birch five feet seven inches in girth.

Larch, or Tamarack or Hackmatack, grows farthest north, even to sixty-seven degrees in America and seventy-two degrees in Europe. It reaches sixty feet in height. Its horizontal branches and pyramidal head and bluish hue not only make it beautiful, but cause it to stand out as a landmark from the sea. Approaching some of the river mouths, for want of artificial landmarks we often steer for a lone larch or for two big fellows in a line. It gives us excellent firewood; but it is the most subject of all our trees to pests, so that thousands upon thousands have been destroyed by the larvae of the sand-fly under the bark. However, larch is becoming numerous again. He is "wet" by preference, a lover of the marshes.

Balsam Fir: This is a dark-green leaved, rapid-growing, soft, perishable wood tree. You can recognize him by the cross-section of the leaf being flat, by the cones standing upright on the branches, and by the balsam vesicles in the bark. He measures fifty to eighty feet and as much as thirty inches across, and is very numerous.

White Spruce: This is our best all-around tree. Forests of these trees, seventy feet high, are fairly continuous as far inland as the Grand Falls. The hanging cones, the four-ribbed or angled leaves, the tree's aromatic smell and its rich green leaves, and the generous way its green branches go right to the ground, making it our best shelter from the icy blasts of winter, all endear it to us. Often enough I have been glad for a chance to sleep in its branches and boil the kettle under its friendly protection. It is easily transplanted, for it has shallow though wide-spreading roots. It lives to a great old age. Its bark is splendid for tanning nets or skins. The resin is used for medicine. The grain is straight, so the wood makes good, strong lumber. Its branch tips, boiled with molasses or honey, make a favourite and healthful drink on the coast. When allowed to ferment, it is called spruce-beer and is intoxicating.

Balsam Poplar is a soft wood, rapid growing, tall tree, subject to great variations, fond of the seaside. The buds are very fragrant in the spring. It grows at the bottom of our bays. The dull white on the underside of the leaves make it easy to recognize it.

Aspen Poplar belongs to the willow family, and like them can be grown from a hard-wood cutting in almost any soil. As the tops are always trembling it deserves its name, Quaking Aspen. It is a gay, bright-coloured, rapid-growing fellow, but very short-lived. It makes an excellent nurse to protect the sterner trees in their slow growth and long youth. It rather gives one the impression of a combination of cheapness and friendliness. Its silver grey of the spring becomes a rich gold in the fall. It is an ornament, and, when it dies, it serves the forest as did the departed Clementine "in a graveyard."

Yellow Birch is said to reach one hundred feet, but amongst our people it is not differentiated from the white birch.

Willows fringe most of our lakes and streams, till in the far north they crawl along the ground and can scarcely be called bushes, much less trees. But they are often life-savers for the traveller, being the only available source of fuel. Many times on the barrens they have served us nobly when we were hard put to it for a fire at night. They also protect and feed our willow grouse in the North, and thus help us find many a needed meal. They nowhere reach a size to make the timber useful, but by continually cutting the lower branches we can make our willows develop a fine, stout stem. Their intricate network of roots does more than any other one agency to hold the soil when it is in danger of being washed away.

Alder is almost more of a weed than a tree, but he is needed to complete the ten who play the game for us in Labrador. His abundant and tangled growth round our river banks has forced many a good fisherman into the cold stream when he least wanted to fill his waders, and has helped the escape of many a fine salmon or

233

trout. He has the sins of others to answer for. However, he has the virtue of lasting well in water, being an admirable windbreak for other trees and plants and forming a "shelter in the time of storm" for some of our fur-bearing animals. In time of need his bark will even afford food to them. He is a rapid grower, and his resilient boughs can well be used for baskets and educational purposes! He grows in shallow soil with rock below, and by spreading his roots widely he manages to still hold on.

Ash: The mountain ash is a useful friend on our coast. He is resilient and tough, and serves well for handles for axes or tools. His beautiful red berries, which we eat, and the brilliant colour of his leaves in the fall add a gay touch to our landscape.

Another surprise of Labrador is the unremitting effort of its actors to cover it all up, from the seashore to the tops of the mountains. Even among a welter of crumbling rock all kinds of saxifrages, whitlow-grass, chickweeds, poppies, mosses, and lichens, often in mass formation, have secured a footing.

A little lower down the hillsides pioneer plants have scaled apparently bare rocks, clinging on, nourished with only a diet of sandgrains, water, and sunlight, and sacrificing themselves to make richer food and victory possible for the next comers—just as Wellington's men at Badajoz filled the moat with their own bodies for the rest to walk over. Around these pioneers now new regiments are camped, varieties of oxytrope, bearberry; the sweet teaberry or maiden-hair, diapensia, yellow arnica, wild rosemary, followed by sundew, pitcher plants, and others which invade the rocky sanctum from the edge.

Right in the dry tundra they have crept into the peaty swamps and settled, making flower oases, in spite of the humic acid, the lack of mineral salts, and the almost impossibility of extracting enough nitrogen. Here the sphagnum moss, so useful in the war, has abundantly established itself to form one vast, water-holding sponge for these little actors.

Especially in the south, reindeer and other mosses carpet the low grounds and barrens so generously that one sinks into them as into soft mud, sometimes above one's boot-tops, and walking over them is a fatiguing matter.

On the sunny slopes there awaits you the welcome of the sweet-smelling, little pink twin-flower, the gay, yellow, pigmy buttercups and cinquefoils, of where there are fourteen kinds, the dazzling blue gentians and especially the snow gentian; while a perfect blaze of glorious red and white fireweeds and bluebells make the hillsides resemble a veritable "trooping of the colours."

The tracery of Nature in Labrador is softened by a subdued green mantle, while its outline is not concealed. Her charm and strength are left naked to observation without the effeminacy of tropical vegetation. When winter comes Labrador's colour schemes are even more attractive. Millions of tiny players don uniforms of bright red, while most of our trees retain their dark green leaves all through the year. The pink faces of our cliffs only show up brighter in contrast when the white snow of the fall picks out the ledges even more vividly than do the foaming grey-white masses of the reindeer moss in summer.

Like the Vikings, Scandinavian plants tried to populate Labrador by the western road. They reached only as far as Iceland and Greenland; and then had to come via the East, as the earliest human actors of our drama had to do. Strange to say, more European plants have had to reach Labrador by this eastern route than by any northwest passage. This "yellow invasion" has successfully made its home in America, being a difficult one to check. But many of the species and individuals have been stopped on the shores of Baffin's Land. There, devoid of international vision and rejoicing in self-contained isolation, they appear to be flaunting an herbaceous Monroe Doctrine at their own ancestors on the other side of Davis Straits.

Labrador's extraordinarily generous harvest of edible wild fruits, their many varieties, and easy accessibility are a startling experience for every new-comer. If a settler's family does not have a supply of cranberries, curlew-berries, bear-berries, blueberries, raspberries, bakeapple-berries, and red currants, and in some localities goose-berries, capillaire-berries, and black currants, it is entirely their own fault. Rowan-berries, bunch-berries and wild pears are frequently eaten. I have seen well-nourished children on a diet consisting almost entirely of wild berries, culled by themselves.

The last group, that of the fungi, is a large one. It is not yet possible to say there are none on our coast that are poisonous, though we have eaten every variety we could find that were not too bitter to be pleasant or too small to be worth while, and have never yet suffered at the hands of any of these friends; who offered a small carbohydrate, and even a protein addition to our all too lightly stocked larders. Some are quite large and meaty, and as tasty as the mushroom so beloved among our home delicacies. The pink-tipped Russula, with pure white ribs on its under side, is the one we prefer. In many of our small woods one can fill a basket with it in a few minutes. Though it looks like one marked "Emetica" in text-books, it has given us many a good meal, without suggesting that quality. The light-brown Boleti, with their honeycomb lungs on the under side, grow very abundant and large on dry places and make an epicurean dish. Some varieties of Agaricus also afford a delicious meal.

It is imperative for travellers through our vast uninhabited areas to be well acquainted with those among our plants which are edible.

An exhaustive and interesting study, "The Outlines of Plant History," suggests that in ancient days, say a million million years ago, there were many more plants in the warmer polar regions. Later the great ice-cap scattered the plants, which were playing around that early May-pole, southward to the four quarters of the globe, then warmer days came back and some of the shivering warriors reascended the mountains, while others perished in the sea, or adapted themselves, just as some animals did, to a marine life. Though this theory still involves hypotheses, the fact remains that many preglacial plants won out where Vikings failed.

Records and remains of former inhabitants of this land are, as elsewhere, hidden away as plant fossils among the rock layers where our sedimentary strata or sand or volcanic ash has preserved them, though to less extent than usual, for these ancient "cemeteries" have themselves been largely worn away. Much of their story of the "dawn of life," of the rise and fall of plant dynasties, still remains, to be translated by the future "paleobotanists." It is quite possible that, reversing the procedure, a primeval seaweed and the whale, the first life in the land, crawled out equally ancient from the "waters that covered the earth" in what has been amusingly called the "Agnostozoic Age."

While life existed on earth in those Pre-Cambrian days when most of Labrador's present-day rocks were formed, there were no definite dividing lines in those humble forms of life between animal and vegetable, nor does geology tell us anything of the origin of life, not even our (Archean) foundation stories of the earth. Science truly understood is not the death but birth of mystery, awe, and reverence.

For the benefit of the more intrepid searchers for botanical data among my readers, I append the following census of our floral actors, as taken by Dr. E. B. Delabarre of Brown University.

FAMILIES *as so far located*	No. of *Species*
Sunflower family, or Compositae	36
Heath family, or Ericaceae	31
Mustard family, or Cruciferae	30
Rose family, or Rosaceae	29
Sedge family, or Cyperaceae	28
Grass family, or Gramineae	27
Pink family, or Caryophyllaceae	26
Willow family, or Salicaceae	19
Rockfoil family, or Saxifragaceae	19
Figwort family, or Scrophulariaceae	14

XII: THE PAGEANT OF THE ANIMALS

"The 'Little Brothers' of the 'Labourer's Land' "

THE marvellous actors in to-day's pageant are the closest to man of all his silent friends. Yet, as this story unfolds, we may, for shame, rejoice that the light is thrown on them, while we watch from the darkness. These "little brothers" once owned Labrador by right of priority. There is no doubt that there they were very numerous; and as men, coming to America, drove them from South and West, many found in Labrador one vast sanctuary. Then came the devastating Mongols from the North, who, finding this happy hunting-ground blossoming like a rose, occupied its whole length and flooded over onto the Island of Terra Nova—as we have seen.

239

Still the animals were able to hold their own. The lessons of the ages had taught them the imperative need for adaptation if they were to survive.

Aeons before man appeared on earth the bolder spirits took to the sea, or took partly to it. Those with less courage took to the rivers. Results show that water has proved to be their best friend. Others still tried to adapt themselves to use air as their refuge in times of need; while some have been able to use air, water, and land. Some of the "little brothers" were able to make a good living within the Arctic Circle, and great communities grew up in the sub-arctic prairies—the so-called "Barren Lands." It took those "lower animals" to make "ice and snow, frost and cold, winter and summer, praise the Lord." They could overcome Nature's moods and circumstances, but with the arrival of Europeans *"in partibus infidelium"* the balance turned against the first actors on our stage.

Gone are the gentle Beothics, almost vanished are the noble Redskins, and the scanty remnant of the hardy Eskimo is but a trophy to the humble efforts of the Moravian Mission. Gone are the "big brothers" before vices and diseases. Gone before literal fire and sword are the "little brothers"; for men did not hesitate to invade the great forest and destroy the very recreative powers through which Nature alone replenishes her ever marvellous stage. Firearms and other emblems of civilization replaced the bow and spear, and with them went many of the primitive virtues which the simple life demanded and evolved.

However, writing in 1758, Captain Atkins of Boston

240

says of Sandwich Bay, "The woods abound in partridge and other game, as well as bears, deer, beavers, otters, foxes, minks, hares, martens, sables, and other beasts of rich fur." He bought hundreds of pounds' worth from the natives for less "than ten shillings in trade." Thirty years later the animals were still so plentiful that Major Cartwright records in his famous diary that he saw thirty-two bears, black and white, in one river pool in one day. He "killed six, but took one skin only." Again he writes that he "could scarcely go ten yards without crossing the trail of a deer or a bear." Even at Cape Charles, where Europeans were regularly carrying on trade, he writes of shooting "four hindes carrying young in one day," without an apology.

From then onwards in the struggle the balance turns against them. The growing fur trade and the incoming of the Hudson's Bay Company turned the tide even more strongly. Not one of the little brothers will ever attack a man unless absolutely driven to it. Hungry wolves have followed lone trappers, but there are no records of their ever killing them. All the efforts of the Labrador animals have been devoted to self-effacement —to be neither seen, heard, nor scented.

We have no poisonous snakes, not even a scorpion or an adder. There are no animals which act as hosts to the fatal tapeworm as in Greenland, to the germs of hydrophobia, to the terrible anthrax so common in other countries. Even the many mosquitoes carry no malaria; and there are no hidden ticks or parasites which kill men from underfoot. Hakluyt writes, "There are no manner of creeping beastes hurtful, except some spiders, which as many affirm are signs of much gold." Another record says of these spiders that "one of our sailors did put one into the hollow of the big horne of a fish we found, which horne grew from its nose. The spider perished, which showed it to be a unicorn"! No such spiders, however, are among the list of our eleven kinds known to-day; and these, judging by the extreme rarity of their capture, are so negligible as to suggest that possibly in the struggle we owe the disappearance of this one poisonous element to the aid of the innumerable hordes of tiny but assiduous winged insects!

The leading actor in this pageant is by all acclamation the dog. His every effort has been to better adapt himself for man's service, till man has become dependent upon him, almost for existence. Sired by wolves, that virile heritage still animates his blood. Still to-day, one way to lure wolves within gunshot is to peg out a mother dog. Like our domestic reindeer, dogs are still so closely related to their cousins of the wild as to mate and have families by them.

To the Husky dog I stand hat in hand. He has become almost human, except that he commits most of his crimes in the open. He occasionally fights. With him it is generally for food, family, or power. How do we differ, except that being a little closer to the wild he still loves it for its own sake? Some have claimed the same for the Irish!

In the fights the dog starts, however, he is always first in the line of danger and takes all the risks personally. He fights fairly and without superior weapons, unless it be his own strength, skill, and courage. He does not leave others to pay the piper in the aftermath. The Husky dog, except that he is a far better gladiator when he does start, when brought up properly, is no more dangerous than any other dog. He has all the claims of a real dog on his master. To make a house pet of him, however, is to ruin him—for his virtues are all those of the great out-of-doors, where he is paramount as man's friend and companion. He can be house-broken, but it breaks his character altogether, so that he runs to fat and ineptitude like a lap-dog.

A good dog standing twenty-six inches to the shoulder and scaling a hundred pounds at three years old, with the mother leading and a dozen of the family in harness behind her, a zero day, the sun shining, a light hickory komatik, a four-pound eiderdown sleeping-bag, an axe, a rifle, a carefully packed bread-box, kettle and matches, a pair of round, Labrador sealskin or deerskin snow racquets, with a fifty-mile run ahead and a chance to help a lame dog over a stile at the end—and what more can any Christian sportsman want!

Two Bible texts we always find hard to swallow literally: "There shall be no more sea," and "Without are dogs." One we understand more readily, "Aha! I am warm! I have seen the fire."

Our dogs never need to be held in with bit or bridle, not even when driven at midday through the crowded streets of Boston, by little Mrs. Milton Seeley, of the Chinook Kennels, from the State-House to the Copley Plaza to help a Labrador Bazaar. Indeed, they can behave magnificently all day long in the foyer of that most fashionable hotel. Yet for hardihood, perseverance, "dogged" endurance, pluck, and cleverness, in following man's trail when there is no trail and no heavenly bodies visible, they run the average Homo Bimana out of the picture.

In appearance the Husky is very striking, like a magnified Pomeranian or Chow. He carries his great, bushy tail curved over his back. As a rule he is tawny like his forbear the timber wolf, but an all black and white dog is far more striking. He is not good on a farm. He yields too readily to temptation when hungry. In one night my leader ate a whole sheep, wool and all, when I locked him up in the wrong shed on a winter's trip. Another made no small stir by catching a goat by the leg as we passed through a little settlement, and calmly dragging him along as we went by without stopping. One of our dogs, always an unreliable character, disappeared one spring, having heard the call of the wild. He was seen later by watchers in a village where three sheep had disappeared. He was a northern dog and must have expected to find our forest "still as of old." Later two more sheep were driven off to islands over the ice and slaughtered there. One carcase, discovered by the edge of a wood, was watched from a blind. True to his wolfish instinct he returned to the prey at night, and so met his fate.

On another occasion a very badly fed team lived five miles from a house where goats were kept. One goat disappeared "teetotally." But the trapper soon traced down the criminals, without, however, sufficient evidence to force his neighbour to kill his precious team. Men with guns kept many long watches; but all the rest of the goats vanished without a single dog being caught in the act. They even returned later and secured the house cat as a savoury. A pack of wolves did exactly the same to a man who had four dogs. These disappeared singly; their own brothers never witnessed the kidnapping.

Even well-fed dogs in harness will take the trail of a caribou which has crossed their path and immediately give chase—an echo of the age-long call in their blood. The dogs take naturally to water in summer. They know well enough how to catch flat-fish. We taught two half-breed dogs to swim to the bottom in eighteen feet of water, by dropping stones wrapped in white rags over the end of the wharf; so that when a seal, killed on the ice in spring, sank, we loosed the dogs from their harness, whereupon they would dive and bring up the much-needed carcase.

The dogs' uncanny ability to find their way suggests a sense unknown to man. If you are caught in a blizzard or fog without a compass and have lost your way, the surest and safest slogan is, "Leave it to Towser." Once a snow blizzard overtook us suddenly when we still had eight miles to go to reach hospital. We had placed poles to mark the way, about two hundred yards apart on the upland barrens, but of course we could not see two yards. Our leader, however, went so straight for home that several times we had to stop and sling some dogs round a pole, the team having gone some on one side of it and some on the other. Another, a half-breed dog, took us a full seventy miles across a country of large lakes, barrens, and woods, deep in unmarked snow, with no blazed trail. No one had crossed that way since my doctor colleague had come with her the previous year the reverse direction. As darkness fell, not knowing where we were, we prepared to camp, but the dog seemed so sure that we decided to trust her. She brought us out safely about ten o'clock, and when we took her out of her harness and gave her her supper, she suddenly put her paws on my shoulders and kissed me goodnight.

Their contempt for cold is like that of the Eskimo. Not only will Huskies go out of a tilt in midwinter to sleep, but they will often lie on the windy side of it, so that the driving snow packs on them till they look for all the world like a row of sugared birthday cakes! They will sleep peacefully in the snow when the temperature is forty below zero, and yet not frostburn. A tenderfoot travelling with me in winter called out one morning that all the dogs had left us and gone home. However, when I whistled, a dozen snowbanks instantly jumped up, wagging their joyous tails at the prospect of another day's work. Their strong instinct as to when ice is safe and when it is not, suggests that they have developed yet another unrecognized quality which warns them against the danger of falling through.

An old trader in Hudson's Bay district with ten dogs and a thousand pounds' weight went one hundred and eighty miles in two and a half days in good going, without the dogs showing any signs of slackening. My own best was twenty-one miles in two hours and a quarter on sea-ice, with whalebone runners on my komatik. On another occasion we covered a hundred and twenty miles with three relays of dogs in about eighteen hours, on a sick call. Once, when crossing a glassy arm of the sea, a cyclone blew us three miles into a snowbank below a cliff at the bottom of the bay—dogs and all, in one mêlée, in less time than I care to recall. Another time our leader somehow missed the trail by only a few yards when coming down in the dark to a village on the land-wash. We all jumped over a cliff at such speed that when we picked ourselves up out of the snowbank below we found that we and the komatik had leaped the whole length of the traces over the team.

Huskies rarely get any diseases, and never suffer from snow and ice blindness, as men do. Huskies discovered long ago that "All are born equal" is not so—very much the contrary. A dictator always rules; and anyone challenging his authority has to show himself a better dog. Throw a fish among a lot of dogs and it may end in several deaths, but not if the top dog is around. I have watched all the team waiting with watering mouths while he selects what he wants, none of them daring to stir. I have seen them lick off the fragments of oil which stuck around his mouth, while he smiled benignly. Yet the same dog would take an only morsel for his pups, laying it down by the mother and standing by to see that his family was not interfered with. Another master dog which used to carry up cods' heads from the fish-stage to his puppies once brought a large cod-head to my friend's baby, who was having an airing in his perambulator. The old dog laid the offering on the quilt and then wistfully marched round and round the perambulator and seemed greatly disappointed that his gift was not appreciated. A trapper told me of his master dog following the trail of another for two miles to the spot where the stranger had killed a seal. After eating his fill, the old fellow brought home two seal flippers for his pups.

One morning, walking along the beach, we met a team of dogs, whose apathy on seeing strangers attracted us. We noticed that every one was swollen up like a round tub, and was only able to waddle unsteadily, for all the world as if affected with the old liver troubles of the chronic drunkard. Their forlorn faces and drooling eyes and mouths fitted the picture only too well. About half a mile farther on we discovered an upset puncheon which had contained cod-liver oil! Another time one of our own dogs came home, an ambulatory sponge of cod-liver oil. His zeal for vitamins had led him into a neighbour's oil vat; and only "when winter came" and his new hair grew out did he get rid of a perfect oil-skin slicker, which for a time made him look as if he were coming to pieces, like the Deacon's One Hoss Shay! Another dog, stimulated by his example, tried the same trick in an oil cask, but going in by accident head-first he shared the princely fate which overtook the Duke of Clarence in a cask of Malmsey wine!

Huskies excel us in so many of those qualities which we rate highly as being attributes of good scouts and sportsmen, with enough spice of our follies and failures, as to make it easy to give them the whole-hearted affection of one "pal" for another. When I think of the day when, after my dogs had saved me from a watery grave by hauling me out of the sea onto an ice-pan, I had to ask three of them to make the supreme sacrifice and give me their lives to save mine, I have no sense of shame in confessing that tears often come to my eyes at the memory.

Robinson Crusoe is said to have recorded of the animals on his island that "their tameness was shocking to see." In Labrador to-day, alas, they not only live in perpetual terror of man, but also of one another; for like their two-legged kinsmen, the "little brothers" prey on one another. Of the wolf this killing of his fellows not only sounds natural but seems to be a law of life among all meat-eaters and carnivores. On the other hand, the caribou, the largest of all the actors, is an outstanding pacifist. The porcupine, beaver, woodchuck, black bear, and muskrat are all in that class, all being herbivores.

Captain Thierry Mallet in *The Beaver* writes as follows of the so-called "Barren Lands," the despised wilderness of the Arctic:

"We pitched camp under the lee of a rock on a sandy beach where the river narrowed to a hundred yards. Beyond the river the country extended for miles and miles without a tree, shrub or rock—just a desert of gray moss rolling in waves away from us as far as the eye could see.

"While sitting round the little fire we saw on the horizon a small, yellow streak which seemed to be moving towards us, like a huge caterpillar. It grew little by little in length and breadth, until suddenly it spread out, and widening and widening, still kept moving in our direction. It reminded me of a swarm of locusts spreading over the fields after dropping in a cloud from the sky.

We soon realized that it was covering many acres. At last in the mass we began to see thousands of tiny dots which moved individually. Then we knew it was a herd of caribou. Spellbound, we remained watching it. On and on it came for the narrows of the river where we were. Its flanks spread a mile or so on each side of the head, which always pointed in our direction. One felt instinctively the unerring leadership which governed the immense multitude. Two hours later they were only a few yards across the river from us. An old doe, nearly white, led by twenty yards. Then came three or four bucks, walking side by side. After them streamed a column of all ages and descriptions, widening like a fan until it lost itself on either side—a swarm so closely packed together that acres and acres of gray moss were completely hidden by their bodies; while the noise of their hoofs and their breathing sounded like far-away thunder. When they reached the water the old doe stopped. The bucks ranged up alongside her, and soon thousands lined the banks of the river for over a mile, and behind them thousands more which could not push their way through stopped also. Then all the heads, of bucks, does, yearlings and fawns, went up. Not a sound was heard. My eyes ached under the strain. I started counting, but at three thousand gave it up. There were too many.

"After what seemed an interminable pause the old doe and big bucks moved slowly into the water and swam across to our cove. In an instant the whole herd had moved; and with a roar of clattering hoofs and rolling stones and churning waters, they were breasting the icy stream till the river foamed. On and on they came. Nothing could stop them or make them swerve. The first ones saw us from the water standing up behind our fire. But they came straight on, all the animals racing up the bank to make room for the next lot. They scattered slightly on either side to give us room, and for what seemed an eternity we were surrounded by a sea of caribou. Finally the last went by—a little fawn with its mouth open—and nothing was left but countless tracks, and millions of gray hairs, floating down to the sea."

The reports of A. P. Low of the Geological Survey of Canada state that the land on the Labrador peninsula north and east of Hudson's Bay to Ungava "carries much vegetation, food for immense herds of caribou." So does every square mile of the now unused lands belonging to the Ancient Colony of Newfoundland. The herds of caribou once stretched from Labrador to Alaska. They have been cut up and divided by man, and by better or worse vegetation. Still there remain plenty in Labrador to show how easily the land supports them.

Our own herd of domesticated reindeer, in spite of no Government protection whatever, and many forced sales to produce funds to help us with their upkeep, out of an original three hundred became seventeen hundred in seven years, proving beyond contradiction the vast and practical possibilities of their adaptation.

Caribou are blood relations of domestic reindeer; and the huge success of domesticating deer in Alaska and now in North Canada makes us blush to look at the Labrador stage to-day and see nothing being done with its vast assets of land, so close by water to European markets.

In the case of our own private herd, we could get, as I have stated, no adequate government protection, the war deprived us of some of our herders, we were terribly short of funds, and had no subsidy from the government. When the war was over only a hundred and forty of our beautiful, great herd were located. Two hundred and fifty animals had been ruthlessly poached in one day. We had constant quarrels with neighbours, and we were the only administrators of law. We had amply proved our contention, but the many calls on purse and time and nervous strength made it impossible for us to continue the experiment unassisted by the country. We therefore transferred the remainder of the herd to Canada, and so Newfoundland lost one of her greatest opportunities for helping her people in the North.

Labrador is an ideal centre for the farming of venison, and growing the invaluable skins of reindeer. It is the shortest distance by water-borne freight to Europe. With the now instantaneous freezing process the excellent and nutritious meat can be served in London as fresh as the day it was killed. In the pageant of the future we can picture just such immense herds of deer as Captain Mallet so graphically described on the "Barren Lands," roaming the "Labrador Wild."

Deer improve the land instead of doing it harm, by making drains on their pathways and by spreading manure. They need next to no labour to care for them. They do not harm any other thing. They are the only animals except the yak and the musk-ox which can make farming the Barren Lands profitable. Both summer and winter, in their contempt for cold, they are the veritable

REINDEER

CAPE WHITE HANDKERCHIEF

seals of the land. They feed themselves easily, all the year round, on the otherwise useless mosses and lichens of our barrens, and have an instinct for finding these through the deepest covering of snow. Wet, cold, arctic winter, scanty food, all mean little or nothing to these animals. Wolves cannot begin to keep pace with them or follow them.

Even beyond the Arctic Circle Peary discovered the White Caribou—our own go nearly white in winter— presumably as a protection against foes. On their feet they have developed large dew-claws which spread out and enable them to run over snow which would hopelessly engulf any of our domestic animals. Their hair has developed a system of air bubbles, so that it keeps them warmer, and floats them high out of water when swimming. They are very fast swimmers and able to go any distance.

One stag is enough for many does, so surplus stags can be used for food, or gelded and made better draft animals. They breed regularly once a year from the second year. To prevent being followed when having their young, the does repair alone to the seaside, leaving the bucks for a rear-guard, and dropping first the scent-bag or gland from the frog of their hoof so as to leave no scent. This gland ordinarily helps them to keep together.

The actual horn of the hoof has developed a hard, chitinous exterior like the tooth of a beaver, so that the soft part, as it wears away, keeps their boot bottoms level and in good repair, enabling the owner to dig down almost any distance after moss through frozen snow.

They are very easy to train for driving purposes. Most important is the fact that on long journeys they find their own food, while at the last extremity they themselves can be used to feed the driver.

Give an Eskimo a seal or an Indian a deer and he has all he wants, for food, clothing, tent, harness, snowshoes, everything, including the best of thread, needles, and fish-hooks, and even a bow.

We owe these four-footed friends another debt, for they have taught us that our cows also can turn the useless old moss, the ubiquitous carpet of our land, into the best of milk. Sprinkle the moss with a little weak molasses and water, and Molly, your cow, eats it with gusto, while by the judicious addition of some dry meal made from the waste of our fish-stages the Christmas sirloin can be made worthy of its knighthood.

The caribou, like the other animals, is pleading for protection for our own sakes as well as theirs, before it is too late, as did the fur seal on the Pacific, with such beneficent results when his appeal was heard and answered. In this mad world we seek satisfaction by every conceivable folly. A wiser era will invest more largely in the "little brothers of the wild."

Brother Timber Wolf is called Canis occidentalis. He is larger than his Husky kinsman. I measured one seven feet eight inches from the tip of his tail to his nose, as against six feet eight inches for the largest dog. His marvellous teeth cut like revolving knives, and are as sharp and hard as steel. They would be the despair and the ruin of the dentist. We have the skull of one big fellow who, when famished, had snapped at a green bough and cut it off simultaneously with both sides of his mouth at once, leaving the middle part of the thick twig bowed upwards between the two great upper cutting teeth against the roof of his mouth. There it gradually wore its way through the base of the skull and eventually slew the biter. The wooden bough piece is still in place even in death, each end having been absorbed into the jaw and made a socket for itself—so that it now rotates exactly like a basket handle.

Neither a wolf nor a dog is swift enough to catch a deer on a straight run. The deer leaps sixteen feet as he speeds. " 'Tis dogged as does it," however, and a stern chase though a long one generally marks his journey's end. We have known of only two wolves actually watched making a kill of a deer. In one case both wolf and deer in the excitement of the death-struggle failed to notice the human observer. The wolf at last caught up when the deer sank on the snow from exhaustion. He jumped up just in time and, standing on his hind legs, laid out the wolf at the first blow. Then his adversary got him by the throat and held on while the poor deer was like one beating the air. The second deer took to the water and easily outdistanced the wolf by swimming; but the end was the same, though before his death the caribou knocked the wolf over three times running. A wolf kills for the pleasure of killing. He will destroy far more deer than he can eat if he comes upon a herd, often hamstringing some first.

Of the little land brothers which wisely sought safety in the water, the otter of our rivers is a real asset to the cast. "Dream memories" of the days when Dinosaurs were faced with the alternative of "Get busy or get out" may have led the otter to a venture fully justified by results; for we still see his beautifully gleaming coat flashing in the sunshine, and his virile, graceful body enjoying life, with still a firm hold on the pleasures of the land as well as of stream. He has taken all kinds of precautionary steps for the sake of "safety first." Entering a burrow or house of any kind entails dangers by which he might be trapped. So he has adopted the corsair life, roaming from place to place. Yet none knows better how to find shelter under impassable banks and osier tangles, or under snowbanks, or to pass you going down or up stream, without your being one whit the wiser. None of his fellows keeps always in such good shape as he. He is always "in fair round belly," and his clothing is immaculate the year round.

The otter clings to a flesh diet—mostly of salmon and trout which are always on tap and easy to get. His teeth are sharp and strong, and in a fight with a fox which happened to try to capture him as he would a rabbit, Mr. Fox departed with a leg practically cut off by one snap of those jaws. He has devised some patent, so that water does not adhere to his hair. Thus he never freezes up. The otter's one mistake is his "rub," the mark left in the snow on the bank, where he toboggans down on his belly in play. Enough patience in waiting silently beside a "rub" will almost always give a trapper a chance for a shot.

Other little actors of the amphibian order are the beaver, and his small cousin, the musk-rat. Both are rodents. Big, heavy, strong, active, and with an almost human intelligence, the beaver is still the gentlest of the wood folk and entirely devoted to peace. He is friendly and less suspicious of man. He is extremely social and shows no fear of owning real-estate. He builds a large, comfortable house, often near neighbours' houses, of camouflaged boughs under a bank, with his front and back doors well under water so that he can come in and out without being observed. His mode of life agrees well with him, and has greatly benefited his size. He rears families in an upstairs nursery, for which he builds a fine shelf-like floor. He is given to hospitality and allows his small cousin, the musk-rat, to use his home. His hospitality is sometimes abused, however, by the meat-loving otter, who will occasionally kill his host.

One day while staking—that is, driving long poles into the mud so as to make a grating in front of the beaver's doors and prevent his getting out—a trapper was lucky enough to see two otters enter their neighbour's house. By removing the top of the house, the inmates and their visitors were captured at leisure. So gentle is the beaver that he will not even bite the hand which is lifting him out of his own home to his doom.

On one occasion a friend was using a brook, dammed up by beavers, to float his logs out to his mill. Finding it a trifle too shallow he raised the dam. This flooded Brother Beaver's nursery, so he simply raised his house like a Chinese pagoda. One day, however, whilst on a constitutional to the dam, he discovered the reason, and immediately lowered the opening. This the logger repaired; upon which, like the gentleman that he is, the

257

beaver simply went farther upstream and built another house, taking his family with him.

His tail has become flattened out and covered with hard scales, so he can use it as a plasterer's trowel. With this he pads down the mud which he brings in his hands to the dam, to stop leakage. This uncouth-looking tool, attached to his stern like a big rudder, ends in the most beautiful fur, which has been developed under the long king hairs of the rat, to keep the beaver both dry and warm even under water. Often he is very hard to see because his outside, streaky brown colour is exactly like the river bank—though the most valuable of all, the black beaver, is also caught in Labrador.

The beaver, like the squirrel and other animals, lays up stores for the winter; and he uses largely the bark of the birch, so beloved by innumerable rabbits. He cannot leave his "pile" on the land, nor can he leave it where it might freeze up. This has given him an additional reason for laboriously building up a dam, and for building it high enough so that the pool shall never freeze to the bottom. The cut-sticks called "browse" he pegs down to the floor in his now unlimited larder.

He can bite down a tree as quickly as some college men whom I have watched could do it with an axe, and leave a cleaner stump at that! Moreover, he never cuts it down where he will have to tow it upstream. He is almost Scotch in his economic housekeeping. A half-finished piece of browse is as rare as a lost bawbee in Aberdeen.

The persistence of this marvellous little brother is not a trophy of any special mission, but of wise and ob-

258

served prohibition laws. The fact that they hold real-estate makes it very easy to exterminate them.

It is unlucky that the Indian has such a sweet tooth for beaver meat and is as determined to have it at the other man's expense as are the rich "wets" to have their liquor. So when a river has improved by the unselfish care and forbearance of the trapper whose fur path it is, a racketeer party of Indians will all too frequently descend and clear out the whole lot in the summer, and at times the other game on the path as well, while the trapper is away on the coast, fishing.

Fearsome as a large black bear looks standing on his hind legs, he is really both gentle and friendly, easily tamed, and never attacks man except possibly in defence of his young. He is always a bear and may play roughly, so it is well to remember it. I have kept several. Only one ever got angry with me. He was standing on the deck with his paws on my shoulders, eating a piece of sugar from my lips. When he pulled on the lump and I would not let it go he boxed my ears and scratched my cheek with his claws—which I doubtless deserved. He immediately ran to the end of the bowsprit and sat watching me as I made a small whip out of a twig, and then climbed out after him. At the last minute he jumped into the sea and swam triumphantly away. I rowed after him in the dinghy and, when I caught up with him, he grabbed the gunwale with his powerful arms and was in the boat in a second. Not satisfied with grinning at me, he shook the water from his coat all over me and then, wet as he still was, calmly jumped up on the seat by my side and cuddled close to me to show that I was forgiven!

One man complained that while hunting on snow-shoes in the early spring, he had come suddenly upon a big black bear just emerging from his cave. He at once gave chase, hoping to save his cartridges by killing the bear with his axe. The poor bear could not escape, for he sank in through the soft snow. Then he ferociously attacked the man, who had to shoot him to save himself. It was the story of the Eskimo over again: "*Il est méchant. Quand on l'attaque, il se défend.*"

We once saw a bear walking around the land-wash towards us, so we hid behind a rock until he was quite near, and then stepped out close to him. The land rose rapidly from the waterside with high cliffs, mounting to several hundred feet. But our sudden appearance seemed to "click" in the mind of Bruin with some painful experience of the past, for the speed with which he climbed hand and foot up the sheer face of that cliff would qualify him for membership in the Mt. Everest Expedition. A trapper friend of ours once crawled into a snug-looking hole to sleep, and on waking found a large bear as high as the roof standing over him, but apparently exhibiting no resentment at his intrusion. The trapper had the ingratitude to shoot his host, and then wait about until he killed the mother and cub.

A bear's desires are very simple, and though he can be taught to drink rum out of a bottle with gusto he greatly prefers molasses. Having a nose for it, as bees have for honey, he plays many a trick on unlucky trappers, who have to make caches for their use in winter along their endless fur paths. Br'er Bear specializes in opening caches, and only a steel safe-deposit box would keep him out if you gave him time. He is an herbivorous animal and lives largely on a diet of berries.

Not only can he climb a tree and sleep in the branches as if he were testing the merits of an aërial existence, but he takes readily to the water, and is an expert swimmer and fisherman. His tough hide and amazing ability to stand "punishment" enable him, when driven to bay on a mountain-top, to curl up in a ball and "roll over the cud," rather than stand like a fool to be finished without a chance. Fool he certainly is not, for he and the little woodchuck have developed a remedy for the troubles of our long, cold winter when food is hard to get, which is unique among our players, and might be useful in a London winter. He finds a nice, deep cave, lines it thoroughly with warm boughs and brush, and then turns in and sleeps till spring comes again. He first takes the precaution to eat enough of the endless berries to wrap himself in a blanket of fat, which incidentally furnishes him with fuel and food, and conveniently lasts six to seven months without his having to stoke the fires or even use them up in the labour of swallowing and digesting.

A baby bear, taken from its dead mother, was once given to a friend. When October came he placed a stout barrel in the bear's run to see if it would know what to do, for it had never had any chance to attend the "school of the woods." He knew all about "caving up," and at once lined the barrel with moss and grass, padding it down well with his paws, far better than we could possibly have done. Dame Nature teaches her lessons thoroughly.

Retiring as he is, black bear is entitled to an honourable place in our pageant. Yet he is abominably treated, being always shot at sight, even in summer, though his pelt is then quite worthless, simply because his flesh is good to eat. I must own that I have tested a good loin of bear many times. With wild cranberry sauce, one could hardly tell it from leg of mutton at its best.

The "struggle" produces strange bedfellows. Who would dream of linking together the great white bear and the little white fox? The skin of one huge polar bear covers the entire floor of my study, while it takes two white foxes to make a good neckpiece for a lady. Yet these two have much in common. Both have retired to make their homes amidst the eternal ice. Both often seek a living through the bitter arctic winter on the frozen sea, often driving south hundreds of miles through the darkness, and living by their wits, skill, endurance, and courage. White Fox is like a dainty little lady. Gentle and timid, amenable to kindness, and harmless, he lives mostly on the kill of others. The disguise of his spotless white clothing is perfect. He breeds later than his coloured congener, having to wait to give his family a home on the land. Sometimes it is an old burrow, sometimes a cleft in a cliff. Once it was under a neighbour's house, where he and his mate brought up seven darling little blue-grey foxlings with an artless trustfulness which, alas, was not justified. Like the polar bear, he is an admirable swimmer and navigator. Once standing on the beach of Nakvak Fjord, at a spot where it is certainly not less than three miles wide, we saw something swimming towards us from the other side. At first we thought it was a polar bear, since through our glass we saw it had a white head. To our astonishment when it got nearer, we realized that it was too small even for a cub. Only when it landed and shook itself dry could we believe that it was a little white fox.

Alas, epidemics, unknown and unsolved, take immense toll of our animals—seeming sometimes to lump them all in one big bunch for victims. Some years Brother White Fox almost disappears in the struggle. Another season he was so numerous as to enable a Labrador trapper to catch three hundred and three, which netted him over ten thousand dollars, a better record than old Samson's, who is reported to have caught three hundred foxes, tied them tail to tail with a firebrand between them, and then loosed them into his neighbour's cornfields. Even an old widow shot two that winter and in the spring brought me the skins to help towards "her debt."

One year, while steaming along the northern Labrador Coast about three miles from land, the watch suddenly called my attention to a seal swimming parallel to the land. On coming alongside we perceived it to be a large polar bear. The surface of the sea was as calm as oil, and though there was much ice about and the sun was shining brightly, Mr. Bruin was so fat that he floated like a boat, and just used his legs to paddle along at leisure. He can, however, not only dive but sink himself almost out of sight, when stalking ducks in the swatches of open water in the sea ice in spring. He, too, has assumed absolute whiteness as his best winter protection. Only his small eyes and nose are black. The latter he is said to poke down into the snow as he stalks a seal on the ice-edge or waits at its blow-hole to catch it when it comes up to breathe. One other trait the two strange comrades seem to have in common—a sense of direction, certainly not possessed by man—for both on the sea and in the forest I have nearly lost my life simply from leaving my compass at home. We once followed a polar bear, which had landed from the ice-floes, for many miles across frozen bays, over hill and valley deep under snow and at last through a long forest, in which one of my colleagues and his young bride nearly ended their lives by being lost in it on their honeymoon. Yet the bear went so straight north through that forest, and thence across the Straits of Belle Isle, that we would only surmise he had a compass in his skull directing his legs.

The immense strength of a polar bear was shown one day in a blubber yard. A large cask made of heavy oak staves had been filled with seal oil and headed up for shipment. During the night Bruin landed from the ice and, climbing over the palisade, decided to sample the brew. An ordinary mortal would find it difficult to break into that ironbound oak cask with an axe, but with a few strokes of his mighty paw he had opened that safe like a gangster specialist, and had transferred so much of the contents to his own interior that he was unable to again negotiate the palisade. He stood close on to seven feet high and weighed nearly three-quarters of a ton.

His marvellous fur coat is proof against any cold. The colder it is the fatter he becomes, till he finally floats as easily as a whale. Indeed, the polar bear is perhaps on his way to follow the example of that former landlubber and become altogether aquatic. At present he must take to the land and hurry "down North" for safety, when the seals have reached their southern limit and are themselves returning "Northward Ho."

Both for their abilities and hardihood and for their courage and ventures of faith, which these little brothers make on their winter voyages, they are worthy of our commendation.

The "little brothers" are singularly free from this malady of possession by evil spirits; but if a vote were to be taken on the question, the lot would certainly fall in Labrador on the Karkajou or Wolverene. Rumour has it that the only good Karkajou is a dead one, when his skin, rightly dressed, fetches quite a fair price.

A Labrador trapper once found a Karkajou held fast and apparently dead, since he had jumped into two steel traps almost simultaneously. The instant, however, that the second trap was released, like a flash Bad Brother Wolverene had his teeth through the man's hand. A common trick of a Karkajou is to sham dead, and then to escape as soon as opportunity offers. Another trapper told me that he was actually carrying a dead wolverene home on his back, but when he opened the bag in his kitchen the "beast had been spirited clean away." It is common knowledge, that if determined to get a luscious bait, wired on the tongue of the strongest "double jumper steel trap," some uncanny power enables him to do it. He has actually been seen to reach in under the tongue, spring the trap, and then sit down and eat the bait.

To catch lynxes a trapper builds a little house of boughs and stakes and, laying the bait inside, buries a couple of steel traps in the doorway. The discovery of such a device seemed to afford intense delight to Brother Wolverene. All he had to do was to dig down and burrow in from the back, and he not only had a free meal but a nice little house all built for him. The habit has grown upon him of following a trapper a long way off, as self-appointed inspector of the efficiency of his traps! A black sable or marten is our poor trapper's greatest prize. A fat sable is a Karkajou's *"bon bouche."* The Indian declares, however, that wolverene never eat trap-caught game, only destroy it for sport. Anyhow, he will take all the victims out of the traps and make away with them; and it is difficult to suppose that he does it as an official of the Animal Rescue League.

One day a lonely trapper hung up in his tilt fourteen marten pelts, the results of his winter's catch. In his dreams he saw himself bringing them home to his wife and family, to whom they would mean almost a year's supplies. Master Karkajou, the Al Capone of the Labrador, came boldly in during the trapper's absence and appropriated the lot.

Brother Wolverene is only a small fellow, after all, and puts in so rare an appearance now in our pageant that help should be extended to him in answer to his S O S. He certainly has merits which strike an answer-

ing chord in an audience with red blood and understanding hearts. Who will fail to appreciate grit and
courage and resourcefulness, even if displayed by a
minor devil?

In his struggle with Br'er Rabbit, Br'er Lynx, Br'er
Trapper Brown and his boys, and with all his many other
too attentive neighbours, Brother Fox jogs along with
his eternal grin on his quizzical face, and his flashing
eye over his cynical whiskers.

For centuries he has held the financial championship
of the world in the fur-collar market. King Edward was
reported as paying eleven hundred pounds for a single
silver-fox skin. Foxes went off the gold standard in
favour of silver long, long ago. For over a century, however, the actual unit for all monetary dealings on the
Labrador was the coat of the beaver. Once two merchants from Liverpool sent out to us to get some pelts
for their own use. One wanted foxes for a rug and the
other otters for a coat. By mistake the parcels got mixed
in shipment; and on my subsequent return to Liverpool
I was met on the dock by a self-satisfied gentleman in a
bright red fox coat which made him resemble a huge
woolly caterpillar. The other recipient had a fine black
otter rug. Neither wished to exchange when I uttered
my astonished protests. So long as red foxes were called
otters in their minds, and vice versa, their value was the
same.

The domestic life of foxes has been thoroughly studied. When fox farms were still considered unpractical
we began breeding foxes in captivity. The memories of
a baby fox which I had caught as a boy and tamed con-

vinced me that they would become almost as friendly as dogs. Soon the first red fox on my farm would scream with delight when I went up to his lonely kennel, and jump into my arms when I entered the wire enclosure. Canada alone in 1931 raised two hundred and sixty thousand silver foxes. One result of this new industry which we did not anticipate was the slump in the prices which our trapper friends had to face, for marten, mink, musk-rat, and all kinds of animal farms sprang successfully into being in the prosperous twenties, followed by apparent over-production which leaves markets glutted and producers ruined.

Few animals believe their own eyes. Foxes, deer, and seals especially "have eyes and see not." Either of the two former, if down-wind, not only will stand and stare at a man who keeps perfectly still in the open but will come close to him through sheer curiosity—like monkeys in a cage around a new arrival. If the man knows their calls and can use them without moving, he will almost certainly lure the animals to their doom. Yet a fox will hear the chirp of a mouse across a marsh, or a deer the crack of a twig stepped on in a dense wood. Once a fox has put his nose into things, he asks no more questions. A strange fact about Brother Fox is that his own scent is so strong that with the increase of our few foxes we had to move the kennels another half-mile from the hospital.

The commoner of our minor actors are, without exception, cannibals. Foxes are among the worst offenders, for if one of two foxes happens to get wounded or caught in a trap, the other will invariably fall on him and devour him; and three times we have had female foxes devour their own husbands in the same pen with them in winter.

The cat tribe are known and feared the world over as masters of egotism, cunning, and ferocity. Yet a small cat will stand up to a large dog to try to protect her kittens. The lynx is the one representative of this family in to-day's pageant. He carries the tradition of the family true to type. Though one of the most invisible of the little brothers, he is among the most destructive. Not infrequently lynxes hunt in couples. This immensely magnified cat has augmented powers of speed and climbing ability, owing to increased relative length and power of legs and claws. Yet we have one record of a single fox that faced and drove off two of these savages of the forest, all by himself.

The lynx is an ardent lover of the spruce-tree pig, or porcupine, and doubtless has been no small factor in his downfall. To the traveller in winter a porcupine often spells life. This humble and slothful "pig" has evolved two new devices to aid him in the struggle. No other of the little brothers discovered the value of converting some of the beautiful king hairs of his coat into invisible barbs, which will prove so painful as well as fatal to the enemy as to create a universal recognition of the fact that it is wise to leave the owner alone. Secondly, while it remained to the rabbit to find out the value of the succulent birch bark for supper, it has been left to the "wood pig" to specialize on the bark of the coniferous trees, which are always to be found in abundance everywhere, whereas birches are apt to be both spotty and scarce. The barbed quills have cost many a wolf, fox, and dog their lives. I have seen a fox whose pelt was so riddled with sores caused by these quills as to be valueless, and also a dog's tongue, from which it was almost impossible to extract them.

The porcupine's great mistake is to retain so sweet and tender a muscular system. If only he could make it smell like a skunk or taste like a musk-rat, he need never go beyond his beloved pine tree to find a safe home. Modern weapons are absolutely fatal to him, however, and treed by an Indian Crackie dog, his black skin and slow movements inevitably seal his fate.

Among the little brothers of the tree folk it would be criminal to overlook the squirrel, beloved of everyone. Champion gymnasts, invariably cheerful and companionable, they are an ornament and joy of every trail. Their very mischief is only one of their attractions. Who but they could rob a Hudson's Bay Company store with impunity! Twice these gay little miscreants carried off by their own small hands nearly a barrelful of hard biscuits, valued at priceless dollars, before ever their raids were discovered. The armed bandit with his big motor car and accomplices is a greenhorn compared with this little brother in his red uniform and enormous plume—even if to our way of thinking the plume is carried at the wrong end.

The coterie, red, gray, and flying, have obviously been lured toward the air and have abjured the price of the valuable wearing-apparel that warrants the expenditure of a cartridge. The flying squirrel is the only one as yet who really flies; and he still has only reached the glider stage. His wings are like webs stretched from his arms to his legs, only not yet so far developed as those of the flying mouse, known as the bat.

In times of famine the shadow of the stew-pot hangs all too ominously over this delightful little group—the pathos being increased by the fact that it takes as many of them to make a square meal as it did of blackbirds to fill the famous pie.

Though we cannot here list the names of all the varieties of mice and rats on the Labrador stage, it is well to remember of what vital value they are to all the other little brothers. One mouse, the tiny leaping redskin, is exactly like a miniature kangaroo, having developed hind legs out of all proportion to his size, so that he seems to walk on stilts and advance like a grasshopper. It is not perhaps scientifically correct to class the contribution of these taxpayers to the general welfare as voluntary. When, through epidemics, they are too few to meet the demands of the annual budget, the whole economic system of the world of little brothers is upset; for then foxes and other overlords are forced into involuntary hunger strikes, and the supreme "Pooh-Bah," man himself, has to suffer severely.

The mink, the marten, and the weasel or ermine, a little group of carnivores, all merit applause from the audience, mixed, of course, with a quota of criticism, unless we agree to turn a blind eye to their peccadillos. As they scamper across the stage they add materially to the well-being of the settlers, as well as to the fortunate recipients of the beautiful coats which they furnish. The mink has made the river waters his home, and resembles a small otter. The marten or sable has not yet finally decided to which element to lean; but much like our polecat, he has a strong liking for land, though he is quite able, if necessity demands, to take to the water. Beautiful in deportment, startling in their agility, with keen, attractive faces and lovely shining coats, they almost persuade us to forget not a few of the ugly habits they share with other raw-meat eaters.

It is pleasanter to turn to the herbivorous Arctic hare and to his smaller brother, also scientifically a hare, but known familiarly as the rabbit. Neither of these makes the mistake of yielding to any urge he may have for owning a home, like rabbits in other countries, or making a temporary cave like Brother Bear or Brother Woodchuck. In summer, assuming the blue-grey colour of the woods and ground, they escape fairly well the attention of the average eye; but their ingenuousness in relying on the same device by turning perfectly white in winter on the snow must one day become obvious to them if they are to survive. For marvellous as is their ability to find food all winter, the telltale tracks in the snow would almost enable a blind trapper to locate their hiding-place. That they have partially noted this already is suggested by the frequency and generosity of their families, which possibly relieve their minds of the spectre of race suicide.

In spite of all the faults and failures of the little brothers of the Labourer's Land, as the curtain falls we can conscientiously pay them the tribute of dubbing them "the good companions"! Still we may hope that one day "the lion will in reality lie down with the lamb"

272

and there will be "peace in all God's holy mountain." The plea of the little brothers is an echo of the old query, "Can wars be made to cease?" The play is in the hands of the audience. If they will to do it, it can be done. The harder the task, the more the credit and the greater the satisfaction. If we face our tasks with the resolution to solve them as so many of the little brothers have done theirs, who shall say that anything is impossible?

XIII: THE PAGEANT OF THE AIR

Νίκη Πτερωτός (*Winged Victory*)

WHO was the first to conceive of the air for a home has not yet been determined. Fishes must have been early entrants for air honours. The world, however, did not wait for "The Road to Mandalay" to develop flying fishes. The fossil remains of the giant Pterodactyls show that the land animals also had faith in very much heavier-than-air machines long before human wiseacres. The first successful human apologist for them, Orville Wright, is still living. When he took his invention to the chosen guides of the great nations he found none willing to make the venture until, when he was actually packed up and leaving Europe for good,

274

an imperial brain-wave ordered him to show it to the Kaiser, who regarded it as possibly a practical factor in war.

Only yesterday mediaeval castles and immense city walls were receiving the sanction of the great of the earth. A bare generation ago an air-minded enthusiast would have been regarded by the public as suffering from a "delusion of grandeur," if not a devil, and would have been held up to the ridicule of his fellows. The same fate would have been accorded him as was to the prophets of an existence apart from a body visible to our physical seeing apparatus, or to a Galileo, who dared to envisage this heavy planet flying round the sun through empty space.

"Other-worldly" minds had conceded to man wings in the next existence—where, however, angels were given no advantage over devils in that respect; but man-kind waited for a transatlantic solo flight of one American youth to finally prove to the world what vast potentials the air offers to us as well as to birds and insects.

The coming of Europeans to the New World spelled disaster to its former inhabitants, but in spite of their having come to Labrador so long ago, species of birds have been listed which still cling to the settings of our aërial stage, and either live on, or journey regularly every year to and from our Coast. Some, however, like the great Shearwaters and King Eider, which are still numerous, save themselves by transferring their nurseries still to far-away lands, where their babies are less likely to be troubled by "civilization." Most birds come to Labrador for their winter, which is our summer, solely to enjoy the vast quantities of easily obtainable food.

Our friend the stormy petrel has adopted exactly the reverse plan. He has invaded Britain at the very headquarters of European civilization and there found the protection which as yet he lacks on the "lonely Labrador." It is only the wanderlust which brings the yellow-webbed Wilson's Petrel to our coast. Only one other of the small petrel tribe, Leach's, still clings to the Labrador as its real home; where, however, being too small to be of value on the dinner-table, and burrowing underground like a rabbit to place his eggs, his danger is not great.

One of our daintiest common "birds of wing" is the Arctic Tern with his cerulean blue cloak, black cap, long dapper wings, graceful forked tail, and an eye like an eagle's. We have often watched him dropping like a flash of lightning from the sky into the sea, and rising every time with a glittering silver trophy in his bill. He is a social bird who enjoys life. The terns' screams of pleasure as they hover over a shoal of herring or capelin fry on a sunny day are a sure cure for the blues. One would hardly believe that so delicate-looking a little fellow is literally such a "man of the world," but none is more so. One youngster banded in summer by Dr. Austin[1] was found ninety days later nine thousand miles distant on the Natal Coast of South Africa, while another was picked up on the coast of Brittany. This ambitious little fellow prefers to fly over ten thousand miles every summer just to lay one egg; or possibly it

[1] Dr. O. T. Austin, Bird Research Laboratory, Eastham, Mass.

is the joy of "hiking home with the family" which gives him so much satisfaction. The ease with which he can store fat for motor energy from the abundant fish supplies is no doubt another deciding factor.

It is characteristic of our fliers, that few find in Labrador an abiding city. The Golden Plover is an incorrigible rover. He visits us regularly every year from his real home two thousand miles away in the Mackenzie River basin, while the little Savannah sparrow comes to us from Mexico every year. So old is the habit with migrating birds of wandering far afield that it is claimed they still fly over ocean paths which by their shallowness suggest that they were dry land when these "exoduses" first began. Possibly some safer magnetic sense guides these birds so infallibly, stimulated by a vestigial impulse, such as certain psychologists think gives rise to some of our dreams and makes the old memories of early childhood more vivid than the experiences of yesterday.

In winter all water birds must leave Labrador; and indeed, most of our land birds follow that line of least resistance. As one watches the fat and cheerful robin feeding at ease on a lovely Boston lawn, one wonders what it is which prompts him so often to fly all the way to Labrador, where we see him in great numbers, hopping about on the snow with his usual infectious cheeriness, in the wake of a noisy flock of snow buntings, or those aërial acrobats, the snipe. These are our very first visitants in May, and sometimes in April, if Jack Frost looses early his grip of the woods, and barrens, or gentle slopes. These little-friends-of-all-the-world cannot be seeking safety, and certainly not food.

Are these and a thousand other similar conundrums suggestions that the climate and conditions of Labrador have special attraction to birds, and that Labrador has possibilities as an international nursery and sanctuary for all the "birds of wing"? Strangely enough, Labrador lies half-way between the Old and New World. In the early days, it was used by seafarers as a half-way house between the two civilizations, and in the era of flying machines, with its endless smooth-water fjords and lakes, the Italians and others have included it in the transatlantic pathway. Labrador, with the distance between land and land, is only five to six hundred miles at any one hop.

Lovers of wild birds cannot fail to regret any decline in their numbers. Within living memory, flocks of the valuable eider ducks made their nests as far south as the Gulf of Fundy. In Norse days immense numbers doubtless nested along the Maine Coast. Primitive weapons made small inroads on them, but now few, if any, rear their families south of the north shore of the Gulf of St. Lawrence; even there the numbers are decreasing, though the bird-protection laws on the Canadian Labrador are well carried out. This is so true that since the imaginary line which marks Canada's eastern boundary was moved to include Greenly Island, the colony of puffins and auks which make their nurseries almost on the actual line has doubled and trebled.

The mere cash value of sanctuaries to America (where in the United States alone sporting clubs and individuals are said to spend on duck-hunting a billion dollars a year), is evident, apart from the value of the ducks themselves in food and feathers. The importance to the world of Labrador as a vast sanctuary would be untold. Settlers, however, would then have, like farmers here, to be supplied with substitute foods for "withholding production."

Everyone who knows the almost incredible work for birds of Jack Miner, near Windsor in Ontario, and has seen the boxes full of bands sent back to him from birds shot over the whole breadth of the North American continent, Labrador included, cannot fail to realize the importance and practicality of more sanctuaries for the members of the feathered kingdom everywhere. If any lover of birds does not know of that worker for the "little brothers of the air," he has a thrill ahead of him. Jack Miner's work was originally begun to carry the Gospel "in partibus infidelium" on the leg-bands of winged messengers, pressing them in hundreds into the service of the harbingers of peace.

Many are the records of the large numbers of birds which frequented the Labrador stage only a few years ago. Writing in 1758, Captain Atkins of Boston states that he found "great numbers of geese, ducks, brant, teal, curlew, plover, sandbirds," and especially he noted robins. In 1789, Major Cartwright writes constantly of the quantities of birds in Labrador. There were then thousands upon thousands of Eskimo curlew. He notes: "On August the 10th we saw a flock of curlews that may have been a mile long and nearly as broad. There must have been four or five thousand. The sum total of their notes sounded like the wind whistling through the ropes of a thousand-ton vessel, and again like the jingling of multitudes of sleigh-bells." In the early nineties we ourselves used to see large flocks of curlews feeding on our innumerable berries, and so unwilling to be driven from any familiar patch that men with muzzle-loading muskets would just sit down and fire away until a whole company was exterminated. No wonder the curlew has been a "missing family" since 1909. A single skin has fetched as high as two hundred dollars.

Where are the great auks? In 1534 Cartier drove them like sheep along planks from the land into his waiting boats till they were loaded. The last of that family was seen in 1852. The beautiful and once common Labrador duck, of which supposedly Cartwright shot many, has not been seen since 1874. Even a skin of one to-day is worth almost any money. It looks as if cenotaphs will soon be required for many more of our birds. On all the Gannet Islands never a gannet is to be seen to-day, and very rarely on the Coast. A casual visitor, the passenger pigeon, has disappeared. Gone, too, are the lovely black and white oyster-catchers with their red legs. The harlequin duck, so aptly named for his striking display of colours, was in great quantities once. Many were taken at Gready Islands. Except in the north they are almost as rare to-day as the proverbial hen's teeth.

For two months the great Audubon visited his Labrador friends. His description of the way in which men engaged in the "vile business of egging" would move to tears any jury which loved birds.

What bird can be more shy than a wild goose? Yet

one day our shot just tipped the wing of a goose, flying high overhead. Our little retriever, seeing it planing down, followed it some half a mile and brought it back to me practically unhurt. It was enough to make any animal hate me. Yet that little lady became one of my closest friends, and would follow me for a walk, if allowed to do so, with the affection of a dog. One of my neighbour's pet wild geese, possibly hearing the honking of a northbound flock and answering instinctively the ancient call of the wild, flew after them. Getting tired after about twenty miles, due to unexercised wings, he landed close to Cape Bauld Lighthouse. The lonely light-keeper, seeing a wild goose in his yard, at once ran into the house to get his gun. When he turned round after loading his ancient musket, to his amazement he found that the bird had followed him into the kitchen to see what he was up to. The keeper guessed the explanation, and when the owner appeared a few days later had so fallen in love with his new chum that, like the Prisoner of Chillon, he could not bear to part with it.

The list [2] of the cast of to-day's pageant includes, as we have said, nearly two hundred species of birds—from the ruby-throated humming-bird and the mourning dove, to that terror of the air, the golden eagle, and that scourge of the night, the great long-eared owl.

Among our game birds are six varieties of grouse, clever enough to change colour with the season, so as to be invisible on the ground, against the snow, or in the wood, which helps one to understand why so many of the carnivores have, like foxes, abandoned their eyes

[2] List by Drs. Townsend and Glover Allen, and Dr. Austin.

for their noses. Moreover, in order to tread softly and warmly on deep snow, like the Snowy Owl, they have clothed their feet and legs in a fine padding of feathers. Only by such ruses have they survived, for they are universally sought after by birds of prey, while every little brother of the land is "out" for their eggs and their youngsters, as well as for the "old birds." Can it be that the snow-buntings, snow-owls, and snow-partridges have suggested the snow-shoe idea to the great big caribou, and even led him to grow his dew-claws?

Many of these birds cross over Hudson's Bay Straits to breed. A ship returning in the fall from the Bay suddenly found her spars and yards covered as by snow—the explanation being a huge flight of white grouse returning for the winter and "getting a lift" for part of the way.

Their undoubted possession of emotions should help us to sympathize with birds. Anyone who has been flighting ducks early in the morning must have noticed how at dawn the young birds keep close to one another, or in fog how thick are the "flights" following some seasoned old leader, realizing their own danger and yet trusting to his marvellous sense of direction. It is common in Labrador for the hunters to trade on these "nerves," for sometimes by making a sudden loud noise when approaching diving birds, they can make them too frightened to dive. Instead, all rush together in a "huddle," which is exactly the worst thing they can do under the circumstances. Yet those same birds are so clever as to be able to keep their entire bodies under water once they have dived, only putting their bills above the surface to breathe. In search of food, I have hunted hundreds of bottle-nosed divers in confined lagoons in my swift-turning kayak, and as they could not, or would not, take to wing, everyone would suppose that they would have no chance to escape a double-barrelled, breech-loading gun. Only experience would convince an audience how easy it is to come home with nothing for supper but a heightened appetite.

Commander Donald MacMillan showed us a motion picture which he took personally of a tiny little moulting diver, unable to fly and caught in a small pond by two great husky dogs. They followed it round and round the edge until the minute bird, getting tired of their attentions, put up a bluff which would surprise a champion poker player. He simply charged head down at the dogs, flapping the water with his wings, whereupon they fled incontinently.

When winter comes and all the water birds and most of the land ones have gone south, those which do stay are all the more dear to us. Three little bright red-capped birds called Redpolls enliven the snowy woods. They are very numerous, very friendly, and well able to live on the cones—like the brilliant pine grosbeaks and the chattering crossbills, who talk to us from the spruce tops. There also stay with us two chickadees, one on sufferance from America and the other our own development. They are so friendly in their yellow and blue frocks that they will almost jump on your hand if you happen to stop on a journey in the woods to "cook the kettle." The chatter of their foreign tongue is hard to interpret, but it is all devoted to timely optimism, and they speak the international language with their bright, sparkling black eyes, which never fails to make us glad to share with them anything we have.

Yet another friend, described officially as "abundant," is the permanent resident, our own Labrador Jay, or "Whiskey Jack," as he is dubbed locally. The jays are the closest animals in Labrador to those "whose tameness was shocking to see." They have a superhuman nose for food, or some even more impelling sense of approaching meal-time. If they spy your komatik turning into the forest, or see it halt anywhere near a wood, they follow it along from tree to tree. As soon as ever the fire is alight they hop so tantalizingly close over the heads of the resting dogs—who do not get any meal until after the day's work is over—that the latter even drool at the mouth as they snap at them in vain.

The custom of having pet names for our birds is really a scientific help, for many, like the Wabby, are internationally known by their soubriquets. He is the red-throated loon, beautiful with a maroon neck-band bordered by bluish grey, as the eiders and king eiders are with their white, green, and black. He alone of all loons can rise direct from the water like a plane. The common loon is a perfect study in blacks and whites. He has a wild, unearthly cry, one of the few noises of our night. On one occasion already referred to, when Sir Hugh Pallisier in his man-of-war was lying in Château Harbour in a dense fog, surrounded by hundreds of Eskimo, this sound was heard by the ship's commander. Taking it for the Eskimo war-cry, he at once ordered the ship cleared for action, all guns mounted, and all hands to their stations to resist boarders, even manning the main-tops.

A recent description of a migration of these loons suggests that their commander may at least have interpreted rightly a martial note in their cry. "Thousands of loons had been collecting in the harbour for weeks. They were evidently preparing for some great event. About nine in the morning they began to gather into great companies under a leader, who kept swimming round and round and chasing stragglers into line, and with shrill orders changing formations. One old patriarch swam about consulting with subordinates and correcting faults in the formation. Sometimes companies were changed to form a battalion, and sometimes a battalion to form a regiment, on which company leaders joined the ranks, leaving a single bird in command. By noon the ranks extended across the harbour in one long black line pointing towards the North. The General and his staff swam a few paces in advance, gave a weird call, sprang into the air followed by the whole army. In two minutes not a loon was left in San Diego Harbour."

The little black guillemot, which is the streak of black and white with brilliant red legs for a trailer, which one sees flashing in every direction anywhere near rocks, is known as the "Sea Pigeon." He has devised such a unique and successful plan for self-protection that he is now "going stronger" than any other bird family in the country. Having mastered the air and the land, he added salt water to his conquest, and has converted the foaming breakers along the rocks into his first line of defence, making his home in the clefts of cliffs and under great boulders, so that no large, prowling animal can get at his nurseries, and no small one dare try. Many of our tiny, feeble folk of to-day's pageant owe their existence solely to the fact that they have scorned to limit their hopes to any one of the three elements, from the tiny dovekie, or bull bird, to the osprey, or great fish eagle.

The auks, or tinkers, make different arrangements. Selecting a narrow rock ledge on the face of a cliff, they place their one great egg on the hard stone itself, with no kind of nest to attract any attention, and laying them in different colours, white, blue, yellow, green well spotted with black or brown—just one more "invisible cap." Incidentally their eggs are pear-shaped, so they cannot roll off; and the different colours help also to avoid quarrels as to whether a particular Mrs. Tinker is sitting on her own property or not.

Some, like the Sea Parrot, suffer from using burrows in the earth for having their families, even on islands distant from the land. They suffer also from their own over-social habit of breeding in thousands close together. This was evident to us one spring, when landing on a densely populated Puffin Island, for our friends were so scarce that we guessed some influenza epidemic had visited the colony. The solution was the carcase of a white bear that had been left on the island in the fall; in the late spring some white foxes on the ice-floe had discovered the bonanza and stayed so late to enjoy it that they were marooned there for the summer. Suddenly to their amazement clouds of adorable fat meat dropped like manna from heaven around them, and they had lived happily ever afterwards, being themselves quite as well able to make and go down burrows as the new arrivals.

With a white front, black back, and huge red nose, Friend Puffin sits upright, wearing great grey spectacles, with only his large feet showing under his white gown. Puffins are the most innocent-looking objects imaginable, and not a few irreverent souls insist on calling them "parsons"; yet they can catch, carry, and bring home to their young several fish at one time in their short, stubby beak. They are much smaller than Antarctic Penguins, and their large red noses make them look even sillier than those of the "Glad Eye." To watch them landing by the dozen and standing cheek by jowl on the edge of the precipices in groups like some chattering "Cackle Club," arguing why the steps of Sister So-and-So tarried so long after having gone down her usual burrow, would have been funnier than any comic opera if it had not been so sad.

Others of our small fry which add to the merriment of our performance to-day are the two phaleropes, or "gale" birds. They are very like common sandpipers; some, however, have lovely red necks and others striking black and buff checks. They fly like the petrels (these latter so named because, like St. Peter, they walk on the water), only the gale birds fly in companies and whirl and twirl very much at the double, with the precision of wooden soldiers and the speed of a gad-fly, exactly as if animated by one soul. Their gaiety becomes more intelligible when we discover that the smaller and drab-coloured birds are all males. The gaily-dressed performers in this marine ballet are the females, enjoying themselves, while the sterner sex are left ashore to look after the family.

There are "pies" and "pies," but our numerous mergansers are universally known as the "pie" bird in Labrador. Being invited by a grateful patient to a dinner of fowl, and arriving with an even better appetite than the perennial one which Labrador bestows, to my dismay I found it impossible to cope with the stewed dumpling, out of which, instead of the aroma of chicken, emerged a distinct odour of mice. I had mistaken the verbal invitation and heard "fowl" instead of "owl." The pie bird and puffin flavour are also a source of trouble till you learn how to forget a mere distasteful savour in anything which helps to satisfy the insistent call of the sub-arctic appetite.

The value of song as one of life's chief adornments has been recognized the world over, ever since the sweet Psalmist of Israel drove the devil out of King Saul with his melodies. Labrador has not been left without divine masters of song; and the very rarity of such joyous experiences makes the song of the robin at dawn on glorious spring mornings, as one glides noiselessly through the forest trails behind the silent dogs, rank with the first-class performances of the art. The songs of the "foxy sparrow," really a gaily-dressed thrush, singing to the morning sun, and of the ruby-crowned kinglet bring to the soul in their matins all that music can afford anywhere. Both in memory and in anticipation, the songs of these birds in the morning and that of

288

Alice's thrush and the hermit-thrush in the evening—
that nightingale of the North—and the cheery music
of that perky little aristocrat, the sparrow, with his
white crown erect like a paroquet's, as he hops on the
threshold, have to be experienced to be appreciated.
As yet we have nothing quite equal to the English skylark, though our horned lark and American pipit are
contesting in his field. Both sing on the wing, towering
high up in the air as the skylark does, and then come
tumbling down out of the blue like a crashing aëroplane, the American pipit visibly rocking to and fro
as he gets near the ground to ease his pace. These
"blithe spirits" of the air know well how to use their
wings as aids in their grand opera.

The value of the power to fly is rapidly being realized. Speed records are being attempted by every nation,
as symbols of superiority, but cruising speed is still
about ninety miles per hour. The fastest record for a
bird is not more than a hundred and forty miles an
hour, made by a falcon. Ducks come a close second,
with easily over a mile a minute. Grouse, quail, and
square-winged birds are sprinters, rising into the air
with the noise of an aëroplane, but getting full speed
almost immediately. Wild geese do not exceed sixty
miles per hour on their long flights. Heavy waterfowl
all have to rise against a wind, as a hydroplane does, for
which reason hunters in Labrador always approach a
flock on the water down-wind. The zigzagging which
a jack-snipe makes when he rises and which makes
snipe-shooting so difficult is not due to his cleverness,
but to his bad balance. When forced to rise any way

but up-wind, his long wings catch the air wrong and cause him to "sideslip." The sudden zigzag is the result of his throwing himself back onto a "level keel" with his strong wings.

Those who have not tasted the lure of the Labrador may wonder that the phœbe, the king-bird, the junco, the wren, the white wagtail, a couple of kinglets, the oven-bird, several thrushes, two swallows, three fly-catchers, and more than a dozen warblers, as well as many another, ever leave the sunny south for the "Land of Cain." This warbler family supply a regiment with green coats donned over yellow waistcoats; but the doyen of our feathered neighbours is his cousin, the glorious Wilson's warbler, with his coat of gold and his glossy cap of jet, which he flaunts as his claim to the title of "Miss Labrador." The scarlet tanager and his golden-robed wife have so far only been recorded as far as Belle Isle.

The hawks, the eagles, the owls, the gulls, the jaegers, the ravens, the gannets, the butcher-bird (shrike), all being birds of prey, exhibit other of those attributes of life which are all too common in civilization. The Golden Eagle, emblem of Germany, of Austria, and of Rome, and the Bald-head Eagle, emblem of the United States, alike honour us with visits. The rapacity of these birds, like that of the lion, suggests that they are perhaps still all too appropriate symbols for great nations. The unbelievable eye of the eagle, which even on the wing affords him a vision as keen as a man's with a tele-scope on the ground, his ferocious face, his irresistible claws, and his superb courage always make an observer feel an inferiority complex in his presence, even though any kingship which that bird possesses is that of the tyrant and of the butcher, and is based on primæval estimates of majesty. Yet to one who has once climbed to his eyrie, it is easy to realize how he has cheated the nations into accepting him at his own estimate of royalty.

Other aces of piratical flight are the osprey, or great sea eagle, which descends from the clouds like a streak of lightning and as surely rises again with a fine trout or salmon struggling in his claws. A more thorough water pirate, however, which can challenge these accomplishments, is the great white gannet, or Solon goose, which fishermen often lure to their stew-pot by towing astern on a long line a flat board with a herring nailed on it. The younger the goose the more likely he is to break his own neck as he hits it.

The "Helicopter" championship is held in Labrador by the rough-legged hawk, which seems to float, poised in the sky over his prey, for minutes at a time without moving. Among the robber barons none excels in personal acrobatic activity the Bosun, or Pomeranian Jaeger. To lovers of athletes, watching one chase a Kittiwake gull which is carrying home his catch after a long spell of fishing to an expectant family, is as exciting as a football match. Turn and twist and tumble and shriek as he likes, the poor "kitty" has always at last to hand over "the goods" to be immediately, and more safely, stowed in the "bosun's locker."

One of our small visitors that is well known on the farms at home should be mentioned in connection with courage. Though he has never been known to kill another bird, he is recognized as a born fighter and called by naturalists Tyrannus, or Tyrant of the Air, and by laymen the "king-bird." One watches with amazement this tiny bird fiercely attacking a big hawk, to which a great big cowardly hen will yield her life without a struggle. Or, if a great bullying black crow comes out into the open on one of his nest-robbing expeditions, the diminutive king-bird is in the air in a minute; a dozen others instantly answer his summons, and so peck and harry the marauder as they dart around him far quicker than he can turn, all the time screaming and shouting their war-cries, that their sheer audacity drives him back to the woods. Thereupon they form a "huddle," all their black crests pointing in the air, as they chatter and cackle over the outrage. The king-bird's métier in life is to swallow harmful insects, and as he can live as far north as Cape Chidley, he may yet become one factor in abolishing the bot-fly, that tortures our gentle deer, and even the scourge of mosquito and blackfly, which he does not despise!

If the title "silly old bird" is ever appropriate, it certainly should be applied to our spruce partridges. They do not even taste "sprucey" enough to prevent their being a table attraction. They are beautiful birds, the male wearing a grey-blue huzzar overcoat and a checkered black and white waistcoat, with a sporty red dab over his eye. His wife affects the latest thing in browns for a coat, and a lace front also of grey and white circles, which might qualify as a "daily hint from Paris." She has about sixteen children annually. They usually keep to the darker spruce woods, and often must escape unseen, or they would have joined the dodo and the two-toed sloth even before "Arms and the Man" appeared in Labrador. Their great idea is to stand still. So single-minded and sincere are they in their eclectic creed that nothing but death convinces them of its fallibility. The natives will scarcely waste a number .22 cartridge at a cent apiece to add this *pièce de résistance* to their menu. All that is necessary is to fasten a small string-noose to the end of a pole and pass it successively over the necks of the various members of the family, to "convince them of their error" by the inquisitorial method of dragging them to their doom. One prisoner of adamantine stolidity we kept as a pet, placing it on the window-sill that it might enjoy the view. It was still there when I last left the country. Occasionally it hopped up and swallowed some heretical fly which disturbed its window-pane; beyond that it remained a pillar of its faith.

On the warmer, though far more northerly, shores of Behring Sea many of our actors of the air penetrate in summer, where the darkness of the night is of only two hours' duration. There they still observe the requisite number of hours of sleep. At nine o'clock the immense volume of their evening song dies abruptly, and silence overshadows the land until three or four in the morning. A visitor reports:[3] "During the long twilight I watched for hours numberless birds sleeping both in the ponds and on the land. Those keeping on the wing were rare, except when parties of Sabine's Gulls passed

[3] *Christian Science Monitor.*

293

by. The day's activities are usually begun by the clanging cries of geese, soon echoed back by a medley of birds' notes in all directions."

The "saddleback" or "burgomaster" may be only a big gull, but he seems always to detect the hunter hiding for a shot, whereupon he circles around screaming at the top of his voice to warn creation, while managing to keep just out of range of whatever gun the sportsman carries. Once when walking on an island where His Honour kept his family, a sudden "swish" like a large club passed close enough by my head to make me jump. It was the burgomaster, camouflaging as a sea-eagle. He was trying the same bluff on me that the tiny duck did on MacMillan's Eskimo dogs.

The ivory gull we call the ice partridge. He nests within the Arctic Circle and has a coat as white as driven snow. The abundant long-tail ducks are known locally as hounds. The harlequin, far the most gorgeous of the lot, we call "lords and ladies." Our chief duck, the sombre brown American eider, and her spectacular green, white, and black mate generally fly in one long line low down over the water, the male bird leading his harem. The barbarous treatment he receives may account for the fact that he always flies with his head down. The gaudy King eider, like the blue goose, scorns to do more than land to refresh himself as he "passes" the Labrador. Each spring their young bachelor drakes come north, first as scouts, and then the older birds follow, flying towards the North Pole.

The gyrfalcon, gleaming white, a startling contrast against the dark faces of our cliffs, remains all winter.

An island south of Hope's Advance bears the name of Gyrfalcon Island, because of the numbers of these birds which breed there. The coots, the rails, the herons, the bitterns, the dozen kinds of pipers, the plovers, and terns, the friendly piping "yellow-legs," the belted kingfisher, eight kinds of owls, half a dozen woodpeckers, the fly-catchers, and many more camp here but come to the footlights and bow. What a showing they would make if we could gather them all together before the bell rings!

To know the other fellow is a big step towards wanting to help him. "Dumb" animals can reveal these emotions they share with man only to their sympathizers. The necessity, alas, for eternal suspicion of man himself has made so wide a gap that few men can bridge it, and the old spirit of "Bill, 'ere comes a stranger; 'eave 'alf a brick at 'im" is all too common still.

The capacity of the performers in this pageant for the greatest of all emotions, "love," is unquestionable. In the will of an English lady, read a day or two after her death at eighty-five years, appears this codicil: "I make no provision for my beloved Poll Parrot, as I know she will not survive me." The bird, which had been her companion for a great number of years, died just twenty-four hours after her mistress.

Natural death is seldom the lot of wild birds. Of four hundred and fifty ducks tagged in three years by Jack Miner, seventy-five per cent of the tags were actually returned to him! One thing is certain, birds will always return to your place if you make it peaceful and safe for them. Geese learn quickly to know a man's voice and trust it, and to actually love him. Miner's stories of "David and Jonathan," and of "faithful unto death" must be read first-hand to be fully appreciated.

Our stage has been so crowded that we have had to neglect many winged friends. But the enormous numbers of those who do not happen yet to possess a bony frame-work are fundamentally so important to Labrador's economy—since without them the others could not exist—that some mention at least must be made of them. How could our fly-catchers live without flies, or our thrushes sing their perpetual hymns of praise without larvæ for breakfast? No, they will not visit us at all if they can get coniferous tree fruit or crustaceans, or dead fish on the beach, any more than our owls will come without mice.

An owl, bred in captivity from the egg, as an adult would not look at a vegetarian diet, and tackled fresh beefsteak with such sparing reluctance that he nearly died of starvation. But his very first mouse, which owls always swallow whole if they can, he hid behind a chair-leg against the kitchen-wall, immediately after sampling the flavour. There he visited it many times, standing staring at it for some minutes on each occasion, till, when darkness fell, he could resist the temptation no longer and swallowed it at one luscious gulp.

It is a common mistake to suppose that a low rung on the social ladder means inefficiency. A certain small fish has earned for himself the title of "lung-fish." When his home stream dries up he rolls up in a ball of mud, keeping a tiny hole open, and so breathes by a lung which he has developed, because his gills are then of no use to him. He has reversed the achievement of that once-upon-a-time dinosaur, our whale.

To grow a new arm or leg, or even his lost tail, is more than any man can do. Yet a lobster can grow one and a lizard the other; while a starfish, if he breaks off a leg, goes even further and grows a new body from the leg! The tiny mosquito drove the French nation out of Panama, and would still be holding that important zone against all comers, if the stimulus of our Labrador climate had sharpened their mosquito wits as it has those of our Coast. For anticipating General Goethals and his lethal kerosene with which he covered the whole surface of the stagnant pools and ponds where those emasculated cousins of the tropics had found such conveniently easy nurseries, our mosquitoes have fooled that plan by each making a separate home of his own, in scattered drops of water everywhere, or even on a snow surface itself. One cannot but give grudging admiration to these mothers who decided on this venture of producing real "snow babies." Nor need visitors wonder at the persistence and endurance of the adult Labrador mosquito. The most infatuated salmon fisherman will admit that the attentions of mosquitoes modify even the joy of a ten-pounder rising to every cast. It is lamentable that there has been practically no research work done on our winged insects. Watch a mosquito on your hand; he is a master of that art!

Our mosquito, to his credit, developed an immunity to the yellow-fever germ, the malaria parasite, and any poison really harmful to mankind. If they would go further and see that their attentions to us did not leave the necessity of scratching, who would grudge them the droplet of blood they need? One lover of animals, whose eyes they had closed and whose face resembled a football, remarked, "I cannot imagine what the poor things did before I arrived on the Coast." The financial reward for extracting this irritant and patenting a rival to Eliman's or Sloan's liniment should alone tempt some reader to answer the challenge of these winged visitors.

The hordes of tiny, blood-thirsty black flies, which leave bleeding wounds on every inch of skin not covered, and which have now learned to crawl in through any chink and repeat the crime on every possible portion of one's anatomy, have also regrettably devised a nursery still impregnable. The venturesome mother deposits eggs which cling to anything immovable under actually running water, so that a Standard Oil main pipe would be powerless against them. They are something like the jelly-fish, whose eggs, fastened to the bottom, just split across like a pile of saucers and float away when they are ready. No greater fame ever awaited a knight-errant than that ready for him who shall destroy this enemy's castle. Explorers have laid down their lives and won immortality by getting "Farthest North"; but these "wings" still hold the championship there against all comers. On the eternal ice-cap of Greenland mosquitoes abound in the dust that becomes mud in the tiniest pools. It is another of the accomplishments of the Arctic Eskimo that he has been able to ignore their assaults.

In Labrador, the whole field of "wings" is still a vast virgin soil offering some of life's really greatest satisfactions. The late Henri Fabre still gives untold pleasure to thousands, and gave facts of enduring value to science, while incidentally adding his own name to the immortals. He himself was far from high up on the social ladder, and his subjects occupied the very lowest rungs. Yet his story of a caterpillar, of a wasp, of a moth, will be classics long after the "best sellers" of today are extinct. Even in the fine natural-history museum at that ancient seat of learning, the University of Oxford, when we sought some information about our Labrador insects, all we could get was the fact that they knew little about them and had scarcely a specimen of:

The Noctuidæ, or night-flying insects (fly-by-nights);
the Hymenoptera, or bee and wasp families;
the Diptera, or two-winged flies;
the Hemiptera, or true bugs;
the Lepidoptera, or butterflies;
the Ephemeridæ, or short-lived flies;

and other winged hosts.

Labrador is not yet demanding a man like the "Scarabee" of Holmes's "Autocrat of the Breakfast Table," who utterly disclaimed any pretensions to be even a Coleopterist (beetle master), being perfectly satisfied to go down to posterity as having been somewhat of an authority on the "hind leg of Meloe." Our condition of ignorance is all the more deplorable since the very future of Labrador lies, so far as man is concerned, in the laps of some of the "Tiniinae," infinitely more so than it ever did in that of the Dinosaurs which have disappeared, or of the whales, which are following them.

One minute fly mother has developed a saw with which she cuts holes in the leaves or bark and deposits her eggs underneath. One nearly annihilated all our beautiful larches. Another attacks the spruces, a third the willow, still another the birch. Two yellow and black marauders of the Hymenoptera family specialize in boring into solid, growing wood. Fortunately another, this one of the Ichneumon family, makes his specialty eating them. Among many more of the constructive types of insects we have seen the slave-maker ant and the black carpenter—very virile specimens.

Tiny insects are capable of carrying messages of death to men and animals, as lice or the influenza microbe, or the yellow-fever parasite. Indeed in Greenland are just such micro-organisms. The dogs act as "hosts," carrying one of the most fatal and cruelly slow-killing ills which affect mankind—the hydatid tapeworm. When the famous Dr. Cook, returning from Greenland, kindly brought to us a present of some specimens of these animals, we felt obliged to destroy them for fear of their bringing infection to our own sledge dogs.

To some extent all animals are bound to be parasitical; but few people realize that not only does every large animal, but every bird and every fish have private parasites of their own:

"Great fleas have little fleas upon their backs to bite 'em;
And little fleas have lesser fleas, and so ad infinitum."

300

Thus some parasites are non-filterable by the finest filters known to man, are as yet invisible through the most powerful microscopes and are undetectable by the most delicate known physical or chemical tests.

The incredible cruelty of some of these little-known winged contemporaries is well illustrated by the bot-fly, which attacks our gentle caribou. The mother is a small fly, so rapid as to be almost invisible in flight. She hit upon the idea that the safest place for her young would be in a nursery which would not merely automatically look after its own safety, but which should have "brains behind" that desirable quality. She decided that the most advantageous spot would be inside the warm moist nostril of the living deer. Her fiendish end is accomplished by two preliminary precautions. First, with maternal devotion, she became a member of the Puparidæ family, which does not deposit the helpless eggs in a cold world to take their own chance. She hatches them out in tubes in her own body, somewhat like torpedoes, and provides each with hooks and spines. Taking advantage of warm, lazy days, she suddenly fires these living torpedoes into the doomed target. Sheep have been so terrified of these bot-flies as to huddle together and bury their noses in mud to escape them. Once in, the invaders work straight through the tissues, and make their homes in the frontal sinuses, next the brain, where they reside for ten months. They then return to the nostril, when the miserable host at last blows them out, thankful to be rid of the tormentors. But it only means that they in their turn soon become bot-flies and replenish the army of the atrocious enemies. Of the many deer I have examined, every one has been affected. Nowadays, however, it is not so easy for the bot-flies. The deer have become scarcer and possibly more wary; so some cousins of the bot have devised a much simpler method and one easier for the mother. They fasten the eggs in a soluble covering, exactly like our tabloids, on the deer's hairs, on the flank or knees, so long as they are within reach of the animal's tongue. On licking his skin he carries the eggs to his mouth. The capsule dissolves. The larvae are swallowed or crawl through the gullet into the tissues, to the warm fat tissue under the skin. There they grow to a large size. Not till some ten months does one bore its way out, drop to the ground, become a chrysalis, and once more a recruit for the hosts of the demons. Among hundreds and hundreds of skins which I have inspected at the Hudson's Bay Company stores or the Moravians' posts I have not seen one skin free from the scars of these fiends; and in many skins there were so many scars that there was not a piece left large enough to make a perfect pair of moccasins. What more worthy life achievement for a lover of animals could be conceived than to discover some means to drive out these devils from the earth?

There are more winged ogres, some day to be banished from the land (like the horse-fly); but, thank God, many more of these hosts are helpful and friendly. Many lovely butterflies and moths add to the beauty and enjoyment of life. Of the former the whites and fritillaries, that feed on violets, are our most common. There are also rare ones to be had on the Coast, some already known that have no small commercial value. We have forty known species of moths; they are masters of deceit, for to survive they must not only deceive man's dull eyes but also the microscopic vision of the hungry shore-lark, pipit, or other winged walker. As the vile cutworms which kill so many of our plants are larvæ of some of these moths, our hearts go out to those that will hunt them down. There are, on the other hand, many others like the beneficent dragon-fly, which are among our best friends, having earned their local name of mosquito-hawks. The harmless pupæ of the dragon-fly live under water, wrapped according to taste in tubes of sand, stones, shells, or bits of plants, and are called Caddis Worms. They are very interesting to keep in glass bowls to watch.

There are forces untold, still unknown and unthought of in the current science of the day. On our little stage lie vast problems, so vast we fail to see them. Records of events show how man still wastes time, talents, and capacities on utterly ephemeral, valueless, and often dangerous and disastrous enterprises, occupations, and pleasure. Here is a great challenge to help, while obtaining permanent pleasure at the same time. Some day some one will win these real prizes. So this pageant really ends as an S. O. S. call. At present no knights have been found to rout their enemies, and as the caption of the legend of our scene suggests, there still remains to be won a real "Winged Victory."

XIV: THE PAGEANT OF FORTY YEARS AND AFTER

Apologia Pro Vita Mea

THE curtain rises on a Bideford-built ketch of ninety-nine tons register, the *Albert*, with a crew of ten North Sea men. The vessel is about the size of the *Matthew*, in which John Cabot made his famous voyage from Bristol. The *Albert* had a little hospital amidships. After leaving Yarmouth she beat down the English Channel and then followed in the wake of the *Matthew*, four hundred years later, but south along the Irish Coast, well south of Greenland, and so across the seas to the harbour of St. John's, Newfoundland, the capital of the "Newlands," which by right of priority of discovery is still to-day part of England's empire, and though her oldest colony, still bears the name of Newfoundland.

304

Her quest was different from Cabot's. She was searching for a great fleet of a thousand fishing vessels. For three days she had been fighting her way through an eerie fleet of icebergs and dripping fog, and a sea which even on the surface was scarcely above freezing. Once inside the great portals of the beautiful harbour, however, a new chaos reigned. Dense columns of smoke blanketed the shores, and the stifling heat was so great that several ships in the harbour had been burned at their anchors. A dozen scattered fires still belched flames heavenwards. The spaces between were filled with gaunt and blackened chimneys, towering over masses of charred débris.

The fishing fleet had gone "down North on the Labrador," carrying some thirty thousand souls. So following them to latitude fifty-two we ran in due west, and, passing a cordon of icebergs, loose ice, and islands, anchored at last in a snug little harbour, among a number of very busy schooners. As there were no wireless stations or land wires in those days, the excitement of the crowds of fishermen which boarded the strange vessel knew no bounds, when they heard of the destruction of the greatest city of which they had any knowledge.

During three months, nine hundred sick folk sought medical and surgical help aboard. Although there were four thousand white folk living on the Coast north of Belle Isle Straits, there was no medical help ever available for them during the months of the long winter. We were called to adjudicate in many troubles, because no law courts existed, to hold religious services, and even to marry one couple eager to legalize their eight children—

305

their explanation being that previously no opportunity to do so had presented itself. The wedding-feast on board had to be ship's biscuit, pork, and a blueberry cake, while distress rockets were sent up to celebrate the occasion.

It was the number of Anglo-Saxons living on the land that astonished us most. All that outsiders knew about Labrador was that "there was not a cartload of earth in the country" and that it was the reputed "land which God gave to Cain." The variety of our discoveries outnumbered Cabot's. To begin with, the country is not a northerly one; none of it is north of Scotland. Three of our hospitals to-day lie south of the latitude of London. The days and nights are no longer than in the British Isles. The snow during seven months, reflecting the brilliant sunlight, makes it so warm that the fishermen are as brown as Eskimo.

When the sea began to freeze in the fall, we were forced to sail south, knowing that we had been given a chance to reënact certain miracles recorded of old.

On the homeward voyage in December, following winds piled up the seas like precipices over our stern, but bags of canvas filled with cod-liver oil, with a drip-hole made by a marlinspike, run out on the ends of our spinnaker-boom, prevented the waves breaking over our craft.

During the winter an invitation came from the Governor and Council of Newfoundland for us to take up regular work in Labrador. This was accepted and our enthusiasm was greatly enhanced by our having learned what preparations to make, and by the generosity of friends who made them possible. Fitted with everything we needed, from square-sail and yard to a portable X-ray outfit and tabloid medicines, with two young medical assistants, we got our anchors the following June with the zeal of a dozen Don Quixotes. Material was sent ahead to finish a half-built house on Caribou Island at Battle Harbour, which had been offered us by a firm of merchants who had carried on business there for over a hundred years. Another firm sent materials for a second simple little hospital unit, to be located two hundred miles due north of Battle Harbour, at their place called Indian Harbour, among a group of islands which formed a "bring-up" for hundreds of schooners and thousands of men and women, on their way either north or south.

Our outfit included also a forty-five-foot steamer, eight feet wide, called by permission after the Princess May, now Queen Mary of England. This we sent out on the deck of a steamer to meet us in St. John's. In it, with an engineer and cook, I cruised the whole Labrador Coast; though, as the funnel had been lost on the voyage over "among the passengers' luggage," we had had to make one of tin. Moreover, as we could carry only a ton and a half of coal, on one occasion we were obliged to burn up the top of the cabin in order to reach a harbour.

That year over two thousand patients received treatment. But for the fact that they had no money this would have been a remunerative practice. However, "they did what they could." Lack of generosity is not a fisherman's fault. But the answer to "Can you pay for your treatment?" had always to be the same which

Peter gave, "Silver and gold have I none." If cod-fish, halibut, and salmon could have met our expenses there would long ago have been not assistants but rivals in our field. But even kings have died of a surfeit of lampreys. The gold standard has been found to have its faults; but the barter system, when one side is illiterate, has the double disadvantage that that side does not know the values of its products, such as a fox skin, or the price of its necessities.

The merchant, on the other hand, occasionally lost heavily through "dealers," who, like Ananias, turned in part of their gains and swore it was the whole.

Arrears of surgery during the first few years occupied most of our energies. Among the high lights, I still remember the blank look of a red-headed Irish lad, with one foot almost completely upside down due to a simple neglected deformity at birth, when I suggested to him that we might make that foot as good as the other. He possessed such abundant Gaelic vivacity that even though the foot was upside down and shorter than the other, he had not learned to "grouse" at his misfortune. Could I do it with a pill? No, I couldn't. Could I "charm it"? Yes, I could, but only if he was asleep. So we "charmed it" during sleep that they had never heard of, with a knife that left no poisoned wound, and with a wrench that the famous Sir Robert Jones had sent us. The leg had to be covered up in plaster while "the charm" was working, but at the end of a month Paddy was already crazy to dance a jig for our benefit.

Two old sea-dogs, who had both gone blind with double cataracts, came to hospital from different harbours almost at the same time. After successful operations they met on the sun porch to discover that they were brothers who had not seen each other for many long years. Again a prospective bridegroom, whose eye had been knocked out when his ancient muzzle-loader exploded, came aboard at sea from a schooner, terribly worried lest his Nancy would not recognize him on his return. Some time later, while passing a group of lads on the beach at St. Anthony, one of them asked me to examine his eye. When I told him to come up to the hospital dark room he laughed. "Guess it's all right, sir, if youse couldn't recognize it. 'Tis the false one t'hospital gave me." One day, while visiting in a cottage on the Canadian Labrador, an old fisherman jumped up and flung his arms round my neck. Unaccustomed to "strangle-holds," my face must have expressed astonishment, for my smiling assailant hastened to explain, "Sure, I'm the man youse carried to t'hospital 'teetotally blind,' and t'doctor gave me back my sight." He reminded me how I had run the hospital steamer on the rocks, in heavy fog. "I thought it was t'Lord's will to punish me for trying to get my eyes back. But after youse put me into a boat, t'steamer washed over t'shoal, and, well, the whole t'ing be as much of a miracle as any I ever heerd tell of, even in t'good Book herself."

New features that soon dotted the landscape were tiny lean-to's, made of old boat spars, on the sunny side of the cottages, with condemned sails that served for curtains. These were for the many consumptives, the victims of poverty and poor food. Those who could keep out in the open air did well, but many who needed the treatment most had neither blankets nor suitable food. Euthanasia would have been far and away better than the only other alternative at times possible, viz., leaving fellow-creatures to die, half fed, in small, dark, damp shacks. Thus one fall, when we sailed away, a consumptive widow with six children was living in a lonely harbour. A year later, when again we visited that harbour, they were all dead, and the shack had fallen in from the wind and weather. Had we given the dying mother a lethal dose, we might have got the children taken care of, but nothing would induce her to part with them. In another somewhat similar case we arrested the three children and committed them to "proper food and schooling for three years." All are alive and well to-day, but the drone critics told the world that I had "better mind myself."

Endless efforts were made to get people to believe in contagion. Individual food utensils, or sterilizing used ones, was impossible. Spitting on the floors of the tiny, unventilated cottages was a national custom. Sorely tried mothers dared not protest even to visitors. Moreover, hooking mats from rags was also a time-honoured custom; so we paid a bonus to all who would make them with "DON'T SPIT" plainly hooked into the pattern, in place of the customary "GOD BLESS OUR HOME."

Catechisms were another national custom. We printed our own and offered prizes for any child able to say the whole, questions and answers, correctly. Thus small children, reeling off:

"Must I spit on the floor?"

"No, I must not spit on the floor."

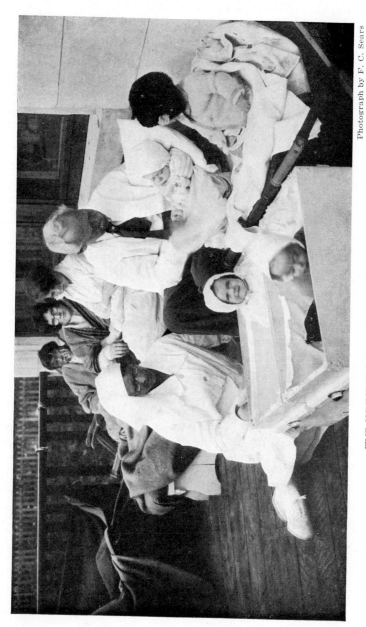

Photograph by F. C. Sears

THE SUNNING BALCONY—ST. ANTHONY HOSPITAL

HARRINGTON HOSPITAL OF THE INTERNATIONAL
GRENFELL ASSOCIATION

ST. ANTHONY HOSPITAL

"Why must I not spit on the floor?"

Etc., etc.,

became yet another "common object of the seashore."

In the winter of 1900 we dragged from the forest at St. Anthony, on the north end of Newfoundland, a third hospital, as that settlement was as isolated in winter as the Labrador. Meanwhile, the little sailing-vessel, borrowed from the English mission, had been replaced by a small steamer. To-day the third in succession still bears the donor's name. This doubled our range of action; and as she can be fired with wood, she allows the people to make that return for her services.

While primarily a hospital steamer, she has been nicknamed the "perambulating providence"; for many a knotty legal problem has been settled on her decks, many orphaned and needy children has she carried to orphanages and boarding schools, many young folks bound to the States or Canada for supplementary education has she transported. She has carried to the end of the nearest railway, two hundred miles distant, specialists in agriculture, in dietetics, in dentistry, in eye surgery, in industrial teaching, in child-welfare work. Religious leaders of almost every attitude of mind, governors, cabinet ministers, and just plain reporters and visitors have all, during the course of the years, availed themselves of the opportunities which the little steamer offers. Thousands upon thousands of fine, warm garments, given by generous friends, has she distributed, always, if possible, for a return in labour, in lonely hamlets the whole length of the Labrador. She has served as a peripatetic library. In short, in her many activities she justifies the claim to supply the proverbial "missing link." To fishermen's families in many an isolated harbour the familiar hoot of the *Strathcona's* siren heralds the event of the year.

The first S. S. *Sir Donald* was crushed in the ice-floes. After years of yeoman service the first *Strathcona* was sunk in a gale off Cape Bonavista, beneath whose waters to-day the legend engraved on her steering-wheel continues to "preach to the fishes" as did St. Francis of old: "Follow me, and I will make you fishers of men." Her successor we bought in England after the war. She was very cheap, and critics considered her so small that we should "never be able to hire a crew to bring her across the Atlantic." The problem was solved, however, as so many of our worries have been, by volunteers! So the critics were partly right; we never did hire anyone. Incidentally, she is the smallest steamer ever to cross the Atlantic under her own power, so far as we can find out.

Canadian friends next paid for a hospital at Harrington, west of Cape Meccatina (famous since Cartier's day), and have maintained it ever since. Recently they erected a subsidiary nursing station at Mutton Bay. As it was found that hospitals on islands, like Battle Harbour and Indian Harbour, were impracticable in winter, since the people have then to move up the big bays for trapping, a small winter hospital was placed a hundred and fifty miles up Hamilton Inlet from Indian Harbour Hospital, in the beautiful woods at the mouth of Northwest River. There it has become the centre of a most thriving settlement, with its fine gardens, its boarding school and children's home, and its industrial activities.

After thirty years of service, Battle Harbour Hospital, like Elijah of old, disappeared in a whirlwind of fire. The loss was due to a lighted cigarette in the village store. So fierce was the gale at the time that even the lofty Marconi pole on the top of the hill was burned. To-day a little model settlement is growing up near by, in the beautiful basin of St. Mary's River, with its cottage hospital, its boarding school, its gardens and domestic animals, its water reservoir, and magnificent salmon-fishing. Behind the special grant of virgin land given us for this hospital station there is still much forest, so a small sawmill is able to supply the lumber for the people to build respectable houses, and to get a little co-operative store started.

Yet another hospital, at Twillingate, in southern Newfoundland, was made possible by the gifts of friends of the Mission; but our directors decided that they were not able to assume its budget, that being a section of the island where the Government and the people themselves could afford that responsibility. The selection of the staff was to remain with us, and help has been given it since it was opened.

A series of small nursing units, combined with industrial work, have grown up at six places in between the various hospitals. One nurse, whose district covers fourteen villages and a hundred miles of coast, has even introduced a riding horse, which makes her dog-teams look to their laurels.

Formerly the great handicaps of the Coast were transportation, communication, and isolation. One might say that all of these have now been conquered. Aëroplanes come north every year. The no longer "Lone Eagle" has visited us with his wife, as did a fleet of war-planes from far-off Italy.

Our survey from the air, begun and carried on for two years by volunteers, has been recognized and assisted by England, Canada, and America. When a volunteer American plane carried British naval survey officers over our coast to help afford our fishermen reliable charts to guide them, a new international note was struck of that chord which alone can insure permanent peace on earth. The hitherto unknown marvels of the Labrador fjords will soon be opened out to the public.

Already "paying passengers" have been carried to and from that world's wonder, the Grand Falls, following up the course of the Grand River, that affords practically the safety of a continuous landing field. A gold rush by airplane is now in progress. Already our doctors and nurses have made many visits in planes, patients have been carried to hospital in them. That one of our doctors never returned was no fault of the coast.

For tourist traffic, the gyroscopic compass and the radio now obviate the dangers of the erratic magnetism of North Labrador; while in the wheelhouse, the fathometer records the depth of the uncharted, irregular Atlantic bottom below the keel. Regular fortnightly tourist steamers now visit us in summer from Montreal.

The handicap of being out of communication has also been removed. Marconi stations, radios, and our own volunteer private wireless stations have enabled us to hear news, music, plays, and sermons from all the world. We can hear Big Ben in Westminster striking the hours. We have listened to speeches in Paris and Berlin.

The persistence of a general peonage system of trade and other inferiority handicaps was the result of ignorance and a cause of poverty. The problem of education was primary. It has been tackled by a number of boarding-schools and orphanages. The educational system of the colony allowed pupils to sit for examination and obtain certificates provided they followed a curriculum which we felt was of limited value to them. Government grants are not given to non-sectarian schools, but those have become yet another feature in our landscape. A combined boarding-school and orphanage in Sandwich Bay, with fifty-five resident children, was suddenly wiped out by fire, the work of a feeble-minded child, but a better building has replaced it, on a large grant of land at Cartwright; now made famous by General Balbo, who was welcomed by Black Shirts from our Lockwood School, bearing the fasces of lictors. Fire protection, running water, and power were installed through the generosity of yet another friend, and the really heroic work of American and English college boys during three summers carried the eight-foot cut through the rock and swamp and clay and forest and mosquitoes and black flies for a mile from the wharf to an everflowing waterfall. The original wooden orphanage of St. Anthony has been replaced by a large concrete building, the pride of which is that though it has all the modern conveniences of running water, electric light, and modern sanitation, it was built entirely by Labrador men under a Labrador foreman, through our own machine-shops, without one hitch.

As no technical training of any kind was ever available for the fishermen, we seized every opportunity of sending our most promising scholars to technical schools in America or Canada, selecting institutions with such backgrounds as would inspire our students to wish to return and give their fellows the benefits of their newly acquired capacities. The plan has amply justified itself by its results. What more valuable asset can any country ask for than inspired and capable citizens?

The father of a young family had been fighting for his life for twelve months in one of our hospitals. He was far from strong, but the tubercular spine was ankylosed and all he needed was good food and weaning back to full working capacity. He had come to say good-bye. The boat was at the wharf to carry him—where? We all love our fellows more, the more we believe we have helped them. It was peculiarly hard to face the fact that our friend was returning to a naked and half-starved family, to an empty cupboard, insufficient bed-clothing, no supplies for the fishery, no gear and no credit to get any. It was easy to give him a little sleeping-draught. Why not? What other alternative was there for him? He could no more pull up a fifty-pound anchor with safety than he could fly. He had no earning capacity. But there was an alternative. What could his wife earn? This query started our industrial department. The finest hooked mats in the world, fine

316

pattern weaving, beautiful skin embroidery, ivory carvings, topical toys, excellent basket-work literally cropped up upon our coast.

For years a skilled volunteer fostered this effort from St. Anthony, where still to-day are its headquarters. It has given work and food and hope to over two thousand poor women in one year, while one of its main branches is offering remunerative employment to cripples and convalescents, to hasten their recovery.

Our hooked mats are of the most perfect workmanship: they last indefinitely; they clean easily. The industrial work spells that redemption of waste labour which is vital to the welfare of any people. Our greatest obstacles are man-made. The ever increasing tariffs in the countries where we try to market these products for the benefit of the fishermen are a constant handicap. The reflex of these industries is seen, not only in the developing of the brains of the workers, but in the increased cleanliness and attractiveness of many little homes, where the housewife realizes she is a direct contributor to the household budget.

To-day this department has a central distributing shop at 370 Fourth Avenue, New York; a shop at 1631 Locust Street, Philadelphia; sales-rooms at 25 Huntington Avenue, Boston, and 82 Victoria Street, London, England. The products may be purchased at 221 Gilmour Street, Ottawa, or at that unique enterprise of Lady Grenfell's, the Dog Team Tavern at Ferrisburg, Vermont, on the Champlain Highway.

Our scene changes to a tiny cove among the trees about a hundred miles south of St. Anthony, our main

317

hospital. The settlement is called Granfers Cove. In a small motor boat we were visiting the villages along that shore, journeying inside the ice-floes which were just loosening their grip on the land. An old fisherman welcomed us warmly. He was in sore distress. The fishing season was just opening; there was endless work to be done; and his two big sons of twenty and twenty-two years old were lying on the floor paralyzed and only able to move their heads! "What can you do, Doctor? Can they be saved?" cried the old man. "Cabbages!" was my answer. He looked at me almost in anger. "Cabbages," I repeated. The two young men were suffering from beriberi, due to lack of vitamins. Already on the Coast I had seen deaths from blackleg scurvy—three grown men in one family. What could have saved them? "Cabbages," or "potatoes, eaten in their skins." They had no cabbages, and the few potatoes which the merchant had allowed them they had chipped raw, fed the peels to the chickens, and ruined the remainder by long boiling.

So our agricultural department came into being, and is steadily becoming a more constructive influence all around the Coast. Formerly seeds were placed in the frozen ground after the snow had gone in early June. Young plants could not put their noses above the soil before July, and our very early fall frosts caught the vegetables unripened. Meanwhile, cutworm, root lice, and caterpillars destroyed unchecked the vitally important food supply. To-day many fine little hothouses in widely separated centres are appearing, so that the seeds sown under glass in March enable the little plants to go into the ground in early June with so good a start that the fall frosts have not arrived before the vegetables are matured. As one result, all around those north coasts new gardens are coming into existence. Many thousands of young plants, two months ahead of time, are now sold, or "worked out" each spring, by the poorest families, and acres of land have come under cultivation. A professional volunteer agriculturist visits the Coast each summer. Exhibitions are held and prizes given for the best results, where once a native potato was unknown, and miserable turnip tops, cut in summer, were the nearest thing to a green vegetable many families ever knew. The champion cabbage so far weighed nineteen pounds; and a steady average of ten-pounders has been maintained.

Following on the agricultural work, invaluable efforts for better feeding have been started. Community canning enables women to bring their own salmon, cod, herring, rabbits, and partridges, greens or berries, to a central kitchen and preserve them for their own use. Anything which cannot be sold or used at once is thus turned to account, and thousands of cans have been placed in homes against the long winter which often only saw dry "loaf," molasses and tea in days gone by.

Better education and the co-operative stores have helped to induce cash dealings and make thrift possible. Whole wheat being cheap and far more nutritious than white flour, we have introduced hand grinders into many little centres, and sent in also hundreds of sacks of wheat to be worked out by needy people, so saving their self-respect as well as furnishing them with most nutritious food at the lowest possible cost. Our reindeer experiment also was a dietetic effort; so have been the highly bred goats sent us by far-seeing friends, the pigs, the fowls, the sheep and the cattle—all of which have been introduced successfully, in so far as funds would permit.

Another terrible handicap of the fishermen was removed when an anonymous friend presented the first repair dock to the coast. On July 26, 1908, a cyclone drove forty-one of our fishing schooners on the rocks near Indian Harbour. As soon as it was possible for the hospital ship to get out, we started on a quest of those in distress. On one strand lay nineteen wrecked schooners. Had there been a dock within reasonable reach we might have saved several of these; as it was, all we could rescue was one ninety-nine-ton oaken vessel. In another gale nine boats went ashore in one bay. All might have been saved—all were lost. Once to test it, we towed a wrecked fishing vessel from St. Anthony to St. John's, a distance of something over three hundred miles. It cost more than it was worth. To-day our beautiful new dock in the north at St. Anthony carries its expenses, has saved several large vessels, and has been a godsend to many. Unromantic as it sounds, it is one of the truest interpretations of love on the whole coast. Thus, last fall we towed in one sinking banker with twenty-three wage earners on board, besides a cargo of fish. She was back fishing in a fortnight. In the old days she would have been lost and the men ruined. Throwing away vessels to get their insurance was winked at under the old conditions. We have been able to make "barratry" an unremunerative temptation. A fleet of boats, given us at various times for various needs, is used to enlarge the scope of our work and as far as possible to lessen the expenses of transportation of people and goods, while ensuring safety and efficiency. The crews of nearly all our boats are volunteers.

Over fifteen hundred volunteers have given their services and expenses, coming from every rank of life and doing every kind of work, from flying, surveying and professional work, to digging, draining, boat running, engineering, preaching and teaching. They have been of every intellectual faith and almost every or no religious label. No purely intellectual viewpoint has ever been demanded. "Love in action" has been the criterion of the faith value coefficient, of which efficiency and unselfishness are the tests. Such services have been given over years as well as only over weeks. The fishermen owe more to the truly Christian spirits of hundreds of volunteers, who have come North through the years to give their services freely for the benefit of their less fortunate "northern neighbours," than they can possibly understand. Were it not for the help these volunteers have given us, the work would never have been possible at all. And yet they invariably claim that they get more out of the work than they put in. Never were the youth of the English-speaking world so chivalrous—so eager to discover an S. O. S. call and answer it when they hear it. Dogma and labels are assuming a truer perspective in the world's recovery scheme.

A large institute at St. John's is the last feature in this pageant that I shall refer to. It becomes ever more and more valuable to the centre of our fishermen, where practically no provision was made for the large numbers who annually visit the harbour. It was to St. John's in years gone by, with the Colony's one dry dock, its own hospital, its one railway, its main road, its seat of judicature, its one poor-relief centre, that practically all the fishermen of the Newfoundland and Labrador Coasts had to go in spring and fall to sell their cargoes and get supplies. For years the Institute has run the only Y. M. C. A. in the Colony, with a splendid department for women. In its fine swimming bath, the only one in the country, many have learned to swim. Its well-equipped gymnasium, its bowling alley and billiard tables, its lecture hall and cafeteria, and its clean, cheap bedrooms, have been invaluable assets to the people and to the community.

"What of the pageant of the future?" you ask. Fifty years ago, Professor Hinde, after crossing Labrador, wrote: "The table-land is pre-eminently sterile. The whole land is strewn with boulders. Language fails to depict the awful desolation of the interior of the peninsula." Elliott Coues, a naturalist from the semi-tropics, writes: "Fog hangs low and heavy over rock-girdled Labrador. Angry waves, paled with rage, exhaust themselves to encroach up her stern shores, and, baffled, sink back howling into the depths. Winds shriek as they course from crag to crag in a mad career, and the humble mosses that clothe the rocks crouch lower still in fear." In contrast to these strictures, Father Browne, Professor of History in New York, who as a boy followed his father to the fisheries on the Labrador Coast,

Photograph by F. C. Sears

INDIAN HARBOUR

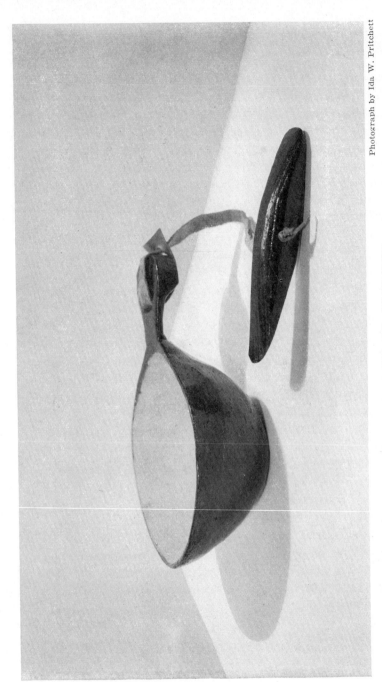

Photograph by Ida W. Pritchett

VIKING DRINKING CUP—BIRCH KNOB

and who knows the land from end to end, comments: "The wealth of Labrador lies in its inexhaustible fisheries, as agriculture on the actual Atlantic seaboard is largely impossible. Lumbering and mining are as yet precarious ventures there. But there is a valuable asset with which Nature has lavishly endowed this fishers' land. Its unrivalled scenery for the tourist, its exhilarating air and balmy breezes for the invalid, its subjects unique for the artist's brush, its virgin forests for the hunter, its limpid streams to tempt the disciples of the 'gentle Isaak'. This land of myriad charms offers every attraction which entices the traveller to the land of the Midnight Sun, and has its additional feature of being within reach of even a slender purse."

We have forgotten the piteous accounts of the sufferings of the early New England colonists. The first Californian settlers must have starved but for the supplies sent them from Mexico. So recently as 1850 the Dakotas were described by an eye-witness as "lands swept by hurricanes, blighted by droughts, cursed by bitter frosts, devoured by locusts, and menaced by savage Indians."

To appraise the value of a country by the failure of its managers to develop it is as sane as trying to hoist oneself to heaven by one's own shoe lacings. It is recognition of responsibility and courage which are needed. Though Cartier stigmatized Labrador as "the Land of Cain" we do well to recall that that was exactly the land Cain needed. The conditions to which our civilization has brought the world to-day suggest that there is something to be said for any country where everyone not only can, but must work. Difficulties, hard physical work and simplicity, are still invaluable assets in evolving the world's most important product—a real man.

One of the last men to whom we bade good-bye as we left Labrador late last autumn was a Tyne-sider. Years ago he deserted from a vessel on which he was deck-hand, because he "wanted to own land of his own." "Good-bye," he shouted at me from a motor boat in which, with his wife and four children, he was starting to go up a long fjord to his winter cottage among the trees. His cod fishery had failed last year, but with salmon he had done well. He was severely gassed in the War, and his tiny grant for this handicap gives him all that he needs from the world outside. To-day as I write he is roving in the woods with his eldest boy, hunting furs, or cutting timber, or building a new boat, while his wife spins and knits, and occasionally snares a rabbit for the cooking-pot.

Four barrels of flour will last a man a whole year. In 1929–1930 a barrel of flour could be purchased for a hundredweight of properly cured fish (dried codfish) a quantity which I have many times watched being taken in one haul from the net. I have seen a fisherman —during wartime—catch enough herring before breakfast to pay for ten barrels of flour, and enough salmon in the course of a day, to pay for the flour for a reasonable family for six weeks. Moreover, such a family can gather enough wild red currants, or cranberries, or blueberries in one week to fill enough empty flour barrels to last them all winter. A barrel filled with plucked and dressed wild ducks frozen solid into fresh water can be finished ready for stowing in a couple of days in a good year. I have known fifty ducks killed by one loading of buckshot in a crack in the sea ice in the spring.

Labrador is now on the direct air-route. Who will wish to go via Montreal, much less via New York, from London to Japan, when to go by way of the Faroes, Iceland and Greenland—where already aerodrome rights have been granted to America—makes the land-to-land flying distance never more than four hundred miles and the total mileage half that of the other routes? From London to Chesterfield Inlet west of Hudson's Bay is the same distance as from London to New York. In Chesterfield Inlet, grain elevators and a railway exist already; and a new transatlantic grain route has already been shown to be practicable.

Labrador still has its fisheries, which are ever producing their stock of wealth. The potential of its geologic formation, with its easily exposed terrain, cannot be forgotten. It is of the same geologic formation as that which has made Canada the richest precious metal producing country in the world.

The timber wealth of Labrador is far from negligible. Not a few pessimists have described it variously as "all stunted second growth," "too full of knots to serve as plank," "too tapering to be of use for spars," "too scattered to be milled profitably." In places it has been badly burned over. Yet to-day the Newfoundland Government claims publicly that it owns forty thousand square miles of good timber in its one-fifth of the Labrador peninsula. In its four-fifths, Quebec undoubtedly owns at least as much. "The world's timber supply of

325

the future will be largely derived from Labrador," says an expert [1] who has spent much time in the country. Our pictures, taken from the air, show large stretches of forest, as well as some burnt areas and barrens. That they will all be a source of wealth in the future is certain. The responsibility for the protection of the forests is a very real one.[2]

Labrador's furs will also always be a source of wealth. Their future depends on their conservation. The trappers are themselves careful of their fur-paths and welcome any effort to protect them. The breeding of foxes in North Labrador has not been as successful as farther south. Mink and other animals which can thrive on a purely fish diet give the experiments at present in progress greater promise. The introduction of herds of reindeer or caribou can be made at any time.

At the moment, however, the chief contribution which Labrador promises to the world in the immediate future is the unique field for tourist traffic. It is close to the United States and Canada, and only halfway to New York from London. It can be reached quickly, cheaply and safely, as soon as the charts of the whole Coast can be relied upon. Those are now finally being undertaken seriously. The British Admiralty is considering completing the hydrographic survey.

The president of the great aluminum syndicate, which has just put a second dam across the Saguenay, thus developing an additional seven hundred and fifty thousand horse power, says that the key to the Labrador situation

---

[1] E. M. Kindle. *Journal of Geographical Society*, Ottawa.
[2] See work of Professor Alexander Forbes, M.D., in 1931, in Labrador.

is transportation, and that that will be provided as the country is explored and prospected to an extent which will ensure a reasonable return on the capital invested in railway construction.

Yet some critic may object that the present fall in the price of our codfish, for which our careless curing, compared with that of our European competitors, has admittedly been a determining cause, the lessened chances of securing large cargoes, and the new substitutes for fresh fish have all caused the fisheries of Labrador to decline so seriously that scarcely a single large firm carries on the business to-day.

In comparison with other countries, our Government in Newfoundland *is* in financial straits. Fifty thousand out of her two hundred and fifty thousand inhabitants had to be fed this past winter out of taxes. We may well reflect at this juncture the following excerpt reprinted from *Harper's Weekly* of New York. It is headed

Be of Good Cheer

"It is a gloomy moment in History. Not for many years—not in the lifetime of most men who read this paper—has there been so much grave and deep apprehension; never has the future seemed so incalculable as at this time. In our own country there is universal prostration and panic, and thousands of our poorest fellow-citizens are turned out against the approaching winter without employment and without the prospect of it.

"In France the political cauldron seethes and bubbles with uncertainty; Russia hangs, as usual, like a cloud, dark and silent, upon the horizon of Europe; while all the energies, resources and influences of the British Empire are sorely tried, and are yet to be tried more sorely, in coping with the vast and deadly Indian insurrection, and with its disturbed relations in China.

"It is a solemn moment, and no man can feel an indifference —which happily, no man pretends to feel—in the issue of events. Of our own troubles no man can see the end. They are fortunately, as yet, mainly commercial; and if we are only to lose money, and by painful poverty to be taught wisdom —the wisdom of honour, of faith, of sympathy and of charity—no man need seriously to despair. And yet the very haste to be rich, which is the occasion of this widespread calamity, has also tended to destroy the moral forces with which we are to resist and subdue the calamity."

The foregoing article appeared in *Harper's Weekly*, Volume 1, page 642, of the issue dated October 10, 1857 —seventy-five years ago. Courage is always the surest wisdom. Confidence that we can make affairs go better is wisdom. We try to make our Labrador watchword, "When two courses are open, always choose the more venturesome."

High tariffs, increased taxation, "bigger and better" walls, which prevent increasingly that "kamaraderie" which alone can bring about the millennium, are now recognized as hopeless makeshifts. Only when it is admitted that the world is a village, and that when one suffers, all suffer, can international mass production be any real remedy for poverty. Each country could confine itself to the output to which it is best suited.

The adaptation of Nature, now that man has such marvellous powers over it, is a password to better days. The basic and essential adaptation, however, is obviously that of man himself. His adaptation to a new era is no more impossible than is flying over the mountains,

328

or than diving under the polar ice was yesterday thought to be. Transportation and communication have already knit the world unbelievably close together, but we still prevent trade from flowing round this globe with equal facility. Even commercial thought for the other fellow must supplant thought for oneself. Not merely those qualities which man shares with unreasoning animals, but those which he shares with God, must become the determining factors of conduct. When that day dawns, Labrador, like the other lands of the round world, will come to her own.

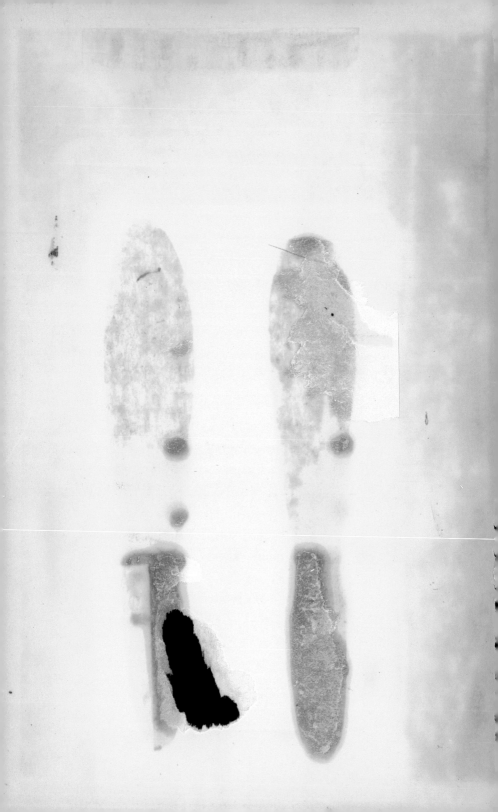